MW01633016

THE
RED
FALCON
TM

Look for these other **Age of Aces Books**

Captain Babyface:
The Complete Adventures
BY STEVE FISHER

The Red Falcon:
The Dare-Devil Aces Years (Vol. 1)
BY ROBERT J. HOGAN

The Adventures of
The Three Mosquitoes:
The Wizard Ace
BY RALPH OPPENHEIM

The Red Falcon:
The Dare-Devil Aces Years (Vol. 2)
BY ROBERT J. HOGAN

Chinese Brady:
The Complete Adventures
BY C.M. MILLER

The Sky Devil (Vol. 1):
Hell's Skipper
BY HAROLD F. CRUICKSHANK

COMING SOON!

From the tattered pages of

POPULAR PUBLICATIONS

by ROBERT J. HOGAN

ILLUSTRATED BY

FREDERICK BLAKESLEE

and **JOSEF KATULA**

AGE OF ACES BOOKS

ORCHARD PARK • NY

All illustrations by Frederick Blakeslee except "Buccaneer Busters" frontspiece by Josef Katula.
The original illustrations in this volume have been digitally edited to better fit the layout.

Edited by Bill Mann
Designed by David Kalb • Art Direction by Chris Kalb
Printed on demand by BookSurge Publishing beginning in April 2008

The Editor gratefully wishes to acknowledge the contributions of
Joel Frieman, Don Hutchison and the great M'Gunda.

ISBN: 978-0-9794092-4-0

TABLE OF CONTENTS

Thunderbolt
Patrol
FREDERICK BLAKESLEE

"Fly! Get away! The world is coming to an end!" The Red Falcon blinked as he heard those pleas. He and Sika had landed in Bocheland, expecting to be captured—instead they found themselves enmeshed in the most amazing adventure this hellion pair ever tackled!

Thunderbolt Patrol

A DEAFENING, earth-splitting crash of lightning and thunder slashed through the night somewhere over Germany. Another and another in one continuous flash of blinding light made the inky blackness like day. But there was nothing to see.

Rain, thick and driving, pounded through to shut off any possible view of the earth far below shrouded in the darkness and the lashing storm. The wind had risen to a sixty-mile an hour gale. Puffy and swirling. Blowing from inland out across Germany and toward the North Sea to the west.

But Barry Rand, the Red Falcon pilot and brains of the strangest outfit that ever roared through the air, didn't mind the storm in particular except as it stung his face. He wasn't worrying. Nothing seemed to trouble the daring Yank outlaw ace.

He squinted one goggle-covered eye around the windshield of that fastest of planes with its Spad wings and Fokker fuselage and Liberty motor. Squinted into the night.

Wicked, stinging drops of water traveling at terrific pace, crashed against his goggles, struck his helmet, smeared over the windshield in great gusts. And it stung his face where the helmet and the goggles did not cover. He ducked under the cowling once more. His lips formed a whistling pucker in the darkness and his favorite tune sprayed out to be drowned by the roar of the giant Liberty engine.

Be down to get yuh with a taxi, honey—

Wam! Crash! A bolt of lightning slithered down the drenched skyways and caressed the tail of the Red Falcon plane. Sparks and flame flickered from every strut and wire of the thundering crate. The tune broke off. Barry's voice came in a laugh and he spoke through the tube that connected with the rear cockpit.

"Sure one rotten night to take a honey to a ball, eh, Sika? Ought to think of another tune for once."

A deep, soft-voice came back through the speaking tube. There was the slightest trace of worry in that voice.

"Not good night for anybody, Master. This kind of night god of jungle roar. You not forget we got to get gas, Master."

That from Sika, the giant Senegalese Negro chief who owed his life to Barry Rand. And for that reason the faithful Sika had sworn himself as the slave and aide of Barry Rand for life.

"Yeah," Barry laughed. "Just right for a murder. And the gas, Sika. Glad you reminded me about that. Almost forgot to watch for a gas station. Tap me on the shoulder if you spot one."

Down to get yuh with a taxi, honey—

Barry's keen eyes flashed over his instrument panel. The luminous dials showed plainly when the flashes of lightning didn't illuminate the whole crimson ship.

Altimeter stood at five thousand. Oil pressure was well up. Tachometer showed the Liberty plugging nicely throttled back to fifteen hundred. Gas gauge showed a quarter full.

"Got a good hour of flying yet," Barry called back. "Then this storm ought to be over."

"It be almost daylight too then, Master," came Sika's voice. "Be easier we get gas in dark if we get out of this storm."

"And speaking of storms," Barry came back, "this is about the swellest sky party I've ever seen the big boy put on."

He was shouting himself hoarse through the tube to make himself heard above the crashing of thunder.

"Never saw a storm hit us quicker either. Out half an hour and circling around trying to find a public-spirited German drome that would like to donate a little gas to the cause and bam, it smacks us without any warning at all. Didn't have a chance of running out of it. Closed in on us from all sides. Good thing we got a good compass to fly by or we might be headed for Berlin without knowing it."

Crash! Bang! Roar! Another convulsion of lightning shook the ship from prop to rudder post. It was cavorting like a spring lamb in the gusty air. Leaping and bucking and plunging. But Barry Rand seemed to be handling the crate with perfect ease. He glanced at his wrist watch, soaked with rain water.

"You're a little off on your time, Sika," he ventured "Won't be daylight for two or three hours yet anyway, I guess. And if this storm goes on we won't be able to see anything when it is daylight. We got to find some place to gas up and it'll be in the dark."

Barry Rand stopped talking. He had been staring fixedly at the watch on his wrist. He shook it. Shook it again.

"What the—?" he cracked. "Damn thing stopped."

He shook it again. It was the only time-piece in the ship. For the first time in the last two minutes his eyes flashed to the instrument board again. They had checked everything else. Now they focused on the luminous compass card.

That time Barry Rand came up with a jerk. His eyes were almost popping out of his head.

"What the hell!"

CRASH! Bang! That terrific clap of thunder came as an answer to his question. The compass was spinning like a top. Round and round and round before his staring eyes. His only contact with the earth. And that was gone now!

The storm was growing worse. The Red Falcon plane was bucking and groaning like a wild horse in the last throws of a bucking contest.

Slowly, Barry Rand nodded to himself and ducked lower under the cowling to keep that hail of water from pouring down his neck. His eyes never left the compass for several minutes. Round and round and round. The thunder bellowed about them. Lightning played about the wires almost continuously now.

"So you're to blame," Barry said to himself, looking up into the face of the blinding light flashes. "O. K but we'll fool you yet. You can't hold out like this forever."

Blam! Boom! The storm seemed to be answering him with still more violence.

Again Barry flashed a glance over his instrument panel. Everything else was working well. Sika's voice came through the tube.

"Where are we now, Master ?"

Barry grinned, but there wasn't quite as much mirth in it as there had been before the compass had gone haywire.

"I can tell you exactly," he said. "We're directly over a large island known as the continents of Europe and Asia. And it's bounded by such famous things as Africa, the North Pole, the Atlantic and the Pacific Oceans.

"Not good time for make jokes, Master. God of the jungle get mad tonight. And—"

"Get mad?" Barry cracked. "For crying out loud. How much madder can he get than this? Hope he doesn't lose his head."

His eyes fell on the altimeter. He'd be lost now. Things came up before him. Flying blind with nothing but an altimeter to tell him what it was all about. The storm battered the fast ship about murderously. He might be traveling in a circle. Or he might be headed in any one of a dozen directions—toward Russia, or Switzerland, or Germany or France. Or worse even than the rest—straight out to sea.

But would that be worse? A watery grave or facing a firing squad? That would be his fate if he were captured on either side of the lines. He'd escaped from a firing squad of his own Yanks when he had been convicted of being a traitor—unjustly. The Germans hated him. They had caught him as a spy enough times to make death certain if they captured him again.

The Red Falcon plane flew straight because Barry Rand was lost. Might as well fly straight if he could do it.

Barry eased back on the throttle still farther. Must conserve the gas as much as possible. He had to ride out the storm before landing, and then—there was no telling what might happen. They might be traveling with that sixty mile wind or into it. He couldn't tell in the air. He could see nothing but blackness about him and feel nothing but the sting of driving rain.

Minutes flashed past with maddening speed. Barry could almost see the gas gauge go down. Lower and lower. He glanced at his watch twice and cursed each time. Shook it. The watch wouldn't run any more.

Sika's voice came through the tube.

"Master, you not fly by compass. Compass not steady."

Barry nodded his head.

"Your observations are marvelous for the time of night or rather morning, Sika. I'll say the compass isn't steady. Spinning like a tornado on the loose. One of those flashes of lightning must have—"

Blam! Crash! Barry stopped and ducked. Again the lightning played about wings and wires that dripped and glistened with a clammy sheen in the brilliant flashes.

"Boy, was that a honey!"

"What we do, Master? Sika not afraid of men when he can fight. But not like storm when god of jungle get mad and roar."

"I've seen pleasanter places to spend an evening, big boy. Get out the instruction book and look up paragraph sixty-six on flying in thunderstorms. See what it says, Sika."

"Huh?" Sika grunted.

"Thanks," grinned Barry. "Now hang on big boy, and if you think you got a drag with that jungle god of yours, start prayin'."

Minutes. Lower gas. Barry dropped the nose and glued his eyes to the altimeter. Down to four thousand. And then to three. And next two thousand. They might be near the Alps for all they knew. But they weren't over them. That was certain. They'd be crashed by now.

"Got to go down through this storm and see if we can pick anything out of the mess," Barry called. "Hang on. Might hit something."

"Yes, Master."

DOWN, down. Barry's hand reached up and pulled the lever for a flare release. One shot from beneath the fuselage of the Red Falcon plane and burst below, shedding a weird light in the slashing rain and driving mist

Barry pushed on the stick instantly. The nose of the crimson crate dropped and the Liberty whined as the speed increased. In tight, diving circles, Barry followed that flare as closely as he could. He allowed it to drop before him. The first sign of the flare stopping its fall would be an indication that he was close to something.

His eyes shifted to the altimeter and back to the flare. Back and forth. Back and forth. He was jumping about the cockpit like a jack in the box following those two.

The flare was still floating down on its small parachute. He could feel Sika staring down into the murderous storm over his shoulder.

But the flare showed nothing. The altimeter showed much. That last showed that they had only two hundred feet from their starting point. That starting point had been the aerie of the Red Falcon on flat-topped Saar Mountain high in the Vosges. They could show two hundred feet and still have plenty of altitude over the flatter parts of Europe.

Barry's eyes were staring. They had dropped rapidly with that flare. Down, down. And his eyes caught something on the altimeter that spelled plenty of danger. The altimeter was down to less than zero. A hundred feet below the level of Saar Mountain. Two hundred feet. And then five hundred feet.

His head was spinning from watching the light and the altimeter. He gave up watching the latter now. It told him nothing except that he was several hundred—almost a thousand feet—under the altitude at which they had taken off in the Vosges Mountains. They were in the flat, lowlands of France or Germany, or even Russia. Had been flying for more than two hours now since their start. Could be almost anywhere, with that gale of the storm blowing them about.

Down, down went the altimeter.

A thousand. Now fifteen hundred feet behind their take-off altitude. The cold sweat was gradually breaking out all over Barry Rand's body. Over a quarter of a mile lower than their aerie. And going still farther down.

The flare was nearly burned out. It was dimmer and dimmer. The storm seemed to have increased in violence with the lesser altitude. He could hardly see the light of the flare at a hundred feet from the circling plane.

He cursed and pulled on the release lever again. An instant later another flare burst out beside the first that was about gone. Down, down, more cautiously. Then Barry was yanking on the stick and staring with bulging eyes at what he had seen. Rough, rippling things they were. Like waves of the sea, long and rolling.

"See that, Sika?" he shouted as the liberty roared in the climb.

At the same time both the old flare and the new one went out completely.

"Sika see something look like waves on water," came the answer.

"Right," cracked Barry. "Those were waves just under our nose. Damn near dragged the landing gear in them. And they're big enough to swamp a house and then some."

Silence except for the throbbing motor. Barry was trying to think. The storm was thicker than ever. He was having a tough time keeping the Red Falcon plane on an even keel. No compass. Over a large body of water. But what was it? Might be the Mediterranean. Might be the Baltic—but that wasn't likely. More probable that it was—

"The North Sea!" Barry hissed at sudden thought. "This storm seemed to be traveling west. We've been driven out to sea. And which way is home?"

Then he was sitting up straight. A flash had come. A blinding flash of lightning. He hadn't been able to see anything but rain and driving mist and more rain by that flash. But a second or so after, there appeared a dull glow of red on his right.

For once in his life Barry Rand felt helpless. The lashing sea beneath him. The raging storm around—and about to run out of gas!

His eyes were staring painfully at that dull glow through the storm.

Sput! Brrrum! Spat! Sput!

The Liberty was gasping now. He shot a horrified but resigned glance at the gas gauge. Knew the answer before he saw the "EMPTY" there.

He dropped the nose of the plane straight for that dull red glow. The Liberty sputtered once more and died cold with a couple of convulsive kicks to make the dying more pained.

That glow. It grew brighter. But what was it? Coming down to a forced landing—where? The glow might be a ship that had been struck by lightning. Or it might be a building on land. In either case it was a thousand to one shot that the landing would be good enough for the two to walk away from.

But down for it. Teeth clenched. A steady hand on the stick.

BARRY'S free hand pulled on the flare release lever once more. His last flare.

Crash! Lightning flashed ahead and then behind them. For that moment it was so bright that he couldn't see whether the flare had lighted or not. Then darkness and the weird, ghastly white illumination of the flare.

But he couldn't circle now. That glow ahead might mean land. That was his only hope. Water had been beneath him when he had yanked out of his dive; he had zoomed and turned blindly away in another direction.

The light of the flare wasn't helping him much. He could feel the faithful giant black Sika leaning over his shoulder, staring silently into the pounding rain and driving mists.

It was deathly still except for the wind racing through the wings and the drumming of the storm against the fabric. Barry could feel Sika's hot breath by his ear.

Crash! Another blast of lightning zigzagged about them. Barry was fighting to bring the plane down right side up. The wind was lashing and driving at a terrific pace.

"Master! Flare gone out!"

That from Sika, who had turned his head to look backward. Barry nodded. There was nothing to go by now except that glow of red through the storm.

Lower and lower. Barry's nerves were going fast. Why didn't they strike something? Why didn't they see something? Darkness like ink about them with only an uncertain spot of red-orange flickering in front.

Suddenly, Barry's whole being seemed to turn to ice. He had heard something ahead. Wild shouting. He felt Sika's hand on his shoulder holding him to silence while the keen-eared, half-savage black man listened with the alert senses of those born to the out-of-doors.

"Shouting, Master. Land. Men shouting as they run, Master."

Barry Rand was leaning half over the windshield staring ahead. A thrill raced up his spine and died at the same moment. For the words that came from below were in German. Even as he listened, there was a terrific lightning blast. The scene below became plain.

Everything was distinct through the rain, because there was no more mist at his level, fifty feet above the water.

He could make out a great loading wharf, faced by a warehouse building. And that building was furnishing the red glow, for it was a mass of flames at one end.

Split seconds seemed like years as he came on down. He could see a little by the light of the flames but being straight ahead, they blinded him and threw a weird prospective of light upon the wharf that was large enough for a landing.

Crash! With another bolt of lightning, Barry spotted his position. The stick came back in his stomach. Wheels touched and rolled. A German plunged headlong into the rolling crimson crate and sprawled with a terrified scream. "*Gott im Himmel.* We all die."

Men were running across the wharf in a mad lunge to escape from something. They were all headed away from the burning building. Mad men with fear ashened faces. They seemed hardly to notice the landing of the crimson plane in their midst. Their only thought seemed to be of fleeing some horrible menace. Something that lurked in that burning building.

The Red Falcon plane knocked over another German and another before it stopped. The Boches ran crazily into it, yelling with fear as they went down.

One German—a short, chunky fellow, the last to be knocked down before the Red Falcon plane stopped—was yelling at the top of his voice. He was back under the tail of the plane straggling to get up. He was obviously a mechanic for he was dressed in overalls and everything—himself and his clothing were smeared with black grease.

His hands went up on the side of the rudder as he tried to get free. Sika whirled to his guns.

"We fight, Master?" he pleaded.

"Hold it," Barry hissed back. "Can't tell yet. They don't seem to *verstehen* anything around here. Gone nuts. No use starting anything unless we have to."

Already, Barry was out of his cockpit and running back to the tail where the German mechanic was held down by the hack end of the fuselage over his thick stomach. The mechanic was screaming something.

His grease-smeared hands had made dark streaks downward on each side of the rudder.

"*Gott in Himmel*, save me," he shouted.

Barry didn't trust his German just then. But something snapped inside him. Now that the suspense of landing was over and they were down anything seemed a relief. Barry laughed. He couldn't help it. He could see the fear on the faces of the Germans as they ran past him, most of them looking back at the building which was blazing brightly now.

The rain was still coming down but not in such bucket-fulls as before.

"*ACH Gott*," went on the German. "Get me out of here. We all die. *Macht schnell*."

Barry heaved on the tail. Sika was out of the crimson plane to help. The German wriggled free. Queer that all of these men should be so scared that they wouldn't even notice the Red Falcon plane and the lack of identification markings, neither black crosses nor the color circles. What did that building contain that frightened them so?

The German mechanic was facing Barry, shaking him by the flying suit that covered the Yank uniform beneath.

"*Gott*. Fly. Get away. Quick. Before it is too late. Take me with you. The world is coming to an end."

Barry stiffened. He stared hard into that white face that looked up pleading to him. He shot a glance sidewise at the burning warehouse and nodded slowly, gravely.

A million thoughts seemed to crowd his brain for recognition at the same time. He could see what it was that frightened the Germans. At least he thought he could. Ammunition was stored in that warehouse. The warehouse had been struck by lightning. It was on fire. The ammunition would blow up any minute. And with the quantity that that warehouse would hold, it wouldn't make much difference whether a human was right there or half a mile away. That part of the earth would be definitely forgotten forever. There was no use running. Couldn't get far enough to make much difference.

Barry hesitated before he spoke. Tried to form his words in German to say what he meant. Then laboriously he gutturaled.

"No use running. The ammunition will explode before one can get away far, *nicht wahr?* Better to stay here and pray, ja?"

The German mechanic flew into a new frenzy of fear.

"*Ach, nein. Es ist nicht* ammunition. It is something in there that will end the world, perhaps. We do not know. A new chemical that when mixed with water separates the oxygen and hydrogen and makes it burn. The whole ocean would catch fire."

Barry stared down at the little fat fellow in astonishment. It was his turn to grow excited. He snatched the German by the shirt front and shook him.

"*Was ist?*" he demanded. "What are you talking about. What is this crazy thing you're talking about?"

"It is true," the mechanic insisted. "Hurry and start the plane and take me away from here for telling you of your danger. The inventor was making demonstrations with the water bombs. They change water to material that will burn. *Ach,* it would end the war for us. But he is the only one who can control it. We plan to burn the whole of the British Isles. Would that not end the war? Now take me before—"

"We're out of gas," Barry stammered. "Where is gasoline?"

For answer, the mechanic pointed to a pile of drums. There were hundreds of them on the wharf near a docked freighter. Barry whirled to Sika. The giant black had been bending down at the tail of the plane where the grease had been smeared when the German mechanic had tried to wriggle free from under the fuselage.

"Gas," Barry hissed, "in those drums. All we want. Hurry, before somebody recognizes this crate."

Barry thought he caught the faintest trace of a smile on the face of the giant black when he said that last. But he didn't take the time to figure it out then. Sika ran for the pile of drums. The German mechanic waddled after him to help. Barry followed and together they heaved a drum to the top of the open filler cap of the crimson crate and allowed the precious liquid to gurgle into the Red Falcon plane's tank,

Sika held the drum upright while it drained. Together they got another and poured. A hundred gallons. Full tank. That second had been brought purposely by Barry Rand. He wanted to stay longer. Fantastic story this about the chemical that changed water to a liquid that would burn. Might be possible. He was going to stay and see anyway. So they brought the other drum and filled the tank to overflowing.

The German was half in the rear cockpit. Barry was taking hold of his padding ready to climb in. The fire was threatening the Red Falcon plane more and more every second. The whole roof of the warehouse was burning madly.

"*Macht schnell! Macht schnell!*" the mechanic was crying. "In another moment the chemical will be loosed by the burning and we will be blazing torches of flame."

Then from the warehouse, Barry saw a group of men filing out. They were passing across the wharf toward the gangplank of the freighter. But they were not running as the others. Rather they were moving at a fast, but careful walk.

There, were five men in all. And each one carried something—a round, steel bottle-like container the size of a gallon jug. Carried it as though his life depended upon it

Barry froze with his foot on the stirrup. He heard a cry of joy from the German mechanic at the edge of Sika's cockpit. The big black, Sika, was poised at the propeller to start the Liberty.

"*Ach,*" cried the German mechanic. "It is all right now. There *ist nein* danger. There go the containers of the dangerous chemical. They will take them to the British Isles—the freighter shall transfer them to a submarine. The whole coast will burn. Rivers will be on fire until they burn dry. But we are safe here. No need to flee now. *Ach,* that was a close call."

The Boche stepped down from the stirrup. Barry Rand hesitated. He flashed a glance toward the freighter. The crew was preparing to cast off even now. Those five men with their deadly containers had gone up the gangplank. The gangplank was being hauled hurriedly aboard.

He whirled to the German.

"*Danke,*" he said.

And to Sika at the front of the plane.

"Let's go, big boy. Got to get on that freighter before it takes off. Got to work fast."

"But the plane, Master."

"Can't think about that now."

They were running across the wharf. The freighter was already pulling out, turning slowly out of the dark, rain-soaked harbor.

BARRY and Sika reached the edge of the wharf at the same time, and together they leaped across a six-foot stretch of space. There was a yell from the crew as they landed on the deck. A sailor in an *offizier's* cap pushed forward followed by four others. He demanded to know their reason for boarding the ship.

Sika hissed something to Barry.

"I fight. Master?"

"O. K.," Barry snapped back. "Let's go."

That came in English. The sailors didn't catch it. Neither did the *offizier*, apparently because he repeated his question in German. But this time his hand moved toward a long-nosed Mauser pistol.

Barry stepped to one side, Sika to the other. As though by signal both lowered their heads and charged with fists drawn back, ready to deal out punishment.

Two men against five. But the odds weren't so uneven after the first flurry.

Sika's great arms shot out. One caught the *offizier* a back-hand stroke that laid him flat on the deck. The other seized a sailor who had come in with lowered head and swinging fists. Before that sailor knew what had hit him, Sika's right fist had caught him behind the ear and sent him sailing over the rail into the water—and eternity.

Three others came in. Barry ducked a sledge-hammer blow to the head and came up with his left. A grunt—and the sailor staggered. He came in again. Sika had spun and snatched that sailor and another in his great arms. He held them at arm's length and then brought them together with terrific force. There came the dull thud of crushing skull bone. Blood spurted and in a moment the deck was slippery from red fluid.

Barry whirled on the other sailor but slightly too late. He had side-stepped and leaped upon Barry while he turned.

Wam! A rock-like fist crashed against Barry's jaw and sent htm tumbling backward. He got up in a bound and came back, cautious now but mad clean through. The German charged him. Barry was a little dizzy, but ready. He backed away at just the right moment and stepped in again in a clever feint.

Wam! His right and then his left finished that argument, with both connecting to the chin of the other. The *offizier* was getting up.

Crack! His Mauser spoke; there was a howl of rage and pain as it flew from his hand. Sika had leaped just a split second before the gun had fired. The arm that had held the Mauser pistol now hung limp and twisted and bleeding.

Sika's left hand came up from somewhere in the dimming light and smacked hard. The *offizier*, too, went over the side of the ship and fell with a lifeless splash into the harbor.

Running feet sounded on the deck. More men were coming. That shot had brought them. Barry whirled and stared about him. The ship had moved well out in the harbor by now and was proceeding at full speed.

He pulled Sika back in the shadow of a ventilating funnel. They crouched there, until the newcomers came to the point where they could see their brother shipmates lying in the pools of blood.

There were exclamations and angry mutterings.

Barry and Sika leaped into the open. The big black was first. His great hands snatched two of the sailors from behind; pulling them apart, he hurled them together again with that same skull-crushing thud.

Barry picked his man and, let go with all he had. But the fellow was big and powerful. He fought like a demon, and yelled his head off as he flailed his fists.

Barry caught one blow in the stomach that hurled him toward the rail. He staggered uncertainly for a moment, then came in again.

Sika stood near. No others were coming for the moment. The Red Falcon leader ducked and weaved and then came straight up with a smashing uppercut; the German's body lifted up, tumbled over the rail and plunged into the sea.

The two Yanks stood panting, motionless, listening on the deck that was strewn with limp bodies. Only one shot had been fired and that by the enemy.

Barry stooped and picked up the *offizier's* Mauser. Making sure it was loaded, he listened again. There was no other sound of men coming. The ship was making good time headed out to the North Sea. The light was growing dim from the land where the warehouse burned. Barry pointed toward it.

"We'll have to swim back there," he said. "And the more time we take for what's coming, the farther we'll have to swim. We've got to get these five guys."

"Yes, Master," Sika said in the darkness about them now.

The storm had ceased and only a light drizzle like heavy mist dampened their leathery' faces.

"One of these five," Barry went on, "is the inventor of this damnable stuff that's supposed to turn water to flame. Remember what that Heinie mechanic said about this inventor being the only one who could control it."

"Yes, Master."

"Then it's a ten to one bet that if we get rid of him the whole formula will be destroyed. Good Lord, Sika! Think what this would mean if it's true. Burning rivers dry. Lighting up and setting the Atlantic ocean on fire. We don't know how this works and we can't take chances with it. But somehow—"

HE stopped short and jerked Sika back into thel shadow of the funnel once more. Voices came from the other end. Two men were walking toward them from the forward deck. From their hiding place, Barry and Sika watched them draw near,

"Not those two," he hissed to Sika after the pair had passed. "Got a hunch. That one bird was one of the five who helped carry the steel containers to the ship. Let's follow them. We've got to get those bottles somehow and take care of them. Don't know what to—"

They stepped out and softly, skirting the cabin edge, crept up behind the two. Barry tensed as he overheard a few words of the conversation.

"*Ach*, it is not dangerous at all to the ship, captain. These steel bottles are perfectly safe to handle except if heated. Of course, the stopper must not be removed until time for their use."

Barry nodded in the darkness. His mind was working rapidly. If he could find some way to protect these bottles against heat or the removing of the stopper—But here before him were the commander of the ship, and the inventor of the fiendish chemical that might turn the world upside down.

"Master," Sika murmured close to his ear as they crept on. "I get um?"

Barry paused for a second. Paused just too long before he gave the final order.

"O. K."

The two just ahead of them stopped and turned sharply. Light shown on the deck from an open door. Sika had tensed to leap. Barry laid a heavy hand on him to hold him back.

All too late. The two had heard the sound behind them and whirled. The smaller man, the inventor, darted through the door. The captain turned defiantly.

Barry ducked past his outflung fist and shot into the room.

He heard the grunt and thud of a man going down. Sika had done his work well on the captain. Barry was in the lighted room. He blinked in the brightness. The Mauser pistol he had taken from the *offizier* on deck was gleaming in his hand.

Five men gasped and stared at him. Five faces whitened as they gazed into the muzzle of that Mauser. Their hands raised.

Barry's eyes flashed about the room. They fastened on shiny, steel globe-like bottles.

Barry moved closer to the steel bottles. He saw the inventor grow rigid, then leap for his precious bottles of chemical.

"*Nein, nein,*" he cried, "you shall not touch my bottles. That chemical is all I have. I cannot afford to make more. And the government will not provide me with money for more until I have demonstrated that my claims are true."

At the same time the little man, pleading, moved one arm down toward a button in the wall. He had leaped before the table and the steel bottles. His arm flashed down abruptly and his finger extended toward the button.

Crack! Crack! The Mauser pistol in Barry's hand leaped and spat flame. The bullets found their mark in the inventor's head. But before those bullets had struck, the German's pointing finger had touched the button.

A loud clanging bell began ringing somewhere. The inventor slumped to the floor in a pool of blood.

Barry leaped toward the table and the open safe. The four other Boches grew tense.

"Back toward that door," Barry ordered. "One by one."

They backed toward the door. Sika would know what to do when they passed that threshold.

Barry held the Mauser in his left hand. With his right he began placing the deadly bottles of steel in the safe. Five in all. He heard the second man cry out as he backed for the door and Sika caught him from behind. The third German was backing through the door before Barry's threatening Mauser pistol.

Bang! He slammed the heavy door of the safe shut, spun the dial. Sound of running feet below decks. That bell had started something.

Barry pointed the Mauser at the combination dial and pulled again and again. Bullets spat and pinged at an angle from the steel door. And the chunks of steel wedged their way to jam the unlocking device.

He raced for the deck.

PING! A bullet slithered past his nose. He ducked back and out again. Gasped at what he saw in the light of the open door. Sika was staggering, pitching over on his face. Running feet were coming from the forward end of the ship.

Barry slammed the door shut to cut out the light. With a mighty effort, he picked the body of Sika from the deck and slid it over the rail, then plunged after it.

In the water, he managed to find Sika where he had come up for the first time. That great black body was limp. Barry held him with one hand while he stripped off his own flying suit with the other.

Lights flashed from the deck of the moving ship. The boat, some distance ahead of them now, began to turn around. Rifles cracked.

Barry was swimming frantically. At the same time he was trying to revive Sika by slapping him in the face with stinging blows as often as he could afford to miss a stroke.

He stared at the ship. It had half turned. Then it had straightened out again. It wasn't coming back. He should have felt relief—but he didn't. Whether the ship trapped him or not, he was still in a terrible jam. The Red Falcon plane sitting on the wharf—Germans would be thick around it by now. There was not a chance of getting off in that. Still, they must go on—must reach shore and get away if they could.

But the ship had to be blown up. That would be the only way of being sure the fiendish chemical was destroyed.

Barry began to feel a little movement of the giant black body he towed along so laboriously.

Ahead the fire of the warehouse was burning down. Fire fighters had it under control by now. It glowed a dull red, far over the water. And beyond that, in the east, gray streaks were forming.

Sika moved and floundered then. That was a thrilling sensation to Barry Rand. He doubted if he could swim much farther with the big Black weighing him down.

Then in the darkness, Sika spoke and struck out. He had regained consciousness.

"This you, Master?" And without waiting for the reply. "Again you save Sika's life, Master."

Minutes later Barry, in his second wind, said, "Looks crazy to keep heading for that wharf where our plane is. Won't be a chance of getting it away. They'll spot it sure without identification marks of any kind. Even over here on the North Sea, they've likely heard of the Red Falcon."

"Maybe not have trouble," Sika ventured. "We try anyway."

Again that suspicion of a smile about the thick lips. On and on they swam together. Then, when it seemed that Barry couldn't take another stroke, Sika's strong hand had him by the collar and was dragging him ashore a little way from the wharf in the gray dawn.

Barry lay there for a few minutes until he could get strength to rise. He got to his feet. Sika had gone to peer over the wharf. He came back grinning.

"Ship still there, Master. Nobody around except one two Boches. Everybody fight fire yet."

"Huh?" Barry leaped to his feet.

"Sika find something else," the big black smiled. "We go bomb boat now. Come. Get big bomb."

Barry followed Sika onto the wharf, and along toward the Red Falcon plane. His face was wrinkled in perplexity. Why had the Germans allowed the most famous plane on the Front to stand on this wharf without guard?"

Sika turned to the right where there was a pile of long, tapered steel-jacketed things with round noses and veined ends. Aerial bombs laying there for transportation. Big bombs for Gothas. Sika picked one up. It must have weighed two hundred pounds. But he carried it as though it had no weight at all.

They walked toward the ship. A German soldier stood back as they approached and looked at them in the dim light of dawn. He had been peering into the cockpit. A shout of alarm went out as he saw the uniform of the enemy on both men. Their flying suits had hidden those before. But those flying suits were floating somewhere out on the cold North Sea.

Barry leaped for the German. He rained everything he had into that howling face. The German staggered back and went down. Barry scrambled to the cockpit. Already Sika had put the bomb in his rear cockpit and was winding up the prop.

Contact!

Crack! Crack! The prop whirled. Bullets whined around them. Men were running toward them from the burning building—the flames were nearly out now.

On the third whirl of the prop blade the Liberty snorted and roared. Sika ducked under the wing and leaped to his cockpit. The Liberty blasted. It coughed and choked and ran fitfully. It was cold but it would soon warm.

Barry raced down toward the other end of the wharf. He spun there before running men could pick them off with their guns and headed back into the wind. The motor was warmer now. Faster and faster—and then slowly into the air with Sika and the big bomb.

Straight out across a pinkish sky they roared. Straight out to the North Sea. Barry's eyes were glued on a trail of smoke that drifted back from the stack of a ship far out at sea. He roared toward it, the Liberty wide open. He dropped the nose. Headed for the middle of the ship.

"Get set, big boy," he called through the tube.

Sika nodded and stood up poising the bomb over the edge ready to let go. Then he heaved it. Barry turned, followed the bomb as it spun downward.

Wam! It struck almost exactly midships. The explosion shot the Red Falcon plane high into the air. Barry grinned and turned back for the mainland. He climbed. They were roaring over the wharf at five thousand feet altitude on their way home. Barry stared down and thumbed his nose at the grunting antiaircraft guns. A puzzled expression came over his face.

"What I can't figure, Sika," he called through the tube, "is how we ever got away with that job there on the wharf. It was daylight when we got there. Why didn't the Heinies recognize our ship and seize it?"

He heard Sika laugh through the tube.

"Ship have markings, Master," he chuckled.

"Huh?" Barry grunted. "The Red Falcon ship has no markings at all!"

"Remember, Master," Sika said, "when mechanic get caught under tail. He have very dirty, greasy hands. He put one hand up on each side of rudder trying to get out. He make two big black marks up and down the rudder. While you talk with him, Sika rub through middle other way. Make marks. That form black cross on each side of rudder."

Barry was twisted round in his seat. The ship was headed for the aerie high on Saar Mountain in the rugged Vosges miles and miles across Europe. But suddenly the ship yawed to the right and then to the left as Barry Rand kicked his rudder bar so he could see both sides of the rudder.

And there, as Sika had said, was a black cross—rather crude and rough, but a black cross just the same, on either side of the rudder. The Red Falcon plane straightened out its course and kept on for the aerie.

Barry Rand grinned and his lips moved.

"Well, I'll be damned!" he chuckled.

Dynamite Devils

"Follow me now as I have followed you—if you can!" A strange crimson ship dropped that message on the Falcon's aerie. Puzzled—but mad as hell—Barry Rand took up the taunting challenge for a whirlwind showdown!

Dynamite Devils

BARRY RAND had no premonition of the giant trap that lay in store for him as he roared homeward from another raid for supplies. His tanks were full. Machine-gun belts and double pans were well stocked with ammunition.

He was light-hearted but a bit weary. It was early dawn. Barry eased back in the bucket seat of the front cockpit of the Red Falcon plane and let his favorite tune moan sleepily from his lips.

Be down to get yuh with a taxi, honey, Better be ready about—

"Master!" That single word came to him through the tube from the back cockpit. Sika, the giant black aide, had spoken, perhaps in warning.

The tune stopped. Barry turned to listen.

"What, Sika?"

Already he had cut the gun and they were gliding down to a landing on Saar Mountain, a flat-topped peak of the rugged Vosges Mountains where was the aerie of the Red Falcon.

"Look behind, Master."

Barry whirled in his seat. In the light of the early morning, Sika was pointing with a great right arm out across the lower mountain peaks toward a tiny speck above the horizon far to the west. Barry's eyes narrowed.

"What the—"

His hand dove inside the cockpit and came out with a pair of powerful field glasses. He raised them to his eyes and stared.

"Well, I'll be a—" he exploded and stopped. "That's funny."

"They see us land if we go in now, Master," Sika ventured.

Barry shook his head.

"Don't think so," he guessed. "We're too far down into the mountains at this end. That crate sticks up in the sky. That's why we can see it. Anyway, we've got the fastest ship on the Front. We'll pull away from him before we land."

"Yes, Master. But how he come this close if we faster than he is, Master?" Sika asked.

Barry had already pushed on the throttle. The Red Falcon plane leaped ahead, plunged deeper into the mountain passes. There was a winding canyon that they tore through, flipped out of it and into a stall.

Barry's face developed a troubled expression while he tore through the canyon and cut the motor again. The stick came back at the touch of his skilled hand, The Red Falcon plane leaped upward with nothing but its momentum to hurl it on.

It slowed. Hovered at the rim rock of the flat-topped Mount Saar and settled lightly the six inches to the edge of the field. The motor roared and the crimson plane shot ahead over the smooth field. Before a snug log cabin it stopped.

Barry got out of the cockpit and stared skyward. He was thinking of Sika's words. He nodded.

"Afraid you're right, Sika," he guessed. He was listening. "Something queer about that other plane appearing like this. If it had come from the side we would have noticed it, wouldn't we?"

"Yes, Master. Sky clear. No cloud this morning."

"Right. Not a cloud in the sky. We were both watching as we came home. Did you see it before?"

The giant black shook his head.

"Sika not see any ship after we bomb that German field far to west and come home."

"Then where did this bird come from?" Barry demanded.

Sika shook his head. Then he stopped short to listen.

"Master!" There was awe, almost fright in that word.

Barry heard it too, then. A low, moaning throb coming from the west. It was high-pitched, almost reaching a scream as it came nearer.

Barry spun round and ran out nearer the center of the field. Sika was beside him. Trees screened the sound from them but they could tell plainly that a plane was coming with plenty of speed.

Barry tensed for an instant. The plane hadn't come into view yet. He raced back toward the Red Falcon ship, yelled at Sika.

"Hurry. Get this crate out of sight so they won't see our field, No one has ever found the aerie of the Red Falcon."

They hauled on the ship. Sika picked up the tail with one hand and with Barry's help they pushed it toward the overhanging trees where it was accustomed to hiding.

They had shoved it nearly into place when the scream became deafening above them. They whirled. Too late. The rear of the fuselage was sticking out from under the trees.

Like a bolt of lightning a crimson streak was shrieking over their heads not fifty feet up. Something hurtled out behind the racing slip stream of the propeller, something that began to fall in a graceful arc for a spot not far from where Barry and Sika seemed riveted to the ground.

Even then, they were both immovable for another full second. The sight before them was the most amazing thing they had ever seen.

SO FAR as they could perceive, that crimson, flashing ship was the double of the Red Falcon plane. It was the same color. The wings looked as though they had been taken from a Spad. The fuselage was at least the same shape as a Fokker D-7 fuselage. And from what they could see of the motor under the cowling it looked like another Liberty.

"Another Red Falcon plane," Barry gasped. He cursed and leaped for the message streamer. Sika was rubbing his eyes and staring again.

"Maybe we crazy, Master, and see things. That just like Red Falcon plane. Even got no circles or no crosses like ours."

The scream of the crimson mystery plane could still be heard. It took on a lower note. The pilot had ducked behind another mountain and was throttling down the engine. Could it be possible that he was going to try to land on Saar Mountain?

They received the answer to that almost instantly. With a high-pitched scream, the mystery plane zoomed into sight again and thundered at them. Barry could see the pilot grinning as he roared ten feet above their heads. Then he dropped out of sight beyond the trees and they could only hear the drone of his giant engine. Barry's fingers flew now into the sack at the point of the weighted Vee streamer. They came out with a note. He frowned as he read it. Then he read it out loud to Sika.

Follow me now as I have followed you—if you can.

The Red Falcon.

"Why, the dirty, low-lived—"

Then Barry stopped short. The crimson devilish thing was hurling back at them from the other side of the mountain. Barry didn't wait to have him pass this time. He leaped into a wild run for the Red Falcon plane.

"The nerve of a guy like that," he yelled. "'If we can!' And signing himself 'Red Falcon,' not that I'm especially proud of the name but I'll be damned if anybody else can throw a bluff about it. Or maybe he thinks he's kidding us."

As he finished, he was in the cockpit, the Red Falcon plane was turned around, and Sika stood at the prop.

"Contact!"

"Contact!"

Wam! The giant Liberty motor caught and roared the first time. Sika ducked flat as the plane slithered ahead. He leaped up when the wing passed and snatched the side of his cockpit.

With a scream, the Red Falcon plane roared across the top of the mountain and soared into the air. The other crimson plane had made a wide turn to the north and was hurling almost across their path, but headed farther on toward the front lines and the west.

Barry sat hunched over his stick and glared across his sights. He saw something else then that he hadn't noticed before. There was a rear cockpit in that other plane, just like the cockpit for Sika. But it was empty.

Wildly, he pushed on the throttle for more speed. But somehow there didn't seem to be any more pep in the old Red Falcon plane. And that space between the nose of Barry's plane and the tail of the other, now that they had straightened out in a race, didn't vary.

Then to Barry's consternation, he saw that the space between them was growing wider. The mystery plane was pulling away from him!

At long range, Barry took aim and tramped down on his trigger button. White tracers and yellow fluttered out front from his four nose guns, the twin Vickers and the two Spandau guns in his wings.

His heart sank. Anger welled stronger within him. Those tracers were falling short. They were dying out before they came near to the mystery ship.

He cursed and tried again. He heard the rattle of the twin Lewis guns firing over his head. Whirled.

Sika was braced behind his flame-tipped guns shooting at random over the top of the propeller arc. His face was set and hard. But there was no sign of satisfaction there. Only disappointment.

He ceased firing and shook his head.

"Think maybe I get him with two bullets, Master," he tried to explain.

"No use," groaned Barry, "for once we're stumped. This guy's got plenty more speed than we have. He's making a fool of us."

Still he hung on. Sika's voice came a moment later.

"You think he German or Yank, Master?"

Barry shook his head.

"Couldn't prove it by me, big boy. But from his speed I wouldn't be surprised to learn he was the very devil himself. Look at that guy go. He's gained a mile on us since we left the Vosges and—"

Barry broke off and stared at the sight ahead of him now. Sika cried out from behind.

"Master. Allied planes. They attack from above."

"Yeah. See 'em."

Through clenched teeth, Barry was hurling on as fast as he could. He pushed wildly on the gun for more speed. It wasn't there.

OUT front two flights of seven Nieuports were streaking down out of the morning sun straight for the tail of the crimson mystery ship.

Both Barry and Sika simply looked—speechless. The Nieuports were streaking down from above, but the mystery plane didn't seem to notice.

"It won't be long now," Barry shouted through the tube.

At the same time he lifted his glasses before his eyes. Another exclamation slipped past his lips.

"Why, that guy flying the red crate isn't even looking behind him. The—"

Something was happening out front then. The red plane had dropped its nose slightly. The Nieuports fairly swarmed about its tail.

Blam!

There was a terrific flash and then a rumbling explosion, the shock of which both Barry and Sika could feel even at the distance that separated them from the fight ahead.

Something was falling. For a moment they couldn't see the red mystery ship, but they saw many others. One Nieuport was tumbling earthward in pieces. The rest veered sharply to the right and left to avoid collision. All succeeded except two.

Three Nieuports gone at a single flash! The others turned, as though dazed, and tried to make another attack at long range.

Blam!

Another blinding flash, followed by a terrific explosion. Another Nieuport burst into splinters; a second crashed into its debris and tore for hell.

Barry cursed. His mind was in a fog. The Nieuports were circling now behind the red mystery crate. After a few moments, they turned east.

Then, through his glasses, Barry saw something else that was strange. The red ship slowed to almost half its former speed, and began to turn in a great arc.

"We know what side that murder crate is on anyway, Sika," Barry growled. "Blast it if you can and we won't worry about any Yanks going down with it,"

The plane was turning gradually more and more, coming back toward the Front and the German side of the lines.

Barry pushed on his gun. He too turned, but he swung in close to head off the other crate. He'd get a shot at the plane this time—and from the side. Something about that tail that was plenty deadly.

He thundered to the attack. Coming closer, he saw the other plane swerve to the east a little more to make a larger circle and be farther out of his way when they came closest together.

Barry hugged in close. He was sighting across his guns when he saw the pilot turn in his seat. The hand of that pilot came up in a familiar motion. Bringing it before his face and extending the fingers, he thumbed his nose at the Red Falcon and then darted ahead with a burst of speed.

Anger flooded over Barry. His thumb tramped down on the trigger button. Tracers slashed out from all four nose guns. They tore straight for the cockpit of that racing machine. But they thudded into the rear of the fuselage because of the sudden burst of speed that Barry, in aiming, hadn't allowed for.

The pilot of the red mystery plane then laughed at him with a showing of white teeth—and roared on.

After that Barry never rose from his sights. His guns began to glow cherry red. But the longer he hugged that other plane, the farther the distance between them grew.

For a moment his shots seemed to be taking effect. They were tearing over Germany, headed northeast. Beyond, if Barry had raised his head from the sights, he would have seen the mountains of the Black Forest.

The red mystery ship was drawing him straight for those mountains. And for once Barry plunged headlong, not noting or caring where he was lead so long as he got a clean shot at that other plane.

"We be careful for something come out of tail, maybe," Sika warned.

Barry's jaws clamped a little tighter. He didn't answer or take warning from Sika's words. His only thought was to get that racing thing before it got away.

The gap between them suddenly began to narrow. Barry flung the Red Falcon plane forward. Suddenly, the other plane dived. They were over the roughest part of the Black Forest. Canyons lay in deep shadow below in the folds of the tree-covered mountains.

Into one of these canyons, a narrow-topped groove between two jagged ridges, the red ship hurtled. Barry didn't wait to look about.

He tramped down on his trigger button again. Glared across the sights. He was staking all on that last burst. He wasn't worrying about what lay ahead.

His tracers slithered out toward the diving mystery ship but were lost in the distance that still separated them. Somehow, that distance had suddenly widened again.

A flood of anger rushed over him at a sudden realization. This pilot was playing with him. Making a monkey out of him and perhaps for a purpose.

He stared at the side and let up on his guns. The canyon widened as he went down. Just that narrow slot of open space at the top to come down through.

Below there was a field where the floor of the canyon leveled out. Ships were there. Other red ships like his own. He caught everything at a glance.

But that glance came too late. He kicked out and jerked the Red Falcon plane into a tight vertical between the narrow walls of the canyon. A cry of warning came from Sika even before he saw his own danger.

"Master. Look up. We trapped."

BARRY whirled in his seat and stared at the narrow opening at the top of the canyon. His eyes bulged. He pushed on the gun. The Liberty responded and the Red Falcon plane leaped into the air in a sharp zoom.

There came a clanging noise from above. A mesh of stout cable, slithering across the top of the canyon, moving as though by the hands of a magician. There was just a narrow slot left. If he could only turn and climb the Red Falcon plane out on one ear, he might make it.

"Master, we crash net!" Sika yelled.

Barry Rand kicked out and let the plane fall off into the canyon again. He took one more glance about him. Men were waiting a thousand feet below. The slit that was the top opening of the canyon was covered completely now by that large cable net, that had been swung across the moment they had passed its bounds.

Barry Rand gave up and prepared to land.

Boches ran eagerly across the field as the Red Falcon plane rolled to a stop. Sika whirled to his guns and shouted a request.

"I fight, Master?"

Crack! A warning shot whined overhead.

"Hell no!" Barry cried. "We haven't got a chance that way. We couldn't get out if we did clean up on a lot of these Heinies. Hold up your hands before they drill us, the devils."

A groan of disappointment came from the rear cockpit. Already running men had Lugers and rifles trained upon them.

Barry, with arms held over his head, was climbing out of the front cockpit. And following his example Sika got to the ground from his gun nest behind.

A grinning German *leutnant* addressed them in English.

"Ach, that was a good chase, *nicht wahr?*" he chuckled. "But you could not know that I was playing with you. To think that I would have the honor to lead the Red Falcon a merry chase!"

Barry nodded. Somehow he couldn't resist the good-natured grin of the enemy pilot he had chased over half the Front.

"I'll say it was a merry chase," he admitted. "But it wouldn't have been so merry if I'd gotten close enough to get a bunch of slugs into your ribs, Fritz."

"Karl is the name," the *leutnant* corrected. "*Leutnant* Karl Steiner. And these—" he swept his arm toward the row of fifteen odd crimson planes, identical so far as Barry could see with his own Red Falcon plane—'"these are my inventions. I have designed them myself and we build them now here in the canyon."

Barry stared about at the row of red planes about the field. He smiled.

"You'd hardly call them inventions would you?" he asked simply. "I'd say they're mere copies of an original. And where do you get that Red Falcon stuff?"

Karl Steiner laughed.

"*Ach, mein freund,* that was merely to make you mad. You see, it was all part of a game. I wanted you to be with me in this new *jagdstaffel* of mine."

"Huh?" demanded Barry Rand. "You want me to be with you?"

"*Jawohl. Aber kommen.* We shall go into my office. I must explain the proposition to you."

The *leutnant* turned and led the way across the field toward a group of buildings. Barry followed, with Sika close at his heels. And behind Sika came Germans with their guns still drawn.

Barry stared in surprise at the buildings that became evident on the floor of the canyon. There was a full-sized factory, houses for the workers, buildings for the flying personnel and the mechanics. It was a fair-sized village, but with only men as inhabitants.

At the door of a building, the *leutnant* stopped and turned. He barked an order to the guards.

"Search the two and then do not follow. They are safe. They cannot get out of the canyon except by the one tunnel entrance and that—" he broke off in a laugh as heavy hands ran over Barry and Sika. Guns were taken away. The guards retreated.

Steiner nodded toward the door and held it open.

"We enter here," he smiled. "We talk now."

Barry and then Sika crossed the threshold. Steiner followed. He ushered them into a well-furnished office. Bringing out a box of cigars, he slid a tray with glasses and a decanter closer to him from the edge of the desk.

"Gentlemen, will you smoke or have a drink?"

Barry shook his head. Sika followed the example of his master. Steiner shrugged and poured himself a half glass of wine. He lighted a cigarette from his pocket. Barry smoked one of his own. The giant black didn't smoke.

"This is my thought," Steiner began. "For some-time, since we got the general measurements of your plane I have been working out the design for copies. The plane which I have designed is faster, but not as maneuverable. *Nein.* We cannot throw it about with safety as you can yours."

Barry looked at him puzzled.

"I must say you're perfectly frank about telling your troubles," he admitted.

"Why not?" shrugged Steiner. "I have brought you here for a plain talk. I have a special proposition to offer but first I want you to understand these things so you will realize what we are after, *nicht wahr?*"

Barry waited without a word.

"So I trick you into following me here," Steiner went on. "With you as leader, you and your aide in the rear cockpit, we would have a squadron that would end the war in no time. Is not that what you fight for mainly, to end the war?"

Barry nodded.

"Partly," he admitted.

"Then hear. Listen to me. You would be in command of this *jagdstaffel* next to me. We have developed planes that look like yours and that fly faster than yours. You would help re-design them or show us how they may be maneuvered with safety. And we would win the war in less than six months! With our one-pound high explosive shells shooting out of the rear of our red planes and exploding in the mere pressure of slip stream, no enemy planes could stand up against us. Think, for the good of humanity. For the sake of the Allies, your friends, this war must end quickly. It is to your advantage as much as to ours, *nicht wahr?*"

Barry shrugged without a word and waited. His eyes were focused sidewise at a Luger that lay on the desk within easy reach of the nimble fingers of *Leutnant* Karl Steiner.

"And not only that," Steiner persuaded. "But there would be money, too, for you and your aide. If you consent to furnish us with the secret of your plane and teach us to use it and become the leader of our great, new *jagdstaffel*, we will pay you the equivalent of a quarter of a million dollars in your money. I have that agreement already for you, signed by the Kaiser himself."

Steiner settled back behind his desk magnanimously. He beamed.

"There. Is that not simple, *mein freund?* For helping to end the war quickly, you get a high commission in the German Imperial air force and receive the enormous amount of money mentioned. What is your answer, Red Falcon?"

Barry had tensed. He was waiting for that question. Karl Steiner was leaning back in his chair smiling; his hands were in his lap, far away from the Luger on the desk.

Every muscle in Barry's body came rigid. He leaped out across the desk. His hand shot out in a blurred movement and came up in the astonished face of Steiner with the Luger in it.

"THIS is my answer," he snapped. "Think I'm going to be a traitor to my country, eh? Well, get this. You hear stories about the Red Falcon, about his being accused of treason. But he never did a thing against his country that he's ashamed of in his life."

He jerked his hand toward the office door.

"Get going, Karl. We're taking a little walk, the three of us, through the tunnel you mentioned. I'm nuts about tunnels."

Karl Steiner's face turned a shade paler. He rose slowly from his chair.

"*Gott in himmel*, what a man you are," he said. "I could maybe make it a half million for you to join our forces. I would do what—"

"Walk," Barry hissed. He prodded him with his own Luger.

They reached the office door. Steiner's arms were up above his head.

"You can drop those hands now," Barry ordered. "And get these orders. I'll go first. My hands will be behind me. You'll cover them with your coat as though you have a gun trained on me. Understand?"

"*Ja, Mein Herr.*"

"And Sika will come behind you. We will walk very close. It will look to the guards as if you are covering me and Sika is merely following. And Sika—"

"Yes, Master."

"I won't be able to see the *leutnant*, not having eyes in the back of my head. I'm leaving it up to you. The first false move he makes, push him against the gun in my hand at my back. When I feel that push I'll blow his insides out, and Steiner—"

"*J-Ja, mein Herr.*"

"Lord help you if Sika stumbles and falls against you, that's all. We're going across the field and out through this tunnel entrance you mentioned. You'll likely have the password. That'll be up to you. March!"

Barry swung open the door. They stepped into a corridor and on toward the front of the building. They walked past guards who presented arms at the front door and presently they were out in the dim light of the canyon.

From every side eyes peered curiously. Some laughed and cracked jokes in German, most of which Barry couldn't understand at that distance.

His finger was tense on the trigger. At the first pressure against the muzzle of the gun that was thrust back in Steiner's stomach, he'd let go. Couldn't take any chances.

They were crossing the field on the floor of the canyon. Beyond he could see the opening of what seemed to be a tunnel. Guards were there, standing before it. Barry walked on with an outward show of confidence, but the short hairs up his spine were rising.

Guards stepped before them and held their guns ready. Barry made a slight jab with his gun farther into the stomach of Steiner. Waited.

"*Ach, Leutnant* Steiner. Bitte. I did not recognize you."

Barry stepped forward. Then something happened. He heard a cry behind. And instead of something pushing against the Luger in his hand as a signal, he felt what it had been pushing against dart to the side.

He whirled in that second. He hadn't dared shoot before for fear of hitting Sika who was directly behind.

"Capture them," yelled Steiner. "Stop them. Do not let them get away."

Guns of the guards came down. Barry let go with the Luger in his hand. Sika leaped aside. Steiner, in that moment of hesitation, had ducked to the right of the gun that had been held against his stomach.

The giant black dived, snatched one of the guards, gun and all, by the ankles and swung him like a club against the others.

Round and round. Barry ducked past a falling guard and into the mouth of the tunnel passage into the lost canyon. Came the wild cry of the great Senegalese chief on the war path.

"*Ki-hu-yi!*"

Grunts and groans and the thud of crushing bone against bone as he swung the unfortunate sentry as a human club.

One shot, two, rang out from behind. Germans were rushing across the field. *Leutnant* Steiner had run out of reach.

He had snatched a rifle and was taking aim at the giant black.

But at that instant, Sika flung the remains of that guard away and plunged into the mouth of the tunnel after his master.

They plunged headlong, down the long, dark, damp- passage. It was large enough for a single track railroad tunnel—and just as black.

Crack! Crack!

Shots echoed and became deafening in the confines, of the passage. Half doubled over, the two raced down the length, knowing nothing of what lay ahead except that Steiner had said the tunnel was the only entrance or exit to the canyon.

In the darkness, they slammed headlong into the side of the passage as it turned sharply.

On their feet once more, they plunged on. The sides seemed more irregular, more like the walls of a cave now than of a tunnel. And a moment later they broke out into daylight.

They were in a narrow pocket canyon with no entrance or exit except the tunnel that had been cut into it. The sides sloped gradually for a space and then went straight up to rimrock that overhung a thousand feet above.

Here and there, either side was dotted by a cave, small or large. Some mere crevasses and others deep enough to hide a man or two.

They didn't stop to investigate. They raced on through the narrow one-track road toward the hole at the other end of the miniature canyon that should lead on out to freedom.

INTO the blackness they plunged again.

Then they came up with a start. That tunnel was short, little more than a hundred and fifty feet in length.

At the far end light showed through. But the light was being shut off; the opening was closing swiftly. There was a grinding of gears and a clanking of steel.

A great iron door was closing before them. They lunged for the crack that was left. Reached it in time to be nearly crushed as the door slammed shut. They darted back, stared for an instant at the barred end.

"This way," Barry cracked. "Maybe we can get out of the top of that pocket canyon back here."

They whirled and started back. From the end of the tunnel at the other end of the small canyon came shouts and yells of running Boches. Barry leaped to the side of the roadway, and crouched behind a rock. Sika flattened out of sight.

Three Germans darted from the mouth of the opening. Barry let go with his Luger. No time to waste.

Crack! Crack!

He took careful aim and his care told. Germans tumbled on their faces or pitched backward as his slugs found their mark. Others came on running headlong.

Barry let them have all there was in the Luger. Empty gun. No more cartridges. Under cover of brush growing on the side of the canyon, he and Sika scrambled up toward the top.

More shouting came from the tunnel. But those near the opening were either dead or dying. Up, up the two Yanks raced breathlessly. Up near where the rim rock fell straight down in a jagged cliff to the more gradual slope below.

In the notch of a shallow cave at the side, they crouched. Sika on the inside, Barry on the outside. They tried to keep out of sight. Barry peered through a clump of brush that shielded him.

Boches had crowded into the canyon, and were already beginning a thorough search. From their excited conversation, Barry knew they were going to comb the place. Sooner or later they would be found. There was no hope of escape.

They crouched there in their hiding place, dead for sleep and growing hungrier by the minute. The Germans were systematically going over every niche in the little canyon. But up until late afternoon, they did not come dangerously close. Then the danger became obvious. The Boches were working their way up the side of the canyon directly toward the shallow cave that shielded Sika and the bush that kept Barry out of sight. Another two minutes and they would be discovered.

In his cramped position, Barry hissed an order to Sika.

"Maybe this'll help," he said. "No use in both of us getting caught. If you can get out, go get bombs and drop all you can carry into the big canyon. Never mind me."

"But, Master—" Sika whispered.

"Orders! Listen. You crowd back into the cave as far as you can get. I'll step out and be captured. I'll tell them that you got through before the door closed. Maybe they'll open it then, and you can get bombs to blow up the place."

"But our plane, Master—"

"The hell with that. We could build another. Do as I say. I'm stepping out right now. So long, big boy. Good luck."

There was a quick, hard handclasp. Then Barry slipped along behind other brush and stepped out into the open. He raised his hands in token of surrender, and started stumbling down the slope.

It seemed at that moment that a million gun muzzles were there for him to look down. But there were only about two dozen Germans in the searching party.

He walked down easily, trying to smile.

"I guess it's no use trying to hold out longer," he ventured, casting a glance about for *Leutnant* Steiner. The Boche wasn't there. "I'll swap my freedom for a square meal," he went on. "Take me to *Leutnant* Steiner."

An *Unterleutnant* stepped before him and jabbed a Luger in his stomach.

"Where is the other, the black one?" he demanded.

Barry shrugged and smiled.

"Search me. I hope he's on his way to get some help by this time. He managed to slip through the closing door before it shut. I didn't."

The *Unterleutnant* stared at him for a moment;

"*Gott!*" he exploded. He jerked his head toward the entrance to the tunnel. "*Verdammt! Kommen.* We go back with you anyhow."

Barry took a deep breath as they marched him through the entrance to the tunnel. Going back to *Leutnant* Steiner. What then? But Sika would be free to work—to do his stuff—if he got a chance.

A group of excited Germans were coming across the field as they broke into the daylight dimmed by the depth of the larger canyon. *Leutnant* Steiner was at the head. He smiled with only a slight trace of malice as Barry, under heavy guard, was ushered onto the field that was rapidly darkening now.

"*Ach*, so you come back," he chuckled. "Perhaps you change your mind. You accept our proposition, *ja*?"

Barry glared at him and shook his head.

"Not in a thousand years," he snapped. "That's final. Shoot the works. I'm set now."

Karl Steiner's face turned purplish.

"*Verdammt Amerikaner*," he rasped. "So you make fun of my offer. You think I am mad to insist. You make it to sound ridiculous? We shall see. Tonight it is getting dark. But at dawn we shall see. You will fly then.

At the head of the *jagdstaffel* as I have requested. But this time you will fly whether you like it or not."

Steiner barked to the men guarding Barry.

"Take him to the lock-up and guard him every second. He is a clever one, but not clever enough."

THAT was the beginning of a night of suspense and waiting. Barry could hardly keep his eyes open. He gave up at length and got some sleep. He awakened to the sound of jangling keys and a hoarse voice.

"*Ach.* You get up now. Time to lead the *jagdstaffel*." Then a laugh and he was sitting bold upright, jerked by the shoulder.

For the moment it all seemed like a dream. But unlike a dream he was awakened from a sleep to become conscious of this thing happening.

Then there was Steiner out on the dark field talking. Planes warming all about the field. Thunderous roars of their motors. Barry tensed. Listened to the throbbing. They sounded like Gothas. Steiner was chuckling.

"Perhaps you wonder where we get all the speed. We hook together by gear, two big Mercedes engines for each plane. That give us more power than one Liberty, *Mein Herr*. And now you lead."

Barry's heart leaped. Were they giving him the chance to take off alone? Surely that couldn't be it. It wasn't.

"We must have this look real," Steiner was saying.

Through the top of the canyon, the narrow slit up there a thousand feet above which the wire net guarded, a grayish hint of dawn came.

"It will be dawn shortly after we get into the air above the canyon. So to make it look real, we have another to go with you. He is here. He will take the place of your Sika, as you call him."

Barry turned in the very dim light.. He saw a huge figure with dark face. He could hardly be told in the darkness from Sika.

Steiner was chuckling again.

"He will do nicely with the black paint on his face. Yanks will see him in your back cockpit and they will not know that he is a loyal German making you fly with a gun at your back, *Herr* Red Falcon."

Then Steiner stared harder in the darkness at the big fellow.

"*Ach*, you have forgotten the helmet and goggles," he said. "They would know when they saw your blond hair, *nicht wahr?*"

The other laughed and trotted off. Steiner went on with his instructions.

"We will take off in line, you first, me next, and so on. When we get to the top and out of the opening we will form in a giant Vee with you at point. Your aide—" he chuckled—"will see to it that you obey or he has strict orders to shoot to kill at the slightest hesitation. He has a chute as you will notice, tied to the side of the fuselage, if necessary for him to use it, *ja?*"

Steiner turned with a trace of irritation.

"*Verdammt.* Where is that *dummkopf?* He should be back by now!"

He paced back the way the other had gone. Called out. One minute, two, three, four passed. Getting slightly lighter. Sound of trotting feet and then Steiner showed up again. He stopped a moment near the tail of the Red Falcon plane to fasten something to his legging—at least that is what it looked like to Barry in the darkness. Then he came on. Steiner saw him.

"*Ach*, you come now. It is about time. Remember your orders. Shoot if you must to carry out orders. *Auf Wieder-sehen!*"

The black turned with a nod, stuck a Luger in Barry's ribs and half pushed him to the front cockpit. They were climbing in. Then the motor was blasting and the Red Falcon plane, leading the others, was roaring into the air.

Up, up they shot. Even under the circumstances, it felt good to be flying the Red Falcon plane once more. His mind was spinning in desperate search of a plan. This big German in the back cockpit blacked up to resemble Sika—his teeth clenched. He wondered just how tightly the belt was fastened about him—if at all. Might throw him out. Have a try.

Where was Sika? He hadn't shown up at all. Perhaps the Boches had got him. He shuddered at the thought. He felt the muzzle of the Luger pressed against his back. He saw the other planes, the doubles of the Red Falcon plane, taking the air at a bound and roaring in his wake. A space of perhaps two hundred feet separated each plane from the other. Up, up toward that slot of grayish light above. Then something seemed to jerk the Red Falcon plane in its climb. As though a rope had been tied to it and had broken loose when it reached the end.

Barry tensed, stared about and upward. His eyes narrowed. He gasped. The wire net that had opened for them was closing again. Giant electrical machines were going into action to spread the great, strong mesh over the top of the canyon. Frantically he pushed on the gun for more speed. There was a chance of getting through this time. A good chance. Up, up—and then he was slipping through the opening, just as the great net clicked into place. There was a blinding flash below. The crimson ship of Steiner had crashed the net and burst into flame. And like the staccato of a machine gun, the other planes crashed against it; they had been too close to turn. They crashed against the net in trying to climb out, or crashed each other as they fell into the canyon.

It seemed then the signal for Barry Rand to throw that Red Falcon plane into a series of convulsions. He must throw that German devil out of the back cockpit if it was the last thing he did. It probably would be his last act whether the attempt was successful or not.

Daylight was above the rim of the canyon. The crimson crate was going crazy. Barry waited for a scream of terror from a falling German or the shot in the back that would tell of his failure. Instead he only heard a low, chuckling laugh from the rear cockpit. He whirled. Sika was grinning at him.

"I overhear about plan for big German to take my place," Sika chuckled. "So when he come to get helmet and goggles I knock him out and take his place. Before that I find out where big switch that control net over canyon top is. I find long piece of rope and tie one end to the switch and other to tail of our ship, Master. I very glad when I feel pull and see nets close. Then I see other ships crash and I think you not know I here. I laugh very much when you try throw me out. That good, try to throw Sika out back cockpit of Red Falcon plane, yes, Master?"

"I'll say it's good," Barry grinned back. "Everything's good except we got to finish that job. We got to have that canyon blown off the face of the map."

Barry was flying the Red Falcon crate with his knees then, as he began writing hastily on slips of paper. He got out message streamers from the side of the cockpit. Some twenty minutes later he swung back over the bombardment field of the 67th, dived low and let go a streamer. Then on to the next bombardment field and another note there.

BOMB K -32 -B-63-14 all to hell. Home of factory and plans of new terror plane of the enemy.

Red Falcon.

They thundered over three bombardment fields in those early hours of the morning. And they could see back over the first when they had zoomed the third. "I wonder if they'll take that tip or—" Barry broke off short. He grinned. "Yeah. There goes the 67th." He turned toward the aerie atop Saar Mountain. He grinned as he saw the second squadron of bombers take the air, like gnats from the distance.

"That's finished," he nodded. "They'll blow everything to hell in that canyon and the Heinies won't have a chance of getting away."

He yawned and stretched. "Boy, could I stand some sleep—but first one of your breakfasts, big boy."

"Yes, Master. Sika hungry too." But the Red Falcon had dozed over his stick and didn't hear.

The Invisible Pilot
FREDERICK BLAKESLEE

Tac-Tac-Tac ... Death slugs flamed from the Red Falcon's guns straight into the head of that Boche pilot. But the German didn't even move; his plane sped on. What was this mystery ship? Who was its strange pilot that bullets couldn't kill?

The Invisible Pilot

HIGH on the top of the great Saar Mountain in the rugged Vosges two figures stood outlined in the light of the setting sun, a good hour before darkness.

One was a little taller than medium height. He had the broad shoulders and narrow hips of an athlete. That was Barry Rand, the pilot without a country who fought a war of his own to end wars.

Just at the elbow of the Red Falcon ace stood a much larger figure. A giant black man—Sika, self-appointed slave and aide to Barry.

The two had been looking out far to the west across the battle-torn area of the Front where trenches on either side of a great No-Man's-Land stretched as far as the eye could reach.

Suddenly the giant black stiffened. His long arm flashed up before his master and his long finger pointed into the air high above the lines, far, far ahead of them.

"Master, look."

Barry stared. He shook his head. He held up his hands about his eyes, cupped them there, to aid him in seeing into the lowering sun. Again he shook his head.

Without taking down his hands he spoke to Sika.

"Get my glasses. Quick! Your eyes are better than mine. Better than any eyes I've ever seen. Hurry, big boy. Something looks queer out there."

"Yes, Master!"

That last came from the running Sika halfway back to the snug cabin that was hidden in trees along one side of the flat top of the mountain.

A moment later he returned and held the glasses out to his master. Powerful glasses those. Barry raised them before his straining eyes.

"That's funny," he mumbled a second later. "What did you see, Sika?"

"Sika see planes flying north."

"Yeah. And what else?"

"One plane far ahead of the rest."

"Like they're chasing him, right?"

"Yes, Master."

"Anything else?"

Sika had his great hands at his eyes now shading them.

"See ship ahead running away from others. They can not catch that first plane. It runs away from the other planes very fast, Master."

"And how, big boy. Phew!"

Barry emitted a whistle.

"Look at that thing go fella. And I can see something through these glasses that maybe you can't see. There are black crosses on that ship ahead, Sika. And it's getting away from—"

Barry whirled and dropped the glasses from his eyes.

"Get the ship started, Sika. We're shoving off. If those Spads that are chasing that Jerry crate can't catch it, maybe we can. We've got the fastest ship on the Front—" he broke off to raise the glasses in front of his eyes once more—"or have we?"

"But Master," came the objection from the great black, "We got only an hour's gas. And it is two hours before darkness. We must wait to get more gas tonight and then—"

Barry never moved from his staring position through his binoculars.

"Get her warm," he repeated. There was no room left for argument.

"Yes, Master."

A moment later the giant liberty in the nose of the ship roared. Strange crate that of the Red Falcon. Barry and Sika had built it from parts of planes that the Vosges had trapped. The fuselage was a Fokker, the wings those of a Spad, and the Liberty motor came from a D-H. It bore no crosses or circles of identification, but this blood-red plane was known and justly feared the length of the Front.

A roar came from the ship half concealed under the trees that hid the little cabin. Barry turned and trotted toward it. He was in the cockpit and testing the motor. Watching the instruments that told of its warming rise all too slowly.

"Hop in, Sika," he called to his aide.

The fuselage trembled a little with the strain of that two hundred and fifty pounds of muscle and brawn that was Sika.

"Hold on. Here we go."

"But Master. The Liberty is not warm—"

The blast of the giant engine cut off Sika's last word. The crimson plane was slithering along the level surface of the flat-topped mountain with increased speed. It lifted. Barry held it down until he reached the end of the runway, then he dropped it into a long, wide canyon.

At the end of the canyon he turned. That was why no plane from either side of the lines had ever found where the Red Falcon hid. That canyon concealed his movements after he vanished into it in landing; and in the same manner it hid his take-offs, since he did not climb until he was well away from the field.

He climbed now. His hand pushed the throttle full open as instruments before him told him it was safe. The Liberty answered with a bellowing roar. Back came the stick and the Red Falcon plane shot upward out of the canyon,

Barry took a long, easy breath.

"That's better," he said to himself. "Afraid she might conk on me taking off so cold. But you're there, old lady, you're there."

His lips began whistling softly his favorite tune.

Be down to get you with a taxi honey. Better be—

He stopped and reached for the glasses. Went on with the rag time song.

Better be ready bout half past eight.

His eyes were staring through those glasses as he went on. The whistle strung out in a long exclamation of surprise.

"Phew! Look at that thing go."

He left off whistling and dropped the glasses. Pushed again on the throttle to make sure that the Liberty was doing her stuff. He mumbled thoughtfully to himself as he thundered on.

"A low-wing job. Never saw one like that. Cant't make much out at this, distance. But we'll soon be closer to her if there's any justice."

They punched on. But as they flew into the setting sun Barry Rand's surprise increased. That strange German ship with its astonishing speed was pulling away from even them.

Already the flight of Spads that had been chasing her were turning back. Barry raced on.

"We'll keep her in sight as long as we can," he said.

BUT it wasn't long. The strange enemy crate suddenly dived into a cloud. Barry raced on. She'd have to come out of that cloud. It didn't look very large from where he sat. But as he came closer he found that it stretched in a sort of hook shape to the north in a long streamer.

Minutes, then Sika's warning voice through the tube that connected the two cockpits.

"Master, you not forgetting we have not got much gas."

"Not while I got this gauge glaring at me," came the reply.

Down to get you with a taxi honey. Better—

The tune went on now sprayed through his thin lips. His eyes roved the sky in search of that ship. It seemed to have vanished completely. Perhaps it was hiding in the cloud.

"Well, we can wait until she comes out then," Barry decided

He circled the cloud once. More precious minutes. Circled it again. He was flying at five thousand feet. They were well behind the lines. Funny that weird crate could disappear like that.

Barry circled the great cloud for the third time. Archie batteries grunted up at them. He broke into a zigzag course to throw them off their aim. Cursed them for bothering him in his search.

More minutes flashed by and again Sika's warning voice.

"Master. Look at gauge. We got maybe enough gas to get back to our drome."

"Huh?" Barry started. "Hell, I was too set on this cloud. Sure is a swell trick that pilot played on us. Yeah, we got enough gas to get back. Then what? We haven't got enough to leave again. And walking doesn't sound very hot to me off that mountain, specially when it isn't possible to do it.

The Red Falcon ace stared downward. It was growing twilight. The sun was just sliding behind the distant rim of the world to the west.

"Look, Sika." Barry was pointing. "See that little field—the one to the east? It doesn't look as though it's very heavily guarded. Let's take a look. We'll clean out the birds there and then—"

He shrugged.

The nose of the Red Falcon plane dropped and the Liberty began to wind up like mad. Down, down they hurled in a screaming dive.

Ahead of them on the field men were running about in wild disorder, pointing upward in terror. The Red Falcon was making another raid. And in daylight.

Instantly, machine guns from the ground went into action. A Pfalz trundled across the tarmac for a take-off. Barry hunched over his stick, aimed his guns at that pilot and punched down.

His trigger thumb poised for a split second while he centered his sights.

Wam! Tac-tac-tac!

The Pfalz crumpled and rolled in a ball before it rose. Barry kicked over. A thin line of ditto marks appeared in the lower wing at his right. Too close.

He ducked to the side and then glared across his sights. A lone German was standing his ground behind that upturned gun. Barry tramped on his trigger button for the second time. Tracers, yellow and white, slithered out front from his four nose guns. The two Vickers and the twin Spandaus.

The gunner crumpled. Others ran for the gun. Sika whirled and his twin Lewis guns spoke out in a demon chatter.

And as they thundered along almost flat on the field, the giant black sprayed the running Germans with Yank lead.

Once more Barry kicked over at the end of the field and came back. Sika spun his guns on their mountings and spattered death among the other Germans who surged out of the hangars.

In that last dash, Barry's keen eyes had caught something. Something that he had been looking for.

There at the end hangar were ranged in rows, drums. Drums of gas, he guessed. The gas that they needed.

Germans were running away from the field now—those that still lived after that murderous slashing of Lewis guns.

Barry kicked again and slammed down for a landing. Sika knew his stuff. The Red Falcon plane rolled on the German field. The Liberty blasted and sent them bounding to the place where the gas drums were stored.

Sika stood his post. Held his Lewis guns ready.

Crack!

From the corner of the next hangar a gun spoke out and the bullet screamed just past Barry's ear.

Tac-tac-tac!

That was Sika answering the shot. And there was no more firing from that corner of the hangar.

Barry raced for the drums. They were heavy, those. Nearby he sighted a funnel. He snatched it, pushed over one of the drums of gas and started rolling it with his foot toward the plane.

Crack!

That shot from behind plucked at his sleeve. He felt the burn as it scratched his arm in passing. The sniper was sheltered from Sika's guns by the hangar.

Barry kicked once more on the drum, sent it spinning toward the ship. Then his automatic was out and he whirled.

He saw a head and part of a body sticking around the corner of that hangar.

Blam!

Crack!

His gun and the gun of the other spoke at the same time as though in angry argument. But Barry had the better aim. He ran on, pushing the drum before him.

"Now your turn, Sika," he panted.

The giant black leaped from the rear cockpit. Barry took his post behind the Lewis guns. Germans were gaining courage—coming back. Barry opened fire on them as fast as they poked their heads in sight.

The giant black was heaving the great drum of gas to his shoulder. A gigantic effort for the average man, but to Sika it was merely child's play.

The funnel was in the filler hole of the tank. Sika turned the drum upward, unscrewed the plug and let the gas gurgle into the funnel.

MINUTES. It seemed the great tank in the Red Falcon plane would never fill. More Germans were coming. But it was growing dark and Barry couldn't see to pick them off as well now.

Then Sika hurled the can to the ground and screwed in the cap. Barry let go with a last burst of fire from the Lewis guns. Then he leaped from the rear cockpit and climbed into his own up front.

"Contact!"

Sika spun the great propeller. The Liberty thundered out and the ship gathered speed as he climbed into his seat.

Then the Red Falcon took the air.

Barry climbed into the night. Again he was whistling his favorite tune. He turned in a graceful chandelle and roared back. He grinned, still whistling in the darkness, and thumbed his nose down at the German drome. Then he climbed higher.

"Not so bad, big boy," Barry shouted through the tube. "Not so bad. Nice work. If I didn't have you I'd have to hire a derrick to help me load gas sometimes when the boys around these filling stations get up on their ear, eh?"

"You have Sika with you as long as he live, Master," came back the faithful reply.

They droned on higher into the night. Barry was whistling again. But, too, he was working his brain overtime.

"I'd like to know," he said half aloud, "where that gang of Spads came from that were chasing that funny crate. There's something plenty wrong there. I could tell by the way they were trying to catch him. There wasn't any love between that Jerry crate ahead and those Spads. Not even the usual love."

"No, Master. They were anxious to catch that faster ship."

"Right," Barry said. "And we've got to find out why."

They were flying generally toward Yank lines. Barry was staring ahead toward a row of pin points that appeared and disappeared in the darkness far below.

"Yank batteries," he nodded. "We're just about over the lines now.

This old bus sure makes time. But I've got a hunch that—" He stopped thoughtfully.

"A hunch, Master?"

"Yes. I've got a hunch that maybe for the first time we haven't got the fastest plane on the Front. That other one that disappeared in the cloud. It was plenty tricky, big fella."

"Yes, Master. It go as fast as we can. Maybe faster."

Barry nodded in the darkness.

"And that isn't any vacation to the cerebral cavity, Sika."

"Yes, Master—er No, Master."

"Very well done, Sika. Don't let those words throw you. I mean it had me worried, in sort of a round-about way. If Heinie's got a plane that can trim us, well—"

"You mean, Master, if that plane faster than us we not do so good?"

"And how," Barry chirped hack. "But don't start losing any sleep about it until we know more about it."

Then Barry Rand was sitting up straight in his seat, pointing ahead through the darkness. And, at the same moment, Sika was pounding on the cowling that separated them.

"See, Master. Lights flashing ahead. Lights into the sky from behind the American lines. What they mean?"

"Hold it. I'm trying to find out. Dots and dashes. There they are again."

Barry Rand was spelling out words as those dots and dashes of light made sense.

O-U-R—H-E-L-P

Barry shook his head.

"Not much sense to that," he mumbled. "Must have come in at the tail end of the message. They're apparently trying to signal somebody up in the air."

He hurled closer. Dropped the nose of the Red Falcon plane and dived nearer.

Sika was pounding on the cockpit cowling once more, Barry's eyes had been glued to that light and nothing else. Sika was speaking through the tube.

"More lights, Master. See? Lights flash all the way to the east, Master. They signal too."

Barry turned his head and stared in the direction of the arm of his black aide. His eyes opened wider.

"Hey," he exclaimed. 'They sure want somebody bad. Trying to flag him down. Some poor sucker is in for a swell job, I'll bet. Look. They are small searchlights strung along a few kilos behind the Yank lines."

Then his eyes were fairly popping out of his head, and he was mumbling letters as the full message was being spelled out again.

R-E-D F-A-L-C-O-N W-E N-E-E-D Y-O-U-R H-E-L-P
R-E-P-O-R-T A-T O-N-C-E T-0 G-H-Q A-T C-A-M-A-I

"Huh?" Barry exploded. "What was that I said about some poor sucker being in for something? And I'm the sucker. Well I'll be damned. First time they've called on us. Must be something mighty important."

"And maybe a trick. Master," Sika objected. "They have tried to catch you, Master. To shoot you because you escaped a firing squad once when you were not guilty. You not forget."

"Sure. Like I'd forget meal time," Barry chuckled. "But this isn't any trick. You don't know Yanks, Sika—at least most Yanks. If the message came with one light I might think that it was some ambitious brass hat without a conscience trying to make a name for himself by capturing the Red Falcon easy. But this is too general."

He came up straight in his seat at another thought.

"Say," he cried, "I'll bet a pan of Lewis lead against a pair of dirty red flannels that this has got something to do with what we saw tonight?"

"You mean the fast ship. Master?"

"Right."

The nose swung to the west through the darkness. He dropped down steeply and zoomed the searchlight as he went on. The light held his crimson plane in its glare. But he couldn't be sure whether those yells that he seemed to hear above the roar of the Liberty were cheers.

HE felt a bit nervous as he turned toward G. H. Q. at Camai. The whole thing was so startling. Perhaps it might be a trick, at that, to capture him.

He shook his head, angry that the idea should have come. No, Yanks weren't like that. There were skunks in the Yank forces who might stoop to such a thing. But not many.

"You going to land at G. H. Q. Master?" Sika asked in concern. "They capture you, they kill you."

"Yeah and what the Frogs would do to you for your long A. W. O. L. wouldn't be anything to laugh off at one sitting, big boy," Barry chuckled. "Yes, I'm going to land. But not at the emergency field at Camai. I know a field a couple of kilos east of Camai. We'll set down there."

He peered through the darkness to make out the landscape. Nothing but dull blotches of dark and darker spots appeared in the night. That was all he had to go by without lights. But Barry Rand knew that war-torn earth better than any other living man. For he ranged the sky lanes at night.

He flew in a great circle to make sure of his bearings. Then his hand shoved the throttle closed and the Liberty idled. Down dropped the nose in a steep glide. He was headed for the little field outside Camai. He'd feel safer with the Red Falcon plane and Sika there than at the G. H. Q. field.

A rumble of wheels rolling and the skid dragging. Then the stop. Barry climbed out, turned to Sika.

"You better hang around and see that the ship isn't bothered," he said. "I'll be going on alone. If I don't come back in an hour or so, better start out after me. But I'm not afraid of anything tricky happening. So long."

"Good luck, Master," Sika said.

Barry walked out of the field. His feet struck the hard gravel of a road that skirted it He headed toward Camai.

A strange feeling of loneliness came over him as he entered the town. He had expected guards everywhere as they usually were where a general headquarters office was located. But so far as he could make out as he walked down the main street there wasn't a soul in sight.

He came to the building that housed the headquarters' offices. The door was open, and to his increased surprise there wasn't a guard on duty.

A prickly sensation of apprehension danced up his spine. His hand fell on the butt of his automatic. If this was a trap there would be plenty of fighting before he was captured. If the Yanks had gotten so low that they were resorting to a trick of this kind it was—

His thoughts seemed to stop stock still as he entered the building. He went cautiously but for only a few paces. His boot sounded slightly on the stone floor.

Another footstep came from an open door to the right of the entrance to the building. A light streamed from the door. A man stepped out before him—the first he had seen since entering the place.

Instinctively, since his nerves were tight at this strange happening, the automatic came half out of its holster. Then he saw that the man was dressed in the uniform of an American major general.

Instantly the general spoke.

"Ah, I've been expecting you. Come in."

Barry felt rather foolish about the half drawn gun. He let it slip from his grasp and drop back into its holster.

He followed the general into the office. The general was smiling.

"You are the Red Falcon of course?"

Barry nodded slowly.

"That's what they call me," he said, "among the nicer names."

"Yes, of course," the general answered. He held out his hand. "I am Major General Parsons."

"And my name, as you may know," the Red Falcon chief nodded, "is Barry Rand."

"Delighted, Rand. You see I was afraid you might think this was a trick. I had everyone removed from the town when the 33rd balloon corps telephoned that you had zoomed their light to let them know you understood. As I said at first I was expecting you. Won't you sit down?"

Barry sat down. So did the general.

"You see," he began to explain, "something has come up that we are at a loss to combat."

Barry didn't move.

"We've called upon you, Rand, because you fly the fastest plane on the Front. It's rather asking considerable favor of you I know, especially after the way you've been treated. Personally I have never believed you were guilty of the treason charge that you were convicted of in the court martial months ago. But some feel differently. I've taken the responsibility of this myself, I may be severely criticized for the move—if things do not work out well."

Barry shifted in his chair, a little tired of the apologies.

"You mentioned something about my plane being fast. Was there something you wanted me to use it for in helping?"

"Exactly," Parsons nodded. "For the past two days a strange sight has been appearing in the sky. It seems to look like a Fokker except that it hasn't any top wing. Our squadrons have tried to down it. But it flies straight over and straight back. Goes like the very devil."

"Any special time?" Barry asked.

"Yes. That's another strange part of it," the general went on. "It comes over an hour after sun up and about an hour before it goes down. We can't catch it. We can't down it and we can't make it out. We can only guess at its mission."

"And that?" prompted Barry.

"Perhaps I should explain a little more at first," Parsons said. "We are massing at Filens. That's eighteen kilometers north of here. We attack tomorrow night at sundown." He lowered his voice ominously. "That of course is in strict secrecy."

"Of course," Barry nodded. "And what was it you suspected of this strange ship?"

"These is only one thing we can figure," the general said. "This low-winged ship doesn't fight. It doesn't turn to right or left. We can't catch it. It simply comes over, makes a turn in the region of our concentration point and then flies back."

"And you suspect that it's taking pictures of the activities?" Barry finished.

"Exactly. No other German planes have come over to observe our activities. We can't figure it any other way."

"Neither can I general," Barry said. He shifted and stared at the toe of his boot. "Just why is it," he asked looking up questioningly, "that you attack at sundown tomorrow? The usual procedure is to attack at dawn."

"That's just it," the general explained. "By attacking in the evening we may take the enemy by surprise. We hoped to before this ship came over. Now, if that ship is taking pictures of our activity, it may not be the surprise that we hope. In fact it may he a failure. This drive must be a success, do you hear—" his fist thumped the desk suddenly, "because other things depend upon it."

Barry nodded slowly understanding. He rose slowly.

"An hour after dawn," he repeated. "I'll be on hand when it comes over. Might be well to keep the sky cleared of ships. I'll see what I can do."

"Your supplies?" the general questioned at the door. "You have enough gas and ammunition?"

"Plenty, I believe," Barry nodded He smiled slightly

"We were just coming back from a raid on a German drome when we spotted the light signals. Good night."

"Good night, and God bless you, Rand." the general said.

GENERAL PARSONS' orders had been carried out to the letter. When Barry stepped from the building entrance to the street and retraced his steps back toward the Red Falcon plane the town was as deserted as it had been on his entry.

He spoke softly to Sika at the little field.

"We shove off now, big boy." Sika stared at his master through the darkness as though he were looking at a ghost.

"Master. You come back. How they let you go?"

"They didn't have me to hold," Barry chuckled. "Sort of like I suspected. They want this mess of the lone, fast enemy plane cleared up. Picked us because we've got the fastest ship on the Front. At least we did have before this low-winged job came along. I'm not so sure now."

"What we do next, Master?"

"We hop for home and some shut-eye. Unless I'm crazy we're in for plenty of excitement tomorrow."

The Liberty roared out in the night. The Red Falcon slithered across the field and took the air with its heavy load. Droned toward the towering, rugged Vosges. Home, and Barry knew that canyon and the flat top of Saar Mountain as well in the darkness as in broad daylight.

There were steaming cups of coffee to top off the evening. Then Barry rolled into his bunk with a yawn.

"We'll want to be in the air at dawn, Sika," was the last thing he said.

And "Yes, Master," was the last thing he heard.

At dawn they were in the air as Barry had ordered, flying southwest toward the ruined village of Filens which marked the point where men in khaki would go over the top when that sun which was now up, went down on the other side of the lines.

Higher and higher the Red Falcon plane climbed until it grew cold and bitter and Barry and his aide snuggled down in their flying suits to keep warm. At almost twenty thousand feet, their movements became slower because of the rarer air.

From there, Barry swung his glasses to his eyes. He checked his time. Not yet quite an hour after sun-up. That was the time that the mystery ship came over, General Parsons had said.

He waited. Flew in a great circle above the spot where the strange, lightning-like craft was expected.

Then suddenly, before he saw it himself, he saw tiny puff clouds appearing four miles below. That meant that the anti aircraft guns of the Yanks were going into action. Something was above them.

Sika was pounding on the cowling. "Master. See ship. There. Look with glasses."

The long arm of the giant black chieftain was pointing to the north of the blasting antis.

Barry swung his eyes in that direction. Yes, there it was. He could make it out plainly. A low-winged monoplane racing into Yank territory. From that altitude it seemed to be crawling along the surface of the ground.

Instantly the nose of the Red Falcon plane dropped and the two hurtled toward the earth.

Down, down with the Liberty going mad. Barry's eyes were glued to that crate. Even at that distance it seemed to be making astonishing speed.

Lower and lower, with the wind howling about them in a death scream. At any moment the wings threatened to leave the plunging fuselage.

With startling abruptness the low-winged plane of the enemy came nearer. Because of Barry's terrific speed, he could follow it easily without the glasses now. He shoved them back into his case.

"I wonder," he mumbled, "why somebody didn't think of hiding upstairs and waiting for the thing and then diving at it. A fellow ought to get in at least a couple of good bursts at the pilot. And he doesn't fight eh? Let's see. This ought to be easy."

He was down to within a few thousand feet of the racing plane. He could see the head of the pilot protruding slightly above the cowling.

And something about that pilot struck him funny. Certainly he could hear that screaming Liberty above the drone of his own—

What kind of a motor was it? Barry couldn't make it out because it was entirely shielded by cowling.

The pilot hadn't moved his head. He sat as though frozen there. Staring straight ahead. Barry could only see his head, but that was enough. And the head wasn't turning to stare back at the attacking Red Falcon plane. The Boche didn't seem to give a damn.

Now Barry was snarling down at close range. He glared across his sights, his thumb poised over the trigger button.

Wam! Down went his thumb as he caught the head of the pilot in his sights.

Tac-tac-tac!

And from behind—

Tac-tac-tac!

SIKA bad been ready. He and Barry let go at the hurtling plane together.

White tracers dashed out ahead. Barry stared before him in amazement Those tracers were going directly where he had aimed them. Straight into the head that protruded from the snug cockpit of that strange plane.

But nothing happened. The low-winged plane with the black crosses hurtled on without so much as wavering. The head remained motionless. Didn't even move from the shock of the many steel slugs that disappeared into it.

"What the hell?" spat Barry.

Then his consternation rose still more. They were heading for a pursuit field in the distance. A Yank field. In plain view of it. And the thing that was driving him mad was the fact that the enemy plane was drawing away from the Red Falcon as soon as the built-up speed from his dive had been exhausted.

Barry cursed and pushed on the throttle. The Liberty was wide open. Doing her best to help win the war. But it wasn't enough. That other craft was leaving them behind. Making them look foolish.

Barry's brain was spinning like a top. Sika was shouting through the tube.

"I shoot him in head Master. He not die!"

Barry gave up the chase. If that plane acted as before it would turn and come back on the same course. He stuck the nose of the Red Falcon plane into the air and let the Liberty groan.

Up, up, he shot. Then he leveled and waited. He saw the low winged ship make a wide turn over the Yank field. Barry poised.

The enemy ship started hack. There was something uncanny about the way it flew and that speed. But Barry had a double plan now. If that was a camera crate taking pictures he'd—

The nose dropped as the low-winged job came on. Down went Barry. Down, down. They were coming much closer this time. But Barry was diving past in front of that roaring thing. The stick came back in his lap.

Wam! Up shot the Red Falcon plane under the belly of the German ship. His guns bucked. The Red Falcon plane shuddered from the recoil of Sika's guns.

Barry's eyes were no longer on that head above the cockpit. They were glued to a little spot at the bottom of the ship. A thing like a large glass eye there sticking through the floor. The camera.

Bam! Slugs and tracers slashed through it. The eye vanished. The plane kept on going. Barry moved the stick while still almost in a stall. He couldn't seem to stop the thing. Bullets that he sent upward into the bottom of the motor cowling spattered off like hail stones against a tin roof. Then the enemy crate roared out of range.

Angrily Barry kicked and stormed down on the Yank pursuit below. Came Sika's warning voice.

"Master. They hold you there, Maybe."

"I don't give a damn. Got a plan. Maybe it'll work."

Then he was landing on the field. A staff car with a flag of stars raced out on the field to meet him. General Parsons was shouting excitedly from the seat even before the car stopped.

"We're licked," he exclaimed, "unless we can stop that thing. Our troops are concentrated this morning. If it's a camera crate with pictures it will—"

Barry hopped out of his cockpit and shook his head. The general stopped short.

"I don't think it will take any pictures back this morning general," Barry said. "I saw the camera in the bottom this last time. She's gone."

"But you should have shot the pilot and downed the plane," the general was crying in a high state of excitement.

"We hit the head that sticks above the cockpit—if that's what you mean," Barry told him. "You saw what happened. Nothing."

By this time colonels and majors were gathered about.

"That's uncanny," a major blurted.

"Good Lord," exploded Parsons, "do you think that head is just there for a trick? There must be someone else flying the plane from some point where we can't see him."

Barry shrugged.

"Perhaps, but I doubt it. Personally, I don't think there's a pilot flying that ship at all. Not a pilot in the plane, that is."

"But how under the sun—" gasped Parsons and others.

"I think I have it, but I'm not going to let it out until I'm sure."

General Parsons confronted Barry angrily.

"I command you to tell me," he cried.

"Command all to hell, general," Barry said. "It won't do you any good. I'll either do this my way or I won't do it at all. I've had enough of brass hat interference."

"By God," Parsons burst out, "if that plane comes over and takes pictures an hour before sunset, an hour before our drive—"

"It'll be over, but I don't think it will go back with any pictures, general. I'll stake my life on it. All I ask is your orders to give me a free hand to have our ship equipped as we like. I want the back seat filled with a special radio apparatus by four this afternoon. Do I get it?"

General Parsons stood hesitantly for a moment. He was baffled, like a man with his back to the wall. Then he gave in with a nod.

"I guess—it's the only way," he said.

"O. K. Let's go. I want the best radio man you've got in this sector."

Presently that man was brought to Barry. Barry faced him.

"Is it possible to install a powerful sending apparatus with variable wave length control into the rear cockpit of my ship?" Barry demanded.

The other thought for a moment, and then nodded in plenty of bewilderment

"I think so."

"But Master," Sika cut in. "Where will I sit?"

"On the ground," Barry smiled, "just this time. Sorry."

To the radio man he said.

"Get going."

Barry watched the installation of that equipment. It was heavy—plenty heavy with large batteries to furnish the power. No, there was no room for either Sika's weight or bulk.

Hours passed. The radio man worked on and on with quick, sure movements. Then he stood up.

"It's done, sir," he said. "But the use of that variable wave length will tangle up all messages being sent in this sector and others during the time you have the power on."

Barry nodded with satisfaction.

"That's exactly what I want," he said. "She's all set, eh? I'll be shoving off."

Sika, with a sad look on his black face, stepped to the prop. He waited for the signal. An orderly came running from headquarters office.

"It's coming," he shouted. "It's coming early this time. Front just called on the phone."

BARRY'S teeth clenched. He nodded and shouted. "Contact!" The Liberty snarled and roared. Barry grinned at the downcast Sika.

"See you later, big boy."

Then he was taking the air. He stuck the nose into the air and climbed. The ascent was slow. The Red Falcon plane was carrying a bigger load than she had ever carried before. No chance to fight now. He'd have to rely entirely on his trick.

Out of the north he saw that strange craft of the enemy coming at a terrific pace. It was drawing nearer. And as it came, Barry kept on climbing and unwound the aerial that the radio man had installed.

Barry's hand was on the controls of the wireless apparatus. There was a switch and a sliding lever that would vary the wave length of the sending.

He tensed as the low-winged thing came nearer. There was the pilot's head sticking up, looking neither to right or left.

Barry was flying to meet that plane at the same level. But he wasn't aiming to crash it. He must come very close to it without the two planes touching.

Nearer and then—

Wam! Barry's hand closed the switch that sent a continuous disturbance into the ether. At the same time he moved the lever slowly from one extreme toward the other. His hand trembled a little with uncertainty. He wasn't so sure. His eyes were glued to that oncoming enemy plane. Nothing happened.

He moved the lever on, shortening the wave length of his sending wireless.

Then suddenly he saw the Boche ship waver in its course. His heart leaped and he moved the lever back to where it had been a split second before.

Something was going on in that low-winged ship now. It was dropping one wing a little. Swerving from its course.

Barry held his breath. The Boche plane kept on nosing down. Then slowly, as though it were trying to correct itself, the nose came up. Up, up it shot until it reached a stall. It turned from there with a quick movement and began to spin straight for the Yank field below.

Down, down and then—*Crash!*

Barry was hurrying to land. His heart was pounding wildly. He felt like shouting for joy. But setting down the heavily-loaded Red Falcon plane took all of his attention.

A mass of shouting, cheering men raced across the field to meet the hero of the hour.

"Marvelous. Wonderful," General Parsons was shouting between gasps for breath caused by his own running. "How did you—"

Barry was climbing out grinning broadly.

"Sort of dumb of all of us not to think of that before," he said. "Let's take a walk over to the wreck and see if I was entirely right."

They reached the wreck a few minutes later. Before they came to it Barry picked up a semi-round block of wood and held it up for the officers to see. It was a nicely carved block representing a human, helmeted head. Barry laughed.

"Looks like the head of the pilot came off in the crash," he ventured. "Let's look farther."

Then he was pointing at coils and gadgets strewn from the cockpit of the plane.

"The motor, I believe, is a super-Mercedes," he said. "And this plane was originally a Fokker D-7. Must have gotten the idea from our crate. The job has Fokker lower wings that have been shortened. It had to be built very light, but strong enough to carry the apparatus which would control it from Germany by radio. They made it bullet-proof by plating the engine cowling. But she wasn't big enough with those clipped wings to carry a pilot. So they just stuck on a head—this one made out of balsa wood—and let it go at that."

They strolled back toward the Red Falcon plane. Barry had left orders to take the apparatus out of his rear cockpit as soon as he landed. Two wireless men were lifting it from the round opening as they came up. But General Parsons stepped before the Red Falcon with determination in his eye.

"My boy," he said fervently, "I can't tell you how much we appreciate this. I'm going to see that you stay with your own people this time. You can name your rank and—"

Barry shook his head a little sadly. Then he smiled slightly.

"Thanks, general," he said. "I'd like to. It gets sort of lonesome up where we live sometimes. But there's one thing that holds me back."

General Parsons frowned. Barry laughed

"You know, general," he went on, "there are a few good cooks in the army, and a lot that aren't so hot. I wouldn't trade the best army meals for Sika's." Barry reached up and patted the grinning, giant black on the shoulder. "Would I Sika? We'll be shoving off now. I want to be over Filens in time to see the drive get going."

And as the Red Falcon plane roared out of the field there was genuine sadness there on the ground. Sadness that the Red Falcon would not come home to join his own. And up there in that crimson crate there was a little sadness in the front seat too. A momentary lonesome feeling for his kind again.

But that passed with the sight below them at the Front. Men surging over and through the German lines in the surprise attack that Barry Rand had helped to make possible. And out of the south came Yank planes to help make the drive a real, permanent success.

Then Barry turned east toward the Vosges. And his lips puckered to whistle his favorite jazz tune, The Darktown Strutter's Ball.

Dynamite Vultures

With his own eyes a Yank peelot saw those Gothas crash into that mountain side. Yet the next night they were flying again—grim ships of death that bullets could not injure. What were these phantom planes? The Red Falcon and his fighting aide, Sika, ride T.N.T. wings to learn the secret of this mystery staffel.

Dynamite Vultures

CHAPTER ONE
Black Drums

VIEWED from the flat top of Saar Mountain, high in the rugged Vosges range, the Front had an ominous stillness. It was sunset and the Red Falcon was preparing for another raid. The light of the sun, as it touched the horizon far to the west like a gigantic gold coin, picked out three forms on the mountain top.

There was the crimson Red Falcon plane, made from parts of German and Allied ships alike. It bore no identification marks of any kind, other than its blood-red color. That was enough to stamp it as the fastest, most feared, and at the same time, most highly respected plane on the Front.

A great, black figure was silhouetted beside it. That was Sika, the giant, black Senegalese aide of the Red Falcon.

Near him stood another figure. A slightly larger than average-sized man with broad shoulders and an athletic build. That was Barry Rand, the Red Falcon, himself. A Yank without a country to live for—but with a country to die for.

The size of Barry Rand was dwarfed by the gigantic figure of his black aide. He looked like a white pygmy as he stood there with Sika towering above him.

"Better check the ship," Barry was saying. "We'll want to shove off as soon as it gets dark."

"Yes, Master," nodded the great black.

While the great Senegalese chief checked the plane and prepared it for flight, Barry Rand puffed on his cigarette and stared out over the strangely silent Front. Stared out past it to where the sun was sinking below the rim of the world.

The Front wasn't entirely quiet, of course. That great area that held more death and destruction than any like space had ever held before in the history of the earth, was never still.

There was the distant rumble of guns and the far-off boom of the shells that those guns had fired. But by comparison to the times when the Front assumed normal action, it seemed still. Threateningly still. Like the lull before the storm.

A tune sprayed through the teeth of Barry Rand. He whistled it thoughtfully, meditatively, scarcely realizing that he was whistling at all.

Then his head began shaking back and forth very slightly,

"Sure looks like something is going to pop," he muttered. "Like either one side or the other is just catching their breath so they'll have more time to raise particular hell."

Then he went on with the tune. This time humming it softly, thoughtfully, while his lips mumbled words.

"Be down to get you in a taxi, honey. Better be ready—"

He broke off with a nod. "Guess that means us, too. Something is getting ready to blow up down there. And, just at a rough guess I'd say it was from the German side of the lines. Well, we'll be ready."

He stamped out the remains of a cigarette and lighted a fresh one. Then came Sika's voice.

"Got a fourth of a tank of gas, Master. We can fly about an hour."

Barry turned from watching the sun set, seemingly, into the earth. It was all but down. Merely the top of the great, fiery disk peeping over the rim at them, could be seen from their mountain,

"How is the ammunition?" Barry asked.

"Your guns got plenty, Master," came the answer from the faithful black. "Sika's Lewis guns need more—"

The great black's voice suddenly broke off. Barry stared at him fixedly. Sika was acting peculiarly. He had turned from a standing position beside his own rear cockpit and now he leaned there motionless, like a great, ebony statue. His black eyes were staring into space. His head was poised at attention like the head of a bird-dog pointing out the game. Watching, listening.

Barry frowned.

"What is it, Sika?" he asked softly.

A huge, black hand stretched out toward him. Remained that way, motionless. A request for silence.

Very quietly Barry stepped over beside him. He glanced up in his face and then turned and tried to see what he might be looking at. Instantly he knew the answer. Sika wasn't looking at anything. Instead, he was listening. Barry grew rigid beside him.

He strained his ears in an effort to hear what his black aide had caught. Nothing but that sluggish rumble of guns, far to the west. He stared again at the black man, fixedly. There was something appalling and, at the same time, commanding, in the way Sika stood there.

His face was immobile, grave. The great, dark eyes seemed sad. Nothing more.

Then, suddenly, the huge negro moved. He knelt down on the ground and placed his right ear close to it. For a long time he held it there.

AFTER a minute or so, Barry knelt beside him. For the first time his untrained ears caught another sound. A throbbing sound that was neither the blasting of heavy guns nor the pulsing rhythm of an airplane motor. It seemed undefinable. A puzzled expression came over his face.

He stood up once more. Sika held his position with his ear to the ground. Barry waited patiently. Then, after another two or three minutes, Sika rose. Without waiting for his master to ask the inevitable question, he spoke. "Drums, Master. You hear them?" Barry nodded, "Yeah, but they might be sending a message in Greek, so far as I'm concerned. What are they and what do they mean, Sika?"

The face of the giant black was shrouded in mystery. He shook his head. "Sika know what they mean, Master," he explained. "But he not know why."

"I don't get you," Barry said. "Who is pounding them? Maybe some Yank outfit has moved near enough to us so we can hear them on their standing retreat, at the setting of the sun."

"No, Master," Sika said. "These not drums of white man. These black man drums. They drums of Wampana. Drums of my people."

"You know what they mean?" Barry demanded.

"Yes, Master, They death drums, Master. We not hear death drums often among my people."

'You mean your people don't die often?" Barry demanded. "Everybody has to die."

"Yes, Master, everybody die, but they not die the way these drums say. Men of Wampana tribe only sound this death drum when some member of tribe die mysteriously. Many Wampana die, just like white people. Some my people die when attacked by Simba, the lion. Others die of sickness, or old age. Not often, some die at hands of own tribesmen. In hate, maybe. Sometimes we are at war with other tribes. Men die then, too. But we not sound death drums when they die."

Barry was growing more and more puzzled.

"Well, who in the devil do you sound these drums for then, Sika?" he asked.

"My people," Sika said, "sound death drums when we find dead Wampana and he not been sick, he have no marks of the spear or the Simba's claws on him. And we not be able to find any cause for death, my people say evil spirits kill him. His body, my people say, are full of evil spirits.

"We burn body at next setting sun. And, as sun go down, we beat death drums until it come up again. You understand, Master?"

Barry nodded a little dumbly.

"Sure," he said. "But I don't get the rest of it. What could cause the mysterious death of one of your Wampana?"

"Sika not know that, either," the giant black nodded seriously. "Those my people sounding drums, Sika their chief. Sika will try to find out."

He eyed Barry anxiously. "If you'll let me?"

"Why sure, big boy," Barry agreed instantly. "But it looks to me as if something is getting ready to pop out there at the Front tonight. I don't want to miss it"

"Sika not know," said the great black, "but maybe strange death of Wampana warrior have something to do with what might happen on Front."

Barry's eyes narrowed.

"Say, that's a hot idea. Sure, we'll look into this thing together. Wait until I get my helmet and goggles and we'll wind her up. I've always wanted to see one of these rites put on by an African tribe."

Sika nodded. "You see, Master, if you come. White man not see death drum ever. But Sika take you."

In another minute, Barry was in the front cockpit pulling on his helmet and goggles, adjusting the throttle, checking the gauges.

"Wind her up!" he called the giant black.

Sika did. He whirled that great propeller as though it were the crank handle of a miniature machine. Then—

"Contact!"

The Liberty roared and warmed. Five minutes later that crimson plane of death was soaring into the skies of evening. The air about them was still fairly light, faintly tinted with pink of the sunset's glow. Barry shouted through the tube.

"Last I remember the Wampana, they were with the French, holding the line around Mornes in the Hosbrock Mountains. Is that where you think they are?"

"Yes, Master. I think drums come from there."

Instantly Barry dropped the map case, like a small desk, in front of him. He shifted maps until he found the one of that sector. Then he inspected it in the lowering light of the evening. He found the location of the line that the French were holding. Found an X nearby.

There were many little X's like that on all of his maps. They indicated possible landing fields where he could set down the Red Falcon plane, if necessary.

Already he had turned the course of the ship toward that spot far ahead. He heard Sika's voice coming through the tube that connected the two cockpits.

"You not forget we low on gas, Master. And it will be dark when we land there."

"O. K., big boy," Barry sang out. "Hang on, now. We're going places. I want to get there before they tune down on this death drum ceremony."

As he spoke, his hand battered the throttle wide open and the Liberty thundered in instant response, jerking the Red Falcon plane at a wild speed.

CHAPTER TWO
The Flaming Corpse

IT GREW darker as they raced on. Grew so dark that before long they could only make out the Front by the pricks of flame that darted up in a jagged line along it—the flames of artillery guns.

Barry's eyes were staring ahead of him into the night. And he softly hummed that tune:

"Better be ready about half past eight. Now honey, don't be late. I want to be there when the band starts playing."

Then, suddenly, he stopped short. And instead of the tune coming from his lips, he emitted a low whistle that was instantly drowned by the roar of the great Liberty.

"Hey! Look what we got!" He was pointing ahead. "There's a fire down there."

"Yes, Master," came Sika's answering voice. "I think that Wampana fire burning body before evil spirits can escape to do harm to others."

"Gee," grinned Barry, "we'll be on time. And it isn't half past eight yet, either."

"We be in time, Master," Sika said.

"But listen," Barry objected. "You say the Wampana will be all around that fire?"

"Yes, Master," Sika assured him. "Wampana be in circle around fire. Others outside keep white man away so they not see. White man laugh and make fun of Wampana. But you not laugh. I take you to see ceremony."

"Yeah, I know. That's nice of you, big boy," Barry agreed. "But how about enemy bombers? They'd have a grand time, laying a flock of eggs on your gang of warriors in the light of that fire."

"They not drop bombs during ceremony," Sika assured him instantly. "Evil spirits inside dead Wampana they burn up in fire. Good spirits and death drums keep enemy planes away."

"Oh, yeah?" said Barry. He was tempted to laugh. But Sika's confidence that he wouldn't laugh at their ceremony, kept him from it

He watched those flames far below. At first it had been merely a flicker of light down there. Now, as they drew nearer, it took on the appearance of a great bonfire. And still, from their altitude, the whole thing seemed so small, so toy-like in size. He could make out an oblong shape, mingled in the flames. He shuddered a little at sight of it.

A human body was being burned down there. There we're nicer things to think about. He struck up the tune once more.

"Be down to get you in a taxi, honey. Better be—"

He stopped. Somehow it didn't sound as good as usual. It was a black man's song of happiness. And here, below him, blacks were mourning. That was the body of a black man that was burning in the flames.

As they came nearer he located the field that was marked with an X on his map. He climbed higher in order to throw off suspicion of his intentions to land and turned more toward the enemy side of the lines. He droned on that way for a short distance. Then, slowly, he pulled back the throttle. Later he cut the switch and dropped the nose.

There was just the swish of wind through the rigging and past the wings now. He turned back for a long glide and prepared to land.

As the Red Falcon plane slipped down through the night, he could make out the field very faintly ahead of them. At first it was merely a smoother blotch of shadow than the rest of the earth. Then it took shape and he could make out the boundaries.

A steep side-slip, then the plane was kicked straight and next came the rumble of wheels. For a long moment Barry sat in the cockpit, listening. He heard Sika's voice coming softly through the tube.

"You afraid, Master, maybe they will not be friendly?"

"Not for my own part," Barry answered. "I was thinking more of you. Sika. This sector is held by the French at present. And don't forget, you're officially A. W. O. L. from your Senegal regiment of the French army. I don't know how they'll take this, if the French recognize you."

"Sika not afraid," came the reply. "We go now to the death drum ceremony?"

"Right," said Barry, climbing out and dropping to the ground. "Let's go."

"Yes, Master. I'll lead the way, you will follow."

THE giant black stalked swiftly and silently across the field, after they had pushed the Red Falcon plane into the protecting shadows of overhanging trees.

They broke through a small thicket and crossed another field. Ahead of them they could make out the blaze of light reflected in the sides above the fire of the Wampana.

"I can't figure that out," Barry breathed as they grew closer.

"What, Master?"

"Why the French let your men put on this ceremony," Barry said. "What a swell target that whole outfit would be for enemy bombers."

"Good spirits keep away enemy during ceremony," Sika insisted.

Barry felt like saying "Baloney," but instead he asked; "And you say your men are keeping the French from seeing the ceremony?"

"Yes, Master. That is our custom, to keep the white man from seeing death drum ceremony of the Wampana because they'll laugh."

"I can't figure that out, either," Barry ventured. "These Frogs don't like to be told where they can and can't go. Especially by a bunch of black subjects."

Sika didn't answer that question. Perhaps he didn't know the answer.

Only a fairly good-sized hedge ahead of them shut off the view of the Wampana warriors about their ceremonial pyre. Abruptly Sika pointed ahead.

The drums had become much louder. They were no longer the mere pulsing of air and the seeming trembling of earth. Instead, they were a distinct booming sound. Real drums.

Tum! Ta-tum! Ta-tum! Ta-tum!

"Beyond that hedge, Master," Sika said softly, "the ceremony of death drums goes on."

"But where are the guards you spoke of?" Barry asked softly. "I thought you said—"

He stopped short. Swiftly, but without a sound, four, huge, dark figures had loomed up out of the shadow of the hedge, stood before them, blocking their way.

So these were the guards who were there to keep the white men from seeing the ceremony. They appeared with such abruptness that they startled Barry for a moment.

Sika strode to them and stopped. Barry saw his right hand extend out and upward. Then he heard him speak very softly in his native tongue.

Instantly, the four guards responded. Two of them turned and broke through the hedge excitedly. The other two dropped behind Sika, one on either side of Barry Rand.

"We go now, Master," Sika said.

As they reached the hedge, that question which seemed uppermost in Barry's mind still baffled him. He had seen no figure, no man, until these black men appeared. No Frenchmen in sight. Then, as he followed Sika through the hedge, the truth came to him.

"That's a hot one, Sika," he said. "I've been trying to figure out why we haven't seen any Frogs hanging about, trying to take a peek at the ceremony. "But maybe they aren't so foolish as they might be. I guess your guards don't have such a tough job keeping them away after all. They haven't your confidence in the good spirits that will hold back the enemy bombers. They are taking no chances of getting blown up."

No answer from Sika.

They broke through the hedge and came out in the light of the blazing funeral pyre. Barry's eyes widened.

He saw before him a flaming corpse on a rack built on stilts. The fire was crackling and roaring wildly. Masses of flame licked up and around the thing that had been a black man and mounted into the inky night.

Several great blacks seemed to be officiating as near to the fire as it was comfortable to stand. They turned as two guards brought the news of their chief's arrival.

The foremost Wampana warrior of the group began bowing and raising his hands up and down while he sang a weird sort of tune in monotone.

About the fire sat many Senegalese soldiers. There was no sign of their uniforms. They were stripped to the black hide, wearing nothing but loin cloths.

As Sika appeared before them, everyone of the blacks who must have numbered four or five hundred, leaped to their feet A high-pitched wailing sound came from their lips in chorus. They turned and faced Sika with hands extended and bowed in rhythm to the pulsing wail.

The sight of these half savage black men in the center of the war-torn lines going through their weird ceremony was startling. Barry blinked his eyes to make sure that he wasn't in a trance, that he was actually seeing these things before him.

Sika stopped short, held out his hands in answering token to his Wampana warriors. He mumbled a few words in his native tongue that Barry couldn't catch. The black men of the Wampana tribe dropped in their former positions and continued to sit cross-legged around the great fire. Those who seemed to have charge of the ceremony came nearer to Sika.

One by one they advanced, bent down and kissed the toes of his boots in supplication. Sika waited until they had all finished the ritual, then he suddenly began stripping off his clothing.

THE under-chieftain, who had been in charge of the ceremony up to now, cried out some command in his native tongue.

Then Barry noticed the drums and the drummers. There were two of them. One drum and drummer stood at what had been the head end of the fire of the funeral pyre, the other at the foot. They drummed in a strange way. Beat the top of the long, cylindrical drum with the right fist and with the left hand seemed to muffle the drum between beats. With the words of the under-chieftain, the pounding of the drums took on a faster tempo. The squatting warriors began to move. Down until their foreheads touched and then straight again. Back and forth to the rapid beating of the drums.

Sika was stripped stark naked now. He turned and motioned Barry to a place in the line of encircled warriors, but slightly nearer the fire.

"You sit down here, Master. Sika lead ceremony."

A low wailing sound came from the assembled black men of the Wampana. It was half whisper, half cry. Hardly louder than the sighing of the wind through a pine grove. It was weird, ghastly. And it sent little prickly chills up and down Barry Rand's back.

The chieftains who had been in charge before Sika's arrival now formed a semicircle of their own before the funeral pyre. Sika was the only one standing. He bowed from the hips in time with the others—with the beating of the drums. It was as though the entire existence of Barry Rand had been suddenly forgotten. He was trying to figure the thing out. Wondering about the death of this black man, who was now nothing but a mass of burned flesh.

But this whole weird spectacle was so fascinating that it held his attention and his thoughts. Kept him, for the time being, from asking Sika to learn more about the death. An hour slipped by. Then another. It was as though these men were untiring machines and not human beings. It seemed to Barry to be beyond human endurance for them to go through such rapid movements for so long a time.

Tum! Ta-tum! Ta-tum! Ta-tum!

His own brain was throbbing with the sound. It made him dizzy to listen to it. Twice he had forced his mind away from this ceremony and had wondered about an aerial attack.

This thing had been going on for more than three hours now, since sundown. The reflection of the fire's light could surely be seen from the German lines. Why, then, didn't the enemy come over with their bombers and blast this perfect target, with its hundreds of black soldiers, into hell?

One or two bombs properly placed would do the trick easily. Could it be that the superstitions of these half-savage natives were founded on truth? That the good spirits guarded them against all evil while the death drum ceremony was going on?

In the strange, weird, atmosphere of it all, Barry suddenly realized that he was almost coming to believe it himself.

Then Sika stopped short. Everyone of the five hundred blacks before him stopped their bowing and waiting. A sudden, ominous lull settled down over the picture.

The drums ceased. Seemed to leave a hole in the air that had been filled before with their throbbing. Barry saw Sika standing motionless, his hands straight out toward the funeral pyre.

The heavy poles at each of the four corners had burned to practically nothing. Sika stood there for perhaps a full minute. It seemed as though that deathly stillness shut out even the rumble of guns on the Front.

But perhaps that illusion was purely mental. Those guns were there, of course, still firing.

Then, as though Sika had commanded it to happen at that moment, the four poles which had held the corpse on its rack, collapsed and the burning body dropped with a hissing sound into the coals of the fire itself.

Flames shot upward toward the sky. Reached higher than they had before. Then Barry sat petrified with fear and astonishment at what he saw.

CHAPTER THREE
The Haunted Mountain

SIKA, still stripped naked, rushed forward as the flames mounted higher into the night. A wild scream belched from his lips. A scream that made Barry Rand shudder as he sat there on the ground.

Every other man of the Wampana tribe leaped to his feet. Sika was headed straight for that blazing inferno. Just before he reached it, the scream died away. Then barefooted, his black skin glistening in the light, he dashed directly into the fire.

Barry was on his feet, too. His eyes were popping out of his head. The flames hid his aide from view; he couldn't tell whether he had stopped in the center of them or gone through to the other side.

The air was filled with wild, bloodcurdling yells, as man after man rushed naked at the fire and plunged into it.

Barry opened his mouth to call out Sika's name. Then he saw the black giant coming toward him, unharmed.

The drums were throbbing in a faster tempo than before.

Tum! Ta-tum! Ta-tum! Tum!

Sika was bowing before him, speaking. He had to shout to make himself heard above the din of screams and drum beats.

"Evil spirits gone now, Master. The fire burned them from us."

Barry nodded slowly. He didn't smile.

"Yes," he said, grimly. "I can imagine."

Sika began to dress. As he did so, Barry put the question that was uppermost in his mind to him.

"How did this fellow die, Sika?"

Sika shook his head, as he pulled on one boot.

"I not know, Master. He die mysterious. That all I know."

"Find out, will you?"

"Yes, Master."

Sika called one of the under-chiefs to him. They had been the first to follow Sika through the fire. Now a long line of the Wampana warriors had formed. One by one they were screaming and running through the flames to cleanse their bodies of evil spirits.

Those that were already cleansed squatted about the circle and continued to bow their foreheads, touching the ground in time to the beating of the drums.

Sika and his chieftain spoke rapidly in their native tongue. Sika asked many questions which the other answered. Then he turned to Barry.

"M'gunda say last night Ogaga sent to stay in house below Sueil Mountain. Watch for something to happen there. This morning he not come back. We go with French to look for Ogaga. Ogaga dead in house. Door open. No knife wounds on body. French doctor say maybe he die of fright. We say evil spirits kill him."

Barry frowned in perplexity.

"So the French say he died of fright, huh?" he mumbled half to himself. "Why was he sent there?"

Sika turned and questioned M'gunda.

They talked back and forth for several minutes. Then Sika explained more.

"M'gunda say last three nights at midnight Gothas come from somewhere to bomb American airdromes. Each night they blow up different field. Last two nights American planes chase Gothas. Then a cloud, like fog, settle around this frame house against side of Sueil Mountain. Gotha disappear in cloud. Each time French think Gotha crash into house or mountain. But when fog clear away in morning, house all right and they not find any wreckage of Gotha."

BARRY'S eyes narrowed. "Sueil Mountain," he repeated. "Let's see, as I remember that's on the present Front."

Sika nodded. "Yes, Master. German trenches halfway up north side. Allied trenches halfway up south side. Wampana sent up last night to help the French hold their lines on Sueil Mountain. They send Ogaga to stay in frame building and see what happen there at midnight. Find him dead this morning."

"Wait now. Let me get this straight," Barry said hastily. "Was there one Gotha or more?"

"They see two Gothas," Sika went on, after questioning M'gunda again.

"And they both vanished into this fog on the mountain?"

"Yes, Master. Whole side of mountain covered with fog."

Slowly Barry shook his head.

"That's got me stopped, big boy."

He cast a glance at the Wampana warriors. Some were still rushing through the flames, others going on with their wailing.

"Do they need you here any longer, Sika?"

"No, Master. Fire dance over. M'gunda can carry on ceremony until dawn."

Barry nodded.

"Good," he said. "Let's go."

Sika drew on his great coat.

"Where we go, Master?"

"We're going to that frame shanty where they found Ogaga," Barry returned. "Find out from M'gunda just how to get there."

"But, Master," objected Sika, "evil spirits there that—"

Barry's fist clenched.

"Listen, big boy," he said, "you said the evil spirits went into Ogaga's body and killed him. Right?"

"Yes, Master."

"And you have burned Ogaga's body. That means yon have burned up the evil spirits."

"Yes, Master."

"And you went through the flames yourself and burned up any evil spirits that might be hanging around you. Then how can they do you any harm?"

Sika nodded obediently.

"I go with you, Master."

He spoke to M'gunda once more. There was much gibbering and pointing by the under-chieftain. Then Sika motioned to Barry.

"Come, Master. I show you the way."*

They walked back through the hedge, the way they had come. Skirting the ceremony of beating drums and wailing Wampana warriors, they moved on through the darkness toward the north. As Barry followed his giant aide, his brain toyed with the one thing that he couldn't get straight. He was convinced that the French soldiers had steered clear of the ceremony and tell-tale fire to avoid the danger of being bombed by the enemy.

And yet, no planes had been heard, either Allied or German. No bombs had been dropped.

It was hours now from the time of the sun's setting. Plenty of time for the Germans to see that fire and send every bomber at their command to blow up the whole regiment of Wampana tribesmen.

But they hadn't done it. Nothing had happened to mar the ceremony in any way. No intrusion by the French. No interference by air from the enemy.

Except for the reflection of the fire against the sky, Barry and Sika walked in total darkness. Ahead of them, now and then, they could make out spurts of flame that marked the positions of Allied guns.

The guns verified the position of the lines along the ridge that was Sueil Mountain. According to the direction taken by their tongues of flame, they were shooting almost straight up into the air.

Their shells then must go high up and come down to explode on the gun placements on the German side of the ridge.

Suddenly Sika stopped, so abruptly that Barry ran straight into his back.

"Look, Master!" Sika was pointing before him.

They had been walking cross country, avoiding roads—such as they might be. No need to have the French down on their necks.

Before them, in a little thicket, Barry could make out a dim form. He struck a match, then blew it out quickly before the light of the flame could draw fire from any quarter.

In that momentary light he saw the grim story of former battle. It had been a machine-gun placement. The body of a dead machine gunner had been missed when the field was cleared.

It was decayed, so that it filled the air with a horrible stench. It lay over a Lewis machine gun. Swiftly, Sika was pawing about at the side of the gun placement. He stood up and spoke, a little choked by the pungent odor.

"Double Lewis pans, Master, seven of them. We need them, Master."

"I'll say we do," Barry said, trying not to breath as he spoke. "Grab them and let's get out of here."

Sika carried them easily in the canvas case he had found them in and struck on through the darkness.

THEY were in the clear now. Above them they could see the stars twinkling brightly. And very dimly they could make out a wide expanse of level ground. Beyond it was the towering, shadowy form of Sueil Mountain.

Barry stamped his feet hard on the earth.

"Hum," he mused, "this would certainly make a good airdrome with a floor like this."

"Yes, Master. But the mountain ahead of us. A plane could only land one way here—toward the mountain."

"I'll say," Barry nodded. He pointed ahead, strained his eyes toward the base of the mountain. "Is that the building, Sika?"

"Y-yes, Master."

They reached it, after a walk of two hundred yards more. Sika hesitated and Barry passed him.

The door of the place was open. Barry stepped inside and stared about the dark interior. He lit a match. To all appearances the building had been a barn. And, in hugging the mountain side so closely, it had escaped enemy gun fire. In fact, it was built partly against the side of the mountain.

But it was much more heavily timbered than any barn Barry had ever seen. Stout, three-inch planks formed the siding. The floor was of wood, but very heavy.

The interior seemed entirely bare. The building contained no windows, only that narrow door, through which Barry had entered.

He called to his aide.

"Come on in, Sika. No evil spirits here now, as far as I can see. Doesn't look as if there is anything else here, either."

Hesitatingly, Sika entered. He followed close on Barry's heels, like a nervous hound, as Barry walked about the place lighting match after match.

The whole place was one big room. Great beams held up the roof. The match in his hand went out. He suddenly thought he could feel a draft from somewhere, blowing on his face. A breath in the darkness.

He struck another match. That match went out like the other as though blown out by the mouth of an invisible person.

Bam!

Something slammed behind them. Barry whirled, struck another match. It, too, went out. Then the place was suddenly filled with a low, moaning sound.

"Wo-o-o-o-o-o-w!"

And, at the same time, he could feel the building move Under his feet.

CHAPTER FOUR
Skeleton Tarmac

ASTER! Master!” Sika’s voice was strained in terror. The interior of the building was pitch black. Barry could hear Sika’s heavy boots pounding on the hard floor. Sika was running for the exit, running desperately—in panic.

Barry raced after him. As he ran he tried to light another match. It went out the minute it was struck. He could feel that draft of air increasing as it swept across his face—as though some monster were following, breathing heavily.

But in the first glow of the match, Barry had seen something that made him wonder for the instant, if there wasn’t something to this evil spirit business that the Wampana feared.

That door, through which they had entered, had been open. They had left it that way after they had passed through. Now, he saw that it had closed. Neither he nor Sika had been near it.

Blam!

He heard Sika’s great body crash against the door. Heard him cry out in panic.

“Master! Master! The door!”

He heard him straining against it. Tried to find another match. But they were all gone.

“The door’s closed, Master. I - I can’t get it open.”

Barry was beside him now. His own hands were shaking a little as they felt about for a knob or a latch. There was nothing there. Nothing by which they might force the door open again.

The weird, moaning sound increased, and at the same time, he felt the draft across his face blow harder. The building was still moving under them.

Barry stared behind him. He heard a rattling sound. Something luminous in the inky blackness was detaching itself from the rafters above them. It swung like a loose-jointed monkey.

Barry didn't wait to see more. He barked an order to Sika in a desperate hope that he hadn't turned.

"Try the door again," he snapped.

Then came the voice of the giant aide, shaking with fear.

"Yes, Master, I try. But—"

A desperate idea flashed into Barry Rand's mind. Sika was very intelligent, but, with his inborn superstitions and inhibitions, he might go mad and die of fright, as Ogaga had done, if he saw that weird form romping about above their heads.

Instantly Barry whipped out his handkerchief. He forced an insincere laugh. There wasn't anything funny about this whole business, but he must reassure Sika.

"Stand where you are, big boy, facing the door," he commanded.

"Y-yes, Master."

"Now, this is all in fun, so don't get any crazy notions. We're going to play a little game here. And I'll gamble that when I take this off, you'll be outside just as safe and sound as when you came in."

"Yes, Master."

He doubled the handkerchief corner-wise and tied it about the head of the giant black, covering his eyes.

"Now, lie down on the floor, flat on your face. And don't be surprised at anything you hear. I'm going to make a lot of funny noises, probably."

"Y-yes, Master."

Sika groped his way to the floor, lay down. Instantly Barry stared up at the weird, unexplainable thing he had seen before. He took more time to scrutinize it as it moved.

It moved with the slow motions which were more characteristic of a giant spider, than a human being. There were the glowing outlines of bones. A skeleton which groped and flopped slowly among the rafters.

Then, suddenly, to his left, another appeared. The whole spectacle was horrible. All the while those two glowing figures were coming closer to a position above his head, where he stood in front of the door.

But the most startling sensation came as he stood frozen there beside the prostrate Sika. It seemed to him that the body of a snake suddenly coiled about his ankle, gripped him tightly, as though it would sever the foot from the leg.

BARRY RAND grew rigid. He moved a little. The grip on his ankle tightened. Then came a voice, Sika's voice. It was shaken with fear.

"You not leave me, Master?"

Barry had to take a long breath before he could go on. So that was Sika's hand holding his ankle and no snake or evil spirit.

"I'll say it's me, big boy, and I'm not going to leave you. But, for heaven's sake, don't grab my leg like that."

"Yes, Master."

The tension relaxed a little. Barry's hand dropped to his automatic and stared upward at the ghastly sight above his head.

Those two weird, phosphorescent skeletons were swinging from rafter to rafter, coming closer to him. The moaning sound had reached a higher pitch.

They reached a point directly over his head. Then, like ghost spiders at the end of their long web, they began to descend upon him. Rattled the loose-jointed, bony arms and legs in a way that sent the chills up Barry Rand's spine.

Suddenly the wild scream of a siren shattered the blackness into bits. Barry's teeth were clenched, his gun out The short hairs along his back seemed to be standing out straight. He could almost imagine that something behind him was just about to reach out and touch him.

He wished he had his back to the wall, but he dared not move and break Sika's hold about his ankle. Even now he could feel the hand tremble. That clutch on his ankle seemed to be the only thing holding Sika to the world of sanity.

To add horror to the situation, the gangling skeletons, with their accompanying clatter of bones, were almost within reach of his face now. Desperately he brought up his automatic.

Those bones seemed to be hanging there now. Just swinging and leering at him with gaping, toothless mouths and sightless eye sockets.

But another sound came to him above the wailing siren call, from somewhere in the rafters. Perhaps it was his imagination. But no, that couldn't be. The sound he heard was the pulsing, droning of airplane motors. Airplane motors not far away.

The floor beneath their feet had suddenly ceased to move. The thunder of the motors increased, until it seemed that the whole building was filled with their throbbing.

As abruptly as the thunder of the airplane motors had come to him it vanished again. The siren died away. Now only that continuous moaning and the draft across his face.

The skeletons continued to dangle and clatter just above his head, as though at any minute they would reach out and snatch at him.

Then came Sika's voice out of the darkness.

"Master, you not make those noises like airplane motors."

For a moment that had Barry stumped. He tried to keep his voice calm as he answered, in spite of the spectacle above him.

"No, big boy. I didn't make those. But there's nothing above evil spirits in connection with airplane motors. Those must be your two Gothas."

"Yes, Master. They come back, maybe, pretty soon."

"That's what I guessed," Barry answered. "You lie still now, I'm going to take a little target practice while we're waiting. Just a little shooting to keep the hand in."

"Yes, Master."

Barry raised his automatic. Pointed it full in the face of the leering skull above his right. He pulled the trigger. A portion of the bony face vanished. It made the remainder more hideous than ever.

He pulled again and again. Aiming through the darkness into what seemed to be the bodies of both skeletons,

Blam! Blam! Blam!

NOTHING happened, except that parts of the phosphorescent glow disappeared. And the agitated dancing of the skeletons increased in activity.

They were coming down threateningly close. They seemed to be reaching out their hands to him. Gaunt, loose jointed hands, but just out of his own reach.

Minutes passed as he stood frozen there. For a long time he had been watching one of those ghastly figures. He took careful aim at the center of it and pulled three times in rapid succession. Put a new clip into his gun and fired two more shots.

Then something happened to that skeleton as the last shot flashed up to the rafters. The middle of it dropped. It hung there with the pelvis bone protruding toward him, and the hands that had groped for him strung backward disjointedly.

Instantly Barry found he could breathe normally again. And with his next breath came a chuckle.

"So it's a trick they do with wires, is it?" he said half aloud.

"What, Master?" asked Sika.

"Oh, just talking to myself," Barry assured him. "Don't you worry about—"

He heard a swishing sound from somewhere in the darkness and then a low rumble. Then, as though that were a signal for the action to begin, the building began to move again under their feet.

The phosphorescent forms danced upward, back into the rafters. And a moment later they vanished.

The moaning sound was lessening and he could feel the drafty wind that had blown over his face die down. Then, almost at the same time, the building ceased to move.

Something large and formidable struck Barry and hit him a vicious crack in the back.

"Ouch!" he cried. "What the—"

Then he turned and stared. The door had burst open. The door they couldn't unfasten before. Barry reached down and grasped Sika by the arm. Guided him to his feet

"Come on, big boy. The show's over and it's our exit."

He took the handkerchief from around the great black's eyes. They stood half hidden from each other as a white mist poured in. It was like fog, but not damp. It was like smoke, but had no odor.

Hastily Barry led Sika out. Gropingly they plowed through the shroud of haze. They could only feel each other, feel their footing as they went on.

Then suddenly they broke out into the clear. And blinding flashlights burst into their eyes.

A voice cried out from the center of the lights.

"I am Major Chapuis, commander of the Senegalese forces. Who are you and where did you come from?"

Barry hesitated. He and Sika could only blink dazedly into the blinding lights.

Before they could answer, Major Chapuis' voice came again, high pitched and excited.

"*Mon dieu!* Name of a dog. I recognize you. You are Sika, the deserter, from my regiment. And you are the Red Falcon. *N'est ce pas?* You are under arrest!"

CHAPTER FIVE
Escape!

BARRY RAND seemed frozen to the spot for the moment He could see neither Major Chapuis nor the others who stood in the shadow, behind the glare.

"So we're under arrest, are we, major?" he said, because he couldn't think of anything else to say. Then his brain began working logically. There were certain things he wanted to know. Things Chapuis could probably tell him. He shrugged.

"All right, we're under arrest. But first, before we go with you, I'd like to find out some things. I'll make you a proposition. I'll tell you what we found out, if you'll tell me what you know."

The lights, one on either side of the central figure, moved nearer to them and around to their rear. The French guards were making sure the prisoners didn't escape.

Now he could see the French major clearly. He was a small fiery little Frog, very cocky and high strung.

"*Mais oui.* Eet eez an agreement, my prisoner."

"O. K." Barry nodded. "Here's the dope. Sika and I attended the ceremony of the death drums tonight. A black man was found dead, in this house which we have just left. A few minutes after we went in it started to move as though it were rolling on wheels. We tried to get out, but the door had slammed shut and locked.

"I believe that everything that went on in there was a trick to scare Allied soldiers out of the place and keep them away from it."

"Then we heard the roar of airplane motors. They were so near that we thought, in the darkness, they were coming right at us. Then they vanished and died away. Perhaps a half hour later we heard a rumbling sound and then the building began to move again. A few minutes later it stopped and the door burst open. Almost knocked me for a loop."

"*Mon dieu!*" the major exclaimed.

"Exactly," Barry nodded. "Now I've told you what we found out. Perhaps you will be good enough to tell me a few things. What is there to this story I've heard concerning Gothas blowing up Allied airdromes, particularly American dromes?"

"Eet eez too terrible," the major exploded, waving his hands. "They do not come from far behind the enemy lines. There are two of them. They attack a different field at midnight, every night. They blow up that field completely. Then they drop a note on another drome, before they return, saying that that drome will be blown up the following night."

"And it always happens?" Barry asked.

"So far, for four nights they have done it. The American airdrome at Carsai was blown up not more than a half hour ago."

"But how do you know that these German planes don't come from the other side of the lines?"

"We have checked every possible landing field, for at least 30 kilometers behind the lines in all directions," the major answered. "The Gothas carry an enormous load of high explosive bombs. They come over then with a small amount of gasoline, because they couldn't carry all those bombs and full tanks of gasoline, too. *N'est ce pas?*"

Barry nodded. "Maybe that building we were in has something to do with it."

"But no," the major objected. "The building, you say you were in it. And you didn't see the Gothas."

"Yeah, but we heard them plenty close," Barry ventured. "I haven't got that part of it figured out yet. But I'd stake my life on it that there's a hook-up somewhere. I understand the Allied planes have chased these Gothas after their raids."

"*Mais oui, mon* Red Falcon. But to no avail. Each time the Gotha dives where our planes dare not go. They dive straight for the bottom of this mountain. And a fog, like this one which is here now, hides them from view as they plunge into it."

"But they don't crash," Barry objected.

The major shook his head. "We have looked everywhere for the wreckage on this side of the mountain, there is none."

"These fields that have been blown up," Barry asked, "how many of them were American?"

"All four have been American fields."

"That's funny," Barry said. "There are French fields here too, aren't there?"

"Oui, monsieur" Major Chapuis nodded. "But perhaps it may have something to do with the fact that very soon—any time now—American troops will be here to take our places, to help reinforce the lines. But come, it will do you no good to stand talking. Remember, you are under arrest, both of you."

Barry threw a bluff; he forced a laugh.

"It would seem, Major Chapuis, that you have not studied your book on international army relations very well. True, you can arrest Sika as a deserter, because he is a subject of France. But don't forget that no matter what my relations may be with my own country, I'm still an American. You can't arrest me."

"Nom du chien!" exploded the little French major. "So you would try to tell me my business! *Mon dieu!* I think I see it now. For long the Allies have suspected you, the outlaw Red Falcon, of aiding the enemy. Your story of what you heard and saw inside the building, it is all a lie. Come, we take you to a place of confinement in the rear, where you will await trial."

Barry moved a little closer to Sika. He felt the giant black stiffen as automatic pistols were shoved against his back.

Major Chapuis executed a very snappy about face.

"March!" he commanded.

THEY began to move toward the south, struck a road and went down it, skirting shell holes and mud puddles.

Far ahead Barry could see the light of the death-drum fire still burning, and around it the great circle of Wampana warriors. On they marched for perhaps two kilometers until the red glow was at their left now—they had come even with it.

Then, at the end of the road, came the low cry of a night-hawk. At the same instant, Sika's lips muttered one word, scarcely audible: "Wampana."

He still carried the heavy canvas case loaded with double Lewis pans.

Suddenly Barry felt the big fellow move beside him. At the same moment he, Barry, was pushed flat on his face in the road.

Sika had spun round. There was a clinking and rattle as the heavy canvas case swung and struck the bodies and skulls of the two French guards.

Then a dark form leaped from the side of the road upon the major, who had stopped to investigate the trouble. The major's light went out and he fell to the ground, crying out threats and sputtering a wild barrage of French oaths.

Barry felt himself snatched from the road at an astonishing rate of speed. Then the whole realization of what had happened came over him.

Sika had swung the bag with one sweep of his great hand, knocking both the French guards to the side of the road. He had pushed Barry flat so that the heavy canvas case finishing its arc wouldn't strike him.

Now the giant black was racing headlong down the road with Barry Rand under his arm like a sack of meal. Barry struggled to get free and Sika set him on his feet. They ran on together.

"Nice work, big boy," Barry panted as they raced on.

"That call of night-hawk Master, M'gunda make that signal. Guards look to see where sound come from. M'gunda take care of major."

"Listen," Barry hissed, "if any of those Frogs are killed, I'll wring your black neck."

"Not killed, Master, just knocked down," Sika assured him. "Hear them shouting now? They looking for us. We go this way."

"But won't M'gunda get in a tough jam attacking the major?"

He heard a soft chuckle from Sika.

"Major not know who attack him. Come, Master, our ship over here."

Sika left the road and broke through the open fields. A few minutes later they came to the place where the Red Falcon plane was hidden.

Hurriedly, Sika was stowing the double Lewis pans into the racks in his rear cockpit. Barry climbed to his own seat, set the controls for a start. Then Sika was at the great propeller.

"Contact!" called Barry in a hoarse whisper.

The prop whirled, the Liberty roared. Sika was racing around the end of the left wing and leaping into his cockpit.

As the crimson plane roared into the air, Sika's voice came through the tube.

"Where we go now, Master? You not forget we only got few minutes gas?"

"I'll say I'm not forgetting it, big boy," Barry flung back. "That's where we're going right now. There's a little German advance training field about 50 kilometers behind the tines. You've got plenty of ammunition now. Well go over and see what the prospects are for gassing up."

"But maybe we not have gas enough to get there," Sika objected.

"We've got to take that chance," Barry said. "It's the nearest German field I can think of. I don't care much about trying any of the Allied fields around here. Major Chapuis will have the message around to watch for and arrest us before we can reach any of them."

They weren't climbing now. Barry was holding down close to the ground. He did let the nose rise a little, as they came to Sueil Mountain. They must just clear that.

As they came down on the other side, Barry sat up straight in his seat and stared below. He saw many lights darting about. They seemed to go right against the lower side of the mountain and then disappear as though they had been swallowed up.

As Barry hurled on, he shouted through the tube:

"See that, Sika? I flew this way on purpose, right on top of that fog covering the building we got trapped in. Then we zoomed the mountain and came down on the other side. What do those lights look like to you?"

"Look like lights in the hands of men running, Master."

"Sure. And they ran right into the side of the mountain and either put their lights out or disappeared. Am I right?"

"Yes, Master."

"The funny part of the whole thing," Barry went on, talking half to himself, "is that that place down there, where we just saw the lights on the German side is directly opposite the wooden building on the Allied side of the mountain. What's the connection, Sika?"

"Sika not know," came back the response.

"You and I both, big boy," Barry said. "But we've got to find out. After we gas up, we're going to stay over here in Germany until we find out. O. K.?"

"Yes, Master."

They romped on through the darkness. Then, suddenly, searchlights slashed the inky blackness, searching for them.

"Hmm," Barry said. "That's something else again."

Tac-tac-tac!

A searchlight caught them in its glare and held them for a moment. A ground machine gun rattled and Boche steel drummed on the covering of the right wing.

Barry kicked to the left and sent the Red Falcon plane wriggling out of the light. Another flash picked them up, and another machine gun began to rattle a hail of death.

Again Barry maneuvered desperately and flung the Red Falcon plane into the darkness. They raced on out of the danger zone. Could see the lights plainly behind, reaching for them. Then—

Sput-sput-sput!

The Liberty engine bucked, coughed and snorted. Then it died altogether. Barry stared at the luminous gasoline gauge. It said empty.

CHAPTER SIX

Behind the Lines

DESPERATELY Barry was trying to pick a landing field. But there was only blackness about. He was gliding down into inky darkness.

Then out of the dark he saw a lighter shadow. The shadowy shape of a field that ran north and south without any apparent obstructions in it.

Everything was staked on that landing. That field might be full of shell holes. It might have rocks that he couldn't see. But he must go down.

"Hang on, big boy," he called softly through the tube. "Here we go."

"Yes, Master." There was implicit faith in Sika's voice as he answered.

They drifted down with the wind humming softly through the wires. That might be the hum of a death chant. No telling until—

Barry jerked the stick to haul the nose of the plane over a tree that loomed up suddenly. He kicked viciously, as the landing gear tore the topmost branches. Then he was side slipping down. The wheels touched.

The field was rough and the plane bounded. The stick came back in his lap and he held off as long as he could. Then—

Carrumph!

The ship rolled slower and slower. As it stopped it lurched to the left, the wheel had dropped into a hole.

Anxiously they climbed out. In the darkness, Barry inspected the plane, more by feel than by sight. He jerked on the landing gear, tested the members for strength.

"Just pure luck, Sika," he said. "I think she's all right. There are some woods down at the south end of the field, where we came in. Let's grab her by the tail and push her back. Maybe we can find a place to hide her."

Carrying the tail, they moved the Red Falcon plane as Barry had suggested until the branches hid her from the air.

"What we do now, Master?" Sika asked.

"Several things," Barry said. "Most important of all, we've got to find out about these lights on the north side of Sueil Mountain. But before we do that, we must fill up this tank. We may want to get going in a hurry."

"Yes, Master. Where we get gas?"

Barry chuckled.

"You're worse than a five-year-old kid with your questions, Sika. But, I've just got a hunch that there's gas where those searchlight tried to hold us. That's an important position, or they wouldn't have all those lights and machine guns there. It must be a supply depot, or something of the sort.

"That's about two kilometers south, I should say. We'll go there first and nose around to see what we can find."

"Yes, Master."

They walked noiselessly cross country toward the point where the searchlights had probed them out of the night. For half an hour they traveled that way. Then, when they heard activity just ahead, they slowed their pace and proceeded with more caution.

They could hear the snorting of great truck engines. The toot of a locomotive. And now and then the shout of a man who was giving orders in the darkness.

"Railhead!" Barry whispered. "That's even better than a supply depot. We ought to find gas there."

"Yes, Master."

They made their way cautiously to the edge of the first track. Here and there a flashlight blinked for a scant second. They kept in the shadow of box cars, moving on down the track.

They heard the rumble of a truck bearing down on them. Barry jerked Sika by the arm.

"Quick!" he said. "In here, under this car."

THE truck rumbled past, just missing them. They could hear a clanking noise, as if two steel bodies were being jolted together. Barry peered out in the darkness from under the car. He motioned to Sika.

"Come on, let's go! Follow this truck. It looks as if it were loaded with gasoline drums,"

The truck jolted and rumbled on ahead of them. They followed closely. It reached the end of the space between two tracks and crossed over to the right one. Its speed was increasing.

Barry grated another order to Sika. "Hurry! Hop up on top of the platform behind these tanks. We're headed in the direction of our plane."

They both leaped, made the platform and crouched behind the steel drums. For perhaps a half kilometer they rode that way. Then the truck turned to the left.

"Quick! Let's pull off one of these drums and beat it!" Barry whispered.

The truck had slowed for the turn, was barely picking up speed again. The giant black reached for one of the big drums, picked it up without an effort and dropped it to the road.

It must have struck a stone when it landed for it made a startling, clanging sound. The truck groaned to a stop. The driver's voice rang out.

"Ach, was ist?"

Instantly Barry snapped another order to Sika.

"Grab the drum and get headed toward the plane. I'll draw his attention in the other direction."

The driver was leaping from the truck, coming back. Instantly Barry struck out down the road and turned toward the railhead.

He saw the giant black place the drum on his shoulders, and dive into a hedge at the other side of the road before the driver could see him.

"Stop!" shouted the driver. "*Was ist?* Stop or I shoot!"

"Shoot and be damned!" Barry yelled back at him.

He was running down the center of the road, the way they had come, A flashlight glare burst out behind him and held him there, for a moment, in the light

Crack! Crack!

That was the Luger of the truck driver, hurling slugs at him. Barry turned abruptly to the left and dove across the field. He was running for all he was worth, now.

The driver wasn't far behind. He was shouting at the top of his lungs, calling desperately for the whole German army to come and help him stop the fleeing figure of Barry Rand.

On and on Barry ran. Germans had come from somewhere in answer to the driver's shouts. The road was at his right. He could hear Jerries coming from that direction to head him off.

He reached the first track, dove through between cars as flashlights caught him again, and rushed on, across track after track.

The great railhead, which had been the scene of orderly work a few moments before, suddenly became a bedlam. Everywhere men were shouting.

Crack! Crack!

A gun barked between the tracks at his right. And he felt the bullet breath against the back of his neck as he plunged between a tank car and a box car.

They seemed to be heading him off from every quarter. Twice Barry thought of stopping to fight it out with his automatic between two of the box cars. But that would be plain suicide with this horde of Germans rushing him.

Then, suddenly, the lights from the electric flashes became dim. For giant searchlights of thousands of candle power, had been turned on about the freight yard, making the whole place as bright as day.

Barry reached the other side of the yard. He had hoped to find a woods there, or a group of buildings around which he could dodge. But the light of the electric torches, as it slashed over the tops of hundreds of freight cars showed him flat, bare fields ahead. No trees, no hedges, nothing that would afford him a hiding place. His heart was pounding like mad against the back of his brain. His breath was coming in short gasps. He couldn't keep up this running forever.

He mustered all of his remaining strength and raced up the line of track. He passed car after car, many of them tank cars. Perhaps they, too, contained gasoline.

Then, as the Germans pursuing him saw him turn and followed, he doubled back toward the east end of the freight yard and began diving under the couplings of the cars, from one track to another.

HE MADE his way in a zigzag course. For the moment, he was shaking off his pursuers. But of one thing he was sure, he couldn't get out of that freight yard. The Germans had it completely surrounded with guards.

He heard Jerries running about some distance away in consternation. They had lost him completely for the moment.

The place where two box cars crossed shielded him from the glare of the search lights. The door of one car was open. Barry made a feeble leap for the opening and crawled inside. Slowly, noiselessly, he pulled the door shut after him.

He was ready to drop from exhaustion, and this place was as good as any.

His feet were treading straw that crackled beneath him as he crept to a far corner of the box car. The floor was covered with a straw a scant foot in thickness. Likely high explosives had been shipped in this car and packed in straw to guard against jolting.

He pulled some of it about him and slid beneath it. He lay there resting, gasping for breath, listening.

Outside he could hear the pounding feet of shouting men. Germans looking for him. His whole body grew rigid and his hand crept to the butt of his automatic as he heard the door pushed open again.

The gleam of a flashlight traveled about the interior of the car.

At that moment he heard a slight rustling of straw; he was sure he hadn't made it. But he didn't have time to determine the direction from which the sound had come. The beam of the flashlight disappeared and he heard a German voice say:

"Nicht Hier."

The door closed and Barry allowed his bursting lungs to take in air once more. For a long time he lay under his covering. The shouting died down outside. So did the pounding of the running feet.

He lost all sense of time. Of course, they would still be looking for him outside. But they were far away from his hiding place now.

Barry moved the straw away from his face so that he could breathe more easily. A little later he sat up. Then he realized that a strange sensation gripped him.

Perhaps it was the recollection of that slight rustle he had heard when the German looked in the door. It may have been pure intuition. But he had the uncomfortable feeling that he was not alone.

Then, as though to confirm his doubts, he heard the rustle of straw once more.

CHAPTER SEVEN
Der Rot Falke!

BARRY remained absolutely motionless, didn't even breathe. Presently he heard another sound. At first it came as sort of a sigh then grew a little louder until it was between a sob and a groan. It choked off.

Barry was sure of the direction from which it came now. It was hardly five feet away from him, in the same end of the box car, but the opposite corner. The inside of the car was inky black.

He raised his right hand, clutching the automatic. Couldn't see it before his face. The sound came to him again. This time it was more of a sob than a groan.

Barry leaped to his feet; his back was against the wall of the box car. He faced the corner from which the sound had come, cracked a low, sharp command in German.

"*Kommen, macht schnell.* Stand up or I shoot!"

A pleading voice answered him. It was not the hoarse guttural that he had expected; instead it was a child's voice.

"*Bitte,* do not shoot, *mein Herr.* And I cannot stand up. My ankle, it hurts so."

Instantly Barry stepped across the straw-strewn floor and crouched down. He could see nothing, but with his left hand he felt around in the darkness. He touched a small body, the figure of a child.

"What the—" he began. Then went on in German.

"Why, you are only a child. What are you doing here?"

"*Ach,*" the voice answered. "I didn't mean to do anything wrong. *Mein Vater* is a great general. I wanted to fight against the *verdammt* enemy. Three days ago I ran away from home and hid in this box car at

Vorstadt. That is where I live, with my mother. I wanted to be a brave soldier like my father. I thought if I reached him, here at the Front, he would let me join his army."

"But your ankle," Barry said. "How did you hurt that?"

"It happened last evening. I was going to jump out when the car stopped. But the door was locked and I couldn't get out. Then, when they opened it, the soldiers came in to take away the boxes of bullets. I hid in the straw in the corner. It was all right until they lifted one of the boxes. It slipped and came down hard on my ankle. Ach, Himmel! How it hurt. But I dared not cry for fear they would find me and return me to my mother."

"Gee," muttered Barry, "but you are a brave *Kind*."

"My ankle has swollen very much," the youngster went on. "I cannot stand on it. Here, give me your hand."

He took Barry's big paw in his small one and laid it on his injured leg.

"See, it's very big.

Barry shook his head slowly in the darkness and drew his hand back.

"A brave *Kind*," he repeated. "And so you wanted to be a soldier and fight the *verdammt* enemy?"

"*Ja, mein Herr*."

"Suppose I take you to your father. Is he near here?"

"*Jawohl*. He is at Dormstech. I saw the address on this car and I know it wouldn't be far to my father's office."

"What's your name?" Barry asked.

"Karl von Grehn. *Mein Vater*, he is General von Grehn."

"*Jawohl*," Barry nodded, "I have heard of him."

"You will take me to him then," the boy cried eagerly.

Barry hesitated.

"I wouldn't guarantee that. But—"

He stopped short to listen. A dull boom had interrupted his last words. The whole freight car shuddered with the blast.

"What's that?" he exclaimed.

"Perhaps," the youngster said sullenly, "the enemy murderers are bombing us."

Barry shook his head.

"*Nein*, I don't think so." '

From outside came wild shouts and screams of pain.

"They are!" shouted the youngster. "They are bombing us! Someone has been hurt."

BARRY was standing now, motionless, staring at the side of the box car. There were cracks here and there through which he could see the flickering light of roaring flames.

That boom had sounded like a reserve tank of gasoline letting go. He had heard it once, before the war when in his home town a whole field of gasoline tanks had exploded.

"What is it?" the boy pleaded. "Are we bombed?"

"No," Barry said, "I don't think so. But we've got to get out of here in a hurry."

He rushed for the door that had been closed by the German, put his weight against it and tried to slide it back. It was locked.

He was rested now from his running; his strength had returned. He stepped back away from the door, then dove at it with all his weight, shoulder first. *Crash!*

The door remained in place. Again and again he hurled himself at it, charging, like a wild bull. Twice more he rushed the door, in the pitch blackness. It held. Finally in the fourth attack, he felt wood give.

Outside he heard the shouting increase. He heard men running about wildly. Heard one cry in German:

"*Gott im Himmel!* We will all be burned to a crisp."

Barry's shoulder ached from the blows against the door. He put the other shoulder forward and rushed again. Solid boards cracked and splintered and gave way. Then he was kicking others aside to make a large enough opening to let them out.

The inside of the car was already getting hot. He could hear the crackling of flames. Then he could see them, licking around the edges of the opening he had broken in the door.

He whirled to find the youngster. There he was beside him on the straw on his hands and knees.

"*Ach du lieber!*" the boy burst out. "You are not a German. You are—"

"No time for that," Barry snapped.

He picked the child up and thrust him through the flaming opening. Then he dove after him. Outside there was too much confusion to notice the Yank uniform on Barry Rand. He snatched the boy from the ground where he had fallen and dived under the coupling of the cars on the next track.

Germans were shouting and fleeing. All running away from the mass of flames which was spreading rapidly. Barry made out the center of the fire. Just as he had guessed. A tank car had exploded. Perhaps the searing heat of one of those searchlights had caught it and had heated the metal of the filler cap.

That didn't matter now. The flames were spreading like wild fire all over the freight yards.

Still carrying young Karl on his shoulder Barry dove through line after line of cars. Many of them were tank cars, many of them burning. Then suddenly, they passed the last line of the cars and broke across an open field to the east, running parallel to the main line of tracks.

Barry heard the boy's voice for the first time since they had left the box car.

"*Aber* you are an enemy. I should kill you."

Barry was tempted to laugh, but didn't feel so much like it at the boy's next words.

"But you are a very brave enemy. You have saved my life. Your country must be very proud of you."

Barry was panting for breath. They were alone, in a small wood. He slowed his pace to a fast walk. "I wish I could say that," he muttered.

There was a hint of fear in the boy's voice as he spoke again.

"B-but where are you taking me now?"

"You have nothing to fear, *mein Kind*," Barry replied. "You are not going to get hurt. I am taking you to your father. You'll get there anyway, whether they catch me or not."

"But they shall not catch you. And if they do they will let you go. I will see that my father orders it."

BARRY strode on through the dark woods and a smile that was tinged with sadness crept over his face.

"I'm afraid you don't know much about war, *mein Junge,*" he ventured.

"I know," Karl said stoutly, "that you're a very brave *Amerikaner.*"

"Yes, but what you don't know," Barry said, "is that I'm the most hated one to your people. *Ach Himmel!* How they hate me, Karl. *Und* perhaps they cannot be blamed for it."

"But when I tell them about you, they will not hate you any more."

Barry chuckled hoarsely.

"I'm afraid you are wrong this time, Karl," he said. "Did you ever hear of the Red Falcon?"

"*Der Rot Falke?*" the boy exclaimed. "But, of course. He is a devil. But you—"

"I am the one they call the Red Falcon," Barry answered. "But quiet now, we are on the outskirts of Dormstech. Do you know where headquarters' office is, Karl?"

"*Jawohl, mein Vater* has written me about it," the boy said, in an awed voice. "He is in the Town Hall. His office is on the bottom floor in the back of the building."

"*Das ist gut,*" said Barry. "Perhaps I can push you through a window and then make my escape before anyone knows the difference."

The town of Dormstech was shrouded in darkness. They moved down a back street and from there, near the center of the town, they turned on into the main one.

There, dimly outlined in the night, Barry could see a building larger than the others, on a little square. That would be the Town Hall.

He carried Karl between the buildings, went through the back yards until he came to the rear of the main building. He had heard the sentry's tread about the front of the Hall but had caught no human movement at the rear. Strange that. Most headquarters were completely surrounded by guards.

He waited for a long moment to make sure, then crept softly up. He whispered to Karl as he saw a light glint from a window in the back.

"I'll hold you up so you can look through the crack to see if that's your *Vater's* office.

"*Jawohl, mein Rot Falke,*" came back the answer.

They reached the window and Barry lifted Karl from his shoulder and held him up to where the crack of light was escaping from one corner of the drawn shade. A tense moment, then Karl's voice:

"*Ja, das ist mein Vater.* He works all night. He is there at his desk, giving orders."

Barry nodded. He was about to lower Karl to the ground and try the window, when a sharp command sounded just behind him. He felt the prod of a gun nuzzle in his back.

"*Die arme hoch!*"

CHAPTER EIGHT
Death Trap

EVERY muscle in Barry Rand's body tightened almost to the breaking point. He could feel the pressure of the gun muzzle against his back, pushing farther and farther into his flesh. Not the slightest chance for escape here.

Little Karl von Grehn spoke first, in answer to the sentry's challenge.

"Take us to my father at once, *dummkopf. Macht schnell!*"

Barry had slowly let the youngster settle to the ground, where he stood on his good leg, clutching Barry's coat to keep his balance.

There came a coarse laugh from the guard.

"*Ach*, foolishness you speak. This *verdammt* one, he is an *Amerikaner.* I can see by his uniform. But you, *mein Junge*, you speak German like one of us. Who is your father, that you are ordering me so haughtily to take you to?"

"*Mein Vater*," Karl said irritably, "is General von Grehn. I just saw him there—through the window. *Mein* name ist Karl von Grehn. Take us to him right now!"

"*Ach Himmell! Bitte*, I did not know," the guard exclaimed. "So you are the young Karl, that your father and mother have been worrying so much about since you ran away three days ago."

"*Ja.* And this brave one saved me from the fire at the railroad yard. You can see it there now."

He pointed to the red glow that showed against the eastern sky.

"*Ja*," said the guard. "*Kommen.* I take you both to your father."

But there was no lessening of the gun muzzle's pressure against Barry Rand's back. As they walked around the building to the front entrance, guards stood aside to let them pass.

They were hurrying down a long corridor. Barry was carrying the boy once more. Carrying him on his arm.

Young Karl pounded eagerly on the door of his father's office.

"*Vater! Vater!* Open the door—let me come in. It is I, Karl."

The door flew open before them and General von Grehn snatched his son from the arms of Barry Rand, saying as the boy nestled close on his shoulder:

"*Ach*, Karl *mein Sohn*. We thought you were lost. For three days your mother has been nearly frantic. Why did you do it?"

For a moment the boy wept softly on his father's shoulder.

"I wanted to be a soldier," he choked. "I wanted to fight the *verdammt* enemy in your own army. I would have come to you before but my ankle—"

They were moving into the office. Barry and the guard followed them. The guard closed the door and stood at rigid attention.

"*Ach*," said the proud general, "*das ist* a noble ambition, *mein Sohn*. But you are so young. Your mother and I have been so worried. I must call her at once and tell her you are safe."

There was a few minutes of silence as the general, with his son sitting on his lap, called the wife and mother and assured her of Karl's safety. Both the father and son talked into the mouthpiece at once. Then the receiver clicked.

GENERAL VON GREHN stared with a puzzled expression from his son to Barry Rand in his Yank uniform.

"But you said, son, you wanted to join my army to fight the *verdammt* enemy. And now it's one of the enemy who saved your life?"

"*Jawohl, Vater*," Karl said. "And he is such a brave one."

He told then of hiding in the box car, of being found there, of Barry's rescuing him from the flames. Slowly a sad smile crossed the great German general's smooth shaven face.

Barry cut in for the first time.

"You see, general," he explained: "Your men came pretty close to capturing me in the railroad yard. I took refuge in the same box car that your son happened to be in."

The general nodded slowly.

"*Jawohl.* I understand. *Und* you, an enemy, saved my son?"

"Yes, Vater," Karl chimed in. "And he is the enemy which we all hated the most—the Red Falcon."

"*Der Rot Falke!*" breathed the general a little awed.

The smile fled from his face for the moment.

"*Und* you saved my son?"

Then the smile returned as he looked at Karl fondly.

"*Mein* son, this is a horrible war. *Nicht wahr?* When we can grow to hate, so terribly, men as brave as this one."

"*Jawohl, Vater.* Could you not do something to persuade *mein freund, der Rot Falke,* to fight with us?"

The smile on the general's face saddened a little. He shook his head.

"*Ach,* Karl. You are so young. A boy twelve cannot understand. This would be impossible."

He looked up quickly at Barry.

"*Nicht wahr?*"

Barry nodded.

"*Und*" the general went on, facing his son once more, "what do you think now, Karl, of joining my army to fight the *verdammt* enemy? To kill men on the other side of the lines simply because they belong to another country and are against us. Would you want to kill this one? This brave *Amerikaner* who saved your life?"

Slowly, but emphatically, little Karl von Grehn shook his head.

"*Nein, Vater.* I would not do it. *Der Rot Falke,* he is my friend. A war like this should not be. *Nicht wahr?*"

Slowly General von Grehn nodded his agreement.

That," he said softly half to himself, "is what I have thought, too, Karl."

He straightened with an apparent effort. For a long moment he looked at Barry Rand.

"*Mein freund,*" he said, "and I mean that sincerely, words cannot express our gratitude for what you have done. However, this is war. And, being war, you are a prisoner."

Barry nodded slowly. He forced a smile.

"*Jawohl, excellency,*" he agreed. "I understand, of course."

The general turned to the guard who had been standing by the door, waiting for orders.

"You will take the prisoner," he commanded, "to the town jail, and you will lock him up in the cell that is there."

"But father," cried Karl, "you cannot. He saved me. He is our friend—"

"I am sorry, my son," von Grehn said gravely. "The ways of war are not pleasant."

Then Barry heard no more for he and the guard were walking down the corridor. Outside he felt the gun in his back again. The guard turned him down a side street.

A few minutes later they stepped in front of a small, solitary building. The guard raised his voice and called for other guards. They came quickly. One produced a key.

In the light of their flashes, Barry could see an old, thinly grated door opening. He walked in without being urged. The door clanged shut behind him and he heard the key turn in the lock. Pitch black in there.

BARRY began investigating the cell; it was quite large. He felt several bunks against the wall. At the back end of the building he found a large opening. But there was no window there.

His exit in that direction was barred by thin strips of metal, partly rusted, as had been the door. Almost instantly the realization flashed upon him of what had happened.

Obviously, General von Grehn had sent him to this prison to carry out a double purpose. He was carrying out his duty as an officer and a soldier.

In spite of the fact that his son had been saved by Barry Rand he couldn't set Barry free, so he had sent him to a flimsy sort of prison that had probably been used by the town fathers to hold drunks and lesser offenders. A jail from which, if Barry used his wits, he should be able to escape before dawn.

He listened at the door again. No sound of watching sentries there. Then suddenly, he tensed. He heard the thud of boots on the paving. Two Germans were nearing the jail. Talking and laughing as they came.

Barry crept deeper into the shadows and strained to catch their words. There was something significant in the way they spoke.

"Ach, you mean yon haven't heard, Max, of the trap that is to be sprung after dawn? It's the greatest one of the war. You have heard of the Gothas in the tunnel. We send them through the tunnel from our side of the mountain. Then we produce an odorless, white gas stream to hide their movement. The building on the other side, which is on rollers and controlled by electric motors, moves away to let them out and back again, after they have bombed the *verdammt Amerikaner* air dromes."

"*Ja, ja.* I have heard of that."

"But that is not the best of the trap. I have just come from Intelligence headquarters. One of our agents across the lines had just sent word that the *verdammt Amerikaner* have moved up with the French in their trenches on the other side of the mountain."

The two had reached a point directly in front of the door of the jail. They were walking slowly. The moment they passed, Barry flattened against the bars of the door to catch all he could.

"At dawn we let it appear that we are to make an attack to begin a drive over the mountain."

The voice was dying away.

"The trap will be set by then. As soon as we have gotten a whole division of *verdammt Amerikaner* on the other side of the mountain—our forces will retreat down the side and run away from the danger."

He could barely hear them now.

"That is when the trap will be sprung. An hour after dawn. Then what is concealed in the tunnel will—"

That was all that Barry Rand could catch of the words. The men had passed on out of hearing.

CHAPTER NINE
"Halt! Or I Shoot!"

BARRY RAND'S mind was spinning in a maze of disconnected thought. Uppermost was the knowledge that he must escape from this jail. That he must get out and, in some way, reach the Yanks and warn them of their danger.

Barry spun round from the door and rushed to the back opening with the flimsy grating. With all his might he shook the thin bars. They bent a little under his touch. But they held. He fought again to move them. Perhaps the rusty iron would give way, if he kept at it.

He was fighting madly, tearing savagely at the bars, when a sound outside the window caused him to stop short.

Out of the blackness came a voice—a faint, whispered voice.

"Rot Falke! Rot Falke!"

At first Barry didn't know whether to answer or not. But the second time he heard those words he was sure he recognized the voice.

"Jawohl," he hissed back. *"Was ist?"*

"It is I, Karl," came the answer. "I have come to help you. Father thinks I am asleep in the repair room. I found sawblades there and I crawled out of the window. Maybe they'll help you cut your way out. Here, *mein freund.* Reach your hand out of the grating. I'd better hurry back."

Barry's hand dropped outside. He felt about, seized the blades that Karl was holding up to him.

"Ach Himmel, Karl," he said. "You are a brave boy. Now hurry back to your cot. And tomorrow you will go back to your mother?"

"Jawohl. Tomorrow I go back to my mother. But I didn't want to go until I knew you'd be safe."

"*Danke*, Karl," was all Barry could say.

He heard a slight rustling behind the grating and knew that Karl was gone. Savagely he tore open the pack of saw-blades and began working on the rusty metal.

Scratch! Scratch! Scratch!

It seemed that the whole German army must hear that sound rasping out in the night.

The first blade broke in his hand. He took another and worked on. Sawed one bar through.

Scratch! Scratch!

That grating sound sent the chills up and down his spine. Any moment a German might pass by and hear it.

Scratch! Scratch! Scratch!

Two more bars separated. The bottom was free now. He began working on the side bars. Got two of them through.

He could bend the lower part of the grating outward. But it wasn't quite enough to let his body pass through. He sawed on. That rasping sound seemed to fill the night.

Then suddenly he heard footsteps out in the street, at the other end of the prison. A German voice bellowed:

"*Was ist!*"

BARRY pushed the grating outward with all his might. He thrust his head and shoulders through; clutched the saw-blades, and the wrappings they had come in, so that there would be no evidence against young Karl von Grehn.

"*Was ist?*" came the voice louder.

Then a flashlight probed the darkness of the prison. The light came just as Barry's hips were squeezing through the opening.

"Halt!" cried the voice. "Halt! Or I shoot!"

Crack!

The shot sounded as Barry's legs kicked through the opening. He sprawled outside. In a flash he was on his feet and running blindly deep into the darkness.

He heard the shout of that one German, calling for others to help stop the escaping prisoner. Barry lunged on, deeper and deeper through the maze of streets and buildings.

The shouts were dying away. But he could still hear them faintly, as other Boche took up the chase.

He took his direction from the stars as he reached the outskirts of the town and headed south along a road. The rumble of a truck came up behind him and he dived into bushes at the side, to let it pass.

Then a desperate plan flashed into his mind. That truck had come from the burning rail head. Obviously, the Germans were trying to unload all they could, before the whole place was demolished. As the heavily loaded truck passed, Barry leaped from his hiding place and up onto the platform.

The load was covered with a tarpaulin. He pulled it over him. He had one desperate plan in mind now. He must warn those concentrated Yank troops of their danger.

The quickest way to get there was through the tunnel of the mountain. He knew what dangers lurked there, but it was the fastest way to reach the Yanks.

The track rumbled on. From time to time Barry peered out from under the tarpaulin. It was still dark. No hint of dawn as yct, but he knew that it wasn't far off. He'd have to hurry.

After long minutes of jolting and rambling along Barry finally felt the truck slow down. He peered out from under the tarpaulin. The commanding voice of a guard boomed out in the darkness.

That was far enough. He slipped out from under the tarpaulin to the ground, moved noiselessly away into the dark.

Before him, a little farther to the south, the great shadow of Sueil Mountain loomed. He skirted the German guard post, where the truck had stopped. Went out into an open, blasted field and approached the mountain cautiously.

As he had seen earlier in the night, when he and Sika had flown over, flashlights danced about at one point, in the center of the base of the mountain. That would be the entrance to the tunnel. Directly opposite the frame building, which blocked it at the other end.

He could see men ahead of him unloading trucks. Many Germans about. And except for the flashlights, where the trucks, were being unloaded, all was darkness so that Barry's Yank uniform could not be seen.

THEN, for the first time, he sighted the dimly lighted entrance to the tunnel. Strangely enough, it seemed empty, All the Germans were outside. Then a great shape was moving toward the entrance from inside. Germans were pushing and hauling one of the two great Gothas that had blown up Yank dromes out of the tunnel.

He watched it through narrowed eyes. He couldn't tell just what power it was that drew him on toward that Gotha. Perhaps it was his subconscious mind that had half recognized one of the figures that had helped to push the giant enemy bomber.

He saw the figure clearly for a moment. A huge man with head bent and a great coat covering him. There was something very familiar about the movements of that man.

Then suddenly he heard a hoarse, German voice.

"Stop him! Stop him! That black man!"

Very dimly, Barry saw the huge man running across the open field ahead of him. Insantly Barry took flight and raced after him. Boche soldiers running from behind.

Barry was aiming to cut off the big fellow, as he headed for the road. And, as he drew nearer, he called out softly.

"Sika! Sika!"

The giant black hesitated for a moment. The came his voice in answer:

"Yes, Master."

Barry caught up with him and they ran on together.

"Master," gasped Sika, "we must hurry and get to the other side of the lines. I have done it!"

"Done what?" panted Barry.

"Quick!" Sika said, "Into this woods and on north. We must reach our plane before it's too late. See there in the east? A gray streak, dawn is coming.

"Hurry, I will tell you. We have little more than a half hour. I tried to get through the tunnel to warn my people, the French, and your Americans."

"What in hell are you talking about?" Barry gasped.

"Listen, Master. I took the drum of gasoline back to our plane. I just finished filling tank when I hear someone call from the side of the field. He speak in English so I go to him. It was an American spy, badly wounded from German shots.

"He had been near when we landed. He hear the rumble of our landing gear, but he too weak to reach us and too far away to call. He tell me what is to happen. He say tunnel under mountain and Gothas only trick to draw Yanks upon mountain. He say whole tunnel planted with tons of high explosive. Tell me explosive controlled by time fuse which runs for an hour after being set off. Then he die."

"I go to tunnel. On the way I knock out big German and take overcoat and hat to hide the color of my face. I plan to find time fuse, set off and then go on through tunnel to other side and warn my people and yours to get off the mountain.

"But other end of tunnel, it was blocked and I could not get out. Must hurry. See, dawn comes, Master."

CHAPTER TEN

Dynamite Patrol

YOU'RE—telling me?" Barry said between gasps. They were racing on together toward the field where they had left the plane. The sky was growing lighter. From the wild shouting behind, it sounded as if the whole German army were in hot pursuit.

Scarcely half a kilometer left between them and their plane. Every foot of it seemed like a million miles to Barry Rand.

They reached the plane and Barry staggered into the cockpit while Sika poised at the great propeller.

"Contact!"

The great blade whirled. The Liberty caught the first time and it roared out as the eastern sky became tinted with crimson. Sika raced around the end of the wing and leaped into his own cockpit.

The plane roared out across the field. Barry turned into the wind for the take off. He uttered a savage prayer and slowly pushed open the throttle. The Liberty gathered speed. Faster and faster they hurled toward those trees at the other end of the field. The Red Falcon plane grew lighter. Then they were traveling, above the tree tops.

Barry was flying the ship with the stick between his knees now. His hands were busily occupied writing notes on large sheets of paper. And the message on each note was the same:

> *Run for your lives, down off the mountain. Mountain tunneled and mined with H. E. Going off any minute. After mountain is blown up, start drive back into Germany.*

They thundered up over the top of Sueil Mountain. A hail of gun fire slashed about them from the German trenches. Looking down, Barry saw masses of Germans out in plain view. That was to make the Yanks think that at dawn a drive was coming from the other side of the lines.

HE GASPED as he looked on the Allied side of the mountain. There were thousands upon thousands of Yank troops. No French there now. Even the black warriors of the Wampana had left as the Yanks came to take their places.

Dropping the nose of the ship he stormed down over the twisting Yank trenches. But even as he started to hurl message after message over the side, he heard the sound of Spandau guns.

Tac-tac-tac!

He whirled in his seat. Four Fokkers were boring in on him, flame spurting from their forward guns. Barry twisted his ship into a zigzag turn and dived toward another section of the American trench line. There was no time to stop and fight it out now. He must get his warnings delivered in time to those Yanks below. Spandau bullets be damned.

Behind him he could hear the savage chatter of guns. That would be Sika, working his Lewis. Like a snarling jungle beast, the huge black man was crouched over his guns, hurling lead at the nearest Boche.

The German came on, straight for the Falcon's tail. Steel slugs hammered into the fuselage. Barry felt the ship tremble as he flung it into a frantic maneuver.

Tac-tac-tac!

That was Sika again. A short savage burst. Barry flung a glance over his shoulder just in time to see the German pilot slump in his cockpit. The Fokker wavered, then began slowly to spin earthward. One enemy gone. But there were still three left—three determined Boches that were coming in now from all sides.

By this time Barry had reached the end of the mountain and was racing back. Glancing below, he saw Yanks reading his message. And beyond he saw other Yanks racing headlong down the mountain side. The whole lower section was covered with fleeing American doughboys and their commanders.

With a grim smile Barry zoomed upward. He had saved those Yanks but three fighting Fokkers now stood between him and freedom.

Barry reached the peak of his climb, whirled around. His eyes popped open. For below him, the mountain had begun to move. It all seemed so slow, so gigantic and at the same time, so horrible. It was as though a giant hand were slowly lifting it from its foothold upon the earth.

Abruptly it broke apart. Huge masses of earth and rock zoomed high into the air. And those three screaming Fokkers were directly in the path of that upheaval. Like three matchsticks they were tossed high into the air; then a moment later went tumbling earthward to mix with the avalanche below.

Barry turned his glasses away, looked off at the American doughboys who had reached a safe distance far to the south.

That terrific explosion seemed to last for fully five minutes. Then the earth that had once been Sueil Mountain settled down again to form a great plateau.

Barry saw the Yank troops surging back, running over the blasted earth. He turned in a great circle a mile up in the air, stayed for a while to watch. The Yanks were moving farther and farther into Germany. Out of the south came Yank squadrons to aid in the drive.

For a moment there was sadness in Barry's eyes as he watched them.

"I hope," he said, with his lips unconsciously close to the tube that connected him with Sika, "that von Grehn and Karl get out before they are captured. But I am sure they will."

"What you say, Master?"

"Huh?" said Barry. "Oh, I was just talking to myself."

Then, yawning, Barry headed the Red Falcon plane toward the rugged Vosges and the flat-topped Saar Mountain,

Sleepily, his toes tapped the rudder bar in time to the tune that sprayed through his lips. The Liberty motor was hurling the Red Falcon back to his aerie to the accompaniment of "The Dark Town Strutter's Ball."

Hell Crashers
FREDERICK BLAKESLEE

A blinding flash—a terrible explosion—screams—and another Yank flight was gone, blasted to hell in enemy air. What was this dread new weapon of death? It had already wiped out eight ships—but Barry Rand tracked it grimly, cutting a blood trail straight into snare-set skies.

Hell Crashers

WHEN the Red Falcon suddenly stopped whistling "The Dark Town Strutter's Ball" and sat up straight in his seat, it was a sure sign that something wasn't functioning according to schedule.

The sun had gone down in a sullen sort of way. Dark clouds had covered it during the afternoon, and there was no red glare or blaze of lovely colors in the west at sunset.

Once the sun had broken through the heavy clouds for scarcely a minute; but no one on that blasted Front had seen it again before night fell.

Darkness had come, black and foreboding, with no stars to break the monotony. There were only flashes of artillery fire. And those were far off—far ahead.

But through that darkness a blood-red plane droned its way. A plane without concentric circles or black crosses. A ship nude of all insignia or sign, except for its color, which could not be seen now in the blackness that surrounded it.

The Red Falcon was out on another raid. A raid of necessity, for supplies.

The thing that had attracted his attention was a flare of light far to the south. The tune of his favorite ragtime selection had died from his lips and he was sitting bolt upright, staring at that flicker of flame.

That light was far off, hardly more than a speck. But instantly Barry Rand recognized it. He called through the tube to his aide, Sika, the giant Senegalese black chieftain who filled the rear cockpit.

"See that, big boy?" he asked.

"Yes, master," the faithful black responded.

"Know what it is?"

"Flame, master. Sika not sure what for."

"Did you see it before?"

"No, master. Sika just see it. They just light it."

While Barry Rand talked, the nose of the Red Falcon plane swung in a ninety degree turn to the left. He had been flying parallel to the lines. Now he was racing toward that dot of flame.

His hand pushed the throttle wide open and the Liberty responded with a bellowing roar.

"It looks," Barry said, half to himself, "like a gasoline trench set off at some field so that ships can get into the air safely."

"Yes, master," said Sika.

Barry went on, seeming not to hear him.

"I can't figure out just why ships should be taking off now, an hour after dark. Observation planes couldn't see anything. Pursuits wouldn't have any excuse to fly in the dark, except in some emergency. And bombers—"

He stopped speaking. Dropping the map case before him, he studied the section.

"Must be bombers," he said. "There's an English Handley-Page field located right about there. It's the 77th bombardment squadron."

"They start off early, master," Sika ventured.

"Right," Barry said. "That's the thing that sort of sticks me. Ordinarily, a regular schedule bombing raid doesn't come off until well along the middle of the night. But this looks as if they're in such a hurry to get going that they don't dare wait any longer."

He stuck the nose of the Red Falcon plane still lower. They were making close to two hundred miles an hour now and were in a dive—a long, shallow dive with the Liberty wide open and going crazy.

Barry reached for his glasses and raised them to his eyes. He wasn't sure whether he could see anything at this distance in the light of that flaming trench or not, But at least he was going to have a try.

HIS eyes steamed through the powerful binoculars. For a long moment he sat there, holding the glasses in his hands, flying with the stick between his knees. Abruptly he removed the glasses and hid them into their case again.

"Not a bad guess, big boy," he said. "I can't make out very much, and that gasoline trench flame sort of blinds me. But I can just see shadows of ships taking the air. And they look plenty big enough to be bombers."

"What we do, master?" Sika asked, a little nervously.

Barry took a long breath.

"Well, being naturally curious, big boy," he said, "we're going to fool around and see what we can learn. Maybe it's just the imagination, but I've got a hunch that there's some special reason for these bombers going out tonight at this hour. I'd like to find out what it is."

"Master," Sika begged, "you not forget we low on gas?"

"No," said Barry. "I'll try to keep that in mind. How's the ammunition, Sika?"

"We got plenty ammunition, master. We not do much fighting lately."

Barry grinned in the darkness.

"That's why I thought we'd see if we couldn't dig up some trouble tonight. Wouldn't do to have our guns begin to get rusty from not being used."

"Yes, master. Sika would like good fight," came back the eager reply.

Barry Rand was studying the air before and below him. Slowly the gasoline trench flame sputtered out. Then all was darkness about them.

He hunched forward now and stared harder. Then his head came up a little straighter and he moved the controls.

The nose lifted abruptly.

"Look, Sika," he cried. "There they are."

They could look down and see glowing exhaust stacks, long stacks that were slightly flame tipped at the ends. Stacks that were in pairs—three pairs of them.

"See, there's three bombers down there," Barry said, as they roared just above them. “Three big Handley-Pages lumbering over to lay their eggs.” They circled once above them. “I wonder what’s up and where they’re going.”

“Sika not know,” came the reply from his aide.

“No,” Barry said, “I didn’t think you would. I was just talking to myself. We’ll go back now and try to find out.”

“You not land on bomber field, master,” Sika said. “They catch us and they—”

“You don’t have to tell me that, big boy,” Barry cut in. “And we’re not going to land on the bomber field. There’s a village right near that field, called Freihoff. It’s about a kilometer from the 77th. I’ve got an X marked on my map just the other side of Freihoff. That means there’s a field there where we can get down—if we’re lucky. Well try it anyway, if you’re game, Sika.”

“Sika go where you go, master.”

“Good boy,” said Barry.

He raised the nose of the plane and climbed higher and higher in a circle.

“I think we’re just above Freihoff now,” he said. “We’ll drop a flare and see if we can locate the field.”

He released a flare, watched it burst into brilliance and begin to settle down. The earth, three thousand feet below them, was lighted with the brilliance of a dull day.

He climbed higher and turned east before the flare went out. In its light he managed to make out the field that he had marked with an X on the map.

“Now if I can remember that exact location,” he said, “we’ll squat there, as soon as we make these Britishers think that we’ve cleared out to the east.”

Slowly he retarded his throttle until the great Liberty was idling. The nose was stuck down in a glide now. He tried to keep his eye on that spot in the darkness behind him. He cut the switch and made a graceful, gliding turn, headed back toward the field that he had marked with an X.

His eyes bulged from straining to see through the darkness. He knew that when he got closer to the ground he would be able to see shadowy forms of obstacles there.

And he must land now. Must land somehow for the engine was dead. He kicked over in steep side-slip. The field was pretty small. He saw a line of dark shadows loom up at him. Kicked straight just at the right moment. Then felt the *carumph* of the wheels rolling and the tail skid dragging.

The plane rolled to a stop. Barry Rand climbed from his cockpit. Sika was dropping his great weight lightly to the ground.

"What I do now, master?" he asked.

"You got your directions pretty well set?" Barry asked.

"Yes, master."

"Then you head for the bombardment field. Go round Freihoff, see what you can get in the line of gasoline. You know about where the supply of petrol, as these Britishers call it, is kept at these airdromes. They don't waste much time guarding it as a rule. Fill up the tanks, if you can.

"Meantime, I'll go down into town and sort of nose around and see what I can learn. I don't believe the Britishers of the Royal Flying Corp are likely to recognize me. If they do—well, I'll just have to get out the best way I can."

They walked together across two fields until they came to the outskirts of Freihoff. There they separated, Sika going around the town and Barry going into it.

HERE and there on the dark streets he saw pilots and mechanics of the Royal Flying Corp. He heard the accents of the British Isles, and several times a strictly Yankee voice from some American who had joined the R.F.C.

He found a group outside an estaminet. He stopped with his back against the building, close to the door, and listened to the conversation.

" 'Ere's 'oping the three old 'ens blast the blooming blighters and the supply depot into a cocked 'at—what?" said a cockney voice. Probably some mechanic.

"Rightho," said another. "It ought to be blooming easy, figuring as how they know just where the dump is located now."

"And if they blast it," said another, "there won't be a bloody thing left of their supplies. The drive that they are figuring for dawn will be a bit of a flop, what?"

Barry's curiosity was satisfied. So these Britishers had news of a German drive coming off at dawn. They had spotted the ammunition dumps—hence the reason for the bombers. But Barry Rand lingered for more. And he got it when another said:

"They'll blow up the dump too, if it takes every bomber of the 77th. If that first flight doesn't make it, there's more ready to go out on the double."

That answered the question of the early departure of these three bombers. They were starting to blow up that enemy dump early in the evening. If the first three failed, other flights of bombers were waiting, ready to leave the 77th field and go over in an attempt to finish the job that the first had tried.

He stood there for some time with his back against the outside wall of the estaminet. The conversation of the men drifted to the gossip of the 77th. An argument rose as to the accuracy of bombers so-and-so and so-and-so.

Barry began to lose interest. He became anxious to be off. But he knew Sika would be some time in getting his supply of gas, if at all. He must kill time somewhere, so he lingered for more information.

The men outside the estaminet talked and babbled and argued on. Then suddenly the sputter of a motor bike could be heard. A motorcycle and side-car took shape in the darkness and squealed up before the curbing in front of the estaminet.

A figure leaped from the side-car and shouted to the men within hearing;

"Attention! Everyone inside the estaminet."

Came the thud of running boots and hob-nailed shoes. The man who had arrived in the side-car bolted through the estaminet doors, letting a stream of light burst out into the street as he passed through.

The soldiers crowded behind him. Barry mingled with them and went in too. Inside, pilots had turned from the bar. Some stood with glasses in their hands. A few showed the effects of intoxication and weaved a little.

The young man who had come in the motorcycle was standing in the middle of the floor. A wide circle was gradually forming about him. He was quite young, a captain of the R.F.C.

"You are to return to your fields at once," he said. "A ghastly thing has happened. Three bombers just went over. We have the report of their fate already. Report says that they were flying at about two thousand feet. Then suddenly the Tommies in the trenches heard a booming sound, like thunder."

"They saw flashes in the sky, and in the light of those flashes they saw the three bombers fall apart as though they were made of match wood. They crashed on the German side of the lines."

A lieutenant pilot, young like the captain, let out a sound that was half wail, half sob.

"My brother. My brother, Gerald, flew one of those planes. Those bloody pigs will pay for this!" His voice reached almost a shriek as he repeated, "They'll pay for it!" Then he dashed like mad out of the estaminet.

An older pilot stepped before the captain.

"What do you make of it, captain?" he demanded.

"I don't know," the captain replied.

"You mean," demanded the lieutenant, "that you haven't a bit of an idea what caused them to be hit? Perhaps the enemy has developed more deadly archies."

The captain shook his head.

"I think not," he said. "There was no report of searchlights from the ground. Everyone up there insists that they simply heard the bombers go over our trenches. Then when they had crossed the German lines and reached a point a little, way behind them, came the boom—and flowers."

Barry Rand was standing in the estaminet near the door. He was on the outskirts of the circle, but he could plainly hear every word that was said.

The lieutenant seemed persistent.

"But there must be some explanation for it," he said.

"I've told you all I know," the captain said. "Everyone of you report back to the field at once for orders. Orders from headquarters. Cheerio!"

Barry edged nearer the door. He tried to keep his face turned away from the others. There might be someone there who might recognize him and again there might not.

He was just going through the opening when a Yankee voice sounded in his ear.

"Your face is familiar," it said.

"You're Yank too, of the American Air Forces, according to your uniform. I've seen you before, but I can't remember just—"

Then the light of remembrance and recollection floated over the face of that Yank who had joined the Royal Flying Corp.

"Hey!" he said suddenly, "I know where I saw you. I was over visiting a friend of mine at the 123rd one day, an American outfit. They had just caught you, you and your big, black aide. You're Rand, the Red—"

SOMEHOW the doorway had clogged with men as the voice sounded. Barry was blocked in passing. So was the other. They were there, facing each other, Barry and this Yank who recognized him.

Instantly the hard fist of Barry Rand slashed out. It struck the Yank full in the mouth before he could continue the last word of accusation. The blow hurled the Yank backward into the men who were coming on from behind.

Barry whirled. He charged those others who blocked the door, charged them with head down like a human battering ram. Men spilled out of the doorway into the street before him. He stumbled over a leg and sprawled on three others as they fell.

He was up and racing on. And from behind him came a shout that spurred him on to swifter speed.

"Stop that guy! That's the Red Falcon! Stop him! He's wanted for—"

The distance that Barry Rand was putting between himself and the estaminet made the words grow dim. The sound of thudding feet and shouts all about him drowned them out.

Barry swerved sharply to the right, ducked up an alley between two buildings, dashed through one back yard and then another. He crossed a street, raced into the middle of another block.

When he reached the next street on the other side he turned left. That should take him in the general direction of the field.

The sounds of shouting and running feet were far, far away now. He had managed to elude his pursuers in the darkness. He reached the edge of town and searched about for the location of the field.

At first, in the blackness, nothing was familiar to him. Then he recognized the building he had seen after leaving the field. And by that he took a new start, crossing lots.

A few minutes later he came upon the plane. He approached it cautiously. He couldn't see any moving figures about it, but it might be possible that some Allied soldiers had chanced to come upon it since he had left.

He crawled through the grass and reached the tail assembly. There he crouched and waited. No sound came to him, no sign that anyone was near. He carefully made a circuit of the plane.

Then suddenly he did hear a sound. It was merely the slight rustle of leaves over near the hedge at the side of the field. He grew tense, crouched and waited.

A large figure loomed in the night shadows. The figure of a huge man carrying something on his shoulder. He came noiselessly, bent half over. Then his voice came ahead of him:

"That you, master?" softly.

"Yes, Sika. You got it?"

"Yes, master. Sika think gasoline supply not guarded like you say. Guard tried to stop me. I have to hit him with fist. Sika sorry."

Barry grinned a little at the thought.

"I don't imagine that will do him much harm, if you didn't hit him with all your might. Most of these guys over here have experienced a few socks on the jaw before."

"Sika glad you not mad, master. I got full gasoline drum."

"Swell," said Barry. "Let's fill up the tank and get going."

"You get news, master?" Sika asked. And then, hopefully: "We fight?"

"I got news all right," Barry answered. "And I rather imagine we'll have a fight on our hands before the night's over."

While the giant black poured the gasoline into the tank Barry told him what he had learned. Of the sudden mysterious explosion of the three planes.

"But, master," Sika ventured, "maybe enemy have new archie guns."

"I don't think so," Barry said. "Archie guns must be aimed, which means their operators must see what they're shooting at. There wasn't the slightest sign of searchlights. Everything was dark."

Sika didn't answer. Barry said no more until the tank was filled and Sika dropped to the ground. He carried the empty drum to the edge of the field and threw it in the brushes. When he came back Barry was in his cockpit.

"Twist her tail, big boy," he said.

Sika wound up the prop and stepped back.

"Contact?" Sika asked.

"Contact," answered Barry.

The Liberty sputtered and roared as the great black pulled the prop through with his giant arms and body. The crimson plane shuddered as Sika climbed in at the rear cockpit.

Barry taxied once around the field to warm the engine because there were no chocks before the wheels. Then he headed the Red Falcon plane into the wind and gave her the gun. The Liberty screamed out, wide open.

The plane bounded across the field and lifted into the air under the skillful hand of Barry Rand. As soon as he cleared the boundary of the field, cleared the shadowy trees that reached up to stop them, he turned toward the Front.

"What we do now, master?" Sika asked.

"One thing we're going to do, Sika," Barry answered, "is to hang over our own lines until more of these British bombers come over. I want to see what happens. I've got sort of a hunch that we're going to have to keep ourselves and our crate in condition to do something about this, after we find out what it is."

"Then we fight, master?" Sika begged.

"Listen, big boy," Barry flung back through the tube, "don't worry so much about the fighting end of it. I think you'll get enough before this fracas is over."

THEY reached a point behind the Allied lines, from whence they could look down and see the pin points of flame from artillery guns.

Barry kept on a little farther. Field pieces of the artillery would be located some distance behind their own trenches.

He was flying at 3,000 feet. Just before he figured that he would be directly over the Allied trenches, Barry Rand turned parallel with them. He kept on climbing. Climbed until their altimeter read slightly under 5,000 feet. At that height he leveled off and turned back, flying above the trenches in the other direction.

Then suddenly he heard a wild pounding on the cowling that separated him from Sika's cockpit behind. And he heard Sika's voice coming through the tube:

"Master! Master! Look! Bombers come! Look to right and down!"

Barry whirled in his seat and stared in the direction that Sika had mentioned. Very faintly he could make out little points of flame and dull glows in the darkness.

He counted five pairs of them. Five pairs in a fairly tight Vee. That would mean that a flight of five Handley-Pages loaded with bombs were coming over.

The black air about them seemed to take on an ominous suspense. Barry was grabbing the stick a little tighter without realizing it, as he watched those five bombers in close formation lumbering two or three hundred feet below him. Heading for the enemy lines and the ammunition dump.

They droned on. One second, two seconds, three seconds. Barry flew a little farther, parallel to the lines, made a sharp turn and then came back. The bombers were too far away for him to see them now.

He guessed he had about reached the point once more where they had droned under him. Then something happened so abruptly that it almost took his breath away. The air was suddenly lighted with the brilliance of day. And above the roar of his motor came a dull booming sound like thunder.

He saw the whole flight of Handley-Pages for the briefest second silhouetted in that light about them. Flashes were occurring all about them. He saw wings being blown to bits. None of the five planes were escaping those terrific explosions. They were all falling apart in the air.

They spattered down. Then as suddenly as they had begun, those rumbling, thunderous explosions ceased. That left Barry Rand staring pop-eyed, gasping.

His next move was more from instinct than from thought. He banked the Red Falcon plane sharply, on a ninety degree vertical, and plunged headlong at the exact place where the explosion had occurred.

He heard Sika's terrified voice.

"Master Master! What you do? We blow up too!"

Barry answered through clenched teeth. He couldn't even explain his movement to himself. All he said was:

"Hang on! Here we go!"

"Y-yes, master," came Sika's shaky voice now back to him.

The nose was down, aiming for that point where they had last seen the bombers over the German Front. Barry Rand was sitting in his seat like a frozen image, holding on, never moving.

He became conscious of waiting for a series of those explosions to occur. Was bracing himself for the shock.

One, two, three, four seconds. Nothing happened.

Five, six, seven seconds. Still nothing happened.

They hurled on. Ahead he could see the spurts of flame from the German artillery.

"Why the devil don't they shoot, if they're going to?" he rasped, half mad with the suspense now. Then—

Blam!

THERE was no explosion but the air about them was flooded with light, the light of a searchlight beam that started far below. Instantly he moved the controls, darted in a wild, zigzag course. Managed to break out of the light and hurl on behind the enemy lines.

Boom—puff!

Archie was going to work now in the old-fashioned style. But the light was no longer holding the Red Falcon plane in its glare. Archie shells burst far away from the racing ship.

Barry flew on, holding the same altitude, just under a mile. He heard Sika's quavering voice through the tube.

"Master! We not get hit!"

"Not so far," Barry said. "And now that I think of it, I can't figure out just why."

"That searchlight, master. Why that not go on before?"

"I can't figure that one out either," Barry answered. "In fact, I'm feeling mighty dumb just about now."

"You not dumb, master," Sika assured him. And then he asked a question. "But why you go where bombers go and not get blown up?"

"I'm not sure that I know," Barry said. "I just acted on a hunch and I don't understand the hunch. I sorta got the feeling when I saw those bombers blow up that something had been there waiting for them."

"What we do now, master?"

Barry Rand was studying the maps of that side of the line. He found several X's on one map in the general vicinity over which they were flying now. One X in particular was fairly close to the place above which the bombers had been blown to pieces.

They had reached a point behind the German artillery now, pretty far back in enemy territory. Barry jumped suddenly as a dim light caught him. A light from above. He whirled around and stared upwards. The clouds had broken away and a half moon was gleaming through.

"We're going to land, big boy. Looks like we're in luck with that moon coming out about now," Barry said.

As he spoke he was staring down over the side, searching for that field that he had marked with an X.

"That field down there?" Sika asked, pointing a little ahead of where Barry was looking.

Barry stared in that direction an instant before the moon was covered with clouds again.

"You're right, big boy," he said.

"Sika remember we land there once before," the big black said. "We had good fight that night."

"Never saw anybody that liked to fight better than you do," Barry chuckled.

He climbed higher, keeping his eye on that field down below. Turning back toward what he considered his own side of the lines, he could look down and see the flame-tipped guns of the German artillery below. Then he throttled back his motor, let it die slowly and cut the switch.

The moon came out through a great rift in the clouds. It helped him to distinguish the field he had chosen for a landing. The nose of the plane dropped into a glide and he turned back.

The Red Falcon plane dropped to a landing and rolled to a stop. They pushed it under some overhanging trees. Barry looked around to get his bearings. Sika pointed in one direction.

"Over there is village. Remember, master? Once before we were here and found headquarters in that village."

"That's what I want," Barry said. "We've got to find out, if we can, what the secret is of blowing up these ships in the air. Then we've got to put a stop to it. I'll go out and see what I can find. You better stay here."

"But, master, I go where you go."

"Right," Barry said. "I always like to have you, Sika. But remember, you're an exceptionally big fellow and you're a black man. Most of these Henries know what you look like well enough to pick you out in the dark. They might pass me up under the same circumstances, in spite of this Yank uniform."

"But, master, Sika want fight."

"I'm not telling you yes or no about going along," Barry said. "You can do what you like. Only if you do come, you'd better trail me, instead of being with me."

"Sika do whatever you say, master. But maybe British get scared and not send any more bombers."

Barry shook his head.

"You don't know these Britishers like I do," he said. "They're the most nonchalantly gutty race I've ever known. Bombers will come sailing over at intervals until they've either blown up the dump—or else. That's why we've got to work fast. We can't have any more blown up."

BARRY struck out across country in the direction that Sika had designated, leading to the village. He walked for an hour across fields, through hedges and undergrowth until he came to the outskirts of the town. There were no lights and the darkness hid his movements. The whole plan of the village came back to him as he walked on.

He recognized the building where headquarters had been when he had made his trip there before. A three-story affair, higher than any other in the town. Now if luck were with him and he could overhear some conversation inside, it might give him the clue that he sought.

Three roistering, German soldiers, happy with potent beer, passed him without notice. Barry stepped in the shadow of a building to let them go by, then dropped in step behind them.

As they passed the corner of the headquarters building, Barry sidestepped quickly into an alleyway. There he tensed to listen.

He heard the three Germans walk past the guard at the entrance. Heard words of greeting exchanged. Then when they had passed on he heard the guards talking in low monotone.

"*Ach Himmell*" said one. "I wish I felt as lighthearted as Hans and Fritz and the other one there."

"*Ja*. I too. I am worried about that *verdammt* plane that was heard to break through the net of bombs," said another.

Blood raced through Barry's veins at those words. A net of bombs. He listened for a long time after that. But that was all that was said, until another one of the guards asked:

"I am new, I have just come up to the Front. I do not understand this net of bombs, as you call it. *Was ist?*"

"*Ach*, you do not know?" said the first guard who had spoken. "You are perhaps as simple as the *verdammt* Allies themselves. But you will see how simple it is when I tell you. We have word that the British have learned of our supply depot. Our scientists were working on this plan for some time before, so now it is a good time to try it out.

"There's a long string of captive balloons all along our Front, hanging at about 15,000 feet, and tied together. At every 3,000 feet on the wire is a very small, high explosive bomb.

"When an Allied bomber runs into these wires it carries the wire with it on its wings and the wire runs upward as the bomber goes deeper into our country, until one of the small bombs strikes the wing. Then, poof, it is all over."

Barry Rand turned to duck down the alley with the information causing his brain to spin. But he only took two steps. A voice before him suddenly commanded:

"*Die arme hoch!*"

Barry raised his arms, but not to answer the command. Instead they struck out in the blackness, straight for the mouth that had spoken.

Smack! Smack!

His fists thudded into the face of the German who had surprised him. A cry of warning left the German as he fell back.

Barry spun round and darted out to the street. He raced headlong the way he had come. The guards about the entrance were running after him. A flashlight probed the night and its beam found him.

Crack!

A rifle bullet pinged past him. Then suddenly he heard another sound. Shouts and cries of pain. The thudding of bone against bone. And out of that tumult of sound came the cry of Wampana:

"Ki-hu-yi!"

Barry whirled and raced back. He could only see dim shadows moving about and one form towering above the rest was knocking down everything before him with his giant fists. Again came that cry:

"Ki-hu-yi!"

Barry saw one form topple over before Sika's savage assault. The great black grabbed the Boche by the hands before he fell; the next second he was swinging him around his head, knocking down the other Boches with his heavy boots.

Barry kept out of range while the fight was going on. Sika, in his lust for fighting, might not recognize him. He called to his aide:

"Sika! Sika! Lay off and come on!" All the Germans in that immediate vicinity were in a heap around the giant black, knocked unconscious. Others were coming. Sika couldn't expect to fight the whole German army.

AT Barry's command, the great chieftain dropped the German that he was using for a cudgel. He leaped over the prostrate forms and followed Barry. Together they ran on toward the ship.

They crisscrossed through the streets as they ran. Then they broke into open country. Later, out of breath, they reached the ship.

"Gotta shoot down a flock of balloons," Barry said, as Sika started the engine and climbed into the rear cockpit. "Got wires strung from them at 15,000 feet all the way down to the ground. Small wires with bombs every so far.

"There will be another bunch of bombers coming over before long."

Blam!

Barry's hands battered the throttle open wide. They raced around the field once to warm the motor and took off. They climbed higher and higher as they neared the lines.

At 19,000 feet it grew bitter cold. Barry pulled his collar about him and his hand was shaking a little as he released the first flare. As that light burst out they say a great roll of small objects extending along the Front below them.

"There they are!" Barry shouted. "We go down after them now."

The nose of the Red Falcon plane dropped. Nose guns chattered. And as they raved over that line of balloons, spurts of flame told that the bags of hydrogen gas were ignited and falling.

Twice they climbed to drop more flares and went all along the line.

"Master, dawn come. See gray in west?" Sika shouted.

"Yes, and that's not all that's coming," Barry shouted back. "There's seven, nine, eleven Handley-Pages down there. See them?"

The air was rumbling and shuddering as though a thunder storm had suddenly come up. The high explosive bombs were shattering the Front along the German lines. And as they watched, a great flight of Allied bombers hurled on over.

Barry waited until he saw those bombers drop their loads and start back. The ammunition dump was blown up now and Allied troops who held those Front lines against the expected attack were making a counter attack—swarming over to take land that was held only by dead Boches who had been killed by their own tricky device.

He saw the troops moving on into Germany, in a great surprise counter attack.

Then Barry Rand stretched and yawned. And as, in the light of the rising sun, he turned toward his aerie atop Saar Mountain in the rugged Vosges, his toes tapped the rudder bar in sleepy time to his favorite tune:

"The Dark Town Strutter's Ball."

Buccaneer Buzzards

An hour before, that German field had been held by a trapped patrol of Senegalese warriors. Now Barry Rand saw just one figure there—a man in a silk hat, digging a hole! And the Red Falcon knew he had hurtled into a strange mystery that only a pair of slashing sky buccaneers could hope to solve!

Buccaneer Buzzards

CHAPTER ONE
Lost Battalion

IT WAS dusk and the Red Falcon was out on another supply reconnaissance. The sun had gone down and darkness was not far off. A dull gray light spread over the Front like a gauze veil.

Through the twilight roared the blood-red plane of the Red Falcon. It had Spad wings and a Fokker fuselage, with two cockpits—a pilot's pit for Barry Rand and the other for the great black, Sika. And when the Liberty motor on the nose opened wide that plane could fly faster than any other on the Front.

Barry and Sika were flying with scarcely a hundred feet showing on the altimeter. From their cockpits they could plainly see everything that was going on below. There was just light enough for that. But from the ground the German soldiers could see that crimson plane, as it slashed the skies, silhouetted against the last glow above. And every Jerry who had a gun was using it to its best advantage as the red devil of the air thundered over their heads.

Barry sat slumped at the stick. He moved the controls with perfect skill and ease, for flying was second nature to him. A grin was frozen on his face and through his teeth he whistled a rag-time tune: "The Dark Town Strutter's Ball."

The plane, in its low, swift flight, flew an erratic course, dodging this way and that, to throw the gunners below off their aim. As he moved the stick, he brought his other hand before his face.

He smiled and bowed, first on one side of the plane and then on the other, like a conquering hero moving down Fifth Avenue amid a cheering throng. But unlike the conquering hero, Barry Rand held his thumb against his nose and extended four fingers. He was giving the Germans the royal razz because they couldn't hit him.

The Red Falcon plane was flying just over the rear of the German lines, at about 150 miles per hour. The two passengers looked across No-Man's-Land toward the Allied trenches. And the earth swept beneath them in a blur as the light of day steadily waned.

Then Barry Rand stiffened in his seat. He looked straight ahead for an instant, frozen like a statue. At the same time came a fierce pounding on the cowling that separated him from the cockpit of his giant, black aide.

"Master! Master!" came the voice through the tube. "Look down! There—under us!"

But Barry Rand didn't need that warning cry from Sika. He had seen the strange sight as it loomed up before him. He whirled to stare as it slipped by beneath.

A perfect hell of rifle and machine-gun fire screamed up at the plane. But for the moment Barry Rand didn't seem to notice that—he was intent on a group of men he had seen below. He recognized them as black men in French uniform—black soldiers from the French provinces of Africa.

But he knew there were many dark soldiers fighting for France, There was Sika's own tribe, the Wampana warriors, from which he had wandered when Barry had found him mortally wounded in the rugged Vosges—the hide-out of the Red Falcon. The fact that he had seen black men alone, on the German side of the lines, isolated and cut off from their own forces, was what had caused Barry to stop his whistling and his bowing so abruptly.

"Master," came Sika's voice, choked and excited. "I think they my people!"

Barry kicked viciously at the rudder and yanked on the stick. The Red Falcon plane flipped in a hairpin vertical and screamed back toward those isolated blacks.

He could see the layout down there, plainly now. In a space occupying little more than five or six acres of ground, several hundred dusky men were fighting. They had formed a great ring and were standing with their backs toward the center. Outside that ring Barry could see what seemed like thousands of Germans, fighting desperately, trying to break up the black's formation.

This was no hand to hand encounter. The Germans had probably tried that before and had learned a bitter lesson, for it was well known that there were no fiercer fighters in the World War than the half-savage men from French Senegal in West Africa.

Several hundred yards to the south, Barry could see a strong force of French and Yanks fighting desperately to get to the aid of the trapped battalion of blacks.

THE light was growing dimmer every second. The machine-gun fire from the ground was growing hotter. But Barry kicked over despite that deadly fire, and screamed in a great circle above the trapped battalion. Black, anxious faces stared up at him—some spattered with blood.

Then Sika was pounding savagely on the cowling once more. And his voice was almost a scream as it came through the tube.

"Master! Master! Those Wampana down there. That M'gunda commanding. My people in danger. I am their chief, master. I must go down to help."

Barry had already started firing his guns. Now he whirled and stared back at the half-insane Sika. He was getting ready to leap out of the cockpit. Barry snatched a monkey wrench from the tool case and brought the wooden handle down sharply on the skull of his giant, black aide.

Crack!

Sika settled back in the cockpit, staggered from the blow. But he was far from knocked out.

"Sit down, you damn fool," Barry rasped through the tube. "What are you trying to do, commit suicide?"

"Those my people," Sika snapped back. "I got to help."

"Sure," Barry bellowed. "But if you think you can help by jumping overboard, you're crazier than I thought you were. What do you think your machine guns are for? Just target practice? Get busy on those Heinies!"

"But we low on bullets, master. We low on everything." Sika was almost hysterical now. "I only got half pan left. We need that to get gasoline at German field."

"The hell with the gas for now!" Barry raged. "Use those bullets and give them hell, big boy."

"Yes, master."

The Red Falcon plane shuddered as the giant black whirled in the rear cockpit, swinging his guns before him.

Tac-tac-tac!

Barry had banked and was swinging back directly over the blacks. Sika was firing from the side into the mass of Germans who choked the warriors off from their own forces.

Tac-tac-tac!

Barry saw countless Germans fall, kicking. Then all too abruptly, the stutter of those Lewis guns, stopped and Sika's voice came pitifully into his ears.

"Master, ammunition gone. What we do now?"

"I got plenty up front in my guns," Barry said. "You hang on."

The nose of the Red Falcon plane dropped. Barry tramped down on his triggers. Two Vickers guns from atop the nose of the great motor and two Spandau guns, one on either side of the motor cowling, broke out with a devilish chatter. He was spraying steel directly into the Germans. They fell.

Then suddenly the men of the Wampana tribe leaped up like savages and rushed forward. They gained a few yards in that attack. A few yards that brought them closer to their own lines. But the gap was still far too wide.

Barry kicked the plane over and screamed back. Again his guns chattered and spat flame, and again Germans fell before his attack, while steel from their guns drummed against the crimson plane in answer.

The Wampana made another advance of a few yards. That was all. For the third time the Red Falcon banked at the end of the line and hurled back. If his ammunition would only hold out—but it was nearly gone now. He must save the last few rounds. And too, it was getting so dark that he could scarcely distinguish the blacks from the Germans.

A wild curse sprayed from Barry's lips as he pulled out and hurled back deeper into Germany.

"Well, we helped them a little," he said a moment later. "Yes, master," answered Sika. "Maybe in darkness they be able to get back. Black men of my Wampana tribe see better in darkness than white man."

Barry nodded, but he didn't answer. He was beginning to give up hope for those Wampana warriors. But he must not let Sika know his fears.

"You not forget we out of gas and ammunition, master."

"Gas is the first thing we gotta have," Barry answered. "And then maybe ammunition, if we can find it. And we gotta get supplies to that gang of yours down below, before they run out."

He was climbing higher and higher as he roared toward the north. He could see dimly, at that altitude, but the earth below was pretty black now.

He dropped his map case before him and checked his position. He knew the area over which he was flying almost as well as the map makers themselves. But just to be sure he located the field he had chosen to raid. It was a little German airdrome, an emergency base with few attendants, about ten kilometers northeast of his present position.

"We're heading for the gas station now," Barry told Sika.

"Yes, master. But how we get gas with no ammunition in my guns?"

"Gee!" said Barry. "I forgot that."

FOR a few minutes Barry Rand didn't say anything more. Sika, if he had listened closely, could have heard the whistled strains of "The Dark Town Strutter's Ball" coming through the tube. A moment later Barry spoke.

"I think I've got it, big boy," he said. "This time you'll go and get the stuff while I hold them off with my machine guns."

"But, master, your guns are stationary," Sika reminded him.

"Right. But the plane isn't. I just worked out a little gadget that ought to do the trick. I'll tie a string on the trigger and draw it back to the tail.

"As soon as we land on the field, you jump out and head for the hangars. Unless they throw a light on you they won't see you coming. Get all the gas you can carry and all the ammunition you can find for my Spandau guns; At least we'll work those anyway. I'll hold back the Heinies."

A few minutes later Barry could see the field through the darkness. He cut the gun and came in to land. The minute the wheels touched the turf a bright light flashed on, sweeping the field.

Instantly Barry smacked the gun open. The Liberty roared, the tail lifted and he pressed his triggers.

Tac-tac-tac!

The light went out. The motor died again and they rolled to a stop. Above the sound of the idling motor Barry could hear shouts and groans.

"Get going, big boy," he hissed to Sika, as they both leaped out of their cockpits. "Here."

He thrust his own automatic into the hand of the giant black.

"You may need yours and mine both before you get going. Now duck into the darkness before they spot you. I'll try to do the rest."

"Yes, master," Sika whispered. Then he was gone.

Barry let the string slip through his hand. The other end of it he had fastened to the trigger. He could go back as far as the string permitted. Then when he wanted to fire the guns he simply had to pull the string. That was all.

He reached down when he came to the tail of the Red Falcon plane and picked it up. In so doing he unconsciously pulled the string.

Tac-tac-tac!

"My error," said Barry. "But we know the thing works anyhow."

He raised the tail high enough so that the guns pointed down across the field.

"Now, you Heinies," he muttered under his breath, "come looking for trouble and you're going to run right smack into it."

The Heinies did come, and they were looking for trouble.

Crack!

A Luger spat flame at the left and the bullet plunked into the fabric of the plane's fuselage.

"So nice of you to let me know where you are," Barry grunted.

He whipped the tail around so that the guns pointed in that direction. Then he jerked the string. Cries of pain and then a scream of mortal anguish rang clear.

"Let that be a lesson to you," Barry snapped. "Come on, you buzzards. Who's next?"

Crack! Crack!

Two rifles sang out over near the hangars. Barry held his fire.

"Wait until you birds get a little closer," he said. "Don't want to hit Sika."

They did come closer, encouraged by their unanswered shots. Then, dimly in the darkness, Barry caught sight of two forms, scarcely fifty feet away, running toward the nose of the plane and pulled the string again. The forms dropped to the ground and didn't appear again.

He heard a German at his right shout:

"Stop him! Stop him!"

Barry swung the ship in that direction and pulled the string again.

Tac-tac-tac!

"I guess I filled that order," he murmured.

A DULL, oppressive silence fell over the field, now. It was ominous, and made Barry crave action. Then suddenly he heard a slight crackling sound behind him—a light foot breaking a twig.

Barry whirled. Instinctively he reached for his automatic, but it was gone of course. He had given it to Sika.

He felt a chill race up his back. Someone was coming up on him from behind. Then his heart leaped as he heard a voice.

"Master."

"O. K.," said Barry in a whisper. "Hurry, big boy."

Sika loomed before him now. He had been crawling across the field, carrying a box upon his back and rolling a gasoline drum before him.

"I not make noise when I walk, master," he said apologetically. "That gasoline drum snapped twig."

"Nice work, Sika. Hurry and fill up the tank. I'll stand guard."

"Got whole box of Spandau ammunition too," Sika grinned proudly in the darkness.

"Swell," grunted Barry. "Now if only these Heinies will leave us alone for a minute. I'll cut the motor so we can hear them coming. Have any trouble. With any of those Jerry mecs in the shed?"

"No, master. Everybody out of hangars to see plane. Not many on this field."

"That's why I picked it," Barry snapped. "Get going."

He cut the motor switch, tore open the case of Spandau bullets and began slipping them into his side gun belts. Suddenly he heard a sharp guttural command, some 20 or 30 feet away and a light flashed.

"Die arme hoch!"

Barry froze.

Three shots rang out in instant answer to the order. They came from Sika's automatic. There was a groan of pain and the light went out.

"Good work, big boy," Barry heaved a sigh of relief. "Keep pouring and I'll fill these belts. And for the love of heaven listen, so they can't sneak up on us again."

"Yes, master."

There was the gurgle of gasoline as the giant black poured it into the thirsty tank. But it seemed that that tank would never get full. Barry's ears throbbed from the strain of listening so hard.

Suddenly twin lights blasted upon them from far across the field. Barry remembered having seen a road over there. Apparently a car had pulled up.

"Duck," he barked to Sika, who was standing on the wing. "Duck while I heave the tail around."

Again Barry lifted the tail of the plane, pointed it full into the lights. A volley of shots screamed across the field at the Red Falcon plane. One breathed in Barry's ear as it passed. He swung the nose, dropped his guns level with those lights and pulled the string.

Tac-tac-tac!

Nose guns sprayed the group behind the lights with death. Barry held the triggers down until the lights were blasted out.

"Hurry, Sika," he said, "it's getting too hot around here. We've got to get out."

"Yes, master. Half a minute and I'll have all gasoline poured out."

Again the sound of gurgling liquid. Then a half minute later the drum clanged to the ground.

"All done, master."

"Swell."

Sika slipped the automatic back into Barry's holster.

"Maybe need it later," he said. "We each got one now."

"Let's go," Barry clipped. "I got my gun belts plenty full."

He dropped to his feet in the front cockpit, Sika poised at the propeller, and just as Barry called "Contact!" more lights slashed across the field and bobbed up and down as the men who carried them came running.

The great propeller whirled, the Liberty motor sputtered and started. As the plane got into motion, Sika ducked under the wing, caught the edge of his cockpit and leaped in.

Barry's steady hand pushed the throttle wide open and the Liberty roared. The Red Falcon plane gathered speed quickly, flying away from the running men—flying into the wind. The stick came back and the crimson plane climbed into the night.

"Now," said Barry, "we're set to go back and help your boys, if we can find them in this dark. I think I can remember just about where they are."

CHAPTER TWO

The Man With a Spade

THEY thundered back toward the lines. Barry checked his time and his course. Minutes crawled by. He climbed higher as he neared the Front.

Far, far ahead he could see spurts of flame, like red pencil points. It was the German artillery as it blasted away at the Allied lines. And as he came nearer the Front he saw the flame tips of the Yank guns, answering the German's deadly challenge.

They were almost over the Front now. One searchlight and then another slashed up through the darkness at them. The plane was rocked by a violent explosion to the left as archies went into action. Swiftly, skillfully, Barry Rand maneuvered out of those blinding lights and hurled on.

He called through the tube:

"We're right up near the Front now, Sika. I'll drop a flare and take a look down. See if you can spot your gang."

As he spoke, the flare burst out behind them in a brilliant blast of light. Instantly Barry stuck the nose of the Red Falcon plane down and hauled to a lower level.

"See anything?" he yelled.

Sika paused before answering. Then:

"No, master."

"O. K. We'll pull over to the right and see what we can find."

Boom—puff! Boom—puff!

Archie was going crazy down below, trying to stop the plane's zigzag course. The first flare was settling. Two minutes—then Barry's voice again: "Peel the eye. Here goes another! Let's hope we find them this time."

And another bright light burst out behind them.

Barry circled and stared down. But he saw nothing but German troops in their trenches, and behind those, supplies being moved up under cover of night.

"See anything?" he asked Sika again.

"Sika not see Wampana," the giant black returned in a worried voice.

"We'll try farther to the—"

Barry stopped short. He had been staring ahead of the plane, in the light of the flare. His eyes suddenly became riveted on something in the center of a small field, just at the edge of the circle of light. It was just a little behind the direct fighting area of the Front.

Abruptly he dropped the nose of the plane.

"What the Hell!"

The figure Barry had spotted seemed no bigger than an ant. It was a man working furiously!

With the nose stuck down and the motor screaming at a high-pitched key, the Red Falcon tore down at two hundred miles an hour. And as he neared it, one of the strangest sights he had ever seen in his life grew large before him.

THE field below Barry was only a small plot of two or three acres. It had once been bounded on three sides by a fringe of woods; but they were no longer in evidence. Gunfire from the Allied side of the lines had long since done its deadly work, so that now only gaunt trunks with a few spindling, arm-like branches remained.

On the fourth side of the field was the remnant of a hedge, which still seemed to flourish to some extent.

In the center of the clearing the last blazing flare that Barry Rand had dropped, showed a strange figure. He wore a unique suit of clothing, considering the work that held his attention.

He was dressed in a cutaway morning coat, a wing collar and a four-in-hand tie. His trousers were dark gray, striped. It was the kind of clothing a well dressed man might wear to church on Easter Sunday. To make the spectacle all the more incongruous, he was working frantically with a spade for a tool—digging a hole, which was even now waist deep.

The man seemed so engrossed in his work that he hadn't noticed the Red Falcon plane diving on him with terrific speed. Then he jerked round and stared upward into the blinding light of the flare.

Barry got a fleeting glimpse of the man, as he dove on down. It was a rather large face with heavy features.

The picture lasted little more than a second. But during that time Barry saw that the hair, what could be seen of it under the high silk hat, was either gray or blonde in color. And on the upper lip there grew a heavy mustache, turned up at each end, Kaiser fashion.

In spite of the incongruousness of a man, dressed in the height of fashion, furiously digging a hole in the middle of a field just behind the front lines, Barry Rand had a sudden feeling that he had seen that face somewhere before.

He pulled the plane out of its dive scarcely twenty feet from the ground. As he screamed over, the man leaped out of the hole he was digging. And, as he turned round in his seat, Barry could see him running for dear life toward the hedge.

A wild burst of laughter escaped from the Red Falcon's lips. "I've seen some funny things in this man's war," he gurgled, "but I never saw anything quite as funny as that."

Then his laughter stopped abruptly. He locked the Red Falcon plane over in a steep chandelle and headed back toward the hedge where the man had hidden.

But now the flare had gone out and he couldn't find the stranger. Darkness surrounded him again. The humor of the situation turned to astonishment and Barry became puzzled.

"Sika," he called, "did you see that?"

"Yes, master," said the faithful black.

"What do you make of it?"

"Sika not know, master."

"You and I both, big boy," Barry shouted back. "That guy looked like a diplomat or a statesman. If it wasn't for that Kaiser mustache he wears, I'd swear he was some congressman on his way to a morning garden party. But that face of his sticks me. I've seen that face somewhere, Sika."

"Yes, master?"

"You bet I have. If I could only think where—"

THEN he stopped speaking and his mouth dropped open. They had circled back in the darkness but this time farther to the north. His eyes were almost bulging from his head as he stared below. At a point which he judged to be about a thousand feet north of where he had seen the man digging, lights suddenly appeared. Lights around a hole in the ground, like a mine shaft. And from that hole men were pouring.

He couldn't hear whether they were making any noise because of the roar of the great Liberty. But he could tell from the way they ran and the expressions on their faces that they were scared. Some warning, had been sounded in that hole in the ground and the men were fleeing in terror.

Barry was prompted to cry out in wild astonishment. But somehow he could only stare, amazed. Then the plane was thundering over the opening of that shaft and he was banking to come hack for another look.

The fleeing men appeared so completely terrified that they didn't seem to hear the roar of Barry's plane at all. They scattered in every direction and the Red Falcon let them go in their fright. Not once did he drop the nose of the plane and trip his machine guns.

At last he found enough voice to shout through the tube:

"Well, if we haven't stumbled on the damndest conglomeration of mystery I ever saw, Sika."

"A guy with a silk hat and morning clothes, digging out in the middle of a field in the dead of night. And now these birds pouring out of a mine shaft about a thousand feet away and scared to death.

"There's something down there that we've got to find out about, Sika. And we can't waste any time about it, either."

"But, master," Sika objected, "you not forget the plight of my people?"

There was a sincerely sorry note in Barry's voice as he spoke.

"Gee, Sika, I did forget them for a minute. Well, maybe this thing can wait. Well go looking for your gang, right now. There may be some kind of a tie up between what we've just seen and your lost battalion. I don't know, but it looks like we've got a man-sized job on our hands."

"Yes, master," came Sika's voice in a relieved tone.

Barry stuck the nose of the Red Falcon plane into the air and they began to gain altitude once more.

"You're better than I am on direction, big boy," Barry called through the tube. "Which way would you say that battalion of yours is now?"

For a moment there was no answer. The giant black seemed to be getting his bearings. Then he said:

"Turn to the left, master. I think they that way."

Barry turned and flew straight for about two minutes.

"Tell me when to drop a flare," he called.

"Yes, master. Little more."

Barry flew on.

"Now drop flare, master."

"O.K. Here she goes."

The flare burst out in brilliance and the ground beneath them shone bright as day.

"There," shouted Sika excitedly. "Down to the right. See, master?"

Barry was staring.

"Yes, I see, Sika."

"Look! The circle is smaller!"

"Yes," Barry said, and the word was sprayed through his teeth.

ALREADY the nose of the Red Falcon plane had dropped. Down, down they screamed in the light of the settling flare. Then, while the range was still long, the four nose guns in front of Barry bucked and rattled, chanted death.

Germans sprawled before the deadly attack.

Tac-tac-tac!

Ground machine guns from all around that lost, black battalion were rattling up at the thundering Red Falcon plane.

Barry had broken into a crazy, zigzagged course as he dove. But in spite of his clever maneuvering, enemy slugs drummed as they pierced the wing and fuselage covering.

The fight looked hopeless to Barry, but he pushed on. He could see some of the blacks inside the narrow circle lying still and dead. He could see others lying flat about the outside, trying desperately to hold the circle intact, trying to keep it from growing smaller.

The Senegalese were appallingly outnumbered by the Germans. They were caught with a horde of Boche soldiers massed between them and the Allied front lines.

Three times, Barry managed to rake over that circle and his guns now were glowing a dull red from excessive firing. He had fed the Jerries hot lead.

Above the din of the roaring motor and the deafening sound of gun fire, Sika's voice, excited and a little panic stricken, came to him through the tube.

"Master, I see M'gunda signaling down there. M'gunda say they are almost out of ammunition."

Bam!

As Sika spoke, the two Vickers guns atop the Liberty motor ceased firing.

"He hasn't got so much on us," Barry flung back. "We haven't any more ammunition for our Vickers guns. All we've got left is the slugs you brought for the Spandaus."

The flare settled low. Suddenly it went out, as Barry nosed down for another wild burst into that mass of Germans. Instantly Barry hauled back on, the stick and stuck the nose of the Red Falcon plane up into the air,

"What you do now, master?" called Sika.

"I'm going up to let out another flare."

He dropped the nose again, and changed his course. He was heading due southwest.

"Changed my mind," he said. "We're going back to the nearest Yank field to get ammunition. We got to help your tribe get out of this. Let's go."

Two minutes went by. They hurled over the Front and on into Allied territory. Then Sika's voice came again:

"But, master, I can't let you go into danger for my people. You land somewhere and I go get ammunition. If they catch you they shoot you."

"I've heard that before and I'm still alive," Barry answered. "We're going back, Sika, and if we can't get in one way, we're going to get it another."

"Yes, master, but you be careful," Sika pleaded.

Barry Rand was studying his map. He found a field that suited his purpose—an American field.

There was a grim expression of determination on his face as he circled the field. At the sound of his Liberty motor a gasoline trench flared.

Boldly he landed and taxied to the tarmac in front of the row of hangars.

CHAPTER THREE
Red Falcon Raid

MEN came running toward the Red Falcon plane as it drew up to the dead-line, their eyes bulging with astonishment.

"Master," Sika hissed, "they'll capture you."

"Not if I know what I'm doing," Barry snapped. "You stay here with the plane."

Then to Sika's amazement, his master turned abruptly upon a mechanic, the nearest of the group of men who had come on the run.

The mechanic was staring goggle-eyed at the crimson, Red Falcon plane, which carried no identification. But that blood-red plane needed no stamp. It was known the length of the Front as the fastest and most deadly plane in the skyways.

"I want to see your commanding officer at once," Barry snapped.

His right hand was not far from his automatic as he spoke.

"Y-yes, sir," stammered the mechanic. "That is, I mean the major ain't here. But Captain Stanton, he's taking his place, sir. I'll show you where he hangs out."

"O. K.," said Barry. "Let's go. I'm in a hurry."

The mechanic broke into a run down the tarmac and Barry followed him. He turned to a small, darkened building. Barry could see a sign over the doorway marked "Headquarters."

"He ought to be in there," the mechanic told him. "If he ain't there I'll show you where his quarters is."

"O. K.," Barry returned.

He opened the door and stepped inside. The outer office was dimly lighted and he went on into the inner office. A young captain with a rather weak chin was seated at the desk. He had the appearance of an overgrown boy who had been fondled by loving but foolish parents long past his infancy. His mouth looked arrogant, suggestive of a sneer.

He looked up as Barry burst into his office and a flush of anger crossed his face.

"What the hell do you mean by breaking in here like this?" he demanded.

"I'll tell you the whole works in a hurry," Barry clipped out. "Then you can judge for yourself whether I am right or wrong. I've just come back from flying over the lines. Maybe you don't know it, but there's a battalion of Senegalese negroes out in Germany who are cut off from their own French forces.

"I have a special interest in those blacks. They are fighting desperately to hold their position until Allied troops can reach them from the front line trenches. They are getting low on ammunition, they may be out entirely by now.

"I advise you to get all planes out from this field at once with orders to dump bombs on the Germans who are trapping these blacks. Then the blacks can get back, or the French and Yanks in the trenches can reach them and hold the advance.

"Do I make myself clear?"

Captain Stanton glared at him.

"And who in hell do you think you are, coming around here giving me orders?"

Barry's eyes narrowed and a dangerous gleam appeared in them.

"Have you ever heard of the no-good, Yankee renegade, called the Red Falcon?" he demanded.

Stanton stared, his eyes bulging a little from his head. He nodded. That was all.

"Well," said Barry, "you're looking at him."

"Yeah?" snarled Stanton. "That doesn't mean a thing to me."

For an instant Barry Rand was tempted to leap out and throttle this arrogant, young, ribbon clerk officer with his bare hands. Then he got control of himself.

LISTEN," he pleaded. "For the love of heaven, can't you understand what I'm saying? There's a whole battalion of Senegalese troops marooned out beyond No-Man's-Land.

"They're about the toughest fighters this war's seen. But whether they are or not doesn't matter so much as the fact that they're Allied troops and they're in a tough spot.

"A number of them have been killed already. We can't let them stay out there without lifting a hand to save them. Be just a regular guy for once, Stanton, and do what I tell you, will you? It's a desperate situation and every minute counts."

Stanton made no move to comply with his wishes. A purple flush spread across his weak, sallow face. Then he said in a rasping tone:

"Listen, you. You say you're the Red Falcon. All right, I'll take your word for that. You've been playing around the Front free-lance for a long time. Too long. From what I understand of your story, you played the trick of a traitor on your own country. You got away from a firing squad that's still looking for you. You've been running around here for months giving orders and making believe you're a great hero. You and that big black numbskull of yours. Well, you've struck a guy that isn't afraid of you, see?"

But his voice trembled as he said that last, and betrayed his fear.

"It might interest you to know that those black so and so's have been sent over there to be trapped for a reason. And that reason is none of your damn business."

Barry Rand's muscles tightened a little.

"You look to me, Stanton," he said savagely, "like a big, babied, overgrown kid that's never had a good licking in his life."

"So you know some secret orders that aren't any of my business. All right, I'll find out my own way then. But any more cracks about these black men like that last one and you're going to get one good licking. And I'm not kidding."

"Do I get my orders carried out or don't I?"

Stanton leaped up from his seat. He was a larger man than Barry Rand. Taller and considerably heavier.

"No, you don't get those orders carried out," he stormed. "If you think I'm going to take orders from a damn traitor just to save a bunch of ignorant black—"

That was as far as he got, for Barry Rand leaped at him like a tiger.

His fists flashed out ahead of him into the captain's face.

Smack! Smack! Smack!

Stanton tried to duck, tried desperately to get out of that vicious attack. But every blow connected. He staggered back, tripping as he went. He went sprawling, and as he fell his hand reached for his automatic.

Barry Rand was upon him like lightning. His foot kicked the clenched gun, nearly broke Stanton's wrist With his left hand he grasped the fallen captain by the front of his uniform and jerked him to a half standing position. His right fist came out like a pile driver and caught Stanton between the eyes.

Then, as he fell back suddenly, gasping and pleading, Barry snatched his gun from its holster. He trained it upon the blubbering man, clicked off the safety and held it ready to fire.

Stanton was cringing before him. His eyes were wavering as he tried to get his bearings. The purple rage of a spoiled boy was gone from his face and in its stead was the dirty, gray color of a soiled towel.

"Get up, you," Barry snapped.

Terror was written on the face of the Yank officer and he struggled to his feet.

"D-dont shoot me," he burst out ,"I'll do anything you say."

Barry nodded.

"I thought you would by now, you yellow dog. Now listen to me. I'm going to give you your orders in plain English, and it's going to be to your advantage not to mess any of them."

"I wouldn't trust you to send out these planes of yours, but at least I'm going back in my own plane and you're going to see that it's fully loaded."

"NOW, get this. I'm going with you and I'm holding your own gun at your back while you go to the supply hangar and order full rounds of machine gun ammunition placed in our guns. You're going to have several cases, let's say six, of ammunition for those blacks placed in our plane so that we can drop them—You're going to have four light bombs placed in our racks for us. Then you're coming to the cockpit with us to see us off and wish us luck."

"And listen, Stanton. I'm not in the habit of shooting Yanks, but a ribbon clerk officer like you doesn't deserve any mercy after what you just tried to pull. I'd be delighted to put a bullet in your back. And so help me, the first mistake you make, I'll do it Now get ready."

Stanton did. They went to the armoring department of the supply hangar. Stanton entered the door but Barry held him back from going farther; he saw to it that those inside, working on machine guns, didn't see the automatic he held.

Stanton's voice was a little sharp as he issued Barry's orders. The men in the armoring room went to work at once, filling belts and pans, carrying the six cases of ammunition and the four bombs to the Red Falcon plane;

When that was at last finished, Sika stepped before the great propeller, while Barry, still holding the gun trained on Stanton, climbed into his own cockpit.

"Contact!" he called.

The great propeller whirled and the motor started. It seemed that every member of that flying field was strung along the tarmac.

Sika climbed to his own cockpit, all guns full now. Everything ready, except—

Barry spoke to Stanton.

"Have the boy lift our tail around so we're headed out into the wind."

Stanton gave the command and the tail was carried around. He followed close to the cockpit, too scared to move away before the muzzle of his own automatic.

"Now," said Barry, "the gasoline trench."

A long blaze flared down the field as the trench caught fire. Barry slipped the safety catch back on Stanton's automatic. Stanton shrank back with a look of terror.

"Here, take it, you fool!" Barry hissed. "Take it as if you were shaking hands with me. I'm giving you back your gun."

The instant Stanton's fingers closed over the gun, Barry pushed the throttle of the Red Falcon plane wide open. A gigantic blast from the whirling propeller threw Stanton off balance. Barry kicked the rudder so that the tail group wouldn't hit him, but the wind knocked him down.

As the plane thundered across the field and sluggishly took the air, a dull boom sounded behind them. Barry grinned. He turned around and thumbed his nose back at the angry captain who was trying to draw another bead on them with his smoking automatic. Then Barry and Sika in their crimson plane plunged into the night.

"Worked pretty well, didn't it, big boy?" Barry called back through the tube.

"Yes, master."

You did a good job of finding those blacks of yours last time. Lets see if you can find them again."

"I think I can, master."

Minutes and more minutes of flying. Then came the pencil points of name marking the artillery fire at the Front.

They sailed over that. Then the German artillery was ahead of them.

"Drop flare now, master. Think we here," Sika called.

Blam!

The night, below suddenly became like day. Both men were staring down from their cockpits. Twenty seconds, and Barry was going lower in a zigzagged circle, while enemy guns grunted up at them.

Then came Sika's strained, panic stricken voice.

"Master, they gone!"

CHAPTER FOUR
Wampana Patrol

BARRY stared about frantically.

"Maybe you're wrong. Maybe this isn't the right place, Sika. Let's try it farther in the east."

"No, no, master!" the giant black aide insisted. "My people they not here now. Circle again. Look down, there, master. You see some of their bodies? You see where circle was? They shovelled up small trenches for themselves."

Barry stared where the black was pointing. There could be no doubt now. This was the place where the Wampana tribesmen had been marooned and lost.

"Maybe," he ventured hopefully, "maybe they got back to their own trenches."

"No, master. You do not know my Wampana warriors. Wampana never retreat. They might be captured, if ammunition run out. That's what happened, master. They have been captured by the Germans.

"Look there between the circle and the front lines? That circle is filled with Germans. See, they are carrying the bodies of my Wampana that fell in battle. I know, master!"

Boom! Crack! Bam!

The Germans were sending up a thick hail of deadly fire about the ship, as they flew in a circular, zigzag course.

Barry suddenly realized that his teeth had been clenched tight. His jaw ached from the strain and he tried to relax—took a deep breath.

The flare was almost burned out by this time, and two searchlight beams suddenly began slashing the sky. He ducked out of one and into another. Managed to maneuver out of that, too, and plunged on into the night.

"Well," he said at last, "if you're sure Sika, I guess there isn't any use hanging around here any longer. We've got a mission in Germany to-night. There's something mighty queer going on.

"I think that guy, Stanton, was lying when he said that trapping your battalion was part of a trick. But thats one of the things we've got to find out.

"We must find your outfit, whether they're held prisoners or not. We've got to find out from them what this secret plan that Stanton talked about, is. I think there's some tie-up between that and that guy dressed up like Astor's pet horse.

"Yes, master," said Sika. "What we do?"

"I think we'll go a little west of here first, to where we saw that bird digging. I believe we're the only ones who saw him. And he may be back at it again. Perhaps we can catch him. There's a field we can land in, about two kilometers north of here, beyond the place where the men were coming out of the mine shaft. Let's go."

Barry turned west and they droned on through the black night. He climbed higher and higher, flying in a great circle.

He dropped their last flare and watched the earth far below. In the glaring light he saw the small field he was looking for.

Deliberately he dropped one of the light bombs. A few seconds later it exploded with a dull boom. He turned back toward his own side of the lines, grinning to himself.

"That'll make them think we just came over to drop a bomb and we're going back now," Barry said.

HE CLIMBED higher as he flew. The flare went out, but he kept the position of that field well marked in his mind, so that he could find it when he returned.

He pulled back the throttle slowly, let the Liberty die so that from the ground it would sound as though the plane were flying south—out of hearing. Then he reached up and cut the switch.

All was still except for the sighing of the wind as it breathed through the brace wires. He made a half turn and headed back for the field. He could only remember its general position. But as he came nearer to it he gradually began to see it clearly.

A steep side-slip over the trees which bounded the south end of the field and he was slithering in for a landing. Wheels and skid touched with the accompanying soft rumble. Then the plane slowed to a stop.

"Come on, big boy," Barry said, as they climbed out of the cockpits. "We've got to make tracks for that field where the guy with the top hat is doing the excavating."

They started out due south, moving cautiously cross country. They heard a rumbling sound to their left.

"That's a road," Barry spoke in low tones. "We gotta keep away from there."

They veered further away and kept on. Minutes passed. Then came a babble of guttural voices. They both stopped and crouched to listen.

"Sika thinks that the mine shaft," the great black whispered.

"You and I both, big boy," Barry returned. "Come on, we'll make a big circle around that and try to hit the field with the hole in it."

They went on, describing a huge arc. The sound of the voices died away. The gaunt spectres of leafless trees loomed before them and Barry put out a hand to stop Sika who was moving noiselessly by his side.

"I believe that's the field just ahead," he said.

They crept on until they reached the edge of the clearing. Crouched there, they watched. Barry felt Sika's hand on his arm. The giant black was staring into the darkness. Next he felt Sika's breath in his ear. Then heard his voice in a very low whisper.

"Man working," Sika said. "See, right there in middle of field."

"I don't see anybody."

"Watch," hissed Sika. "Not see man but see something come up out of ground. Shovel of dirt, maybe. Something shiny just then. Just above edge of ground."

Barry strained his eyes. Gradually he could see what his black aide was trying to point out to him.

"Man have hole deeper now," Sika whispered. "Maybe it the hat that shine."

"By George! You're right!" Barry hissed back. "Listen, we gotta get that bird and find out what he's there for. The whole thing looks crazy to me.

"You go round one side of the field, Sika, and I'll go round the other. We'll come at him from opposite sides."

"Yes, master," said Sika. Then he was gone;

Barry crept noiselessly in a half circle toward the place where the hole was being dug. Now, as he came within ten feet of the hole, he saw a mound of dirt all around. Saw shovels full come up.

The hole was deeper and he couldn't see the hat above the mound, but he could hear the dink of a spade, as it struck rock, or the faint thud as it plunged into hard earth.

He crept closer—reached the bottom of the mound of dirt. He began to dimb over when something came hurling through the air straight for him.

Bam!

He caught a shovel-full of dirt squarely in the face. A curse nearly sprayed from his lips, but he managed to hold it back. Now he moved a little to the right of the danger zone, as he crawled to the top of the pile of dirt.

HE WAS looking down into the hole; could hear the heavy breathing of the man as he worked. Digging, digging, digging.

Then he saw another figure coming over the mound on the other side of the hole. He recognized Sika's great head and shoulders.

Barry put on his best German.

"*Mein Freund*," he said in a hoarse whisper.

The digging stopped instantly. The figure standing at the bottom of the hole grew motionless.

"*Mein Freund*," Barry repeated, "we've come to help you, if you'll let us—"

"*Gott im Himmel!*" gasped the man. "Help at last!"

"*Jawohl*," said Barry, in the same low tone. "But first come out and tell us what you're doing."

"*Ja*," came the answer. "Give me your hand."

Barry and Sika both reached down. Then suddenly, for the first time, the queerly dressed stranger saw Sika's form bending over him.

"*Ach, Himmel! Was ist* this one?"

"He is a friend also," Barry explained. "*Kommen*. We help you out."

"*Ach, ja*. So Bismarck still has some friends after all, *nicht wahr?*"

"Bismarck," repeated Barry, as he and Sika hauled him up over the edge of the hole.

"*Jawohl*" answered the stranger suspiciously. "Do you not recognize me?"

Then Barry did remember. There had been something very familiar about the face he had seen in the flare. It was the stern face of Bismarck himself. But Bismarck was dead, or Barry was off on his history.

"*Kommen*," the man in the silk hat whispered. "I'll tell you. You can help me."

He led them to the scraggly hedge which had screened him from the place where Barry had seen men pouring out of the tunnel, or mine shaft. In the scant shelter of that hedge, the three crouched, and the stranger talked in excited whispers.

"So you're still faithful to your ruler, Bismarck. *Ja. Das ist gut.* But these other—these who call themselves Germans—they are traitors. They are trying to win the war for the *verdammt* Kaiser. But I—" he struck himself on the chest—"I am still the ruler of this country. But they are trying to get it away from me. And because they are not loyal subjects of mine, I am going to ruin their plot to win the war."

"Good," Barry said. "That's swell. And we'll help you, too. But what's that hole got to do with it?"

The stranger lowered his voice to an almost inaudible whisper.

"Listen to me," he said. "These *verdammt*, disloyal Germans have developed a fire gas. They have tunneled under the lines and the mouth of their tunnel is near here. This fire gas is highly explosive. I'm digging a hole that will go down almost to the tunnel."

He rapped gently on a box beside him.

"I have here boxes of dynamite. I dig a little farther and then I set off the charge. It will blow up everything. The fire will consume them. And I, the great Bismarck, will be avenged."

"Holy gee!" Barry whispered. "I mean, *Gott im Himmell* We'll sure help you, Bismarck. Do you want us to dig for a while?"

"*Ja, ja*, I have been digging long. I am very tired. Besides, it is beneath the dignity of a ruler like Bismarck to dig when he has loyal subjects to help him. *Jawohl*, you will dig now."

They got up from their crouched positions. They had taken little more than a step from the hedge when lights filtered through the foliage and guttural voices could be heard.

Then, for no apparent reason, the stranger in his top hat let out a wild cry and struck off in a dead run down along the hedge. Barry and Sika were after him like a flash and so were the Germans who had come upon them, apparently by accident

The further they ran, the louder the stranger yelled. Then lights flashed on them from all sides. They were trapped, cut off from retreat.

The stranger stopped.

"Gott im Himmell!" he howled. "Caught again! I thought perhaps with the shouting I could keep them from seeing my hole."

CHAPTER FIVE
Black Wireless

CRACK! *Crack! Crack!* Rifles blazed from several different angles. Bullets pinged close to the three fugitives. A guttural German voice commanded that they "Halt or die!"

They had been running abreast, Barry between Sika and the stranger in the silk hat. He reached out suddenly and caught both his companions by the arms. Stopped them.

"Wait," he panted. "We're surrounded. It won't do us a bit of good to go on running. They'll shoot us down like rats."

"*Jawohl*" nodded the one who called himself Bismarck. "We will be captured now and later we escape. *Ja!*"

"*Ja*," said Barry, "maybe."

The dancing lights, held by running Germans, were closing in on them from all sides.

Sika whispered to Barry.

"We fight, master, when they get close enough?"

There was a pleading eagerness in his deep voice. An eagerness to fight these Germans, to revenge his own black men. But Barry shook his head.

"No," he said. "Not yet, anyway. I'll tell you when there's fighting to be done, Sika. Before we do any fighting we've got to learn some things."

He spoke in a low whisper so that the Germans who were coming nearer couldn't hear him.

"We've got to find out whether this stuff about the flame gas in the mine is true. And we've also got to learn about these secret Allied plans that that cocky captain hinted about."

"How you do that, master?" Sika asked, puzzled.

"Wait and see," said Barry. "Not another word now. The Heinies can hear you."

As he finished speaking, a big, arrogant Prussian *Offizier* swaggered toward than. Then a boisterous laugh exploded from his lips.

"*Gott in Himmell!*Look now. It's the *wahnfinnig* Bismarck. The crazy one who thinks he is our old ruler."

"*Ja,*" said another *Offizier,* coming up beside him. "But who are these other two? This big black man and—"

"*Lieber Gott!*" exploded the first Jerry. "*Der Rot Falke!*"

The *Offizier* glared furiously at Barry.

"Am I not right?" he demanded. "You do not deny that you are the Red Falcon?"

"That's what they call me," Barry said.

"*Ach, verdammt* one!" exploded the Prussian *Offizier. Und* what are you doing with this crazy one who thinks he is Bismarck?"

Suddenly Bismarck, himself, spoke up.

"You see?" he said. "You see what I have told you? These *verdammt* ones, they are impostors. They say they are Germans, but they are not loyal to their old ruler. They think they will win the war with this new flame gas aber—"

"Silence!" bellowed the Prussian. "No more talk about the tunnel or the flame gas. *Dast ist* a secret."

But the man in the silk hat did not remain silent. He was yelling at the top of his voice, laughing in fanatic glee.

"*Ja, ja.* A secret. *Dast ist* funny. As funny as you think that I am crazy. You thought I did not know. *Ach, Himmel,* what dumb subjects you *schwein* would make. When I get back into power I'll have you all beheaded.

"So you thought I did not know about your tunnel and your flame gas that you plan to release very soon, now that the north wind blows. You thought I—"

The German *Offizier* leaped at him. His arm flashed through the air and his fist struck Bismarck squarely in the mouth, before he could finish.

Smack!

THE insane man's top hat flew from his head and he fell backward. Then the Prussian *Offizier* shouted a command to men about in the circle.

"Take this one back to the insane asylum from where he escaped. *Macht schnell!* And see that he does no more talking. How he got out and learned our secret I do not know. For one so crazy he is a clever one!"

Men came forward. They jerked the madman to his feet, still sputtering angrily, and bore him off through the throng.

The German *Offizier* faced Barry once more.

"You think you have heard our secret." He shrugged. "*Ach.* That doesn't matter now. For very soon the war will be over. Already we have captured the worst battalion of fighters on the Allied side. Not two hours ago we succeeded in taking prisoners the Wampana troops."

He jerked his head toward Sika.

"Perhaps your black man here is interested to know that."

Barry Rand could feel the muscles of his giant aide tighten as he stood close to him. He pressed his arm.

"Take it easy, Sika. Let me handle this."

The great muscles relaxed a little. Then Barry spoke directly to the Prussian Officer.

"You say you have captured this Wampana battalion?"

The *Offizier* grinned triumphantly as he nodded.

"*Ja.* Less than two hours ago."

"That," said Barry in chilled tones, "is a damn lie. We saw those Wampana warriors about twenty minutes ago still fighting in their circle."

The Prussian *Offizier*'s face darkened ominously. His hand crept for his Luger butt and he drew out the gun. Long since eager hands had snatched the Colt automatics from Barry and Sika.

"*Ach.* That is an insult!" the Prussian flared. "To call me a liar in peace-time would be to demand a duel. But now in war-time I—"

"Just a minute," Barry cut in. "Don't let that hot head of yours make a damn fool out of you. There's a much better way to decide whether you're a liar or not.

"If you're sure that you're right, the most conclusive way of proving it would be to show us these Wampana. If you refuse to do that, I will continue to call you a liar for the rest of my life."

"*Und* you wouldn't believe what I have seen with my own eyes? You, the *verdammt* Red Falcon, would have me prove it to you?"

Suddenly the German *Offizier* seemed to get control of himself.

"Very well," he said. "You will be shown. *Kommen.* It will not take much time, my car is at the roadside. But I warn you, at the first false move you will be shot. *Verstehen Sie!*"

Barry nodded.

"Quite," he said.

The *Offizier* called the names of three German soldiers and they stepped out of the circle. They were huge fellows, these three—big and powerful. Notwithstanding, they looked intelligent

"*Kommen*," said the *Offizier*. We go. My driver and car waits."

The circle broke way for them to pass. The Prussian *Offizier* led, Barry and Sika followed. The three stout German guards brought up the rear.

The car was a large touring model with the top down. The two extra seats were dropped down and Sika and Barry were directed to take their places.

The three guards climbed in behind, their Lugers held at the backs of the prisoners. The *Offizier* dropped into the seat beside the driver and gave him directions. Then the car moved off.

THE car moved swiftly through the darkness without the aid of lights, and Barry watched every turn in the road like a hawk. They were moving back, generally northeast. Barry judged that they had gone about three kilometers when the car drew up before an enclosure. In the light of the electric torches which flashed about he could see three circles of high, barbed wire fence. Guards stood about a great gate in the front. Dimly in the darkness, by the light of the stars, shadowy figures could be seen moving about inside the enclosure. The *Offizier* pointed proudly. "So," he said. "I am a liar, *nicht wahr?*" He called to the guards. "Flash your lights on those black devils in there so that these prisoners can see that I speak the truth about the capture."

Lights flashed. The blacks of the Wampana glared into them through the three thicknesses of fence. Barry was standing very close to Sika. He spoke to him in the lowest of whispers.

"Ask them what the secret move will be by the Allied troops."

In answer to his command, Sika's voice boomed out into the night. "M'gunda!"

Then he gutturalized words to his under-chief in their native tongue.

"*Was ist?*" demanded the German *Offizier.*

"Nothing special," Barry said hastily, "My aide here is just calling a greeting in his own tongue to his people. Nothing very wrong about one prisoner saying hello to another, is there?"

The Prussian didn't answer. He was merely staring now. For inside that enclosure the warriors of the Wampana tribe suddenly broke into a wild native dance.

Two of the blacks there, not having drums, pounded in a fast, rhythmic tempo against the side of the sole building. *Boom-ta-ta! Boom-ta-ta! Boom-ta-ta!* And the guards who held the lights upon them seemed so transfixed with the strange spectacle that they remained motionless, staring.

Boom-ta-ta! Boom-ta-ta!

And through the barbed wire, Barry Rand made out the giant form of M'gunda, himself, leading the dance, but staying ever on Sika's side of the enclosure so that every movement of his could be seen plainly.

Barry felt the giant black beside him stiffen. M'gunda was going through a series of contortions. Holding his arms this way and that. Spreading his legs, bringing them together again. Bowing, standing erect. And behind him the warriors of the Wampana danced and hopped around like wild Indians in a savage war dance.

Boom-ta-ta! Boom-ta-ta!

Then Barry felt the hand of his giant black upon his arm. Felt the finger tips pressing and releasing him rapidly, as though they were working a wireless key. Sending a message in the wireless code that Barry Rand had taught him.

Instinctively Barry began spelling out the words Sika was sending him.

A-l-l-i-e-s p-l-a-n s-e-c-r-e-t a-t-t-a-c-k a-t d-a-w-n
M-a-n-y Y-a-n-k-s a-t F-r-o-n-t n-o-w i-n d-u-g-o-u-t-s
s-t-a-r-t a-t-t-a-c-k a-t d-a-w-n

M-g-u-n-d-a s-a-y W-a-m-p-a-n-a s-e-n-t o-v-e-r
a-t-t-a-c-k s-o G-e-r-m-a-n-s t-h-i-n-k t-h-a-t w-h-a-t i-s
c-o-m-i-n-g w-i-l-l b-e o-v-e-r w-h-e-n
W-a-m-p-a-n-a d-r-i-v-e-n b-a-c-k

B-u-t W-a-m-p-a-n-a f-i-g-h-t t-o-o l-o-n-g g-o t-o
f-a-r g-e-t t-r-a-p-p-e-d

CHAPTER SIX

Torture Chamber

SUDDENLY a cry of rage left the lips of the German *Offizier*. "Stop it! Stop it! Turn off your lights! Those black devils are sending a message to their leader out here, in signs that we can't read."

He whirled to face Sika and his Luger jabbed the giant black in the stomach.

"You, you big black *Schwein!*" the Prussian exploded. "You are going to tell me what they said. You will tell me or I will shoot."

Barry felt the muscles of his aide grow hard as they knotted.

"Take it easy, Sika," he advised. "No use fighting here."

Then Sika said to the *Offizier*.

"Sika not know any message they send. The dance Wampana do is the Dance of Sorrow. They are sad that we have been captured. That is all."

"*Dast ist* a *verdammt* lie!" cried the *Offizier*. "But I will make you talk.

"Your man has told you of the Allies' plans. We must have that information. I have a way of getting it out of you. *Kommen!* Back into the car."

Lugers jabbed in their backs. There was nothing else to do but to climb into the car. The three guards crowded in behind them in the back seat, the *Offizier* gave an order and the car moved away.

They drove for what Barry figured was another kilometer. Then a great, shadowy form loomed before them and the tires of the car crunched on the gravel of a drive.

They drew up before a building that was partly in ruins. From what they could see of it, it appeared to be the remains of an old castle along the frontier of Germany and France.

The *Offizier* got out.

"*Heraus mit,*" he snapped.

Barry and Sika obeyed. But now Barry was not so sure of his position.

The *Offizier* led the way with a flashlight to light his path, the rest followed. They went down a long, winding, stone staircase that was permeated with a dank, musty odor. Cobwebs brushed against their faces.

Then rusty hinges creaked as the *Offizier* opened a heavy door and went into a great, vaulted, underground chamber.

In the beam of his electric torch they saw the interior of an ancient dungeon.

There were chains with bones in rings hanging from the walls, and machines of torture littered the floor. There was a strange, gigantic, wooden contraption, the like of which Barry Rand had never before seen; it was made of a long, rectangular framework, perhaps ten feet in length. In the middle of it was a drum of wood, about three feet in diameter.

The *Offizier* jerked his head toward it.

"Place the big one on it, on his back," he ordered. "You two," he designated the two nearest guards, "will work the device. You," he nodded to the third, "will cover the Red Falcon with your pistol. *Verstehen Sie?*"

"*Ja, ja,*" answered the three.

At the point of a gun Sika lay down over the wooden drum. Strong arms seized his wrists and ankles, bound them to ropes which were attached to wenchlike round timbers at either end of the frame.

"Now," commanded the *Offizier*, "work the machine. Perhaps when the pain becomes bad enough, the giant black *Schwein* will talk."

Barry saw Sika's eyes roll as the men strained at the handles of the machine. One worked either end until Sika's arms and legs were stretched tight and the wooden drum, which was his only support, was cutting into the small of his back.

Frantically Barry was trying to think, trying to figure out some means of escape. Some way out of this. He knew that Sika would never tell what he had learned. He knew as well that his great, faithful, black aide would die on that torture rack if the *Offizier* had his way.

"Listen," Barry Rand snapped, "you can't get away with this. This is against all international agreements of war."

And while he spoke he knew that his words were futile. He was merely stalling for time.

"None of the countries in the war," he hurried on, "have degraded themselves to the point where they torture information out of prisoners from the other side."

"Nein?" said the *Offizier*, as he surveyed him coldly. "You speak like a child, *mein Freund*. But remember, this is a seperate case. And no one will ever know of it.

"Besides, I have my personal reason for wanting to get this information. It will be a 'feather in my cap,' as you *Amerikaner* say. For getting this information I will receive perhaps a medal and a raise in rank. And no one but my three men here and myself will know how it was gotten."

He whirled around to the two guards.

"Now, you bring up the drum into his back, slowly."

Barry Rand stared, almost gasping, as the wooden drum came up into the small of Sika's back. The great Senegalese chief was being bent over that drum, his hands and his feet held solid. Enough of that and it would break his back.

And Barry knew that there was fierce pain racking that body on the torture machine. But Sika's eyes merely stared at him. His lips were tightly shut. But behind those lips, his white teeth would be tightly clenched in grim determination not to give up.

The *Offizier* glared down at him.

"Now," he said, "perhaps you are ready to tell me, before we go farther."

Sika merely glared at him.

"Very well," said the *Offizier*, "If you do not choose to talk we will get it out of your other black men. We will put every member of your tribe on this torture rack. We will kill them one by one, until they tell us what they have told you."

Then something happened so swiftly that it astonished even Barry Rand. Sika, stretched out on the rack, had suddenly grown tense. His body was contracting. On his face was the look of a maniac, and from his lips came a bellow of rage.

There came the sound of rending timbers and the round, wench-like beam, about which the ropes that held Sika's hands were fastened, tore loose from the frame.

Sika jerked upright. His feet dropped to the floor, as he flopped off the wooden drum that had been pressed into his back. The leg ropes were long enough to permit his legs that freedom.

The *Offizier* let out a warning cry. A cry, mingled with sudden terror.

"Shoot! Shoot!" he commanded.

The instant his voice echoed through the dungeon, the great, round beam to which Sika's hands were tied, swung in a wide arc.

Crack! Crack!

His aim was perfect. The heavy timber crashed against the skulls of the two guards who had trussed him up.

Barry saw the one remaining guard raise his Luger to take aim, at the command of his superior. He leaped for the gun.

Blam!

Barry knocked the Luger down just in time. The bullet struck the floor and ricocheted off with a scream. In the light of the torch, Barry saw the *Offizier* reaching for his Luger.

He started a lunge for him—then changed his mind and ducked. The wild, blood-curdling battle cry of the Wampana rang through the room.

Ki—hu—yi!

The heavy beam on Sika's hand was swinging again. It was descending like mad toward the head of the *Offizier*. The Prussian tried to dodge, but he was too late.

Crack!

The beam struck his skull and bashed it in. The light dropped from his hand, rolled to the floor.

As Barry Rand dropped he felt the figure of the other German plunge upon him. The weight of that great body almost knocked the wind out of him for a moment. Then he heard Sika's voice.

"Master, we fight!"

Barry tried to answer, but he couldn't get his breath in sufficient quantity to utter a word. The German was choking him. He heard something sizzling through the air.

Then consciousness all but left him. He heard a groan and the body on top of him went limp amid a sound of crushing bones. Barry was struggling to catch his breath, to throw that heavy form off. Then the weight disappeared and he was lifted to his feet.

Sika was staring at him with a pleading, worried expression on his face. He had gotten his hands free from the beam, but as yet his feet were tied to the other end of the rack.

"You hurt, master?" he asked.

"No," Barry gasped. "I'll be all right if I can get my breath. Everyone taken care of?"

"Yes, master. But Sika scared when he killed last one on top of you. Not mean to hit him so hard. Sika hear you go *'oof'* and think kill you too, maybe."

For the first time in several minutes Barry Rand grinned.

"To tell you the truth, big boy, I've been in more comfortable positions. But we gotta get out of here."

"Yes, master. We go back and try to free Wampana?"

"Not just yet, Sika," said Barry. "First we gotta set off a certain flock of dynamite in a certain hole that a nut was digging.

"Let's gather these Lugers and that flashlight and get going. Did I get that message straight that M'gunda gave you: that the Allies are attacking at dawn with a flock of Yanks who are hidden at the Front in dugouts now?"

"Yes, master."

"Good Lord!" Barry exploded. "You know what that means, don't you? It means that if we don't blow up that mine before they make the attack, this east wind will carry that flame gas right on down to Paris."

CHAPTER SEVEN
Prison Ace

BARRY and Sika were picking up the four Lugers the Germans had carried. Barry had the flashlight of the *Offizier* grasped tightly in his fist.

"Yes, but master," Sika objected, "maybe you not notice wind change. Wind blow from south now."

Barry stared at him an instant, before they started up the ancient, stone steps.

"You wouldn't kid me, big boy?" he demanded.

"No, master. Wind change. You see when we get out."

Barry started up the steps at a bound. They reached the open air. He wetted his finger and held it up to tell the wind direction. He felt his finger cool toward the south.

"By George! You're right, Sika," he hissed. "That's swell."

"You not forget driver in car, master?"

"No," said Barry. "You go around the car and sneak up on him from the other side. I'll ask him a question and when he turns to answer, you let him have the butt of one of the Lugers."

"Yes, master."

The next thing that happened came without the slightest warning, from somewhere at the side of the ruined doorway through which they had just passed.

It was the shrill, warbled note of a signal whistle. Both Barry and Sika whirled and crouched, a gun in either hand.

Barry was fumbling for the switch of the flashlight he had picked up in the torture chamber. But a blinding light caught them full in the face. Instantly the Lugers in their hands spat flame. One of the slugs hit the light and put it out

Again that whistle sounded. This time it came from farther to the left. Either the blower had moved or there were two men there. Again Sika's Lugers barked in the direction of the voice.

So quickly had come that warning signal that it rather unnerved Barry Rand for the moment. He was trying to hold a Luger in each of his hands, shoot them and turn on the flashlight at the same time.

A long, drawn out, guttural cry of pain came from the lips of the man who had blown the whistle. He had been hit. But he still had strength enough to let out a piercing cry for help.

Barry cursed under his breath, cursed his confusion. He grasped both Lugers in his left hand and then snapped on the flashlight. He directed the beam to the place from whence the groaning was coming.

He and Sika both leaped up and moved toward a figure in German uniform which was writhing in pain on the ground.

"Look," Barry said. "It's the driver. We gotta get out of here in a hurry. Gotta get to the car down there in the drive before—"

"Germans coming now," Sika cut in.

Barry tensed for a split second. He could hear them plainly. Could hear guttural shouts. And he could hear, too, the pounding of running feet.

"Quick!" he said. "To the car!"

Already Sika was running beside him. They dashed headlong down what had been once a sloping lawn. Raced toward the place where they had gotten out of the car.

Lights were coming from near there now. Bobbing lights held by running men. Doubled over, Barry and Sika were running straight for the auto in the face of those oncoming lights.

Crack! Crack! Crack!

Guns barked at them. Then Barry felt himself snatched half off his feet. The great black had almost jerked his arm out of his socket and was running wildly to the left, pulling Barry after him.

Crack! Crack!

More bullets whistled about them. They broke into a clump of trees.

"Hey! What goes on here?" Barry panted.

"Sika see just in time. Car not there. Was not time to warn you with words."

"That driver must have moved the car after we got out," Barry ventured.

Blam!

Sika stopped short as he finished speaking. He moved to the side quickly.

"This way, master. Men coming from ahead."

"I don't hear anything there," Barry said.

"Sika feel men over there. Come, this way."

They turned and ran on a few more paces. Suddenly the giant black stopped again. He tensed there to listen. Then, in the darkness, Barry felt the black drop down beside him. Felt himself being drawn quietly down.

"We surrounded," Sika whispered in his ear.

"Where? I can't hear them," Barry hissed back.

Snap! Snap!

One twig and then another broke. The snap seemed to come from fifty or sixty feet away.

"There. Hear that, master? Sika hear more as we run. We surrounded, master."

"O. K. big boy," Barry hissed back, "if you say so."

Then came Sika's whisper in a hopeful, pleading voice.

"We fight, master?"

"And how," Barry said. "But we'll stay here. If you're right and we're being surrounded, we'll wait until they get close to us. Close enough so that we can make out their movements. Then we'll see if we can shoot our way through one side of the ring."

"Yes, master."

So they crouched, tense, and waited. All about them came the sound of twigs crackling. Germans, who had come running at the signal from the driver of the car, were stalking them—cornering them in the little clump of trees. But Barry Rand and Sika had the advantage. They had trees to protect them and to hide behind.

Nearer and nearer came those crackling sounds. Barry felt the pressure of the great black's hand on his arm. Then slowly, cautiously, a lone figure showed through the trees.

"See, master?" Sika whispered. "Men moving outside tree."

"Right," Barry breathed "They'll be turning their lights in here in another minute."

"Yes, master. They come closer."

The two fell silent. Barry's brain was spinning. He was trying desperately to formulate a plan. They must move at just the right moment—before those lights flashed.

Looking through the leaves of the underbrush now, he could see very dimly the shadowy forms coming closer. They were at the very edge of the trees now. Not more than twenty feet away.

Barry turned his head very slowly.

From all sides he saw those same shadowy forms closing in on them.

He put his lips close to Sika's ear.

"Get set," he whispered. "When I give you the signal, we run for it—straight ahead, shooting as we go. I'll press your arm, then we go."

He felt Sika's head nod.

Another and another second passed by. The Germans in the circle were just about to enter the clump of trees. They were closing in very slowly, with great caution. When they entered the clearing their lights would go on. Barry was sure of that.

He pressed Sika's arm.

Blam!

Together they leaped from their hiding place, dove for that line of Germans.

Blam! Blam! Blam!

Flames spurted from their Lugers. There were groans and cries of pain from the Heinies,

Crack! Crack! Crack!

A volley of shots bellowed out in the night from the Germans' guns. Bullets pinged past and thudded into trees. Then Sika seemed to forget that he had a gun in his hand with which to shoot

In the fight of flashlight beams, Barry saw the giant black plunge headlong at a big German who was trying to level his Luger at him. Barry swung his Luger and pulled.

But the German, mortally wounded from that shot, never fell. Sika picked him up before he dropped. He grasped him by the ankles and swung him like a great club. And as be did so, the old battle cry of the

Wampana blacks rang out in the night

Ki—hu—yi!

There were wild shots and the thudding of feet. More Germans came swarming in.

Crack! Crack! Crack!

Guns bellowed and barked. Lights flickered. But it seemed nothing could stop that great black from swinging his human cudgel. There came the sickly crunch of skull meeting skull.

Round and round Sika hurled that big German, holding him by the heels.

Thud! Thud! Thud!

Ki—hu—yi!

As more Germans poured in at close range, Sika knocked them over, crushed them with the force of the swinging body pounding against their own.

Barry Rand had emptied both his guns. He was trying desperately to make a break. He was following the hole that Sika was cutting through the Boche circle.

Ki—hu—yi!

The giant, black chieftain was half mad with the thrill of fighting. Germans fell before him like hay before a mowing machine. Then suddenly the great black staggered. And the next instant he fell, flat on his face.

Barry struck out with his bare fists. He knocked two Germans kicking before he realized the futility of that course. He suddenly stopped and let the Germans overpower him, before they shot him where he stood.

The Boche soldiers swarmed about Barry and the fallen Sika. Lights flashed in his face, but he was staring down fearfully at the figure of his aide. Saw a patch of blood ooze out upon the thick, black, curly hair of Sika's head. It was spreading very slowly. The great body was still.

"*Ach, du lieber!*" exclaimed one. "What a fighter he is, this one we have killed."

For a moment that word struck terror in Barry Rand's heart. What if they had killed Sika? Everything was at stake. That tunnel with the flame gas. In fact, his very existence from now on. He realized suddenly how much he had counted on Sika, how lost he would be without him, and he felt lonesome.

Then his heart leaped for the great black man moved. Instantly a half dozen Lugers were trained on him. Slowly he turned over and sat up, shaking his head dazedly. Then Germans were jerking him to his feet.

Sika's great eyes rolled in his head for a moment as he stood up. He managed to catch his balance and in the light of the electric torches he saw Barry Rand's face before him—read the worry upon it.

"Sika all right, master. Head ache a little. Sorry I could not go on. If you want, I fight some more now."

Barry shook his head.

"No, big boy. We're caught and that's that. They'd make sieves of us now if we put up a fight."

A German *Leutnant* spoke then, in an attempt at English. He bowed from the waist, a perfect Prussian gentleman.

"*Jawohl.* You are *sehr* brave fighters, but it is well that you know when it is time to stop. I congratulate you both on your good judgment. *Kommen.* We take you to confinement."

The Germans led them then back across the open space and some distance down the drive. There they found the car in which they had come.

Again Sika and Barry were placed in the two side seats. Three Germans took their places behind them, and two sat in front, the one driving. The car moved off.

It did not go far, perhaps a couple of kilometers. Again Barry kept careful track of directions. The car drew up before a small building.

"*Kommen,*" said the *Offizier.* "We go now into the jail. *Und* I think you have company waiting for you."

Two guards stepped aside from the door of the jail. A key turned in the lock.

"Ach, *Himmel,*" said a voice. "*Was ist?* This key does not turn, does not open the door."

And then, after another try:

"*Ach, ja.* I have it."

Rusty hinges groaned as the grated door swung open. The way was lighted by electric torches and Barry and Sika stepped inside.

As the lights still showed the interior, Barry stared at the figure already in the cell.

"Well, I'll be damned!" he exploded.

CHAPTER EIGHT

Boomerang Dynamite

YOU are surprised, *mein Freund*, to find me here," the deep, throaty voice said. "I am surprised that you find me here, myself."

"Well, if it isn't Bismarck in person," Barry said.

"*Jawohl.* And you, *mein Freund*, to recognize me as such, *das ist gut.*"

"Wait," Barry hissed in his ear. "Listen."

Outside, guttural voices had come to them. He heard the *Leutnant* speaking.

"We go back again," he said. "It is only a little way. No, no. You need not take the car. I will advise the high command of what has happened. We will await his decision concerning the prisoners. You two guards remain. The car will be sent for later. *Kommen.*"

The sound of heavy boots faded away. Then came the voice of Bismarck.

"Haw-haw! They are fools, all of them. You are the only true ones. I almost fooled them before, but I will do it now. But the guards must not hear me say this, bring your ear closer.

"The hole which I was digging, I am sure it is deep enough. I must get there and blow up the dynamite."

"But how are you going to get out of here?" Barry hissed.

"Sh-h-h. I'll tell you. Once already, a little time before, I had the lock picked. I am an expert at locks. *Dast ist* how I have managed to escape so often from the asylum where the *verdammt* fools placed me.

"They brought me here tonight because they didn't want to take the trouble of driving me all the way back to the institution. When you arrived just now the *Leutnant* had trouble unlocking the door with his key. *Ach.* The *dummkopf* didn't know the door was already unlocked. *Eines Minuten, bitte.* I will pick it again."

Bismarck, in his tall, sleek, silk hat, a little the worse for being knocked about, crept to the door. His movements were noiseless as he picked at the lock. While he worked, Barry turned to Sika.

"You're sure you feel all right, big boy?" he whispered.

"Yes, master." came the reply. "My head is very thick. I have a little headache. That all, master. It was only a little tap. Blood does not flow more."

"Good," said Barry. "You had me worried plenty when you went down."

"Sika was not so happy at that time, either, master," Sika grinned in the darkness.

Bismarck came back, quietly.

"The door it is unlocked now. We go. I will go first."

"O. K.," whispered Barry. "But wait. This door creaks. It's got to be opened in a hurry, Sika, you do that and follow us. We will make a break and run into the darkness."

"Yes, master," Sika said as he stationed himself at the door.

"Now," whispered Barry.

Squeak!

The door was flung open. Bismarck dove through first. Barry was hot on his heels and Sika came last. There was a cry from the guards as Bismarck passed them.

Crack! Crack!

Flames spurted from gun muzzles. The two guards fired directly at the mad man and he toppled over.

Barry leaped sidewise, half crouched, and raced away in a zigzag course. He heard the shouts of the guards who were coming after him. Then their cries rose into screeches of pain and horror, died away and were no more.

A giant figure was catching up to him.

"Guards not bother us any more," Sika said.

"Swell. But what about Bismarck?"

"He dead, master, I am sure."

"Quick!" Barry hissed, "to that car now. We've got to get away from here in a hurry."

THEY whirled and raced back to the car. Barry got into the driver's seat, Sika beside him. Barry managed to start the engine, got the car in gear. Strange controls in these German cars.

The car started off, but not very rapidly. Barry had to pick his way and he must remember how they had come. He must get back to that field near the tunnel shaft opening, where they had seen the lunatic digging.

Dimly, above the throb of the engine, he heard men shouting. But went on and the shouting died away.

Barry drove back around by the old chateau. He broke out on wider road and drove faster. His eyes were becoming more accustomed to the darkness. He made a turn to the right, which he remembered, and another to the left. Lights suddenly blinked ahead of them.

Barry felt for the switch of the car lights and turned them on. The road was suddenly bathed in their bright light. He saw four German guards lined across the road, blocking their way.

"What we do now?" Sika asked.

"Hang on, big boy," Barry grated. "We're going through."

He gave the big, purring motor all it would take. The car leaped ahead in a wild burst of speed.

Then Barry said:

"Duck! They're going to shoot!"

And at almost the same instant they heard the crackling of gunfire and the tinkle of glass, as the windshield shattered. Then there was the scream of a German, as he stood too long in the way of the onrushing car.

They raced on. Barry came to a fork in the road. He remembered that they had come from the right before. He drove to the left and switched off the lights. Then, with lights still off, he backed up and turned right.

He drove on as fast as he could with safety. Suddenly Sika pointed toward the left.

"Look, master. First sign of day."

Barry stared.

"Gee, that's right," he said. "We gotta work fast now."

"And look there," said Sika. "There trees around the field where man was digging."

He had pointed ahead, to the right.

"Right again. I can just make them out," Barry said.

They ran the car into the ditch and got out. Then they hurried across the field, each carrying two guns.

"There may be some Heinies lurking around, watching for something to happen," Barry warned. "That nut, Bismarck, said the hole was deep enough."

A few minutes later they stumbled on the dynamite. There were four full cases of it.

They carried it under their arms to the center, of the field and placed it gingerly in the bottom of the hole. One of the boxes had been broken. Barry felt inside. He drew out a long coil of fuse that was attached to the end of one stick.

"That fuse ought to last for about five minutes," he guessed.

"We maybe almost make field where plane is," Sika said, "by that time."

"That's about my guess," Barry said.

In the shelter of the mound of earth around the hole, Barry struck a match. Then as the fuse sputtered, the two dashed away toward the field where they had left their plane.

"I don't know what's going to happen to the tunnel," Barry panted, "when that dynamite goes off. Maybe it won't take. Maybe the hole wasn't deep enough.

"And if it does go up, I haven't the slightest idea how this flame gas is going to work. We may get caught in it ourselves, Sika."

"Yes, master," replied the giant black, running beside him. But there was no fear in his voice.

"We've made about one kilometer already," Barry said. "It's taken us about three minutes, at a rough guess. At that rate we ought to be almost to the plane when the dynamite goes—"

SUDDENLY he stopped talking and put on a burst of speed. Ahead of them lights had flashed. Men were coming toward them. Men, whom they would have to pass in order to reach the Red Falcon ship.

"Quick! This way!" Barry gasped. "We've got to dodge them if we can."

They swerved abruptly to the left. They were running half doubled now, trying to keep out of those long flashlight beams.

Then a shout warned them that they had been seen. And a moment after came the crackle of gun fire. Bullets whistled about them. But the men who were shooting must have been shooting on the run, for their aim was none too good.

There were shouted orders for Barry and Sika to stop. But the only effect those commands had on the swiftly running pair was to make them double over more and more as they raced on.

It was slowly growing light now and that first streak of gray in the east was illuminating the whole sky. They could see the Germans almost as plainly as the Germans could see them.

"Ought to be almost time for that thing to go off," Barry gasped.

"And we ought to be almost at our plane, master," Sika answered.

"Yes, but we must not let them know where it is," Barry countered, "unless we've got time enough to start it and get it off the ground before they catch us."

Guns continued to spit at them. The Germans had spread out in a desperate line across their path. They were forced to swerve still more to the left.

"We can't dodge them. We'll be lucky if we keep away from them. We've got to—" Barry stopped short.

Suddenly they heard the muffled boom of an explosion back toward the south. And with that, almost instantly after it, came a roar. The earth under their feet trembled and the air about them shuddered.

Barry heard a sharp cry from the lips of Sika.

"Master, look! The flame gas!"

The Red Falcon turned his head and looked back. The whole sky had suddenly become bright with flames. Flames that were sweeping at them with the speed of the wind. Flames that decorated the ground as they came and then mounted toward the heavens.

Instantly Barry swerved toward the plane.

"Run! Run!" he panted. "We've got to make it. We've got to reach the ship before that flame gas reaches us or we're done for."

They were running straight for the Germans who had been in hot pursuit. But the Boche saw the same danger the Red Falcon and his giant aide had seen. They turned suddenly with apparently no more thought of pursuing. They too were fleeing for their lives, heading back for the car they had left a little way off.

Several times Barry looked back over his shoulder as he plunged on. There was a good, stiff, southerly breeze blowing. The flames were gaining upon them.

Barry and Sika broke through the undergrowth that skirted the field where their plane stood. It was there just as they had left.

Barry leaped into the front cockpit as he reached the Red Falcon plane. Sika grasped the propeller, whirled it around to suck the gas. Barry yelled "Contact!"

The propeller swung again. The motor caught and died. The flames were gaining on them. Even now they could feel the heat of that fiery gas.

"Contact!" Barry yelled at the top of his lungs for the sixth time.

The great propeller spun around.

Blam! The Liberty barked. Then it died.

CHAPTER NINE
Buccaneer Patrol

ALREADY the flames were coming across the next field. It would be less than five seconds before that fire would reach them. The giant black was shiny with sweat from his exertion. He pulled the great propeller twice more. Then: *Blam!*

The Liberty caught. It emitted a deep throated roar, bellowing out a challenge to the flames. Sika slipped under the right bottom wing and snatched at his cockpit as the ship started to move.

The plane was galloping across the field. All odds were against them now.

The ship was weighted down with its cargo of ammunition and bombs, and they were trying to take off with a cold motor.

Barry didn't open the motor wide. One choke and she would load up on them.

Two low trees barred his way at the other end of the field. They stood so close together that it would be impossible to break through. And worst of all, they were taking off down wind, because Barry didn't dare fly into the flames.

Barry was three-quarters of the way down the field now. He tried the stick, but the wheels didn't leave the ground. Those trees stood stark ahead, blocking them. He didn't have enough speed, enough lift,

In desperation he pushed the throttle wide open. The Liberty took on a higher note, she began to grow light. But would it do any good now—they had almost reached the end of the field.

The ship lifted—she was flying. But Barry Rand was holding her nose a few feet off the ground. He must get more speed. An instant before he reached those trees he banked the plane gingerly to the right.

And, cocked on one wing, scraped through.

Sput!

The Liberty gasped and back-fired. Barry's heart sang as he eased back the throttle again to humor the motor a little. It picked up and ran on. He climbed a little now that he was free. He took a long breath and looked down to the right. The flames were sweeping across the field below—shutting it out from view.

In his ears came the terrified voice of Sika—begging, pleading.

"Master, master, my Wampana! They get burned in their prison!"

"Not if we can help it," Barry called back through the tube. "We're going up there now to see what we can do about it. We're headed that way. Keep an eye peeled for the prison yard."

They were climbing higher as they went. Here and there, Germans who had escaped the first blast up near the Front, were running about in terror. Barry watched their flight, horrified and yet at the same time speculative. He watched them falter and saw them overcome by the flames.

Then a call from Sika made him stare ahead.

"Master! Master! The prison. There my Wampana. See, master?"

Barry saw. He looked back at the oncoming flames. He glanced ahead at the temporary prison camp. He guessed the distance between the flames and the captured Wampana warriors. It was probably about two kilometers. That would be enough if he reached them in time—if his plan worked.

HE dropped the nose of the plane down, straight for the prison gate. He called through the tube to Sika.

"I'm going to fly low and then cut my gun," he said. "When I do, you tell your men to run to the other end of the prison yard—away from the entrance. We're going to bomb the gates."

Then he was flying low. The motor died to an idle as he glided fifty feet above that barbed wire enclosure. Sika shouted the message down in his native tongue. Barry saw the blacks rush to the back end of the prison yard as he gave the ship the gun and began his turn.

Now guards outside, the prison saw their danger from the oncoming flames. They were fleeing in terror, leaving the prisoners alone to their fate.

Back came the Red Falcon, flying low. Barry grabbed his bomb release lever. And just at the right point, an instant before they came over the gates, he pulled.

Blam!

One of the gates burst and disappeared.

Instantly Barry cocked over in a tight vertical and hurled back. He pulled his bomb lever twice.

Blam! Blam!

There was not a trace of the gates left now, only a gap in the wall. Barry saw the blacks rushing from the other end of the enclosure for the opening.

He shouted an order to Sika.

"Tell them to run from the flames. Tell them to run for dear life."

He cut the gun again and glided down low so that Sika could shout his orders. Then Barry opened the throttle once more and circled higher.

He saw the black warriors of the Wampana tribe pouring out of the prison yard and fleeing north, in the wake of the Germans.

The flames were within half a kilometer of the prison now. But there was something about them that drew Barry's attention and held it. It didn't seem to him that they were nearly as strong as they had been.

Then for the first time he realized that those flames must die out sometime. The gas which was feeding them could not last forever. The fire gas was gaining on the Wampana, but at the same time it was dying out.

Suddenly a frantic hope welled up within Barry. For the third time he dived down toward those warriors and told Sika what to tell them. And for the third time Sika did.

He told them to keep away from the flames until they died. Then to turn and go back over the land that had been swept with the burning gas.

And after that Barry Rand gunned his motor and raced toward the Allied side of the lines.

The flame gas died out as he made that desperate run. He stared down in horror at what it had left in its wake. Everything was smoldering and smoking.

Trucks, timbers, earth, trees and—men. There was not a moving, living thing in that area all the way from the front line of the German trenches back to where the Wampana warriors had been.

And even before he reached the Front Barry saw that the Yanks had taken their cue, and had begun their drive at dawn, as planned. They were pouring over into Germany. Over that great area devastated by the German's own weapon.

Barry Rand climbed higher and higher, watching the Yanks as they moved deeper into new territory. And there were French troops helping them. French troops to whom the lost battalion of the Wampana had been attached.

Barry waited until his giant black aide could see his own people back with the army to which they belonged. They joined about the center of the devastated area—the Wampana with the French and the Yanks.

And those great, black, fighting men, receiving new weapons, turned to carry on into Germany. And Yank planes came roaring out of the south to hold the air.

Then, and not until then, did Barry turn the Red Falcon plane back toward its aerie, high on flat-topped Saar Mountain in the rugged Vosges.

He yawned after he had made that turn and spoke through the tube to Sika. "I'm hungry as the devil, big boy, for some of your wheat cakes."

"Yes, master," Sika grinned "Sika make them for you like you taught me."

Then the Red Falcon droned on, a smile on his face. And his feet beating the rudder bar in time to the tune that sprayed through his teeth—

"The Dark Town Strutter's Ball."

SOS
Buzzard

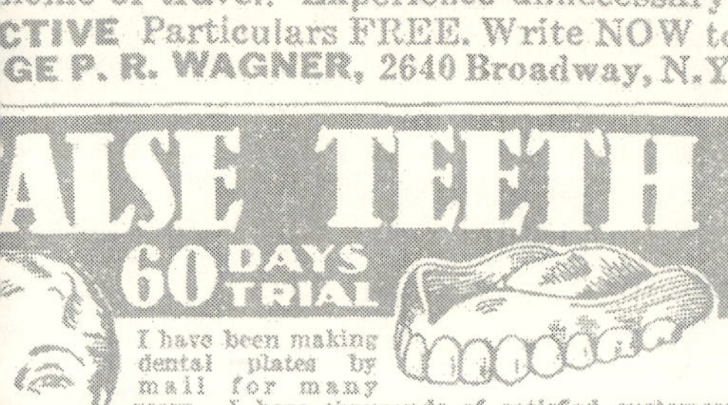

At dawn thousands of Americans
would walk into that death snare.
Only one Yank knew the danger,
could hope to warn them in time.
But he was a helpless prisoner,
ar behind the German lines!

S.O.S. Buzzard

"B*E DOWN to get you in a taxi, honey, better be ready 'bout half past eight. Now honey—*" It was morning and the Red Falcon had turned to fly back to his aerie after the night flight. Tanks and machine-gun belts and pans were full. He was happy. His lips moved as he softly hummed his favorite tune and his feet tapped the rudder bar in time to the rhythmic strains. But suddenly the tune stopped.

Barry, with his big black aide, Sika, occupying the cockpit behind him, had been flying over the Front at 10,000 feet. Below puffy clouds dotted the sky. At the moment that the song died abruptly on his lips he had just come over the edge of a particularly large cloud and found himself looking down on the rear Yank lines.

His voice rang through the tube that connected him with Sika.

"What the hell goes on down there, big boy? Look."

Sika was looking. Together they stared and what they saw was this. Some 5,000 feet below them a Yank observation plane circled slowly. Below that observation plane a tiny, white square appeared and disappeared on the ground.

Barry throttled back his motor, snatched his high-powered binoculars and peered through them.

"That's a shutter panel down there," he told Sika. "It's sending up a message. Y r-e-c-e-i-v-i-n-g. I got that much."

He spelled out the words as he decoded them.

> *"Y r-e-c-e-i-v-i-n-g i-n-f-o-r-m-a-t-i-o-n f-r-o-m o-u-r s-i-d-e o-f l-i-n-e-s. W-e h-a-v-e a-l-l r-a-d-i-o c-o-m-m-u-n-i-c-a-t-i-o-n c-h-e-c-k-e-d. W-a-t-c-h-e-d f-o-r c-a-r-r-i-e-r p-i-g-e-o-n-s i-n a-i-r. S-h-o-o-t d-o-w-n a-n-y-t-h-i-n-g t-h-a-t l-o-o-k-s s-u-s-p-i-c-i-o-u-s. V-e-r-y i-m-p-o-r-t-a-n-t."*

An aerial wire was lowered from the observation plane; he could see the lead fish dangling at the end of it.

"Hmm," he commented.

Then Sika handed him a slip of paper.

"Here, master. I took down message as you gave it to me."

Barry stared at the sheet.

"Good boy," he said. "I didn't know you were a secretary too." He studied it. "Wish I had gotten in on the first part of this thing. Let's see. Y is the only-letter I got in that one word. I have it. That must mean enemy. Enemy receiving so and so and such and such."

"Yes, master. Sika think you right."

"So some enemy spy is sending information across the lines and they're looking for carrier pigeons, eh? They would, just when I thought we were all through work for the morning."

He paused to deliberate, swinging the plane in a large circle over the Front.

"For about two cents I'd let that Yank observation plane and the rest of the crowd chase this wahoo bird themselves. I can't see much excitement in chasing a carrier pigeon, can you, Sika?"

"Sika think we not find much fight chasing pigeon."

"Right," Barry said.

He cocked over and headed for the Vosges Mountains once more. But suddenly he banked the plane again.

"Where you go, master?" Sika asked.

"Just for fun," Barry said, "I'm going to take a turn around the back area. Like a drive through the park on the way home, big boy. It might be possible that we could spot that bird."

"Yes, master. I go where you go."

They swung lower. Barry dropped the nose and held it in a gentle dive until they reached 3,000 feet. He had made one, two, three circles over the back country behind the lines when there came a wild drumming on the cowling behind him. Sika was pounding and shouting into the mouthpiece.

"Master! Master! Look! A bird fly! A black bird, master."

Barry whirled and stared in the direction of Sika's pointed finger.

"Where?" he said. "I can't see it."

"There, there, master. Down below. It has gone now into that building in the patch of woods."

Barry was still staring, straining his eyes.

"You mean that flimsy shack down there?"

"Yes, master. A big black bird. I see it fly into the window."

BARRY dropped the nose and hurtled nearer. He roared over the building twice. Saw no movement around it. No sign of the bird that Sika had mentioned. Frantically he cast about for a place to land near it.

"If we could get down," he exclaimed, "somewhere within striking distance of that place, we'd look into it. But all there is, is clumps of trees spattered around for a couple of kilometers or more."

"But master, that bird not fly toward German lines. It come to the house."

"Gee, that's right," Barry said. "I didn't think of that. A spy wouldn't send information about our activities to a house behind Yank lines. That doesn't make sense."

He flew higher, spiraled in a big circle above the shack. But as he turned, he kept his eye constantly on that isolated spot.

The sun was bright this morning. It shone down through the puffy, drifting clouds in a clear, brilliant light. And suddenly he saw its rays being reflected from some shining object on the side of that shack. Coming lower, he saw a man's head and shoulders leaning out of the window. A man who was flashing a message into the skies with a mirror that reflected the sun.

"We got it! That's it!" Barry yelled. "He's sending a message to—" he broke off abruptly and stared down with his mouth agape. "Hey, what the hell! That guy there is sending a message to us. Take it down as I spell it, Sika.

> *"R-e-d F-a-l-c-o-n. G-e-t b-o-m-b-s. B-l-o-w u-p a-m-m-u-n-i-t-i-o-n d-u-m-p i-n e-x-a-c-t c-e-n-t-e-r o-f w-o-o-d-s t-w-o k-i-l-o-m-e-t-e-r-s s-o-u-t-h o-f G-e-n-s-v-i-l-l-e. T-h-i-s i-n-f-o-r-m-a-t-i-o-n j-u-s-t r-e-c-e-i-v-e-d b-y c-a-r-r-i-e-r p-i-g-e-o-n f-r-o-m o-u-r a-g-e-n-t o-n e-n-e-m-y s-i-d-e o-f l-i-n-e-s. M-u-s-t b-e d-o-n-e a-t o-n-c-e t-o s-t-o-p d-r-i-v-e.*
>
> *"T-i-m-e i-s i-m-p-o-r-t-a-n-t. I-t w-o-u-l-d t-a-k-e h-a-l-f a-n h-o-u-r t-o g-e-t t-h-i-s i-n-f-o-r-m-a-t-i-o-n t-o a b-o-m-b-i-n-g s-q-u-a-d-r-o-n a-n-d h-a-v-e t-h-e-m i-n t-h-e a-i-r.*
>
> *"O-n-e b-o-m-b p-r-o-p-e-r-l-y p-l-a-c-e-d w-i-l-l b-l-o-w u-p t-h-e w-h-o-l-e d-u-m-p. I a-m o-n-e A-m-e-r-i-c-a-n w-h-o h-a-s g-r-e-a-t c-o-n-f-i-d-e-n-c-e i-n t-h-e R-e-d F-a-l-c-o-n. G-o-o-d l-u-c-k a-n-d s-u-c-c-e-s-s."*

The message ended. Barry saw the man wave his hand in final greeting. Then he drew inside the shack once more.

"Master, Sika think maybe look fishy, like you say. How he know we come along just now?"

Barry shook his head.

"I think it's O. K., big boy," he ventured. "Of course he didn't know we were coming along. We just happened along now and he thought he could save time by giving us the job to do, instead of waiting until he telephoned to G. H. Q. and it went through all that red tape.

"Got a couple of hand bombs back there in that rear cockpit, Sika? We're heading for Heinie land and we're going to blow up that dump, if possible."

"Yes, master," Sika said meekly. "I have three bombs."

Barry turned abruptly and headed northeast. He dropped his map case, got out the map of the sector that contained Gensville and studied it. He struck a true compass course straight for that place and thundered on.

He reached his own lines flying a crazy, zigzag course. It wouldn't be long before guns were belching up at that crimson Red Falcon plane. He wanted to be in practice to avoid their aim.

And guns did boom and bellow up at him as he crossed the German side of the lines. He was flying too high for ground machine-gun fire to have much effect, but at just the right altitude that pleased archie the most. And arch was doing his stuff!

Some of the bursts came so close that they made the Red Falcon plane buck and gallop like a wild bronc gone crazy. Then they were out of that danger area and hurling deeper into Bocheland.

Barry was staring ahead, searching for the patch of woods south of Gensville. He had little trouble in finding it. He dropped the nose and spoke to Sika as they roared over the woods just above the tree tops.

"Keep the old eye peeled, big boy, for something that looks like an ammunition shed. You watch over the right side, I'll watch over the left."

"Yes, master," came back the faithful response.

Both were staring down. At that moment there was no thought of a sudden attack by enemy planes from above. As they roared over the woods for the first time, Barry's face became puzzled. He banked and swung back.

"That's funny, Sika. I couldn't see a single building. In the center I could look right straight through the trees and see the ground underneath. Get ready this time to drop a bomb."

"Yes, master. They may have low roof camouflage to look like ground."

"That's what I was thinking," Barry said.

As they hustled toward the center of the wood again, Barry tensed.

"Now!" he called to Sika.

Blam!

The concussion of the explosion booted the plane higher in the air and slightly off balance. Barry and Sika stared behind, hopefully, hoping that that first explosion would be the beginning of a gigantic upheaval there in the center of the wood. But nothing happened. The trees that had been blasted settled down. Barry swung around and again, at his command, Sika dropped a second bomb. Then—

Tac-tac-tac!

From close range came the sudden staccato of Spandau guns. Barry whirled in his seat and stared upward. He saw two flights of Albatrosses. Their round, bullet-shaped fuselages were painted a brilliant canary yellow. Their wings were black.

Two flights of them. Seven planes each. One coming down out of western skies and the other coming out of the east.

"Why the dirty—" he commenced.

Then he flung the controls hard over and back. The Red Falcon plane leaped upward. Barry pushed the throttle wide open and the great Liberty screamed. Albatross planes tried to follow them, but they couldn't climb as rapidly as the Red Falcon.

IT looked for a moment as though Barry were going to try a loop and come down on them. Instead of that he held his zoom, stared back over his tail angrily.

Tac-tac-tac!

Spandau guns belched frantically as they climbed away. Sika was facing the tail of the crimson plane, hunched over his guns, giving them all he had. One Albatross went down. Still Barry Rand held his zoom. Then came Sika's pleading voice:

"Master, you go too fast for me to fight back. You got me out of range now."

"I'm just getting altitude, big boy," Barry told him. "Counting out that Albatross you just sent down, that's thirteen to one against us. I'd rather have more space underneath me."

"But we come back and fight?" Sika asked to make sure.

"Bet your life," said Barry. "This looks to me like a trap. And we're not going to run away like a bunch of scared school kids."

The altimeter went up 3,000 feet. The Albatrosses were circling, following him up, trying their best to get within range once more. 13 against 1. Desperate odds, but Barry had a plane that would outrun any of them, and outfight them, too.

When the altimeter reached the 3,000 mark he kicked over in a split S and plunged down on them. He glared across his sights. One red-nosed plane stood out among the others; it was possibly the leader of the whole *Jagdstaffel.*

Barry caught it in his sights. But he was still out of range. He must get closer to make sure. He hurled in, doing almost 300 miles an hour in that power dive. Almost within range now.

Suddenly the red-nosed Albatross flipped over and lunged away behind the other planes. Barry cursed. He plunged on down, swerved the nose so that his sights were on another cockpit. Had that one dead to rights.

Tac-tac-tac!

He heard Sika's Lewis guns exploding in his ears. The giant black had whirled round and was shooting over the top wing, directly above Barry's helmet. It was then that Barry Rand clamped down on his own triggers.

Tac-tac-tac!

The four nose guns on the front of the Red Falcon plane chattered crazily. White and yellow tracers slashed out through the clear blue morning air. Two of the Albatrosses went down.

Then the dogfight broke into a wild tangle. Eleven planes romped wildly about them. They were completely surrounded, above and below and on all sides by wings that came in with the deafening chorus of death.

Yellow tracers formed a dim haze through which the Red Falcon plane whirled. Several times Barry tried to draw a bead on one or another of the enemy planes. But each time as he did so, holding a straight course for a split second, bullets came so close that he had to hurl out and try again to save himself and Sika.

Then with the startling abruptness of a bomb bursting in the middle of a peaceful garden party, the Liberty engine coughed and died cold.

Barry knew better than to turn and start toward his own lines. That wouldn't do any good. He only had 2,500 feet now and those lines were three or four kilometers to the southwest.

He did three things with great speed. He threw his hands up in the air, flying the ship with his knees—a token of surrender. He shouted to Sika to throw up his hands. And he looked for a field below that would be suitable for a forced landing.

The instant that his hands went up into the air the chatter of Spandau guns on those Albatrosses ceased. The enemy planes swung around and hovered about his tail. The red-nosed ship raced past and pointed to a field a little way to the east.

Down, down went the Red Falcon in a swift glide. He kicked over into a dizzy slide slip, straightened after he crossed the boundary of the field and brought the plane down for an easy three-point.

Four of the enemy planes were also landing. But the red-nosed one lingered above with the others. No use fighting now. If they made a break and ran for cover, those seven E. A.'s still in the air would riddle them with their guns.

"I guess we're cornered," Barry said to Sika, as they climbed out. "Better take it easy. These birds would be tickled to death for a chance to blast us with their guns."

"Sika fight if you say so," the giant black said stubbornly.

"Maybe later, big boy," Barry told him, "but not now. We haven't a chance. I'll tell you when, if any."

The four enemy pilots who had landed in the same field had climbed from their cockpits. They drew their guns and approached them.

"You are our prisoners," said the first to reach them.

"Okay," Barry nodded. "Where do we go from here?"

"We go," the German replied, "to the car that is waiting under the trees, two fields away."

"Just as I thought," Barry said. "This whole thing was a trap to catch the Red Falcon. You had a car waiting here. You must have felt pretty sure you were going to get us."

The four Germans only smiled.

"*Kommen*," said the one who seemed to be in charge.

THEY climbed over three fences, crossed the two fields and found a seven-passenger German staff car waiting under the overhanging branches of some trees. Barry and Sika climbed in, took the two side seats. Three of the pilots climbed in behind them and one took the front seat beside the driver who had come with the car.

"Back to the airdrome," commanded the last to get in.

The driver nodded and the car moved away. Barry watched their course as they moved along the road and turned left at the next road. Then suddenly a thought struck him and he turned to Sika and spoke in English.

"Listen, big boy," he said, "are you sure that you saw a black bird? Not a carrier pigeon?"

Sika shook his head.

"Bird was black," he said, "bigger than carrier pigeon. Twice as big maybe."

Barry nodded.

"Thanks. That sort of teams up with my idea of the trap, although I can't figure all of it out."

The German pilot who had taken his seat beside the driver had turned his head as they talked. Apparently he understood English. But he didn't answer; he only smiled wisely.

A few minutes later the car turned in at an airdrome. Barry had seen it from the air a little north of Gensville. Yellow fuselaged planes were taxiing across the field to the deadline. The car drew up before what looked to be the officers' mess of the airdrome.

"We get out here," the German pilot beside the driver said in good English.

Barry and Sika dropped to the ground.

"Inside now we go," he said.

Other pilots were climbing from their planes. Two chairs were brought and placed at the head of the table for Barry and Sika. They stood there at the command of the German. Other pilots filed in and took their places.

Three vacant chairs seemed to yawn at everyone else. The chairs of those three whom Barry and Sika had sent to their death not long before. A waiter filled glasses all around. Thirteen of them. The eleven pilots and Barry and Sika.

A small, cocky, arrogant pilot took his place at the other end of the table. He had a selfish, sneering curl to his lips and a weak chin. He wore a monocle in his left eye. He held up his glass, everyone else followed.

"*Erstlich*, a toast to the departed ones. *Hoch*."

The glasses were held high. Another of the German pilots, the one who had taken command of the capture of Barry and Sika, said in a steady, soft voice:

"To those already dead and to us who will follow."

Reverently, Barry and Sika held their glasses in a toast to the men whom they had killed. Silently thirteen glasses were drained, bottoms up. Except for the arrogant little figure at the end of the table, the other Germans sat down. The one with the monocle remained standing and nodded to Barry and Sika.

"You may be seated also," he said. "Then I'll begin what I have to say."

The Red Falcon and his aide sat down. All was still as they waited. The little one cleared his throat.

"Perhaps by now," he said, "you have suspected that this was a trap, Red Falcon. A trap to catch you and your *verdammt* black aide. Was it not a clever idea, *mein Herren?*"

"Damn clever," Barry nodded, without smiling. "But I'd like to ask you one question, if you don't mind. What's the connection between that black bird and this trap?"

The German smiled delightedly.

"So you know. *Ach,* but that is beside the point of what I have to say. You think you are so very clever. You should have found that out before you were captured. Let me introduce myself. I am the Baron von Gilder. A great ace of the war. You have heard of me, of course."

Barry shook his head.

"Not until just now," he said. "Sorry if it spoils your opinion of yourself."

"*Ach, verdammt Schwein!*" the baron exploded, glaring at Barry. "Now I can say what I was about to with a clear conscience. You think, Red Falcon, that you're the cleverest one on the Front. But I'll tell you this. If it wasn't for your black aide you'd be helpless.

"You are both my prisoners. I'll prove how helpless you would be by taking him away from you. Without him you are nothing but a yellow dog."

Barry's eyes narrowed.

"Perhaps," he said. "But being that way, I do not feel that I can be compared with you, von Gilder. I saw you in the fight a little while ago. I saw you duck from danger and run behind your men, like the coward that you are."

"Silence!" barked von Gilder.

"Silence hell!" Barry flung back at him. "I am talking now and I am going to keep talking until I get through. You look like a damned imposter to me.

"I doubt if that 'Baron' you call yourself belongs to you. Much less the 'von' that you choose to put before your name. You aren't that type of gentlemen. But if it's so, I'll gamble your whole family's ashamed of you. You're as yellow as the fuselage of that red-nosed Albatross you fly."

Then Barry Rand stopped. Tiny yellow and red flames of hate seemed to leap out of the eyes of von Gilder. He was shaking with rage. He tried several times to speak and failed. Then finally he found his voice.

"Listen to me," he barked. "You have already insulted me. I have said you would be helpless without your black aide. There are thirteen of us at this table. Someone is due to die, according to superstition. Tomorrow morning at dawn you will leave him. He will be shot."

The air grew tense in the room as he stopped talking. Barry Rand felt the great muscles of Sika bulging. He laid his hand gently on the arm of the black.

"Take it easy, big boy," he warned. "There's lots of time between now and tomorrow morning."

Then von Gilder's voice cut in.

"Take the two away. The black one, take to the prison at Gensville. The other, take to the old cell in the back of the stone building where I have my quarters. I want to have him where I can return the taunts that he has flung at me. *Heraus mit.*"

PILOTS leaped up from their seats at the table. Again Lugers were drawn. Barry and Sika rose. The great black turned with sad eyes, held out his hand to Barry.

"We part now, master," Sika said. His eyes grew misty. "Perhaps some day we meet again where the God of the Jungle has prepared a place for those who are good hunters."

Barry slapped him on the shoulder. He forced a grin.

"I'll see you before then, big boy," he said. "Tomorrow morning is a long way off yet. Almost twenty-four hours. Use your head in the meantime and don't take any wooden nickels."

Sika forced a grin at that. Then the two groups of guards parted them. Four pilots walked Barry straight across the airdrome toward a little stone building. Behind it were the ruins of a few other stone houses. Once, before the war, that had been a town. But guns had made a waste of it and left standing only this one building.

They entered it through the front door. Apparently the front quarters had been once occupied by the village law officer. The rear portion was shut off by a heavy, rusty, iron grating that had been the village prison.

Barry glanced about the walls in passing; they were plastered with strips of fabric from Allied planes.

The German who had been in command of the capture was in charge now. Barry grinned at him.

"I'll bet this guy who calls himself baron picked up these Allied insignias from a pawnbroker."

The one in command smiled and answered in English.

"Perhaps I shouldn't say it," he said, "but you sized up our commander neatly this noon, *Herr Rot Falke.* He has a strong political pull somewhere in his family. The 'von' is perhaps correct and the 'baron' also. But he doesn't act quite like the gentlemen that the titles would imply.

"Many times we have acted as his hounds, *verstehen Sie?* But of course this is war and we are under him."

He unlocked the iron-grated door, swung it open. It groaned on its hinges.

"You will step inside now, *bitte, Herr Rot Falke.*"

Barry nodded and followed orders. The door clanged shut and as the German locked it again, Barry said:

"You know, sometimes when I meet guys like you, I wonder why we're fighting you."

"And I also," said the other. "*Auf wiedersehen.*"

"*Auf wiedersehen,*" said Barry.

When he was alone, the Yank surveyed his quarters. There were only the two openings. The grated door that opened directly on the quarters of von Gilder and a small window at the back with bars spaced wide apart. Barry looked out that window, tried the bars. They were more than an inch thick.

"Damn!" he said. "If I were about thirty or forty pounds lighter I could almost squeeze out between them."

Von Gilder didn't show up that afternoon. The hours passed slowly, sluggishly. Barry tried and tried to formulate plans but he couldn't figure any way out. He felt lonesome without Sika.

So they were going to shoot Sika at dawn. He didn't bother to think about the reason they would use. Von Gilder was the type who would think up something logical. But he must get out and go to Sika's aid before that hour came.

Toward evening he heard footsteps outside. He rose from his cot where he had been sitting between paces about the small cell. Perhaps this was von Gilder. But it was an orderly instead carrying a broken glass containing water and a half loaf of black bread with spots of mold through it.

Barry tasted the water, drank a little of it. It wasn't particularly good. He was hungry but he couldn't eat that moldy, black bread. He flung it out of the window so as not to draw the rats to his cell.

It was growing dark outside. A little later von Gilder came in. He switched on the light in his quarters and peered through the grating.

"So," he said, "*verdammt* coward, I have you as a guest, *nicht wahr?*" Then he laughed.

Barry tried to keep calm.

"You must feel *viel mehr* helpless without your black aide now. *Ja?*"

"I'll get along," Barry said.

A KNOCK sounded on the front door. Von Gilder flung it open and a *Kapitan* came in. He bowed, then he looked past the baron, saw Barry in the dark cell.

"*Ach,* baron. I thought I would find you alone," he said. "I have important orders. Perhaps I can give them to you elsewhere?"

Von Gilder chuckled.

"This is only my prisoner, *der Rot Falke,* whom I captured this morning. He is perfectly helpless now and perhaps he would enjoy hearing our plans."

"Very well," said the *Kapitan,* "if you wish it. D*er Rot Falke,* eh? Let me have a look at him." He peered through the bars curiously at Barry. "Hm, he looks perfectly harmless, eh, baron?"

The baron chuckled again.

"He is harmless—now. Proceed, *Kapitan.*"

"Very well," the other began. "It is about the river trap. We have given indications to the enemy that we are weakening our position on the north side of the Muesell River. In fact, it is the truth.

"The *Amerikaner* hold the lines on the south side of the river. They command a good position on a slight bluff, while our men occupy a level plain. We have drawn off many of our men to protect them from the deadly fire of the *Amerikaner.*

"We expect the Allies to make an attack before many days. The sooner the better. We have stationed large quantities of kerosene along the banks. When the Allies advance we'll cover the surface of the river with oil—a match will be applied and poof! They'll all be burned in crossing."

Suddenly Barry Rand realized that his heart was banging away at double time as the Kapitan went on.

"It will be up to you and your *Jagdstaffel, Herr* baron, to be ready to take off as soon as we receive word of this attack. You will strafe the Allied troops from the air and keep them from escaping the fiery river.

"When they have been destroyed and the fire is out, our forces will storm across the river and will take the bluff. *Verstehen Sie?*"

"Jawohl," grinned von Gilder.

"Das ist alles," said the *Kapitan.*

The two saluted. When the *Kapitan* had left, von Gilder turned to Barry.

"I'll leave you now for a short time to think that over. I'm expecting—" his grin broadened and became fiendish in its delight—"a special message shortly. I'll be back to receive it."

Then he left, closing the door behind him.

Barry Rand's brain was throbbing. He paced the floor. The whole enemy plan had been revealed to him. A most hideous plan. To burn thousands of Yank troops in a flaming river as they crossed it. But there was no way of getting the news back.

Minutes passed. A half hour. It was pitch dark outside. Then he heard the rustle of wings outside his window.

Flap! Flap Flap!

A bird was flying about the building, trying to get in. But the door was closed. His only means of entrance was the grated window in Barry's cell. Presently, dimly outlined against the slightly brighter out-of-doors, Barry saw a form, black and foreboding, alight on the sill. It stood considerably higher than a pigeon. It craned its head this way and that.

Noiselessly Barry crept toward it. This must be the bird Sika had seen. There was some connection between this German drome and that shack deep in Allied territory.

As Barry drew nearer to the bird he suddenly froze with astonishment. A strange voice was coming from somewhere, apparently from outside the window. It was not a human voice, and yet it spoke a sort of a bastard German that was hard to catch. It came in sort of a rasping, resonant sound.

It reminded him of something. The voice of a parrot, that was it. And yet it was not a parrot's voice. The words were less distinct. It was saying two words over and over which Barry finally worked out.

"Attack dawn. Attack dawn. Attack dawn."

He gasped as the meaning struck him. This bird had come to tell the Germans that the Americans on the Mucsell River were attacking at dawn. He made a lunge for it. This black thing must not live to reveal his message.

But the bird fooled him. Instead of flying away, it made a strange croaking sound, stopped talking and hopped directly into the cell. In the pitch blackness Barry couldn't see it. He could hear that strange croaking sound, could hear its wings flap as it moved about—but that was all.

Again and again he plunged for the bird in the inky blackness. Or rather, for the place where he heard it. But always his body came up with a bang against the hard stone sides of the cell.

Then he heard a faint sound from the front quarters. The door was opening. Someone was coming in. The light switched on and he saw von Gilder standing beneath it. At the same moment he saw the bird. A big, black crow. He made a lunge for it, but it hopped just out of reach of his hands through the grating of the door.

"ACH Himmel, Adolph. You come early," von Gilder said.

The crow hopped up on his shoulder, kept on making those croaking sounds. And then out of the croaks came those words in German.

"Attack dawn. Attack dawn."

Von Gilder reached up, took the bird from his shoulder and looked at it.

"*Was ist das?*" he demanded.

"Attack dawn. Attack dawn."

"*Gott im Himmel, das ist news.*"

Von Gilder leaped across the room and snatched the phone.

"*Ach, ein's Minuten,* Adolph, and you get your reward. Here—" he was shouting into the phone—"give me Second Army headquarters, *macht schnell.*" Then a moment later—"*Ja, wie geht's. . . .* The Baron von Gilder speaking, *Jagd-staffel siebenundsechzig.* The bird has just returned with good news. The *Amerikaner* attack at dawn. . . . *Ja. . . . Danke.*"

He hung up. The crow had its beak diving into von Gilder's pocket. Von Gilder reached in, drew out a half handful of cracked corn.

"There, there. Eat until you blow up, you black angel. *Und* then you sleep for a time and grow hungry again. And before dawn I send you back to get more corn from our friend across the lines. *Verstehen Sie?*"

The crow couldn't bother to reply now. He was busy eating.

"*Und* in the meantime," von Gilder said, "you learn to say 'ready' to tell our friend that we are prepared and have received the message."

During this scene, Barry Rand had been hanging on the bars of the cell door. Von Gilder turned to him now with a smile of triumph.

"Is it not *wunderbar?*" he said.

"I'll say," Barry said. "But—"

"*Ach,* I know what you are going to ask," von Gilder cut in. "You are so clever, I should let you figure it out for yourself. You want to know how we get a crow to talk. *Nicht wahr?*

"Have you never heard of a tame crow with his tongue slit just right? A crow is a very intelligent bird. Much more intelligent than some of you *verdammt* human *schwein.* We teach them to talk like a parrot and they'll fly miles for this corn.

"Your plane motor has been repaired with another magneto that was damaged in the fight. Hereafter, your fastest plane of the Front will be my plane. Und here, while I think of it, you may like to try to reach the key to your cell. I'll lay it here on the table six feet away from your door.

That will perhaps aid you in having a pleasant night's sleep, *Rot Falke*."

The baron turned to the crow.

"Come, Adolph," he said. "To bed."

The baron took off part of his uniform and hung it up carefully over his cot. The crow had finished eating. He hopped up on a roost in the corner. Then the baron switched off the light. Shortly Barry heard his measured breathing.

All was still. He felt dead for sleep himself, but knew he had to figure out a way of escape. Some means of saving Sika and getting the news back to the doomed Yanks. He tried the bars on the door and the window with all his might. They stood solid.

In a last effort he tried desperately to reach the key that the baron had placed on the table. He couldn't get his hand within four feet of it. He tried to find some wire or rod that would reach it. There was none. Finally, worn out by the loss of sleep and the suspense, he lay down on the cot.

He was astonished hours later to find that he had been asleep. Light filtered in through the grated door. It was yet dark but the baron had just gotten up and had turned on his light. He heard him talking to the crow, repeating one word over and over again. The crow repeated it after him.

"*Fertig!*" The German word fou "ready."

"Now," said von Gilder, walking toward the door with the crow in his hand, "you're hungry. I let you go. Tell our friend across the lines '*fertig*.' Go"

He opened the door. There was a flutter of wings. A last squawked "*fertig*" from the crow as he flew out into the darkness just before dawn. Then a giant, black figure charged out of the night into the room. Sika was there, slamming the door behind him.

For a split second he glared about him. The light blinded him at first. Von Gilder's hand reached for his Luger. Sika snatched it away from him before he could draw it. Then he grabbed the small baron's body, flung him across the room.

He lunged for him as he crashed there. The body of the baron was limp, but Sika wasn't taking chances. He lifted him high above his head and crashed him against the stone floor. Barry could hear the skull crunch. Then Sika was staring at him like a wild beast that had just come out of a trance.

"Master, I get you out the same way I get out. Tear bars apart."

"No," said Barry. "I'm afraid these are too heavy and there is a quicker way. There's the key to the door on the table."

Sika whirled, snatched the key. There was a click and then the groan of old hinges and the door swung open. Barry bolted out. Sika caught him in his great arms and gave him a bear hug that almost squashed the wind out of him. When he could speak Barry said:

"Quick! We'll put off this petting party until later. Got to get to the plane."

They dove out into the night. Gray streaks were forming in the east as they raced toward the spot where the plane had been left. They slowed as they reached the border of the field.

"I guess," admitted Barry, "I would be lost without you, just like the baron said. Look, Sika, there are two guards holding our plane. You circle the field. When you get up behind them I'll let out a yell to attract their attention. Then you do your stuff."

There were a few minutes of waiting, then Barry saw the dark form of Sika slinking through the grass behind the two guards. He let out a wild yell. The guards turned and stared, their backs to Sika. The giant black leaped at them, brought their skulls together with sodden thuds.

Barry raced for the plane as the two guards fell. A moment later the engine was started and they took the air.

He hedge-hopped all the way to that bluff over the Muesell River that the Yanks held, and while he flew he wrote a brief note.

> *TRAP LAID. GERMANS GOING TO FIRE RIVER COVERED WITH OIL. MAKE BELIEVE START ATTACK AND THEN DUCK BACK OUT OF DANGER. DO THIS FIVE MINUTES AFTER READING THIS NOTE. MAKE ATTACK AFTER FIRE DANGER GONE.*
>
> *RED FALCON*

He swung low over the bluff and dropped the note. He had seen Germans with great tanks behind shields already pouring oil on the waters of the river in the gray light of dawn. He turned abruptly and roared up the river.

"What we do now, master?" Sika asked through the tube.

"Plenty, if you can hit a mark with that one bomb you've got left, big boy," Barry said. "There's a dam up here about ten kilometers; power dam. That one bomb ought to blow it up, if you hit it in the right place."

"Yes, master."

Minutes of flying. They sighted the dam, swung low over it. And as they reached the middle Barry shouted through the tube.

"Let her go!"

Boom!

The middle of the dam crumpled and a great wall of water swept down through the Muesell valley. As Barry hurled back above that rushing water, he saw flames down the river. Already the Germans had set it on fire. Then came the water.

He saw the Yanks running back up the bluff out of danger. The wall of water was striking the section of the river where the oil was on fire. Sheets of flame rolled up. But the great tidal wave from the burst dam was carrying that flaming river on below and stretching it out all over the flat country that the Germans held.

He climbed higher and higher as the sun came up until he saw the flames go out. Then as the river receded, the Yanks swept across to go on and on into new territory, with nothing to hold them back.

Barry Rand yawned and turned west, toward the high Vosges.

"Now for some sleep, big boy," he said.

"Yes, master," said Sika.

Buccaneer
Busters

One man had learned the secret of those camouflaged roads—and died. But that didn't keep Barry Rand and Sika from trying, didn't stop them from thundering down a corpse trail straight into a Boche hell trap.

Buccaneer Busters

HIGH in the rugged Vosges, where the Red Falcon had his aerie, the air was heavy and ominous. Even at those altitudes there was no late afternoon breeze to drive out the oppressiveness of fog. All day long that heavy mist had hovered over the mountains, had lingered low over the war torn Front.

Barry Rand and Sika had been sleeping most of the day. It was early dawn when they had returned from a successful raid for supplies and gasoline and oil tanks were full. They had collected plenty of ammunition. There had been a fight with the enemy, of course, when they had taken these. Then with dawn they had returned home to rest and await further developments.

They sat now eating a late afternoon meal in the cozy cabin on the edge of flat-topped Saar Mountain. Neither had spoken for some time.

Barry finished his meal and pushed back his plate. He lighted a cigarette. He got up from the table and walked with a slight air of impatience toward the door through which traces drifted of fog.

He stood there staring out for almost a minute. Staring out into the white, smothering blanket that hung in the motionless air. Then he spoke.

"Well, big boy, it doesn't look like there's going to be much flying until this pea soup thins out. Lord, you could cut it with a butcher knife."

"Yes, master," Sika replied, as he got up from the table and began clearing away the dishes. "Thick fog this morning."

Barry chuckled.

"Morning, big boy? Well, I suppose you're right. We do our work at night, so to us this is daytime. And when we get up, of course, that's morning."

Sika's face beamed, and his great, likable smile spread across his countenance.

"We sleep days so many times, master, Sika forget this is afternoon. This looks like morning fog we have in my country, sometimes."

"So you have fogs in Africa, too, big boy?" Barry asked.

"Not often, master. But sometimes in early morning."

The rattle of dishes continued. Barry stood in the doorway leaning up against the casing, smoking. Usually, on Saar Mountain, they could hear the distant rumbling of the big guns of the Allies and German forces. But now all seemed still in this grim, smothering moisture.

Then suddenly Barry straightened. He stood motionless, listening. He had heard the faint sound of an airplane motor's drone. It came louder and then almost died away. Once more the hum increased.

Barry didn't turn and he didn't hear Sika come up behind him, either. But a moment later, as the drone of the motor increased, he felt the black directly behind him in the doorway. He turned to glance at him. The big man was standing there, listening too. The sound came nearer, died away and came nearer again.

"What that, master?" Sika asked.

Barry shook his head and the expression on his face was a sad one.

"Some poor devil lost up there in the soup."

"That sound like our motor," Sika ventured.

Barry was striding out in front of the cabin to enable him to listen better. Sika followed like a giant, black shadow.

"Might just as well be our motor," Barry said. "It's another Liberty."

"That mean the plane is Allied, master?"

Barry nodded without speaking. He was listening more keenly than ever. The ship up in the fog blared out as its exhaust stacks turned toward the listeners. Then it veered away as the sound died to a dull, staccato moan.

"They're coming nearer," Barry observed.

"Who you think they are?"

Barry shrugged.

"No telling. They're Allies, there isn't any doubt about that. And they're in plenty of trouble."

"What can we do, master?" Sika asked anxiously.

FOR a moment Barry Rand didn't answer that question. He was staring up into the fog thoughtfully. Dampness sprayed upon his upturned face, dampness that was half fog, half drizzling rain. The noise came closer again. The plane lost above was making a series of circles and in each one it came closer to Barry Rand's field.

B-r-r-r-r-am!

That last roar, as the plane turned, shook their ear-drums. Barry whirled to face Sika, and snapped a command.

"Start the plane!" he shouted. "We're going up to guide them down."

"But, master—" Sika began.

"No buts, get going. We're going to help them down."

"Yes, master."

As Sika finished he was racing for the great propeller on the front of the Red Falcon plane which stood a few feet away. Barry leaped into the cockpit as Sika stepped back.

"Contact!" called Barry.

A warning cry from Sika was his only answer.

"Look out, master! They come down on us!"

That warning was unnecessary. The roar of the Liberty motor above became deafening. The plane was very close and coming down. The pilot was making a desperate effort to get out of the fog and try to land somewhere.

"He can't make it," Barry shouted, "He doesn't know he's over the mountains. Poor devil he'll—"

But the thunderous roar of the Liberty drowned the words at his lips. Instinctively, Barry Rand ducked. Ducked and stared over his shoulder in the direction of that ship. He thought he saw the form of the plane very dimly in the fog.

B-r-r-r-r-am!

The motor screamed out louder than ever as it shot past their heads. Had the pilot in that cockpit seen their field on top of Saar Mountain? Barry heard the plane make a turn after it had swept over. It was coming back. Then—

Bam!

The motor was cut, and they heard it idling.

"He saw it!" Barry shouted. "He's coming in to land here. Thank the Lord for—"

He stopped short to listen. Standing there in his cockpit, he could still hear the sound of the idling engine, but it sounded too far away and too low to make the field. Came the roar of the Liberty once more, but for only a second or so.

Crash!

He heard the rending of metal, wood and cloth. He leaped from the cockpit, was running toward the location of the sound. Out of the fog, at that end of the field, a mass of wreckage became dimly outlined. He got a glimpse of it as it rolled sidewise, the wings torn off, and stopped its forward motion.

A sickly feeling came over him, as he saw a form hurtle through the air from the back cockpit and strike rolling. Then it seemed to untangle and was still. Sika and Barry reached the figure at about the same time. It lay between them and the wreckage of the plane.

They stared at it. Bent down. It was the body of a man in the uniform of a German *leutnant.* Barry felt of the man's pulse. The heart was still beating.

"Just knocked out, I think, Sika," he said. "Let's have a look at the plane and what's left inside."

They hurried there. Found a ghastly sight when they reached the wreckage, fifty feet away. The pilot was still in the front cockpit. His body was smeared with blood that had come from a hole in the side of his head, made by a strut broken in the crash. Barry shook his head soberly.

"Poor devil. And he was so close to getting down alive. Damn the fog anyway."

"Fog bad, master," the Sengalese agreed. "Sika glad we not have to go up to try to bring them down."

"Right," replied Barry. "That was sort of a fool idea of mine, but I believe we might have made it. We might have saved this guy's life if he'd hung around a little longer. You better get your shovel and dig a grave for him."

"Yes, master, I go." Sika half turned, then he stopped. He frowned in a puzzled expression.

"That funny, master," he said. "This plane a D.H., two-seater with Liberty motor."

"Yes, I know," nodded Barry. "And it's got black crosses on the wings and the pilot is dressed like a Yank and the bird out there who came with him is dressed like a Heinie. Don't you know the answer to that, big boy?"

"No master."

"Just dragging over a spy," Barry said. "I've heard of the Allies using black crosses on their wings when they land a spy in broad daylight."

BARRY left Sika to take care of the dead pilot and went back to the man who had been thrown clear. Now he put his ear down upon the fellow's chest and listened. The boom booming of his heart was plainly audible.

A little red abrasion on the forehead of the man showed where he had struck in his fall. Perhaps some rock had knocked him out. Barry slapped his face gently. A few minutes later the eyelids fluttered and opened. He was a wiry little man, this one in the German uniform. But he spoke slowly, as one quite sure of himself.

"Thank God we're still on the Yank side of the lines," he said. "I see that uniform you have on."

He struggled to a sitting posture, raised his hand to his head, swayed a little dizzily while Barry held him.

"Take it easy, old man," Rand said. "There's no hurry."

"Indeed there is a hurry," replied the other.

"O. K. I'm ready to listen. What's the story?"

The man with the German *leutnant's* uniform stared at him searchingly for a moment.

"I must ask who you are first," he said. "And what happened to my ship and pilot?"

"That's all quite simple," Barry told him. "But the last part isn't particularly pleasant." He jerked his head toward the wreckage. "There's your ship. And over there at the edge of the field is my aide, digging a grave for your pilot."

The man shuddered a little as he nodded.

"I see. Apparently I was thrown clear."

"And very fortunately," Barry observed. "That was a nasty crackup. But about the story."

"And to whom am I addressing myself?" the man stalled. Barry smiled very slightly. "It may be," he said, "that after I tell you who I am you won't want to tell me what your mission is. However, after you learn the details, I think you'll agree that we're the ones best fitted to help you in your venture.

"You see, you happen to have crashed on a field from which there's no way out except by air. And we have the only plane here."

Then for the first time the man in the German uniform saw the crimson plane without any identification marks—other than that plain, blood-red color.

"Good lord!" he exploded suddenly. "That's the plane of the Red Falcon!"

"Right," replied Barry "And, as a matter of fact, you're talking to the one they call the Red Falcon right now."

The man looked a little startled at first. Then slowly he answered Barry's smile with his own.

"This is indeed a pleasure." He held out his hand. "My name is Marston. John Marston."

"And mine, Barry Rand."

"I have heard a great deal about the Red Falcon," Marston said. "I have thought what a grand painting you'd make, although I've never seen you before."

"A painting?" Barry inquired with a chuckle. "A painting of me?"

"Yes," answered Marston. "I'm an artist, you see. That is, by profession. But I must confess I am somewhat disappointed in you, Rand. I expected you to be a very wild, fierce looking character, with lots of scars on your face to make you look like the devil you're supposed to be."

"Sorry to disappoint you, Marston," Barry grinned. "But about this mission you're on. If it's particularly important, there may not be too much time to waste talking about incidentals."

"Yes, of course." Then for a long moment Marston studied Barry Rand.

"I've heard about you, the length and breadth of the Front," he said. "I believe you can be trusted. In fact, I am sure of it, in spite of some of the stories I have heard to the contrary about you siding with the Germans."

"To be truthful," Barry replied. "I have sided with the Germans once or twice. But never even in those cases have I taken sides against the Allies.

"It is true I was convicted of treason. Or rather, framed by some of my superior officers. I escaped a firing squad, and was extremely bitter toward my own country, Marston.

"But I am still a Yank at heart—it's in my blood. And Uncle Sam's interests are mine. Now will you tell me of your mission? We may be able to help you."

"Yes, gladly," Marston nodded.

HE moved to rise and Barry helped him. For a moment he moved his legs and arms speculatively, after he had stood up.

"How do you feel?" Barry asked.

"A little sore in spots," replied the artist. "But I am quite all right, I am sure."

"Let's go into the cabin where we can sit and talk comfortably. I doubt if there'll be any flying until this fog clears. We don't want another accident like you just had."

"No, indeed," Marston agreed.

They walked to the cabin and went inside. Then when they were comfortably seated, Marston began telling his story.

"You see, Rand, this whole thing started sometime yesterday. I don't remember the exact moment, but an observation plane sighted something strange going on about the Carsi sector.

"This plane carried a few light bombs and it was sent up to watch enemy activities which had been increasing on that Front. The ship carried orders to find the road, if possible, by which troops were being moved up to Carsi. Then after these roads had been discovered, heavy bombers were to be sent up last night to really finish the job.

"Well, the observation crew came back with a very strange report. And this in turn was verified by the pilots of the five plane flight of Nieuports which convoyed them.

"They could make out more troops than usual in that sector. But every one of them said that there wasn't a single highway or railroad anywhere visible that connected with that sector. Not at least that they could see from the-air."

Barry looked puzzled.

"That's funny," he said.

"Of course it's funny," agreed Marston. "Well, to make a long story short, last evening the brass hats held a conference. They have decided that the only explanation is that the Germans have discovered a clever way of camouflaging their roads.

"I have been working more or less with Intelligence for some months, although I have not been commissioned as a special agent. But they picked me for this job because of my profession.

"You see, I studied art for four years in Germany and six years in France. I understand the German people and language quite well. I was to go over at dawn this morning, but the fog was so thick we couldn't get off. We've been waiting all day.

"Now in the middle of the afternoon we got a little break. But just before we reached the lines, the mist closed in on us and we became lost. So here I am."

Barry got up and strode to the door, looked out. The air was just as thick as ever, but it was growing a little darker.

"I think," he said, "luck is going to be with us before long. This fog's about spent. In fact—wait a minute."

He stepped out on the field, away from the shelter of the cabin. He stuck his index finger in his mouth, wetted the end and held it up in the air.

"Yes, I am right," he announced. "There's a breeze coming up. One usually does after the sun goes down. I think that by the time it is really dark the fog will all be blown away."

"Excellent," said Marston. "Then perhaps you'll take me over?"

"That's exactly what I had in mind," Barry replied.

He led Marston back in the cabin again. Sika had finished digging the grave for the pilot, and Barry could dimly see him going toward the wreckage to get the corpse. No need of Marston seeing that. The man needed all the nerve he had.

They sat and smoked and talked for more than an hour. Sika came in, started a fire. It was getting cooler.

"Wind come up, master," he said. "Drive fog away."

"Yes. I had hoped for that."

"We fly tonight?" the black grinned.

"Right, big boy."

It was nearly an hour after that when the Red Falcon plane with a heavy load of three men thundered out into the clear night. Before that Barry and Marston had been poring over Barry's maps.

"Do you remember just where you were going to land?" Barry had asked.

Marston had nodded, studying the map. Then he pointed.

"I believe it was right there. You already have a cross marked at the field."

"Yes," Barry had nodded. "I have a cross on every field on both sides of the lines where it is possible to land."

SO now as they thundered out over the Front, Barry had his map before him and that field marked with an X well in mind. It was a little clearing surrounded by what had once been a wood, several kilometers behind the German lines. Near that field a road that lead toward the Front was marked.

Barry spoke through the tube to Sika.

"Put the earphones on Marston, I want to talk to him."

"Yes, master."

Then Marston was speaking. "Hello, Rand. What is it?"

"Your plan, as I understand it, is to land at this field and inspect that nearby road."

"That will be part of it," Marston answered. "If I find what I'm after about that road location, the method of camouflage, I mean, I'll be back to signal you to give you the details of what I have found. If not, then I'll have to go on. You'll drop me at the field and take off again."

"Right," replied Barry. "I hope you get away without having all the Heinies in the country on your tail."

Barry Rand had reached the Carsi sector. From his altitude, now, he should be able to see the field he sought. He was headed north. Behind, he saw the specks of flame where German guns belched death. He released a flare, climbed higher as it settled and in its light located the field.

The nose of the Red Falcon plane dropped as the light went lower. He spotted the clearing and cut the motor for the long glide. Germans would hear it and suspect. There could be no doubt of that.

But on the other hand he would merely land and pull off again. It would be hard to apprehend Marston as a spy, dressed as he was in a *Leutnant's* uniform. Hard, that is, if Marston was clever.

The flare struck the ground some distance behind the Front and went out. Barry could begin to see the field dimly as his eyes became accustomed to the darkness once more.

The Red Falcon plane was heavily loaded. She would land fast tonight. He cocked over on one wing and slithered in under the trees in a steep sideslip. He kicked straight as wheels and skid touched the ground. The plane rolled and Marston was climbing out. He hesitated an instant beside Barry's cockpit.

"I'll signal in one hour if I need you—if my venture is successful."

"Right," replied Barry. "We'll be upstairs waiting for you then."

Then Marston disappeared in the darkness. And Barry gave his ship the gun and took off.

Fifteen minutes later he was landing on flat-topped Saar Mountain. No need wasting gas hanging around upstairs waiting for that hour to pass. Barry lit a cigarette and strolled about the plane on his own field.

"Well, so far so good, big boy," he mused. "I'm wondering what we'll find out when we go back."

"Maybe we find fight, master?" Sika ventured hopefully.

"I am afraid," Barry replied, "that you're in for a quiet evening, big boy—if this bird Marston finds out what he's after."

"Sika want fight," the giant black persisted.

'Well, keep your shirt on," Barry said, "maybe you'll get it after all. Only remember, I'm no fortune teller."

He glanced at his watch from time to time. Then a little less than a half hour after they landed on Saar Mountain, the Red Falcon plane took the air again and turned back toward that German field.

Flying at 5,000 feet, Barrry Rand looked down into the blackness that was Germany. He sat hunched over his stick a little tensely, his eyes roving that blank space below him. Then suddenly he sat up. A tiny light was blinking at him from far down. A light that said something that he couldn't quite understand at first because the dots and dashes seemed to all run in together.

At the same time Sika's giant fist began pounding the cowling back of his head.

"Master! Master! See signal!"

"I see it," Barry said, "but I can't make it out. If that's Marston down there shooting that stuff up to us he's either in an awful hurry and not being careful or else he doesn't know the code. Looks like a drunk guy is getting them all—"

He stopped short and his mouth opened. The dots and dashes came closer. Then he could make out letters. Letters that didn't run into each other quite so much.

"He send letter S," Sika shouted through the tube.

"Shut up!" Barry barked. Then: "There's the letter O!" He tensed an instant. "An S. Good Lord, Sika, he's sending us an S. O. S.!"

"Yes, master. He had trouble. Maybe we fight now?"

Barry's teeth clenched.

"I wouldn't be a bit surprised, big boy."

He climbed higher and tried to orient himself as those dots and dashes continued—slower and slower.

S. O. S.   S. O. S.

HE distinguished the field where he had landed before. That blinking light was coming from a distance of a half-kilometer away from the field. Without the slightest hesitation he reached up, closed the throttle and cut the switch. The Liberty died.

Silence hovered about the plane as it glided down. Then, as before, he was cocked over on one wing, slipping in under the trees and kicking straight for a landing. The landing came with a gentle *carumph,* as the landing gear touched the ground.

Barry leaped from the cockpit. Sika was down beside him. They tensed a moment beside the plane, listening—making sure that the field wasn't being watched. Satisfied, they moved on in the direction of the light they had seen from the air.

Suddenly Sika stopped short. He was listening. Then he was whispering to Barry.

"Master, hear trucks over there where road marked on maps?"

Barry listened too. Very dimly he could hear the rumble of heavy motors and the jolting of trucks as they dropped into chuck holes.

"There's a road over there all right," Barry hissed back. "But how in the devil do they hide it? We've got to find that out. Got to hurry to Marston. Let's go."

Half crouched, they made their way noiselessly across that field and across another and another. Then Barry stopped to make sure of his directions again. Sika pointed a little bit to the right.

"Master, Sika think light came from over there in corner of field. I go see?"

"We'll both go," Barry ordered.

They went on. Halfway there they stopped short. This time to listen. A sound had come to them from the corner of that field. A half gasping, half groaning sound. Neither spoke. It came again. Then both broke into a run.

Crouching down, they found Marston lying in a pool of his own blood under some bushes. Barry shook him gently.

"Marston!" he said softly. "Marston, what happened?"

For a moment only groans answered him. Barry lifted Marston's head a little. Again he begged:

"Marston, what happened? Can't you tell us?"

The artist seemed to tense. He was trying his best to get strength enough to talk.

"They—got me," he rasped in a hoarse whisper. "Crawled—here."

Barry half lifted him.

"Come on, Sika. Take hold. We'll take him back with us."

"No—don't!" pleaded Marston. "I'm dying. Listen—roads camouflaged with—"

The last word trailed off without meaning.

"Yes, yes," Barry urged. "Road camouflaged how?"

Marston seemed not to hear him. He was trying to get strength enough to speak again.

"Enemy—move up supplies for—"

The last word died in a bloody gurgle. Desperately Barry Rand shook Marston. Tried his best to revive him. But the body went limp in his arms. Marston was dead.

Barry rose. For a moment he stood facing Sika, silently. He jerked his head then.

"Come on, big boy," he said. "I guess you're going to get your fight, after all. Marston found out what he was supposed to, but he died before he could get it out. Now we've got to learn the same thing over again. And we've got to do more. We've got to get this information back to the Allies."

"But how you do that, master?" Sika inquired.

"I'm going to take a dangerous chance," Barry said. "We're going to walk right out on that highway where you heard the trucks. Come on. I'm not sure what's coming off just yet. But you're in for a fight, big boy.

"We're going to walk right into the lion's mouth and if we're lucky, we're going to come out running—and fighting."

They could still hear the rumble of trucks plainly. They headed in the direction from which it came. The strong southwest wind had blown the air completely free from fog and now it was clear and cold. They could see quite plainly.

They crouched as they neared the rumbling trucks. They were fifty feet away, now, from the edge of that camouflaged road. Barry remembered the location of the road on his map. The map gave it as a main highway that ran between Carsi and Voucourt.

THEY drew nearer in the darkness, crouched at the very edge of the ditch. From there they could see truck after truck moving up toward the Front, rumbling and jolting as it went.

"Those trucks are carrying supplies," Barry whispered into Sika's ear. "See they're covered with big tarpaulins. They probably wouldn't have those covers on if there were men inside.

"Look up above the truck and the road here. Some kind of covering over it, 'cause we can't see the stars through it. That's the answer to the camouflage. They've got a canopy spread over the whole length of every road in this sector."

"Yes, master, Sika see."

"But we've got to make sure of the enemy's plans," Barry mused.

"How you do that, master?" Sika demanded.

"If it works it will be easy," Barry grinned. "Quick! Here comes a squad of German soldiers now, walking down the side of the road.

"We're going to walk out and make believe we've stumbled into them. I'll handle everything except the fight. When I snap my finger, Sika, you fight and how."

"Yes, master." There was an eager thrill in that voice.

Barry leaped up to the side of the road, and drew Sika beside him. They stepped out beside the grumbling trucks and began to walk boldly in the same direction as the squad of German soldiers. But Barry made sure that he and his aide were walking at a slower pace.

They strode on perhaps a hundred yards. They could hear the clink of heavy German boots upon the hard, rocky road. Coming closer, closer.

Bam!

A flashlight caught them in its beam from behind and held them. Intantly Barry turned around. He swung Sika with him so that the Germans could easily recognize the big black.

"*Ach du lieber!*" exploded one of the Germans.

"*Gott im Himmel,*" said another.

Then several chorused together, "*Ach, Gott. Der Rot Falke!*"

Barry held Sika beside him. He shouted out of the corner of his mouth.

"Surrender, big boy, without an argument. But, remember, when I snap my finger—"

"Yes, master."

And it was just then that a commanding voice of the German shouted: "*Die Arme hoch!*"

Barry and Sika had already raised their arms shoulder high. Now they put them up above their heads. In another second they were completely surrounded by more than a half dozen Germans. Drawn Lugers prodded them in the backs and in their stomachs. Swift hands searched them and took away their guns.

"*Was ist?*" demanded the *Offizier* in charge.

Barry shrugged as a flashlight played in his face.

"I guess you got us this time, *mein* corporal."

"*Ach Himmel!* The insults of this one," raved the *Offizier*. "I a *Leutnant* and he calls me a corporal."

"Sorry, *mein Herr*," Barry replied, "but you look like a corporal to me."

He gazed up at the canopy that covered the road.

"Hm-m," he said, "nice little roof you have over these trucks. Too bad we got caught before we could get back and tell the Allies about it."

There was no mirth in the voice of the *Offizier* as he laughed. It was more of a triumphant, rasping chuckle.

"*Kommen!* We take you with us. You are our prisoners, of course. So the Red Falcon comes to find out why he can see no roads from the air leading to our place of next attack. *Ach*, you didn't even suspect what these roads meant.

"Listen, you *verdammt schwein*. Now that you're our captives and have made fun of my rank, I'll tell you what you do not yet know. Already we have moved troops along this highway to the Front. They are massed there, ready to attack at dawn.

"*Und* now, a half hour ago, begins the movement of the ammunition and supplies.

The *Offizier* broke off into another rasping chuckle of delight.

"A mistake was made by the High Command. They sent up troops without the proper supplies for the drive. And only now begins the truck trains of supplies. If your *verdammt* Allies knew this fact, they would be swarming over to blow up this road and cut off the supplies.

"But I tell you because you're prisoners now. Because I would laugh in your face. After all, you, the smart one, are the *dummkopf. Nicht wahr?*"

Barry was moving as though to march willingly, easily, at the first command of the *Offizier*. He nodded soberly.

"I guess," he said, "you beat us to it. The joke is sure on us, Herr *Leutnant*. And it looks as if the Red Falcon will scream no more."

Then—snap went Barry's finger. It was the signal for Sika to go into action. And with that Barry dropped to the ground, before the astonished Germans knew what was going on. Sika was left standing.

Flashlights swept about in the darkness but they didn't pick out Barry. He was thrashing about like a wild man, kicking with his feet, grabbing with his hands. Tripping up Germans as Sika lunged at them.

TWICE, three times he was stepped on, but the fight was at its height and Barry didn't seem to mind.

"Ki-hu-yi!"

The piercing, age-old battle cry of the Wampana rang out in the night. The giant black grasped the *Offizier*, jerked him off his feet, whirled him around like a drum major's baton.

That fight only lasted a few seconds. A shot rang out from a passing truck. Came the sound of running feet and shouts from up the road. Then Barry, standing now, grabbed Sika by the arm and plunged into the darker recesses of the field that bordered the road.

Together they ran across that field and another. They turned left and made for their plane. Everywhere, flashlights probed the night trying to pick them out.

The plane was standing alone. Barry grasped the edge of the cockpit and climbed in. Sika leaped to the propellor.

"Contact!" Barry called.

"Contact, master!"

Then the propeller whirled. Four times Sika spun that prop before he got a snort out of the Liberty. Then it caught and droned out in the night. It was still warm but they must get down to the other end of the field and turn in order to take off into the stiff breeze.

From that end of the field came running men. Men whose light bobbed up and down.

Crack! Crack! Crack!

Rifles and pistols bellowed in the night. Bullets whistled about them.

And the Liberty answered with a deafening roar as Barry shoved the throttle ahead—gave her the gun.

Tac-tac-tac!

Barry pressed his triggers, sent a rain of lead hurling into those Jerries. Then he was roaring over and through them as they fell. He reached the other end of the field and turned. Down the turf, which was strewn with dead Germans. The plane grew light and lifted. And as he climbed, Sika spoke.

"Too bad we've got to leave Marston, master."

"Right," Barry said. "But if I were dead I don't know that it would make much difference whether I was left in Germany, France, Hell or Hoboken."

The Red Falcon was in a hurry now. He didn't bother to climb for altitude as he roared out across the lines. Two, three searchlights pierced the darkness, trying to catch him as he thundered over the rear of the German trenches.

Then over No-Man's-Land and the Yank trenches. He was flying almost entirely by compass.

"Where we go now, master?" Sika asked through the tube.

"We're going to the field that Marston's plane took off from," Barry answered. "That's observation squadron 167. I hope they have a sensible commanding officer, that's all."

He began to circle in the general location of the 167th. A moment later, over to the left, a gasoline trench flared at the sound of his Liberty motor. Instantly, Barry dived for it. And in the light of that gasoline flare he saw the field he sought.

With motor cut, he glided down for a landing.

"Where's the commanding officer?" he demanded.

"Captain Thomas," said someone, "he's—"

"Right here," spoke up another voice. "What's up and who are you?"

"Name is Rand," Barry said quickly.

"Good Lord!" the last voice to speak exploded. "The Red Falcon!"

"That's what they call me," Barry hurried on. "But there isn't time to argue about that now, Captain Thomas. For the love of heaven, listen to what I've got to say and believe me.

"Late this afternoon a D.H. from this field took off carrying a man in a German uniform who was going over as a spy. It crashed at my secret airdrome. The pilot was killed."

"And the other?" demanded Thomas.

THE other," Barry said, "the spy, was taken behind the lines by us shortly after dark, when the fog cleared. We landed him. He told us to fly over that spot in an hour and he would signal to let us know whether we were to pick him up and bring him back or not.

"He did signal. Sent us an S. O. S. He tried to tell us some things when we got to him, but he was dead before he could get it out. Then we had to learn the whole business ourselves and fight our way free.

"The Jerries are planning an attack at dawn. Through some slip at German headquarters, the men were brought up first and now they have just begun to bring up supplies for the drive. They are carting those up over the straight road between Carsi and Voucourt.

"That highway is shielded with a canopy that makes it look like the rest of the country. But the bombers should be able to find the location of it from their maps, if you believe me, captain."

"If I believe you!" exploded Thomas. "Of course I believe you. What do you want me to do?"

"Inform the nearest bomber squadron," Barry said. "Send your whole squadron over with light bombs to help out. I'll tell you the rest as soon as you send those orders."

"Right," snapped Captain Thomas. He bellowed to his men. Every observation plane and light bomber was to be warmed at once and to be equipped with bombs. He rushed into the nearest hangar. Even out on the tarmac Barrry Rand could hear him shouting into the mouthpiece as he called a squadron of heavy bombers.

Then Thomas was back before him. "I have another idea to work with that," Barry said. "It might be well to tell headquarters that you received this information, not that you got it from us. If they knew the Red Falcon told you, some of them might spend the next six months arguing the question."

"Yes, of course," Thomas agreed.

"O.K. Here's a whole mess of Germans up on the Front waiting for supplies so that they can start a drive at dawn. Our trenches across the lines from them are filled to the usual strength, I believe.

"If we succeed in blowing up the road, they'll be cut off from supplies at least until they can get the roads repaired again. If, in the meantime, our men bring a counter attack, there'll be nothing left for the Germans to do but retreat."

"By George!" Captain Thomas exploded. "You're right, Rand. And a mighty clever idea. I'll call and advise that it be done at once."

"And I'll be getting on," Barry said. Thomas shook his head. "Oh, no you won't," he said. "You need ammunition, gas and oil for your flying. Here you—" He whirled to mechanics about the place. "Fill up the tanks of this Red Falcon plane. And make sure the gun belts are filled too, while I send this report."

He strode off. Barry watched the mechanics work over his plane in the light of their electric torches.

Then Captain Thomas returned. He held out his hand to Barry.

"I wish," he said, "I could do something to get you back into the service. But I guess you're doing more for the cause now, Rand, than if you were here, hindered by a lot of orders from brass hats."

"That's damn nice of you, Thomas," Barry said, "and thanks. I think we'll be shoving off now."

He and Sika climbed back into their plane. The motor was started and they took the air. They followed the light bombers of the 167th out of the Front. In the light of flares they made out the location of that straight road between Carsi and Voucourt.

The earth and the air above it shuddered with the bursting of bombs. Then the whole squadron of Handley-Pages came over to finish the job. Barry waited until he saw that it was done properly.

Then when the bombers turned back for their fields, Barry banked over and headed for his aerie.

And the tune of "The Dark Town Strutter's Ball" sprayed from his lips as the Red Falcon winged his way home.

Explosion
Buzzard
FREDERICK
BLAKESLEE

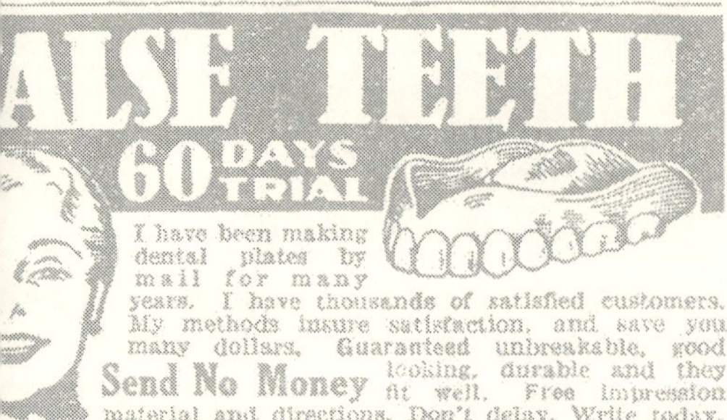

"Ach Himmel, help has come in time," gasped the German, But he had no idea that the rescuing plane was the Red Falcon, that its pilot was Barry Rand, Yank outlaw—and that the two of them were due to go hell-bent on a dynamite sky mission!

Explosion Buzzard

BARRY RAND surveyed the low-hanging clouds from the rim rock of flat-topped Saar Mountain. The sun would be setting just about now but there was no evidence of that fact in the west. No blazing sunset, only the slow dimming of light. It would be dark soon. A very light breeze blew the smoke behind him as he took puffs of a cigarette and exhaled. He was humming a tune softly to himself. His favorite.

"Be down to get you in a taxi, honey, hum-hum, hum-hum, hum-hum."

Apparently he didn't have a worry in the world. But he started as Sika, his great black aide, came noiselessly behind him and spoke.

"Not look like good night for flying, master."

"Fact is," Barry said, "it is very rotten."

"We fly tonight, master?" Sika asked. "I was just trying to figure that out." Then almost instantly he nodded. "Yes, we fly tonight, Sika."

"Master make up his mind in a hurry," said the big black.

Barry shrugged. "Just sorta got a hunch."

Sika waited. "About what, master?"

"Don't know exactly," Barry said. "I'm not naturally superstitious, but there seems to be something drawing me out there in that mess and I don't know what it is."

"But, master, the fog," Sika objected. "Clouds hang down low. We not see lines or anything from here."

"Sure, I know," said Barry. "But maybe it will be okay when we get down."

"We need gas, master," Sika said. "Got plenty bullets."

Barry didn't answer. He was staring out into the dimming gray twilight.

"We'll get gas," he said finally, "but I was just thinking." He smiled a little. "I'd like to try one of our own gas stations this time. Just sorta for fun, Sika."

"Maybe you think it fun to get caught and shot, master," Sika warned.

"I'm not worried so much about that. If the Germans capture you as a spy, they'll line you up and shoot you the next dawn.

"But the cautious Yanks, they're too afraid of killing the wrong man. So there's usually a lot of red tape about being shot on our side."

He glanced at the Red Falcon plane standing nearby under the protecting branches of the trees.

"How is she, Sika, all set to fly?"

"Yes, master, but she low on gas."

"How much have we got?"

"About enough for an hour and a half. Maybe not quite that."

Barry thought a moment. "I think that's enough. I'll put on my flying togs, then we'll go."

Two minutes later, Barry returned from the cabin carrying two sets of helmets and goggles. He handed one to Sika and stepped into the cockpit.

"All right, big boy," he said. "Wind her up."

Several turns of the giant prop caused the Liberty to blast out. Barry let the motor warm while the instrument needles pointed to satisfactory figures. It had grown darker in those minutes of preparation. A blinding cloud of fog drifted over the mountain top, smothered them with gray mist and then passed on.

Barry's hand pushed the throttle ahead and he kicked the rudder, turning the ship to taxi out on the field. His eyes were a little anxious now as he looked about in the gathering darkness. Sika spoke to him through the tube from the rear cockpit:

"Maybe fog too thick, master. Maybe we stay home tonight."

Barry didn't answer for a few seconds. He wasn't so sure of the fog and mist himself, but he shook his head. "No, I've got a hunch we ought to be out there. Hang on, big boy, here we go!"

"Yes, master," came the answer, a bit nervously.

The great Liberty roared. The Red Falcon plane shot ahead and a few seconds later it was alone in the gray-black clouds, without the slightest sign of earth anywhere about them. Barry turned in a general westerly direction. He let the crimson crate climb higher and higher. He must make sure of a safe altitude.

At 3,000 feet above Saar Mountain he leveled off. That would give him about 5,000 feet above the lower country of western and central France. He dropped the map case in front of him, looked over maps until he found one showing the area south of Paris. He smiled a little.

"How would you like to see those great training fields at Issodun, Sika? There used to be quite a bunch of fields while I was there, months and months ago. All sort of different and still all hooked together."

"Why we go there, master?" Sika asked. "There be many men there."

Barry nodded. "Of course there will. That's why I picked it. There'll be so many men that, as usual, there'll be a lot of confusion."

"But maybe there be so many men we get caught," Sika said.

"I hardly think so," Barry explained. "Whenever you want to keep under cover, big boy, get in the biggest crowd possible. Get right in the middle of it and usually every one is so interested in everyone else that he won't bother to ask you a lot of fool questions."

"But master, we have to get gas and you tell me I not fight or kill Americans."

"You're damn right I did and do," said Barry. "I don't think we're going to have to fight about this. Not if I can get rid of you somewhere, big boy."

MINUTES passed. They rolled on into a half hour and then an hour. Barry was watching his gas gauge more and more anxiously. It was beginning to jiggle dangerously toward the empty mark. He pushed the stick ahead and the nose dropped.

He stared tensely out, struggling to catch any glimpse of land that might come through the heavy clouds. But no such sight came to him. He dropped 2,000 feet. The clouds, thick, foreboding and black, still clung about them.

"We ought to see something that looks like earth pretty soon," Barry said.

"In pitch darkness now it be hard to tell from mist," Sika ventured.

"Right," snapped Barry.

He struck up his favorite tune again, whistled "The Dark Town Strutter's Ball." He dropped 500 feet more.

"I think I see a break, Sika. Seems to be getting thin down there. Look—"

Sika's voice cut in.

"Master! Master! Lights below!"

The air was getting clearer. Barry Rand didn't have to follow the pointed finger of his black aide to see what he was shouting about. There were flashes of light, blue like those from an electric arc, coming up rather dimly through the bottom of the cloud bank in which they flew.

Barry dropped the nose into a steeper dive. Suddenly the ship broke out into clearer air that was hazed by a light, drizzling rain. They could see the blue flashes plainly now.

"What is it, master?" Sika called.

Barry hesitated to answer. And before he could get near enough to see them distinctly, the flashes stopped.

"They heard us coming down," Sika warned.

Barry shook his head.

"Maybe, but I don't think so."

He was circling a thousand feet above the spot where they had seen those arcing flashes.

"There! More flashes, master!" Sika cried.

Barry could see them as the big black spoke. But they weren't in a hot, bluish flame now. Rather they were orange, tipped with crimson and they were on either side of a fairly wide area. Furthermore, they were accompanied by the crackle of gunfire which came to the Red Falcon and his aide dimly above the thunderous roar of their motor.

Barry jerked back the stick and zoomed almost up into the clouds again. From that altitude he released a flare. It burst into brilliance and lighted the earth below them. A strange scene was being enacted down there.

"Look!" Barry yelled, "it's a prison camp. A camp with a flock of Heinies penned up in it. See their quarters in the middle and the big yard and the rows of electrified barbed wire around it? Somebody has escaped."

Sika's excited voice cut in there.

"There he goes, master, running north across open field!"

"Yeah, and those guards with their guns going off aren't so very far behind him, either."

The flare was settling, settling. Before long it would burn out. But in its light they saw the running figure. They saw him stare upward, then extend both arms toward the plane as though in supplication. But he didn't stop. He crossed the field, reached a low hedge just as the pursuing guards came upon the other end.

From above Barry and Sika saw the fleeing prisoner turn abruptly to the left and run along behind the hedge, using it as a screen. The guards were going on across the field. They reached the hedge some twenty or thirty seconds after the man they pursued had dodged to the left. They broke through and started on across the next field.

Then suddenly they stopped short. Barry and Sika could see them running about excitedly. At that moment the flare went out and darkness hovered over the ground once more. Then they saw tiny lights like fireflies pricking the gloom, dancing about. Barry was grinning as he stuck the nose of the plane into the air and climbed again.

"That Heinie has plenty of guts to cut his way through a bunch of highly charged barbed wire and escape," he called back to Sika. "I've never done much to help the Jerries against my own gang, but I'd sure like to give that fellow a boost. A guy like that deserves a break."

He reached a point close to the bottom of the clouds. His hand went to the flare release lever and a moment later the earth was lighted brilliantly once more.

"If we spot him this time," Barry called through the tube, "don't shout too loud, Sika. Your voice might carry to those guards hunting him."

"Yes, master," said Sika softly.

Down, down they plunged. They saw that the men who made up the searching party were spreading in all directions. Barry grinned.

"I guess," he said, "he's given them the slip. Maybe we can find him and give him a lift. I'm curious about this whole business."

He flew in a lower circle to the east in the direction the fleeing prisoner had taken. They passed a woods, a small patch of trees.

"I'll bet he's in there," Barry said.

He climbed a little higher and circled twice.

"Damn that flare," he said. "I wish it would keep going a little longer."

"Master," Sika called softly, "there he is, see him? He comes out of edge of woods."

Barry stared.

"Yes, I see him. Duck, Sika. Duck down in your cockpit. I don't want him to see you."

He roared low in front of the fringe of woods. He pulled back the throttle. The nose of the Liberty died. Then Barry called in his best German to the man he could see dimly there:

"Hold on, I'm going to land and pick you up."

THE prisoner had a good lead, but his pursuers would find him soon now that the plane had revealed his whereabouts. As Barry circled and came in to land he called through the tube to Sika:

"Listen, big boy. I hate to do this, but you gotta get out for a while. Slip out before this bird sees you. I got an idea for getting some gas at Issodon. I know this prison camp and Issodon isn't far off. But if you're along they'll spot me instantly. With this Heinie, maybe I can get away with it."

"You mean, master, you land at Issodon with this German in my place?"

"Right," said Barry. "Now be a good guy and hop out and don't ask any more questions. Make a big circle to the west and south and back again to this field. Be here in about twenty minutes. I'll be back to pick you up then."

"Yes, master," said Sika obediently.

The flare flickered and died, but Barry had his direction well in mind. He slipped over the eastern border of the little field, and landed in the darkness. Wheels touched and rolled. He felt the fuselage shudder a little. That was Sika climbing out.

He heard a hastily whispered, "Goodbye, master. You not forget Sika." Then his black aide was gone in the darkness.

A few seconds later he heard the swift footsteps of someone running and next, a panting voice in German:

"*Gott* be praised. Help has come in time. Who are you?"

"Never mind that," Barry replied in German. "Hurry, climb in before it's too late."

The man was climbing with all possible haste into the back cockpit. There was a thunderous roar as the Red Falcon plane leaped down the field and once more took the air.

Barry turned toward the field where the group of guards had last been seen. Blackness all about them. But now shafts of light flashed upward and there came the dim *crack! crack! crack!* of rifle fire above the drone of the Liberty. Tongues of flame, tiny pencil points in yellow and red, were spitting up at them.

"*Ach,* my pursuers," said Barry's passenger. "They are no doubt very angry."

"Ja," said Barry. "We fooled them."

"And now we go instantly back to Germany?" came the inquiry from behind.

"We do that very shortly," Barry assured him. "Just as soon as we can replenish our gasoline supply."

"*Himmel,* you would stop on this side of the lines for gas?"

"Got to," said Barry.

"But we will be caught and I will be made a prisoner all over again," said the man.

"Not if my stunt works," said Barry. "I speak good English. I believe I can tell them a story at Issodon that they will believe." He climbed higher as he talked. "The prison camp should be below us here and Issodon?"

"*Ja, ja,*" said the other. "It is only four or five kilometers to the south. I have seen men in training fly over while I was in camp."

"Right," said Barry. "In another couple of minutes I'll drop another flare."

"But this plane you fly," objected the man behind him. "They will see the black crosses and they will—"

"You're wrong *mein Freund*," he cut in. "This plane I fly has no markings of any kind—no crosses and no circles, like some of the training planes that are used far behind the lines. You'll just sit still in your cockpit and let me do the talking, *verstehen sie?*"

"*Ja, ja,* I will sit still, but—"

"I'll see to it," said Barry.

He released a flare that flooded the earth below, revealing the great expanse of fields that comprised the training depot of hundreds of Yank pilots. Issodon was just ahead. He cut the gun. The Liberty motor died. Then he was gliding down in the light of the flare to land. Men came running out to the deadline as he taxied up. Some carried flashlights. They looked curiously at the plane and the two men inside.

"I want to see your commanding officer at once," Barry said. "Tell him it's very important."

Two men left to find him. The others hovered about. Barry eyed them a little coldly.

"I think," he said, "it would be well for you birds to be out of sight when the C. O. comes. I have some very private things to talk over with him."

Grudgingly the crowd broke up and men moved to a respectful distance, but continued to watch. Five minutes elapsed. Then a motorcycle pulled up. The flare had long since gone out and it was dark once more. A figure climbed out of the sidecar and strode to the edge of the cockpit.

"I am Major Sparks. Who are you and what do you want?"

"Come, closer so I can tell you, major," Barry requested. "I must whisper. I am on a special mission tonight. I have a spy in the rear cockpit whom I must drop over the lines. But, unfortunately, when we left our field our tanks were not full. The fog is very bad over our field so we were forced to land here to refuel. If you will see to it at once, major, we will be eternally grateful to you."

"Of course," said Major Sparks. He raised his voice. "Hey, you on the gas crew, get out the trucks and refuel this plane immediately."

After a moment's scrutiny of Barry and the man in German uniform, the light of Major Sparks' flash went out. Barry sat with a half grin on his face as he heard the truck pull up before the Red Falcon plane. Then gas was gurgling into the tank. It seemed to take a long time to fill it.

"You've a large capacity for gasoline," Major Sparks ventured.

"Yes," said Barry. "The plane was specially built for this work. There's no markings on it of any kind. But isn't that the way this war goes, major? They build this plane with extra large tanks. Then put a dumb mechanic on it who forgets to fill them."

"Right," snapped Major Sparks. "It's those things that drive the commanding officers crazy. Yet some of these birds think we have a snap of it."

"Isn't it the truth?" Barry grinned in the darkness.

Finally the tank was filled. The cap was replaced.

"I think you're all set," said the major. "Here, one of you men throw the prop."

Four men strung out, hand in hand, before the great propeller in the darkness.

"Contact!" yelled Barry.

The Liberty sputtered, roared and then idled.

"Good luck to you," said the major.

"Thanks," Barry answered. "We'll probably need it."

BARRY roared down the field into the wind and two seconds later he was flying again. Climbing higher and higher, he headed for the field where he had left Sika. Surprised to see his altimeter go up to 3,000 feet, he kept on for more altitude instead of leveling off.

"*Ach*, we are in luck, *mein Freund*," he said. "The storm clouds are lifting. Did you notice back there at Issodon the rain has stopped?"

"*Ja*," answered the other. "Look. Up there is a little light in the sky. The clouds already are breaking away. *Nicht wahr?*"

"*Jawohl*," replied Barry. "*Das ist gut*."

"*Ach du lieber*, that was a clever trick you played on the *Amerikaner* back at Issodon field. How did you do it?"

Barry's muscles tightened for a split second.

"How do you know it was a good trick? Do you speak English?"

"*Ach, nein.* And besides I couldn't hear you anyway. But would it not be very clever for any German to come down on a field with his plane and get gasoline in his tank with so little trouble?"

Barry relaxed.

"Yes, I guess you're right," he said.

At 4,500 he ran into clouds, but an instant later came quickly out of them. He was high above the field where he had dropped Sika. He pulled the release lever and another flare dropped out. Far down they could see the earth. Then an explosive cry from the back seat.

"*Gott im Himmel! Wast ist!* Why do you drop a flare to show the enemy where we are? *Ach,* you are going down now. I thought we were going back to Germany."

"Not so fast, *mein Freund,*" Barry said. "I have to make one more landing before we go."

"But I do not see what is the reason for another landing."

"Don't forget," Barry said, "I'm running this show. I just saved you from those guards who were chasing you. That ought to be enough to give you some confidence in me. *Nicht wahr?*"

"*Jawohl,* but—"

"Don't bother to say it, we're going to land anyway."

As Barry spoke he was diving down past the little, glowing parachute flare.

Diving down for that little field where he had landed once before that night. As he flew he drew the automatic from his holster. Keeping his head turned side-wise, he watched out of the tail of his eye the man behind. The occupant of the rear cockpit must have noticed his move for he made no more objections.

In the light of the flare Barry saw a great figure moving and waving at the edge of the field. He kicked over on one wing and slipped down for a landing. As he did so Sika came running across the field toward him.

"Master, you not forget Sika," he said.

At this, an explosive voice came from the back cockpit, this time in English.

"Hey, what goes on here?"

Barry whirled and stared at him in the light of the flare that was still drifting down. The man was half out of the cockpit. Sika grabbed him just before he had a chance to leap out.

"You stay until my master tell you to go," Sika said.

Barry glared at the German, then spoke in English.

"How come you talked like a Heinie up to now and all of a sudden you start spouting perfectly good Brooklyn English?"

The man was staring from Sika to Barry and back again.

"Oh, now I get it," he snapped. "You're the Red Falcon. I didn't recognize you without your black man here. Well, what are you going to do with me now?"

"Nothing very serious," Barry said, "unless you won't talk. But we got to get out of here right now. Hang on to him, Sika. We're going back home and talk this thing over. And you better keep your hand over his eyes when we get close to home so he won't see where we have our hideout."

The Red Falcon plane had been shuddering as the black had climbed into the cockpit. Now he was seated with the German garbed stranger on his lap.

"Yes, master," he answered.

"Wait a minute!" exploded the other. "There isn't time for a lot of monkey business and talking. I've got to—"

Suddenly he fell silent. The crackle of rifle fire had sounded from the other end of the field. One bullet pinged past and two thudded into the wing covering. The Red Falcon plane shot ahead. It rumbled, grew slowly light and then lifted sluggishly with its great load.

Barry shouted through the tube as they turned toward the Vosges Mountains and home.

"Hello, Sika?"

"Yes, master," answered the big black.

"Put our friend on the other end of the tube. I want to talk to him."

"Yes, master."

Then a moment later Barry was saying:

"Just what was that you started to say when I interrupted you?"

"Nothing," said the man.

"Okay," said Barry. "Keep it to yourself if you want to. You'll talk before long or you won't eat."

NO ONE spoke for the next 45 minutes. Barry Rand flew that Red Falcon plane wide open, straight for his aerie on flat-topped Saar Mountain. The storm clouds had cleared and the fog was gone. There was a half moon out to light their way into the mountains. A few minutes before they landed Barry called back: "Better cover up his eyes now." "His eyes covered, master," Sika assured him.

"Okay, big boy. Here we go." With the moon to light the way, Barry swung low over the flat top of Saar Mountain. He turned into the wind and dropped the plane lightly on the field, taxied under the trees and stopped.

"Okay, Sika," he said. "Now I guess you can relieve the blinders from our friend's eyes and help him to the ground."

The man in the German uniform glared at him in the light of the moon as he got out.

"Listen," he snapped, "you can't do this. The lives of thousands of Americans, maybe some of them your friends, are at stake."

"Then," said Barry, "the faster you start telling us everything, the greater chance they will have of coming out whole. Let's go in the cabin and build a fire. That was a pretty clammy ride in the fog."

"Yes, master," said Sika and trotted off.

The two sat down before the fireplace and a moment later flames licked up inside and sent a cheery glow about the interior of the cabin. Barry studied the man in the German uniform for a moment.

"Just why," he asked, "did you stop talking and refuse to go on when I picked up Sika?"

"Well, of course," the other said, "you must admit some strange things have been going on tonight. You saw me break out of a German prison camp, picked me up as one whom you thought was an escaped prisoner, and gave me the idea that you were flying back across the lines.

"I think it was the sudden realization that you were the Red Falcon that stopped me more than anything else. You see, we've heard a lot of stories about you. Some of them aren't any too complimentary. Understand me, I'm not saying they are true. You know how things get about."

"Yes," Barry nodded bitterly.

Barry shifted in his chair. The other passed him a pack of cigarettes and Barry took one. He struck a match and lighted both.

"Look here," Barry said. "We may as well understand each other from the beginning. My name is Barry Rand and I've never done anything that any other true, red-blooded American wouldn't do under the circumstances.

"When I picked you up tonight I did think you were a German, fleeing a prison camp. I dropped Sika so that I wouldn't be recognized as the Red Falcon so readily. I picked you up for two reasons. I can't tell you how much I admired your nerve in cutting your way out of that electrified barbed wire as you did.

"You see, we were coming out of the fog looking for the ground when those flashes of light attracted our attention. I said to myself that any man, Heinie or Yank, who had guts enough to make the break you did to get free deserved to be saved.

"Then I figured I'd pose as a fellow German. Of course, in this teddy bear outfit of mine it's pretty hard to tell which side of the lines a pilot is fighting for, if he hasn't any markings of identification on his ship.

"I figured as a comrade German you might confide in me some secrets that would help my side of the lines. That was really the important reason for trying to help you get away."

Barry settled back in his chair.

"I think," he said, "I've been quite frank with you. I believe it's your turn. First, would you mind telling me your name?"

The man smiled.

"I am quite satisfied with your explanation," he said. "The truth is, I have no name in the war. I am an Intelligence officer and as such I am known as S-17."

"Huh?" Barry showed surprise.

S-17 laughed.

"I thought you'd get a kick out of that," he said. "Here's the dope. This afternoon a bunch of German prisoners were rushed from the Front where they were captured to the prison camp here near Issodun. I joined them dressed as a German.

"We're expecting a drive sometime in the next few days in the Versette sector. These prisoners came from one end of that. Intelligence decided it would be best to conceal my identity even from the guards.

"You see, for some time we suspected these prisoners were working a signal system between their camp and the coast. It's relayed by lights or in such a way that it reaches all the way across France to a submarine somewhere in the English Channel. We are practically positive of this, but as yet we haven't been able to put a stop to it.

"That was why it was necessary for me to escape as a regular prisoner and run my chances of getting free. Of course, I was given the added privilege of smuggling in insulated wire cutters and naturally, that did the trick.

"But if the Germans in the prison camp suspected that I, as a spy, had gained the information I have, they would have immediately relayed the messages to the submarine telling their Brass Hats to change their plans."

Barry frowned.

"Yes," he said, "that's all very well. That's a good story, S-17, but there's a hitch in it. Why were you so concerned when you found I wasn't going back to Germany?"

"It does look a bit fishy, doesn't it?" S-17 admitted. "But here was my plan. If a Boche pilot took me into Germany that would be a way of getting there without suspicion."

"But how would you get word to our own troops about what you had learned?" Barry demanded.

The smile on S-17's face broadened.

"That would be a very simple trick," he said. "I have here in my clothing a thin messenger streamer and also pencil and paper. In fact, I had already started to write a message when you decided to land and pick up your black aide here. That's one reason why it gave me such a start. I hadn't figured on that."

"Oh, I get it," Barry said. "Pretty simple of me not to guess it before. You were going to write a note telling all that you had learned in the prison camp and then drop it into the Yank trenches as we went over the lines. Right?"

"Perfectly," nodded S-17.

"IT LOOKS," Barry chuckled, "as though we all had pretty much of a surprise party. But about this information you learned." His face suddenly clouded with uncertainty. "I hope you're ready to spill it now."

"I have complete confidence in you," S-17 said, "if that's what you mean. And having that confidence, I am prepared to tell you what I have learned. In fact, I believe you can be a considerable help to me."

"Good," nodded Barry. "Now we're getting some place. Will you begin, S-17?"

"Yes," nodded the agent. "As I told you before, we have expected a drive somewhere along the Versette sector. But I learned something else that's even more important.

"They are going to make the drive, all right, and they are going to make it at dawn. That isn't so important because we've been preparing for it for some time. However, here's the thing that is of great importance.

"There is a hill with a gradual slope from the south. It ends in a rocky bluff facing the north, overlooking the plain where the Germans will come in this drive,

"Here's what the Germans are terribly afraid of. With the aid of bombs to blast out the reinforcements from the top of that hill the Yanks can storm up it easily and take possession. Our Yank generals have thought of that, but they haven't figured on the bombers to help them out.

"And I learned from the Germans that their artillery is entrenched so deeply on top of that bluff, which is known as hill 63, that our guns, outside of a possible howitzer battery, can't do more than just throw dirt in their faces.

'We've got to get the bombers over them in order to drop bombs down on them effectively. After that there'll be nothing to it. If this takes place just before dawn, the Yanks can be firmly entrenched and with their own artillery and machine guns ready to hurl back the drive of the enemy at dawn. Do I make myself clear?"

"Do you!" Barry shouted. "I'll say so." He was already on his feet.

"Where are you going?" S-17 demanded.

"Where would I be going?" Barry flung back. "Over to the German side of the lines to tell them to lay off? Don't be foolish. We're going to the nearest airdrome. It will be dawn before we know it. We've got to work fast."

S-17 was standing, too.

"Excellent. I know the airdrome we should head for. It isn't the nearest one, but there's a field of big bombers pretty well south of the Versette sector. We'll go there first and get those started before dawn. Then I'll notify the Yanks to follow them up."

"Swell," said Barry. All three turned to the door. "Hurry, Sika. Wind her up," Barry called as they ran toward the plane.

He leaped to the cockpit. S-17 climbed in behind. The motor roared. The moon had settled low so it was almost pitch dark, as the Red Falcon plane rumbled into the air. Barry called through the tube as he climbed and headed west.

"Sika? Let me talk to S-17."

"Yes, master."

"What squadron is that? The 181st bombers?" he asked.

"Right," said S-17, "you've got it."

Barry did have it on the map before him in the dim light of his instrument board lamp and he was heading for it as fast as the Liberty motor would hurl him through the air. Minutes sped by. Twice Barry turned and stared into the black eastern sky.

"I hope," he said to himself, "we get this job done before dawn. It comes earlier this time of year."

The Red Falcon plane was traveling at top speed, and it was faster than any other plane on the Front. But it seemed to the tensely nerved Barry Rand that they were little more than standing still. At last they romped down on the field of the 181st bombers. He made out dimly the gigantic hangars that housed the great Handley-Page lumber wagons.

It was pitch dark, the darkest hour of the night. The hour before dawn. He circled the field to make sure, waited for a gasoline trench to flare up at a far corner of the field as men below recognized the Liberty motor's bark. Then he came down to a swift landing and taxied to the deadline. Mechanics and a ground officer came running out.

"I want to see your commanding officer at once," Barry said.

And at the same time S-17 said, "I want immediate transportation to the Front and divisional headquarters there."

The kiwi officer studied them in the light of his electric torch. He blinked twice at the German uniform of S-17.

"Don't stand there like a dummy!" the Intelligence officer shouted. "I told you I wanted transportation immediately and my friend wants your commanding officer."

"Yes, but," began the kiwi.

"Damn it! You're not supposed to think," snapped S-17. "Not when your superiors tell you what to do. Get going!"

"Y—yes, sir," obeyed the kiwi. He turned abruptly and vanished into the gloom.

"Hell!" barked S-17. "I suppose I'll have to find transportation for myself."

"I guess that Heinie uniform you've got on has him stumped," Barry grinned.

S-17 then vanished in the darkness. A few minutes later the roar of a car starting came to his ears. And about the same time a motorcycle sputtered and screamed to a stop beside the Red Falcon plane.

"What the devil goes on here?" a commanding voice roared. "One of my lieutenants tells me the Red Falcon just landed in his plane with a German aboard."

Barry nodded.

"That's right," he said, "except for the German part of it. Your lieutenant shouldn't jump to conclusions. Remember, all those who wear German uniforms at times aren't Germans. This happened to be S-17 of the Intelligence.

"He has some damned important information. He's just left in a car for divisional headquarters in this sector. He left me here to tell you to get the bombers started at once."

The captain in charge of the field glared at Barry Rand.

"So I'm to send out a flock of bombers on the say-so of a man who's a fugitive from his own country? A deserter from his own army? Is that it?"

"You wouldn't have to take my word for it," Barry snapped, "if it wasn't for the fact that S-17 was in such a hurry. The German artillery placements on hill 63 have got to be blown up. They can only be reached by airplane bombs. They're down too deep.

"As soon as they are out of the way our troops will be ordered to storm up, take the hill and place their guns. All this must happen before dawn, it is—"

Barry half turned and stared. There were very faint streaks in the east now.

"Hells bells!" he exploded. "It will be dawn before I get through arguing with you."

"There will be a million dawns before I'll send my bombers out on the word of a renegade like you," the captain flamed.

AS HE finished speaking Barry saw him shift the light from his right to his left hand. Then he saw that right hand move downward significantly. Barry Rand moved with lightning speed. His foot came up and kicked the light out of the captain's hand. And as it fell he jerked his own gun from its holster, leveled with the captain.

"All right, you lousy example of an American officer," he cracked. "One false move out of you and I'll drill you with pleasure."

With his eyes still on the officer who was reaching for sky now, Barry reached down and recovered the flashlight. He straightened.

"Now," he said, "turn around and show me where the bombs are kept. If you won't send over bombers we'll take them over ourselves. And, Sika, you climb in the back cockpit and if anyone so much as lays a hand on this ship, you know what to do with them."

"Yes, master," said the giant black.

"Now, about face, forward march, Captain," Barry snapped.

And the captain obeyed without a word. There was no trickery from the captain. He marched ahead of Barry into the nearest hangar. Two mechanics were working on a plane in a dim light.

"Get out six light bombs," the captain ordered. "Put them where I tell you to."

The men obeyed. Each carried three, ahead of the captain. Barry walked behind him, his automatic against his back. They reached the ship.

"Now put them in the racks," Barry commanded.

They obeyed.

"You just stand off to the side, Captain. And you birds," he nodded to the two mechanics, "wing her up."

They did. The Liberty responded with a roar.

"Watch him, Sika," Barry called over his shoulder. "Keep your guns on him and don't let him make a false move."

He spun the Red Falcon plane on its front wheels, covering the sputtering captain with dust. Then they were roaring across the field. Slowly, grudgingly, the Red Falcon plane lifted with its heavy load.

"Master, look. Almost daylight."

Barry glanced to the right.

"Right," he said. "Why couldn't that squadron commander have been a regular guy? Most of them are in the air service."

Barry pushed on the throttle again and again to make sure it was wide open. Would they never reach the crest of hill 63? It seemed that hours passed before they could see it, but actually it was only a very few minutes. Barry climbed to a thousand feet and held that altitude. Once, twice he heard the crackle of gunfire from behind the Yank lines.

"Some poor damn fools got to be shooting at something or they aren't happy."

But there were no shots fired when he dropped altitude and flew low over the Front lines of the Yank forces and just south of hill 63. There seemed to be nervous tension in the air. A nervous tension that broke suddenly at sight of that crimson plane bearing no identification markings. And Barry Rand was flying low enough so that the men in the trenches could see the bombs in their racks. He couldn't hear their shouts, but he could see them waving frantically.

Then a deafening rattle burst forth. A rattle accompanied by the drumming of steel on wing and fuselage covering. The machine guns along the breastworks of hill 63 had stuttered into action. But Barry had sensed what was coming an instant before that deadly fire broke out.

The Red Falcon plane began to buck and leap like a thing possessed, throwing the gunners off their aim. He swerved in a tight vertical to the right along the hill. He swerved back again in 180 degree turn. Now he was thundering over the crest of the hill. He could look down and see the gun placements. He pulled the bomb release levers twice.

Blam! Blam!

The Red Falcon plane shot up, pushed high in the air by the explosion. Instantly Barry was hurling over in a steep chandelle, racing back at those gun placements. He saw two deep holes there and three disabled guns at the other end. Again he pulled his bomb levers.

Blam!

BARRY hurled the crimson plane over on one ear. Fokkers had charged out of the north. He crouched over his stick and took aim. Pressed his triggers. White tracers fluffed out. Another Fokker went down. He straightened his course, tramped on his triggers again and kicked the rudder viciously, spraying the remaining five Fokkers with his lead. They veered away to dodge his fire and as they turned Barry banked over and screamed down for the third time on the enemy gun placements on hill 63.

Tac-tac-tac! Tac-tac-ta-c! Tac-tac-tac!

Sika was raving from the side of his twin Lewis guns. Then Barry was romping down over the three remaining guncrews in their deep entrenchments. He pulled the bomb release, let go his two remaining eggs.

He whirled and stared back over the tail. The whole hilltop was gutted now except for two or three machine-gun nests. Sika was firing behind, holding back the Fokkers as Barry climbed. He swung to look the other way and down. Yanks were storming out of their trenches in front of the first of those three machine gun nests.

Barry whipped over, opened his guns as he dived and poured lead and death into those three nests. Then he zoomed again, high out of reach of the Fokkers as they tried desperately to follow him.

Barry saw Yanks of the infantry storming up that hill. Saw them take possession. And a moment later guns were being moved up in their wake. Artillery guns that had been waiting under camouflage. He stared north of the hill. The German drive was starting. He saw Boches by the hundreds running across that plain to back up the advance of the men in the Front line trenches. The advance that wasn't doing so well.

Then Yank guns were going into action along the northern crest of hill 63 and the attacking Germans began to fall before that deadly barrage.

Then Barry Rand turned the Red Falcon plane back toward the rising sun.

"Well, I guess that's that," he said through the tube to Sika.

"Yes, master," came back the reply. "But why you not wait to see the full victory?"

Barry shook his head.

"Too much blood," he said. "I want to get back while I still have an appetite for breakfast."

FREDERICK BLAKESLEE
The Apache Patrol

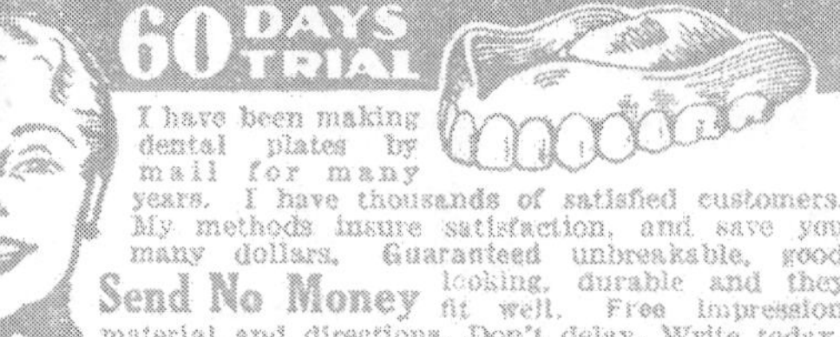

Steel churches strung out in a line behind the German front—They puzzled Barry Rand, but it wasn't until he was locked in jail in a terror-mad Paris, that he knew their purpose, that he realized the Red Falcon must defy death to fly a buccaneer, T.N.T. patrol!

The Apache Patrol

THE strains of the Darktown Strutter's Ball sizzled through the teeth of Barry Rand. The Red Falcon crate, fastest on the Front, was screaming through enemy skies, but there was nothing grim about her this morning. The Red Falcon was in a cheerful mood. And Sika, his giant black aide in the rear cockpit, was even more eager than Barry Rand himself. For Sika was standing there, grinning from ear to ear. He had been that way since they had taken off from their mountain aerie shortly after dawn.

Then, slowly a troubled look came over the face of the great black Senegalese chieftain.

"Master," he called through the tube, "we not headed for Paris. We over Germany. Going deeper into Germany."

Barry Rand didn't stop whistling until he had finished another verse of his favorite tune.

"Thought we ought to take a turn around enemy country before we set down at Le Bourget. You never can tell when there's something going on."

"Yes, Master. But we be late for getting the medals," Sika objected.

"If it hadn't been for you wanting those medals so badly," Barry said, "we wouldn't be coming to Paris for this excursion. You'll find, big boy, that medals don't help much when you want to buy bread and butter."

"Yes, Master," Sika objected. "Sika know that. But maybe it would be better if we come back and accept invitation of Allies to take us with them again. Maybe they mean all right this time."

"Maybe the ones who invited us mean all right, but there are others," Barry corrected.

"But the high commanders, Master. They asked us to come and receive medals. The high commanders have the say, Master."

Barry nodded.

"Maybe," he said. "But some of those birds are like women. They have a right to change their mind."

The Red Falcon plane soared on, snorting defiantly high above the back German country. Five minutes later Sika raised another objection.

"But Master," he said, "we not even headed for Paris now. We going back farther and farther into Germany. We not get there in time."

"We're parallel to the lines, Sika. See the smoke line to the south of us? We're running even with that. And what if we are late? Let the brass hats wait for us a while. I've spent too much time waiting for them. All you're thinking of is the string of medals you can get on your chest."

"But Master," Sika said softly, almost hurt, "Sika can't help feeling proud of such things. Of being even a small part of you, the great Red Falcon, Master."

Barry Rand chuckled.

"If you weren't so black, Sika, I'd say that there was some blarney Irish in you."

Then he stopped, straightened and leaned over the edge of the cockpit. The Red Falcon was staring down, down several thousand feet. Down at a red glow which, even from that distance, was almost blinding.

"Hey," he called back to Sika, "what do you see down there? No, on the other side. See it? A red glow that almost blinds you."

"Sika see, Master. Sika not know."

"Neither do I," snapped Barry all alert now. "We're going down and find out. It comes from that building. Funny looking thing. Damned if it doesn't look like a church."

They tore down, down for the spot on the earth. Then Sika called out as they raced.

"Master! Look to left and farther to west. See? Another red glow. Another building like that one."

Barry swung over to the other side of his cockpit and stared.

"You're right," he agreed.

They were racing nearer and nearer the first building.

"Master," exclaimed Sika, "the second red light gone out now."

"So has this one. No! It is on again in another part of the building. If that isn't the—"

Barry Rand stopped short and gaped. They were at least ten miles behind the Front at the point where the lines dipped down to the south and then swung back up along the Belgian front.

"Sika!"

"Yes, Master."

"See anything queer about the place?"

"Everything queer," came the answer.

"Yes, but I mean do you see any men about that building?"

A pause for a moment and then came a "No, Master," through the tube that connected their two cockpits.

"No, sir," Barry agreed, "not a soul outside that building. Wait a minute. There goes a truck moving north. A truck that, I've got a hunch, just dropped a load at that church."

"You think it a church?" Sika enquired.

"If it isn't I don't know what it can be," Barry flung back.

He was leaning over, examining the building from an altitude of five hundred feet now. He was still in his dive, hurtling down at full speed with the Liberty running wide open and the plane was shuddering with the strain.

Bam!

He pulled up right in front of the church. The red glow had vanished and the bare edifice stood, apparently deserted.

Jerking upward in a long zoom, he roared for the second building, at the same time yelling to Sika.

"Say, big boy. There was someone watching us through the crack of the front door. I saw the door open just as we roared past."

"Somebody inside all right. Or how would red light come?"

"I can't figure how it would shine through, anyway," Barry said.

"That building is built of steel. And how a light could shine through steel is beyond me."

They were tearing for the next church building, which was situated almost due west from the first. Then Barry's eyes caught sight of a third. It was in line with the other two and about three miles west from the second. And a red glow was coming from it.

He thundered past the back of the second church, saw no movement, banked, chandelled and came slamming past the front of the building. Nothing there either. The place looked deserted.

Just then Sika let out a yell.

"Master! The church we just left has red glow again."

Barry spun around in his seat and stared back. That was true. The blinding glare was coming now from a corner of the edifice.

He shrugged and his brow furrowed in perplexity as he screamed toward the third church.

It was like the first and second both in abandoned appearance and the fact that it gave out a blinding red glow from one corner.

He dived down, passed and climbed again. Then to his amazement he saw another and another of those churches stretching in a straight line parallel to the Front while he stared Sika pounded on the cowling that separated them.

"Master! Master!" he shouted through the tube. "Enemy planes. Fokkers. Come out of the sun."

BARRY whirled in his seat and stared behind. Raising his thumb before his right eye, he closed the other eye and squinted into the sun. Yes, Sika was right. Enemy planes were diving out of the sun. Five of them. No, seven.

The Red Falcon bared his teeth in a grin. Here at least was something to break the monotony of trying to figure out the reason for this line of churches.

He whipped over in a tight vertical, pushed on the throttle and prepared for the fight that was to come. Seven against one. But the odds were about even because the Red Falcon had proved many times that these German pursuits were no match for his two-seater.

Two and then a third Fokker suddenly banked and turned back

when the pilots came close enough to recognize that blood red crate. The other four held their course; Spandau guns rattled as they warmed them.

Barry Rand clamped down on his triggers. All four front guns bellowed in answer to the challenge—the two Vickers on top of the Liberty motor and the twin Spandaus, one on either side. He was ready.

Tac-tac-tac!

The shots of the leaders' guns cut toward them, streaming yellow tracers. Barry Rand moved the controls ever so lightly. The Red Falcon plane answered instantly to his touch. Then he was spraying all four in the formation with the lead from his four nose guns.

Bam!

Two of the Fokkers zoomed and two banked and hurled away from each other in steep turns.

Tac-tac-tac!

Sika's guns burst into action. There was a blast of Lewis chatter and one of the Fokkers plunged. Another was stalling at the top of its zoom. Barry had gotten that one. The other two turned back and raced for their home drome with all possible speed.

"We chase them, Master?'" Sika yelled eagerly.

"Haven't time," Barry grinned. "You've forgotten our date with the generals, big boy. Remember those medals. We've got just time to make it from here if you want to. Personally I'd just as soon not show up."

"The medals, Master. Sika forgot," came the reply. "Sika want the medals."

"Okay, then, here we go. And while we fly to Paris, you figure out why all those churches are strung out in line ten miles behind the Front."

But when they circled Le Bourget Field an hour later and came down to land, neither Sika nor Barry Rand had been able to figure out the answer.

There was a crowd of Allied soldiers waiting for the famous crimson plane. Men packed about them when they climbed out of the cockpit. Men eager to shake their hands.

A big staff car, boasting a starry flag on the radiator cap, was waiting for them. They were ushered into it with much dignity. An American general was waiting in the rear seat for them.

His face was beaming and he greeted them with much enthusiasm. A band was playing when they left the field.

Barry glanced past the general at his giant black. Sika was sitting there, a marvelous specimen of a man, straight and broad-shouldered and powerful. And his intelligent black face was wrinkled in a constant grin of pleasure that showed his perfect, even, white teeth.

That ride through the streets of Paris to the parade grounds could not have been more grand if it had been the triumphal entry of a monarch to his throne. Even Barry began to thrill as two Yank bands struck up the marching tunes that he had known when he was in regular standing with his outfit, months before.

At the parade grounds, soldiers of every Allied nation stood at attention with arms presented as the medals were pinned on Barry Rand and Sika. There were three medals—one from France, one from Great Britain and one from Barry's own United States. Citations were read before presenting each medal—read in a mumbled or shouted tone that in either case was hard to understand.

After that there was a review of the troops, with Barry Rand and Sika standing proudly among the high commanders while the troops passed to martial marching music. Then—

Barry's heart seemed to be a huge lump in his throat as he stood and listened, scarcely believing his ears. For the review march pepped up to double time and the massed bands played, not the Star Spangled Banner, nor any martial air, but his own favorite ragtime tune, "The Darktown Strutter's Ball."

And how that band could play it! He had a hard time keeping his feet still. Generals with twinkling eyes shot sidelong glances at him to see how he was taking it. And they could tell easily because Barry Rand was grinning from ear to ear and his eyes were misty.

Then the crowd broke up and he was hurried into the same car with Sika and the general who had conducted them from Le Bourget.

A banquet followed. Speeches. Barry Rand and Sika were called upon, but they were both stumped.

The black officers of Sika's Wampana warriors were present, too; the men who had known him for years as their chief. Barry Rand tasted some things that he hadn't eaten since he had fled to his mountain aerie. And the broad grin never left the great black face of Sika.

The banquet lasted until well along in the afternoon. Then came a conference with the great commander and two lesser generals. The commander addressed them gravely.

"Rand," he said. "I believe you've been approached before on this subject, and have turned it down. But we are asking you once more to join us with full pardon. You and your aide will be given high commissions. You, Rand, will be made a colonel and your aide, Sika, will be commissioned a major. If you accept you will never again be forced to obtain your supplies by the pirate methods that you have been forced to use. We want you both, Red Falcon.

BARRY RAND squirmed uneasily. He had seen this thing coming, had seen it tried out before. And it hadn't worked. Even high commanders were too human. They would be suspicious—watching for a slip-up. But still he yearned to be back with his own, to be working directly with the Allies with all of their resources at his command. He thought of what he could do with a set-up like that.

He stood up to speak.

"I'll take a little time to think over the offer, general," he said. "I'd like nothing better than to be able to come out of hiding and fight alongside of my own people instead of playing a lone hand. It sometimes gets rather lonesome. We're outcasts and we know and feel it, gentlemen. Yet we want to be sure that we're doing the right thing—for everybody concerned. As I say, we'll consider the matter and let you know. In the meantime I want to speak of something that seems of much more importance."

There was a dead silence in the room while Barry paused.

"On the way over this morning we flew about ten miles into Germany, and we saw something very strange. Have you any record of five or six churches, in a straight line parallel to the Front?"

The general's eyes widened.

"Why, no," he said. "Churches? I don't quite understand. You mean they are new buildings?"

"They seem to be," the Red Falcon answered. "But the queerest part is that each one of them sends out a blinding red light that shines right through the roofs and the sides of the buildings.

"When we came close enough the red-glow went out and there was only the church there, with not a soul nearby although we spotted a truck that had just left the first one, and saw someone peering out at us through a crack in the slightly open front door."

The eyes of all three of the high commanders opened wide with interest. Then came perplexed frowns. They wagged their heads.

"I can't understand such a thing," the general remarked. "Have you any idea what it might mean?"

Barry Rand shook his head.

"I can't figure it out at all," he replied. "I thought perhaps you gentlemen might have some information from Allied Intelligence agents on the other side of the lines."

The general shook his head sadly.

"I'm sorry to report," he said, "that in one sector our spies have not been doing so well. We haven't heard from them in the Mareus sector for more than a week."

Barry Rand stiffened a little.

"That makes it look all the more as though those buildings are more than mere churches," he said.

"What makes you say that?" demanded the general.

"Because," Barry said, "the churches are right north of the Mareus sector, and it is very obvious that the enemy has made a complete cleanup on the poor devils who have been spying for us there."

The general took a long, deep breath.

"We can't let this excite us too much. Nothing has happened from those 'churches', as you call them. Queer things occur every day of this war and you must not let this prey on your mind."

Barry Rand shrugged his broad shoulders and nodded.

"I'd like nothing better than to forget it for the time being, myself," he said, "but I can't get it out of my mind—can't think of anything else, in fact."

"I'll tell you something that will get it out of your mind for a time at least," remarked another high-ranking officer—General Single. "Let me conduct you and your aide through the Paris night life. I can assure you that there will be diversion in that."

"Good idea," agreed the commander. "General Single is well versed in the night life of Paris. He can show you everything from the Folies Bergere to the low dives that are frequented by the apache. He took me down through the latter section one night and I can assure you that my head was swimming before we were through. I wouldn't want a great deal of it but one night is indeed something to take one's mind from war and its horrors."

Barry nodded with a grin.

"That certainly would be a treat for us, wouldn't it, Sika?"

The big black chief nodded eagerly.

Dinner at the Crystal Palace was followed by a visit to the Folies Bergere, and toward midnight, started to invade the lower quarter of Paris, the section where the apaches and sewer rats swarmed until dawn.

As they left the Folies Bergere and stepped into a cab, Sika bumped against Barry Rand.

"Master, someone follow you," he whispered. "He get in cab right behind. Not a man with money, Master—very bad looking."

General Single turned and stared through the rear window of the cab.

"That is queer," he admitted. "That fellow doesn't look any too good to me. They come tough, these apaches."

Barry turned too and got a glimpse of the man Sika had seen. He was a slim, but sinewy figure, with an ugly face, his nose bent to one side, one ear gone completely and dark, ominous eyes.

Barry Rand laughed.

"He looks tough," he said, "but I'll gamble he isn't so tough when things begin to get hot."

"Just the same," General Single ventured, "I don't like it. Don't know but we'd better give up this trip to the underworld. That is, for tonight. It looks almost as though he has us spotted."

"Spotted for what?" Barry demanded.

The general shrugged.

"One can never tell about those fellows. They'd cut your heart out and eat it for a franc. And for a hundred francs they'd take on the President of France, guards and all."

"Swell," Barry grinned. "Let's go. I've heard about things like this but never seen them. I could handle a little excitement tonight."

The general looked at him strangely. Then he shrugged again and spoke in French to the driver of the cab.

They rolled off. The streets grew narrower and narrower. Now and then General Single glanced nervously back through the rear window.

"That cab that the apache got in is still following us," he said. He leaned forward to the driver and ordered. "Turn back for the main part of Paris."

The cab turned back and they started back.

"Now," ordered the general, "turn this way and that—try to lose the cab that is following us."

The driver did what he was told. Single continued to stare back. He shook his head.

"I don't like it," he said. "If I had my choice I'd go back to my hotel and stay there. That fellow hasn't any good in mind, I can assure you of that."

Barry grinned.

"I've got my heart set on the apache dives," he said. "The driver will know the way, general. If you wish, we'll take you back to your hotel and then go on ourselves."

General Single hesitated.

"You're sure you wouldn't mind?" he said. "Wait, I'll ask the driver." He asked him in French if he knew the dives of lower Paris well. The driver grinned and nodded emphatically.

"In that case," ventured the general, "I think I will return to my hotel. I—er—have some work that I should get done tonight. I just thought of it."

"Sure," said Barry Rand. But he was thinking. "So you're the stuff that they make generals of?"

THE cab returned to the general's hotel. He apologized again at leaving but Barry only laughed. Then Barry and Sika rolled away out into traffic and the cab behind continued to follow them. Barry looked back now and his brow furrowed.

"Just the same," he said, "I do wonder what that guy is shadowing us for. Maybe he's going to try to get revenge for something he thinks we've done."

Sika said, "He look like bad man, to Sika."

"Yeah," agreed Barry, "but my curiosity is aroused. I'm going to find out what he wants."

He ordered the cab to stop at the curb. The other taxi stopped right behind them. Barry Rand got out, Sika beside him. They were a formidable pair as they walked the few feet along the dark sidewalk to where the Apache was getting out of his cab.

The fellow was smiling, an ugly smile that showed rotten teeth in the front of his mouth. But it seemed a friendly enough grin at that. He bowed and his words came swiftly in French—so fast that Barry had difficulty in following him.

"*Monsieur*, I have tried to see you. But always the general, he is with you. I have something that I believe you will be interested in. Something about the war, *monsieur*."

Barry nodded.

"Okay," he said. "Let's have it."

The apache looked around with his ugly dark eyes under the brim of his slantwise cap. An angry gleam came into them.

"*Mon dieu!*" he exclaimed, "we cannot talk here. You will come with me to a place where I will lead you, yes?"

"Wait," said Barry. "You say this is about the war?"

"*Oui, monsieur*," the apache nodded eagerly. "It is something—that I find out—something that will have a great deal to do with saving Paris, *monsieur*."

Barry Rand didn't hesitate for a second then. A third cab slowed by the curb behind theirs and stopped. A group of soldiers came swinging along through the darkness. They were singing a strange song in a strange tongue. Yet Barry thought he had heard those words and that song before.

"Okay," he said. "Let's go."

The apache turned toward his car, saw the other behind his, and turned back.

"If it will be all right I will pay my driver, *monsieur*, and then go on in your machine."

"Okay. But let's get going," Barry answered.

The driver paid and the apache returned and slipped into their cab. Then they were snorting through the narrow, dark streets, the driver being guided by the stranger.

Twice Barry looked back. He thought there was a car following them at a good distance. The apache noticed it too. He turned.

"*Monsieur,* do you know who is following us?"

Barry shook his head.

"Perhaps friends of yours, or the police?"

"So far as I know, nobody knows we're in this car," Barry said.

They rolled on among the narrow streets once more. Then the apache ordered the car stopped before one of the most dilapidated and filthy structures Barry had ever seen. He got out, waited while Barry paid for the cab and it drove off. The other car slowed and came nearer. Then it picked up speed and pulled past.

Barry tried to look into the rear windows as it rounded by but he could see nothing distinctly. Nothing, that is, but the driver and the faintest hint of faces in the rear.

He turned and stared about in the night for the apache. He had gone. Just then swallowed up in the darkness. Then he came out of the shadow without explanation.

"We go in here, *monsieur,*" he said.

He led them through a low, slanting doorway. Sika had to bend almost double to make it. Inside it was dimly lighted. A nearly naked woman danced a hideous dance and ghastly looking humans sat about at tables, drinking and talking as though they were bored.

Barry felt the eyes of most of the patrons following them as they entered. Yes, they would soon know that the Red Falcon was in the dive with his aide. Few could help but recognize Barry Rand and Sika.

The apache led them to a table in a far corner. They sat down. There was a restless movement in the dive. Other figures, even more ugly looking than the stranger that sat with them, began moving to tables nearer them.

Barry Rand slipped his hand to the butt of his automatic. It wasn't any too reassuring in here. Then when his hand touched the holster he straightened with a start. The automatic was gone.

He whirled and faced the apache angrily but the stranger had already anticipated him. He smiled that ugly grin again.

"*Monsieur* misses his guns? Both are gone. We could not take the chance, monsieur. We must talk without danger."

Barry took a long breath. The other horrible looking filth-mongers of the underworld were creeping closer to them. They were completely surrounded by now but no one was very near, though they all seemed to be in on the plot—whatever it might be.

The apache began talking in a harsh whisper.

"One of us has gotten information from the house of a German spy—the headquarters, *monsieur,* for the German spies in Paris.

Barry nodded with interest.

"Okay" he said. "Let's hear about it?"

The apache grinned greedily.

"I first tell you this—that Paris is in great danger. An hour before dawn the entire city of Paris will be—"

He broke off in a cackling laugh.

"But not so much. Perhaps this way; Paris is in great danger. Germans plan to destroy Paris and the destruction will begin an hour before dawn. The method is known to us here, for we have heard the plans. We know how this destruction can be stopped. You will stop it. We will tell you where it comes from so that you can fly with your plane and do the work."

"I'm waiting to hear about it," Barry Rand said.

"But not yet," grinned the apache. "This will come when you have gotten us the money for our work. We sell our services to the rich *americains.* It is not reasonable? We will get the money, you will receive the credit and Paris, it will be saved. Everyone will be satisfied."

Barry Rand surveyed the situation from where he sat. Neither he nor Sika had guns. Besides that, the others in the room, and the number seemed to have grown greatly, were crowding up in that end.

THEY wouldn't have a chance in a fight, even with Sika to help for there was another Apache who was even larger than Sika, not six feet away. Might as well play along until he found out all about things at least. Perhaps these cutthroats did have something of great importance. It would be just as well to listen.

"Just what do you want me to do, go to the commanders of the Americans and ask them for the money?" he demanded.

"*Oui*," nodded the other. "*Oui, monsieur.* You were with a general when I saw you tonight. Go back to him and tell him that we will help by giving our secret if he will arrange payment at once.

"And the price?" Barry Rand asked.

"Twenty thousand francs," came back the answer instantly.

Barry Rand was a bit stunned by the meagerness of the figure. Why, that was less than five thousand dollars in American money. That shouldn't be hard to get.

He got up from his chair with an air of finality.

"I'll see what I can do," he said. He knew there was no use asking for further information about the menace that threatened Paris. "You will, of course, give me the information as to where the German spy headquarters is located in Paris?"

"*Oui oui, monsieur*," the Apache replied.

Sika rose and followed the Red Falcon to the door. The apache moved ahead of them with a cat-like stride. The others parted and made way for them to pass between the tables.

Barry reached the door and stepped outside. Sika would be right behind him. He half turned to make sure, heard a scuffling sound and then:

Thunk!

That sound came from a heavy club descending on the great head of his black aide—from behind. The blow had been dealt by the giant apache who had been sitting within a few feet of them when the conference was in progress.

Barry tried to leap back into the dive. But the door slammed in his face and he heard a bolt slam home. Then the voice of the apache who had followed and talked to them came through the heavy door.

"We keep the black one here—until you return."

Barry Rand stepped back, got a running start and hurled himself against the door. It trembled only slightly as his shoulder connected with it, that was all. His shoulder felt as though it were broken. He stood close to the door and shouted back.

"You'll let me in or the deal is off. I'll have a dozen *gendarmes* on your necks in five minutes."

"We are leaving now the way that is not known to the *gendarmes, monsieur.* Do not waste time. The sooner you return with the money the sooner your black man will be returned to you, monsieur."

Barry stood outside that door, his hands opening and clenching convulsively. He stared at the door as though it would show him what was going on on the other side. A choking sound came up in his throat, half cough, half sob. Sika in there, out cold. He had seen him falling. And he with nothing to do but try and make the deal. And it must be made at once, too, to save Paris.

Never once did Barry Rand doubt that these apaches knew the truth about something threatening Paris. He thought of the churches. There was something strange there that he couldn't fathom. He dared not take chances.

He turned and ran down the narrow dark street. Shadows vanished before him as he ran—vanished into recesses between ancient and tumble-down buildings.

He ran for blocks before he saw a cab snorting along a wider street. He hailed it and dropped into the back seat, breathing as though his lungs would burst. He shouted the address of the high commander. The cab cackled off through the darkness again.

Later, after a series of squawking horns and weaving in and out of traffic, he leaped out in front of the hotel where the general was staying. He paid the driver and raced for the entrance.

Inside he was—on inquiry—admitted to the suite of the general. The general stared at him, frowned.

"You look as though you'd seen a ghost, Rand," he said. "What in the name of heaven—"

Barry Rand told him what he had seen and heard.

The general's face flushed angrily.

"Rand," he barked, "I'm disappointed, but this is just what I've been told to watch out for in you. So you'd stoop this low to get twenty thousand francs, would you?"

The Red Falcon stiffened. His thin lips came back and his eyes fairly shot sparks.

"You—you think this of me?" he cracked. "You think this is some idea of my own? Why, you—"

"Stop," bellowed the general. "General Single called me after he reached his own hotel tonight. He told me how anxious you were to meet that apache cutthroat. He told me to watch out for something."

"Listen," bellowed the Red Falcon. "Don't you realize what it means? For the love of heaven, general, don't be a fool. If Paris were destroyed the French holding the Front might go crazy and start pushing for the city to try and protect their families. They might—"

He stopped short breathlessly. The general was lifting the phone.

"That's right," he said calmly. "Send up a squad of guards. I've got a madman up here. Yes, at once."

Barry's mouth dropped open. Then he snarled a curse.

"Why, you brainless idiot," he roared. "I'm not in on this. I haven't a thing to do with it. These cutthroats know something.

"It's perfectly reasonable that they should pick up information the way they say. Remember those churches? That may be a part of it. I can't figure it out yet, but—why twenty thousand francs isn't much. You spent more than three times that amount to train every Yank airman that you've got at the Front."

"Yes," the general bellowed back. "Airmen. And what good are they? They come over here thinking they're the pick of the States and they don't know right shoulder-arms from left shoulder-arms. They can't even salute properly."

"Yeah," Barry shot back. "I suppose that damned right and left shoulder arms and the saluting makes men who can knock down spying Germans. That's the trouble—the air service has done wonderful work in spite of you, not with your help. Why, one airman with a good ship—which we never had—could do more than a couple of companies of infantry. And you know it but you wouldn't admit it. Maybe because you haven't even got guts enough to fly."

"To fly?" snarled the general. "That doesn't take guts. The pilots are yellow. Conceited. They want the world on a silver platter and then expect to get decorated for it. Why—"

But that was as far as the great general got. Barry Rand flew at him with fists flailing the air furiously. The general tried to shout a command to stop: tried to cover up when he found that that would do no good.

He went down. The Red Falcon jerked him to his feet again. Let fly with a terrific right to the jaw that sent him hurtling backward just as the door burst open and the guards came in.

They picked Barry Rand up bodily. Four of the guards had to hold him while the other four worked over the punch-drunk general. The general was coming round. He got up with the help of the others.

He stared about him, bewildered for a moment, then his angry eyes rested on Barry Rand. He pointed his finger at him.

"Behind the bars with him," he cracked. "If he isn't shot for this attack upon me I'll miss my guess. But watch him—that's the Red Falcon."

They did watch him closely, too—watched him until they had him behind the barred door of a jail three blocks away. And then two guards stood at his door to make sure that he would stay.

Barry Rand looked out of the little window at the back of his tiny, ill-smelling cell. He began pacing the cell. The two guards watched him. One said to the other:

"He doesn't look so dangerous from here."

"Not half as dangerous as what is going to happen to Paris very shortly," Barry snapped.

"Yeah? I suppose you're on the inside and know all about it. Maybe some of your German friends told you about it."

The two laughed at that. Barry lighted a cigarette. Thoughts were tangling in his brain; a mixture of wild thoughts of Sika and the churches and the menace and the apaches.

AN HOUR passed. A guard yawned and stretched outside the cell, but inside the cell there was a baffled fighting demon, a famous fighter who was at the end of his wits to know what to do.

Then something happened. Something that jerked Barry Rand and the guards outside to an erect position. There came a screaming sound from outside.

Wheeeee!

Then:

Brammmm!

The building they were in rocked from the terrific explosion. Sounds of screaming came from the street. A perfect bedlam started outside. The guards before his cell door cried out in fear.

"The guns," Barry Rand shouted instantly. "Why didn't I think of that before? That's what the apaches heard about—long range guns, and in those churches behind the German lines! That's what it is. I'm sure of it now. Let me out. Quick! I can do something about it."

But the guards had already broken into a run and were part way down the hall in front of his cell. From outside the building, out there above Paris, came the whine of another long range shell.

Wheeeee!

Brammmm!

When Barry Rand heard that scream it sounded too close. He ducked into the corner of his cell, hoping for protection behind the steel-lined walls.

But even with that protection the explosion knocked him half unconscious. A blinding flash in the hall and the building rocked and heaved and seemed to settle again.

It must have been the steel cage he was in that saved him. He was bewildered and shaken. Everything was pitch dark now. All lights had gone out. He heard a groan before his cell door, crept to it.

Wheee!

Brammm!

Another shell burst closely but not in the jail. Barry Rand was feeling through the bars of the cage. He felt a body; felt blood. Then he felt other things—an automatic in a holster, and a bunch of keys.

The explanation was plain. The guard had been blown back against the cell door by the explosion into the other end of the building.

Barry Rand's fingers were trembling a little in his excitement as he took the bunch of keys and the gun. Feverishly he tried one key after another in the lock of his cell door. Then he had the right one. The door opened.

Barry Rand dashed out into the darkness of the blasted hall and felt his way to where he remembered the stairs had been. They were still there, shaky and partly demolished. He crawled down while shrieks and cries rang from outside.

And now the shells were screaming over the city, one every few seconds. And Barry Rand knew the answer. If he could only do something about it!

He had a plan and he was putting it into action as his feet struck the walk outside the building. Here and there a light flared. People jostled. He ran for the hotel where the general was stationed. If the general were there he might—

People were pouring out of the hotel as he reached the entrance. Gun in hand he leaped up the stairs into the lobby, staring at the frightened faces of the people there.

The general was there pulling on his coat as he ran from the stairs into the lobby and for the front door.

Barry Rand stepped aside, then behind the general as he ran. He stuck the gun at his back.

"Quick!" he snapped. "About face. Upstairs to your office. One false move and I'll let you have it, you murderer."

The general turned just enough so that he could see Barry Rand's face. His own was white and strained. Then without a word he turned and started up the stairs again. There was so much bedlam in that lobby that no one seemed to notice the Red Falcon with his gun at the back of the general as they raced up the stairs.

"You'll pay for this," the general panted.

"Maybe," snapped Barry, "but the rest of the people will thank an airman. Get going on the telephone. Order every big bomber at Le Bourget out on the line with a full load of bombs and plenty of flares. We may have to work before it gets daylight."

The general nodded, picked up the phone, and repeated the orders that Barry Rand had given him. When that was done he slammed the phone on the hook. Barry gave more orders.

"We go outside and into our car. We're going to Le Bourget."

They got out of the car as the bombers, three dozen of them, were warming.

Barry walked through the grayish dawn beside the general. He had the automatic under his arm stuck in the general's side as the general shouted Barry's orders to the bombing pilots.

"We'll lead the way in the Red Falcon plane. Follow us. We'll show you where to drop the bombs. When you see the churches ten miles behind the German lines, let go. Blow those churches to hell!"

They reached the Red Falcon plane. The general hesitated.

"You really don't mean that I'm to go with you?" he asked hesitantly.

"Nothing else but," snapped Barry. "Climb into the front cockpit where I can watch you. I'll fly from behind, this time. And maybe you'll see why a bunch of yellow, conceited prigs can't make pilots. Hang on, we're off!"

The Liberty thundered and they were racing across the field, taking the air while the bombers rose sluggishly with their huge loads.

Barry throttled the motor back and climbed above the bombers. Stayed with them. And while he climbed he ticked off a message of general orders on the wireless of the back seat.

> *GENERAL ORDERS TO ALL PURSUIT SQUADRONS WITHIN FIFTY MILES OF MAREUS SECTOR. TAKE OFF AT ONCE. JOIN BOMBERS AND CONVOY TEN MILES NORTH OF LINES IN THAT SECTOR.*

THEY hurled on. It was growing lighter and lighter. They were tearing across the lines and No-Man's-Land at five thousand feet.

And while they hurled on, Barry's thoughts were divided between the churches ahead and Sika somewhere under Paris in the sewers. A lump rose in his throat. They'd kill Sika sure. They'd—

He came up stiff in the seat. Stared ahead. Enemy planes were coming at them and this Red Falcon plane was the only convoy the bombers had.

He shouted to the general through the tube.

"We'll try your hand at target practice now and see how you go with those nose guns. I'll try to give you some shots."

"Thank you," the general said meekly.

He went straight for that five-plane flight of Fokkers.

"Get ready and pull the triggers when I tell you to, general," he shouted through the tube.

"Right," snapped the general. He was hunched forward glaring over the sights. They tore on. Closer. Spandaus warmed now.

Tac-tac-tac!

"Let 'em have it, general," Barry shouted.

At the same time he squeezed the stick between his knees and dropped his twin Lewis guns and let drive at the Fokker on the right tip of the formation.

Two Fokkers went hurtling down. Then a flight of Nieuports came screaming out of the sky above and the Fokkers turned and ran for it.

Barry pulled over and caught sight of two churches below. He screamed down past the bombers and pointed them out. Two of the bombers dived for closer attack; and while they bombed those two buildings the Red Falcon led the other bombers on and on toward the other church-like structures in the line.

And when he saw them go up in flashes of flame and smoke and saw great guns sticking out in the wide steeples he knew all the answer. The blinding red glows had come from welding torches from the inside; that was it. Those churches were made of steel, welded together quickly, and only the great bombs carried by the big boys of the army could do the trick.

One after another, those church-like structures were blown to bits. The giant, long-range guns that had been battering Paris were bent and destroyed. And then the end of the line was reached.

With a sinking feeling, Barry Rand turned the Red Falcon plane back toward Le Bourget. He felt he would never see Sika again, but he'd do his darndest to find him even if he had to plow Paris up by the roots, if he could get the general's permission.

But no word came from the general until they landed at Le Bourget. Then it was quite unexpected.

"I'm sorry, Rand," he said. "Mighty sorry. I was wrong—wrong about everything, airmen and you."

Barry nodded solemnly.

"I think with you generals changing your mind like a bunch of women," he said, "you can understand just why I don't line up back in your outfits as you suggested. I think it's better as it is, general."

"As you wish," said the general. "And will you shake my hand now to show that there are no hard feelings, Rand?"

"Gladly," said Barry Rand.

But before he extended his hand he ripped off the three medals that he had received, and when his hand came away from the general's after a short shake, he left the medals there.

Then before either could speak, something caught his eye. It was a group of blackmen running toward him and the Red Falcon plane. And Sika was leading them.

They flung arms about each other and danced about like lunatics in their joyous reunion. And when Sika had time he explained.

"Wampana follow me," he said. "They afraid something happen to me in Paris. Some of my under chiefs were in car that followed. Then they waited and saw you come out alone and saw me get hit over head. They went in. All my Wampana. Master, that was a fight. Apache against Wampana. Men of sewer get licked. My people bring out Sika this morning. You all right, Master?"

"Never better," Barry grinned. "And I'm just prime for one of your breakfasts, Sika. We've got time to get back to the camp for it and it's a swell morning for flying to work up an appetite."

"Yes, Master," Sika grinned.

They climbed into their cockpits, Barry in the front and Sika behind. The giant black stood up in the rear cockpit where his medals glistened in the sun. A cheer went up from his Wampana blacks, and they were not the only ones who came in on that cheer.

Then the Liberty blasted and Barry Rand waved good-by to the gang—to a life of closer contact with his fellow-men, his own kind, which might have been—but just wasn't to be.

He was silent for the first few minutes. Then the tune began to take shape on his lips and he sat back while the Liberty boomed and let go in full-throated song—the Darktown Strutter's Ball.

The
Tom-Tom
Ace

Boom-boom-boom! Through the twilight beat the throb of savage drums—an S.O.S. call from the Wampanas. And the Red Falcon, rushing to their aid, didn't guess their full message, didn't know that before the night was over he and Sika would be slashing flame gorged skies on a madman's mission!

The Tom-Tom Ace

FROM the top of Saar Mountain the setting sun looked like a great gold disc standing on edge on the western horizon.

Under the trees beside the little cabin that was the home of the Red Falcon and his giant black Wampana chieftain, Sika stood motionless.

Before him, more than waist-high, was a big African drum. The black's hands lay lightly upon it and he was tense, listening.

Barry Rand, coming out of the cabin, spied him. A smile spread over his weatherbeaten face. He began creeping up behind the black giant very softly.

As he approached, the Red Falcon stooped and picked up a small handful of pebbles. He crept up, step by step, then he tossed the stones gently toward the drum.

The stones showered down on the drum head with a resonant plunking sound. The big black's body never moved. Only his head turned on his massive shoulders, and his black eyes focused on his master.

Then the head shook back and forth in the negative.

"Shhhhh," he whispered, "Sika listen. I tell you in a minute, master."

Barry Rand came closer. He stood beside the drum, motionless, but at first he could hear nothing.

His eyes wandered and then focused on the drum head. Some of the pebbles that he had tossed had remained on the drum head. Suddenly, inexplicably, they began to move in a rhythmic, dancing motion.

Barry leaned over, fascinated. The big black lifted his hands from the drum head and the movement of the pebbles increased. They danced and jarred from the center of the drum until they were fairly hopping up and down.

At that moment, with his head bent over close to the drum, Barry Rand began to hear the throbbing beat. It seemed as he listened that he felt its pulsations through the air more vibrantly than he could hear them. It was the cadency of the very air itself.

"Master," Sika announced, "my people, my Wampana warriors, are in trouble. They want me to come to them and give them advice."

Barry looked up quickly for a moment, then his eyes shifted instantly to the drum head once more.

He nodded. He heard what Sika said, but something else was holding his interest at that moment.

"Look," he said, "at those pebbles doing a dance on top of that drum."

Sika nodded with little show of interest.

"Yes, master," he admitted, "always do that when drums in tune. Beating of other drum in same tune as this vibrate through air and make head of this drum vibrate, too. You cannot hardly hear other drum beat, many miles away. But Sika, with hands on head of this drum, can hear."

"You mean feel it, Sika," Barry corrected.

The big black shrugged.

"Maybe feel, maybe hear, master. Maybe both. My people say—"

"Yes, I know," Barry nodded. "We'll take care of that in a minute. But this is a new one on me. You say that if the drums are in tune the beating of one will vibrate the other?"

"Yes, master."

"How in the devil do you tune a drum?" Barry demanded.

"Same size drum, master," Sika explained, "then draw skin so make same noise. Like you tune piano or fiddle, master."

"I never thought of that, Sika," Barry admitted. "I suppose a drum head does have a certain note just like the string on a musical instrument. Look there—almost all the pebbles have bounced off the top of the drum onto the ground."

"Yes, master." Sika nodded. "Would do that with bigger stones if other drum was closer."

"Say, that is something, isn't it?" Barry ventured.

"But, master," Sika began, "my people in trouble. They send message."

Barry turned his eyes from the drum head quickly. All the pebbles had been shaken off.

"Right," he nodded. "I guess I've got this other thing settled in my mind. Damned interesting, but about this message. What's wrong with the Wampana?"

"Wampana in trouble, master," Sika repeated gravely. "M'gunda tell me on drum. French officer in charge of Wampana regiment want to make them go in fight where no white man go."

"Huh?" queried Barry. "What's that?"

"That what M'gunda say, master," Sika repeated solemnly.

"Yeah," Barry frowned, "but is that all?"

"That all M'Gunda say except 'please come quick, Sika."

The Red Falcon gave a short nod.

"Okay," he said. "Wind up the old red crate and we'll shove off. Are they in the same place they were before?"

"Yes, master—" hastily.

The giant black chief picked up his message drum. With it tucked under his arm he strode around the corner of the cabin to the door. Barry went in first. They both came out with their helmets and goggles. Sika carried the drum to the Red Falcon plane hidden under the trees on the other side of the cabin.

"Going to take that along with you?" Barry asked.

"Yes, master," Sika answered—then—"if it all right with you."

"Sure, if you got any place to put it."

"Sika put it behind his cockpit. It be all right."

He stowed it away and then stepped before the prop.

"Never know when maybe need drum at time like this. Maybe they not let us see M'Gunda and have to talk to him with drum again."

"Okay, big boy," Sika called. "Switch off."

The great propeller whirled and there came a hissing sound from the engine as gas was sucked into the motor.

The big black stepped away.

"Contact!" Barry roared.

Wam!

The great prop spun. The Liberty motor in the nose of the Red Falcon plane crackled and barked and then throbbed.

A few minutes for warming. Barry tested controls and watched his instruments while the motor warmed. He glanced at the sky; the sun was just visible over the top of the horizon.

Barry Rand taxied out on the flat top of Saar Mountain and turned into the wind. The Liberty roared out and they thundered into the air, then dropped into the canyon that led them secretly from their hideout.

As they broke out of the lower end of the canyon into the open and screamed three thousand feet over the flatter country west of the Vosges Mountains, Sika's voice came through the tube.

"Master, you not forget that we need gas."

"I was thinking about that," Barry answered. "The Wampana are stationed ten miles behind the Front at the Greville sector, aren't they?"

"Yes, master," Barry called.

"Right near there, beside a field where we've landed before, there's a truck and tractor depot. Ought to be able to get some gas there."

"Maybe they try to arrest us, master."

"I don't think those Frogs will try to pull that until we try to leave, anyway," Barry ventured. "Got to take that chance. But about your Wampana warriors—I can't figure out how any human being would send your men in where it would be certain suicide—where he wouldn't send white men. He must be a fine kind of a skunk."

"Something wrong, master. Sika not know."

"Well, we're going to find out mighty soon." A pause and then Barry shouted, "Hey, what's that. Maybe—"

THE Red Falcon plane had been screaming through the air at a good hundred-and-eighty when he spoke. He had turned his head so that his eyes traveled toward the northwest. The sun was out of sight and they had only the twilight to show them the way.

Barry was pointing to a high ridge of rock far off in that direction. Even at that distance they could make out tiny points of flame coming from the top of the mountain.

"Isn't that Gardemont, as the French call it?" Barry asked. "The Mountain that is naturally guarded?"

Sika stared.

"Yes, master, that Gardemont, all right."

"The Yanks and French must have pushed the Germans all the way back to that mountain and they can't get any farther. The German lines were five or six miles to the south of that two days ago as I remember."

"Yes, master. Sika remember. Wampana maybe help push line back then. Guess now they rest."

"Yeah. But, say, do you figure, maybe—"

He stopped short with a scowl on his face. He shook his head vigorously in the negative.

"No," he snapped, "that wouldn't be human. It's unthinkable. I—"

His hand flew to the throttle and he pushed on it to make sure that the Liberty was doing her best.

"Let's just have a look at that mountain before we go to the aid of your warriors," he barked.

Barry swung the Red Falcon plane over and headed for that mountain of rock that rose up like Gibraltar from the flatter country.

Boom-puff! Boom-puff!

Archie fire from the top of the mountain screamed up at them. Barry swung his crimson crate this way and that to keep out of the line of aerial shells while continuing to study the formation of the mountain.

To the north the mountain dropped away with an abruptness that made it difficult, but not impossible, of ascent. But on the south side of the ridge-shaped mountain, the face dropped almost straight down.

He tore in from above in the dimming light of day, while archie and ground machine guns went crazy with rage, trying to knock him down. The Red Falcon could see the entire top of the mountain bristling with German artillery. Line after line of them ranged along that ridge, the larger guns in the back, the smaller field pieces behind them. And along the edge of the rocky face, to the south, were stationed a double row of machine guns, commanding the entire valley occupied by the French and the Yanks.

He kicked over and slammed at the one end of that long row of machine guns.

Tac-tac-tac!

That last rattle came from the twin Lewis guns that Sika handled. The big black was firing over Barry's head at the machine-gun nests beyond.

They saw Germans tip over and flop upon their guns. Barry zoomed upward at the end of the line and wriggled for altitude, then he kicked over and headed deep into Germany.

Archie fire followed them as they traveled. They slammed back, flying due north from the impregnable mountain. The eyes of the Red Falcon were narrowed as he studied the ground beneath them. The firing from below lessened.

"They seem to have staked everything on the mountain, master," Sika ventured. "No concentration of troops back here."

"Right," Barry flung back. "They've got a pretty sure thing in that mountain. Any bunch of men that can get past old Gardemont deserves all the medals in the world. Why, we could throw a million men against that mountain and they wouldn't have a chance of getting past it and driving the Germans off the side of it."

"Yes, master. We go back now. My people wait for me to help. And we almost out of gas."

"Okay, big boy," the Red Falcon nodded, turning in a steep bank. "We'll go back and look into this, now that we know the lay of the land."

He swung back over the lines at a much higher altitude, maintaining his twisted course of flight until they had passed the danger mark. They stared down into the French and Yank trenches before the face of the mountain.

Barry shook his head.

"Those trenches are too close if my guess is right," he said. "Those poor ground rats down there under these guns are catching plenty of hell and they haven't got a ghost of a chance of doing any good by being there."

It was so dark now that they could scarcely see the ground.

Behind the Allied lines there was the ruined town of Greville from which the sector took its name.

Sika's long arm flashed out past Barry's face, pointing ahead and down.

"There place where Wampana are, master," he called.

"Okay," Barry nodded, "and there to the right is the field where we're going to land."

He cut the motor and kicked over in a steep sideslip. Down, down they tore for that emergency field, wind screaming through the rigging.

Then wheels and skid were touching at the same time and they were rolling to a stop beside the truck and tractor depot between the field and the road that skirted it.

As Barry Rand climbed from the front cockpit he heard Yanks shouting as they ran toward the plane.

“Hey—look who’s here—the Red Falcon! Isn’t that his plane?”

“Yeah, but watch that so-and-so. Maybe he’s goin’ to pull some funny stuff. I wouldn’t trust—”

“Nuts, he’s fightin’ with us. Look at the stuff he’s done. Remember the time when—”

The first of the Yanks came running up to Barry and Sika.

“This is the Red Falcon plane, ain’t it?” he grinned.

“Right,” nodded Barry, “we just stopped in to fill up with gas. Hope we don’t have any trouble getting what we need. We’ve come on important business and we’ll be shoving off directly. I hear the Heinies got you birds in a tough spot.”

That seemed to reassure all of the doubting Yanks. Heads nodded. The one who had reached them first, a sergeant, Barry observed, spoke again.

“I’ll say they have!” He cursed. “Right up against a stone wall.”

“Fill up the tanks with gas and we’ll see what we can do to help,” Barry promised.

“Damn right,” sang out the sergeant. “We’ll get you fixed up if some shave-tail doesn’t butt in and change orders.”

Barry and Sika swung off across the next field at a rapid gait. They came to the outskirts of the rest camp that the Wampana regiment was occupying.

The first blacks they met suddenly rushed up to their chief, bowing before him. And when he stopped to talk to them they knelt down with frightened gestures. Some knelt down before Barry, too. He shooed them away.

“You don’t have to do that to me,” he laughed. “Come on. Tell us what’s happened. What’s the trouble.”

“We take you to M’Gunda,” said two at once. “He tell you. M’Gunda know. M’Gunda very much worry. He send drum talk this afternoon to Sika.”

“Okay. Let’s go.”

THEY were led through the streets of the rest camp. Everywhere blacks were standing, and as they came up to them the blacks snapped to attention and then bowed to Sika as he passed.

They came to one of the smaller camouflaged buildings and stopped. Black guards stood in front of it. They presented arms and then, like the other blacks, bowed down before the great chief.

One of the guards spoke.

"French colonel inside with M'Gunda now," they said a little uneasily.

"What's he doing?" Barry demanded.

"You hear, maybe," said one of the guards. "Listen. Can hear sometimes out here. Very angry."

They did listen. And when the hum of thick lips about Barry Rand had died away he could hear an angry voice spouting French inside the building.

"*Mon dieu!* Are your men cowards? I am commanding you to do this."

Then, above that sound of the French colonel's voice came another voice, a high-pitched cry, almost a scream.

Barry Rand tensed and listened to that second voice. It didn't come from the building they stood in front of, but from down the street a little way.

He couldn't make out what the man was saying, though he thought he was shouting in English.

"What's that?" he demanded of the guard in front of them.

The guard shrugged.

"It is nothing," said the guard. "One who is insane. He escaped from his hospital near Paris yesterday and came up here shouting a wild story. No one can make much out of it. Something about mountain."

"You mean Gardemont?" Barry demanded.

The guard bowed and nodded.

"The colonel says that it is nothing. The hospital sent out a warning that the man had escaped. He is insane from shell shock."

Barry shook his head with a sad gesture.

"Poor devil," he murmured.

He turned to Sika and jerked his head toward the closed door of the building where the angry voice of the French colonel was coming from.

"Come on," he said. "Let's go in and find out about this."

The guard before them hesitated.

"The colonel be angry if I let you pass," he ventured.

Barry grinned, put his hand on the fellow's barrel chest and pushed him out of the way.

"Tell the colonel that I sneaked in," he chuckled. "Come on, big boy."

With Sika right behind him, the Red Falcon reached the door, turned the knob and pushed in.

The chatter of the colonel's raving voice ceased. He was a small, excitable Frenchman with a sharply waxed mustache and beady eyes.

"*Mon dieu!*" he barked. "Who are you and what is the meaning of your bursting in unannounced."

His eyes widened as they took in both the men standing before him in the lighted room.

Barry grinned at him tantalizingly.

"You've heard, perhaps, *monsieur le colonel*, of the Red Falcon?"

The eyes of the little Frenchman almost popped out of his head. Then, as quickly his eyes narrowed and he spoke very slowly.

"That is it. So, M'Gunda, you were sending a message to this outlaw chief of yours when you beat the drums this afternoon?"

The great M'Gunda stood like a statue. Only his finely chiseled black head bobbed back and forth.

"*Oui, monsieur le colonel*," he admitted.

"*Oui*," said Barry. "You see, colonel, we heard that the Wampana regiment was having some rotten deal put over on it and we thought we'd better look into it."

The French colonel fairly jumped up and down in his rage.

"*Dieu de dieux!*" he piped. "You will go back where you came from before I place you under arrest. This is no affair of yours. If I want to give orders for the Wampana to attack in the dawn, that is nothing to you."

Very calmly Barry Rand took out a cigarette and lighted it.

"That's where you're wrong, colonel," he said in a puff of smoke. "We heard there was trouble and we came down to find out what it was all about."

His eyes flashed to M'Gunda's face and he gave him a reassuring smile.

"Now, M'Gunda," he said, "what's the story on this?"

The colonel's eyes blazed. He started for the door, but the giant form of Sika barred his way. The colonel stood trembling for a moment. Barry pointed to a chair.

"Better go and sit down before you get hurt, colonel," he advised. He turned once more to M'Gunda. "Now let's hear about this trouble, M'Gunda."

"Not take long, master." M'Gunda bowed. "My Wampana soldiers work with American outfit and drive Germans back to mountain. To Gardemont. Germans already there with big guns mounted. You know Gardemont, master?"

Barry gave a short nod.

"Just flew over it," he declared.

"Then, you know, master, it is impossible to take Gardemont from this side."

Barry nodded again.

"*Monsieur le colonel,* he order the Wampana regiment alone to take the mountain. We can only attack from this side. We are not afraid. We have prove that before in our fighting, but I do not wish to order my men to go into a fight which I am sure will be certain death to all of them—when it can not possibly do any good."

Barry glanced at the French colonel and nodded very slowly.

"I figured it was just about this," he muttered. "You decided that you wouldn't risk your white soldiers. You'd send these black men to do the dirty work."

The colonel cowered before him as Barry strode over to him.

"It is because, *Monsieur* Red Falcon, the Wampana are such fierce fighters. They could take the mountain if anyone could, *monsieur.*"

"How do you know?" Barry snapped. "I'll bet you haven't been in sight of Gardemont since the Germans armed it and stopped the advance of the Allies there."

The face of the colonel flushed fiery red.

"You make *zee* insult," he flared. "I will have you arrested. I will tell you, the Wampana regiment is black. Why should not they rather than white men go to fight against the mountain? They are half savages. They are like animals."

"You don't deserve to be called a human being, you rat," Barry shot at the colonel.

He drew back his right hand and when it flashed out again his palm was open.

Smack!

The blow struck the colonel across the face and echoed through the room. The colonel went sprawling backward.

Barry turned for the door, jerked his head to Sika to follow him. He paused there and eyed M'Gunda.

WE'LL take a look over the Front again," he announced. "I've got a hunch that the mountain can be taken some other way. Perhaps it can be surrounded, although that doesn't sound plausible just at the moment. Anyway, we'll have a look. Keep the colonel here until we get going or he's liable to try and stop us."

M'Gunda glanced at the colonel, who, although breathing, was still lying on the floor.

"He not look like he run after you, master," the big African ventured.

Barry and Sika stalked out of the place. Blacks twenty deep gathered about their chief. Sika spoke to them.

"The master and I go see what can be done," he explained. "You not do anything until you hear from us."

Blacks bowed as they walked through a wide line of them. Then they turned and followed the Red Falcon and his aide to where they had left their crimson crate.

Several times while they walked to the edge of the rest camp, Barry had heard the yells and screams of the insane man who had escaped from the hospital.

At the field he turned to the blacks.

"I feel sorry for that poor devil back there waiting to be sent back to the nut house," he said. "I knew several boys who went that way from the shells. Any of you know what his name is?"

For a moment there was silence. Then a big black lieutenant stepped up.

"Think name Hartson or maybe Hart or—"

Another cut in.

"Name Harten," he said. "I take message from hospital back near Paris."

Barry shook his head.

"Don't know him," he said. "Maybe it's just as well. Thought maybe I might have been able to help him in some way."

Yanks of the truck outfit gathered about.

"She's all set to sputter," the sergeant announced with a grin. He held out his hand sheepishly. "Could—could I shake hands with you, Red Falcon?"

"Sure," Barry nodded. "Anything just so you don't try to kiss me on both cheeks."

In the ripple of laughter that followed, Barry climbed to the front cockpit while Sika whirled the prop. The Liberty started and roared out in the night. Sika climbed to his cockpit. Someone spilled gasoline on the ground and touched a match to it and, in its light, they droned into the air and turned toward the impregnable cliffs that were Gardemont.

High above the mountain top Barry cut loose a flare and climbing above it, stared down at the earth bathed in the weird light.

Vainly he searched from one end to the other of that mountain for an unguarded sector. He dropped another flare and continued the search. But it was useless. He spoke to Sika through the tube. "I'm afraid of one thing," he called.

"We can't save your Wampana warriors from being sent into battle if that colonel insists upon it—that is unless we could get the order countermanded by the high commander himself. And you know what chance we'd have of doing that."

He glanced at his wrist watch.

"It's early yet," he said. "We've got the whole evening before us. Let's take a turn around back of the mountain like we did a while ago. Maybe we can pick up some idea."

"Yes, master. Sika not want to see Wampana all killed."

"Neither do I, big boy. And we're going to do everything that we can to work out something. You can see yourself, though, there ain't a chance of attacking from either side. Those Heinies have got every possible attack cut off on each end of the mountain. I'll gamble that their strongest trench forces are there below on the flat lands at either side of Gardemont."

The flare had almost burned out, but Barry Rand saw something in its light that made him sit up in the seat a little straighter.

A moment later when the flare had gone out he was looking down, studying the light and dark shadows below intently. At length he made a decision and called through the tube.

"We're going to land. There's a field about two miles north of Gardemont. This afternoon it didn't look as though it were guarded. The Germans are paying plenty of attention to the mountain, but the back area just behind seems pretty well deserted."

"Yes, master. You think we fight?"

"Don't know," Barry flung back, "but at least I want to have a look around this area. We've got to figure out some way."

He climbed higher and higher as they droned back behind the enemy lines. He began turning in a great circle as he climbed, then very slowly he throttled back the great Liberty. They began going down. And all of the time the eyes of Barry Rand were focused on that one field two miles behind the German lines.

The switch was cut and they were gliding down.

The Red Falcon plane landed with a low rumbling sound and rolled to a stop. Barry Rand climbed out and listened. Sika waited for his word.

"Come on, let's go," Barry hissed.

"Where we go, master?"

The big black dropped down beside him.

"I think first we'll head for a lone house I saw this evening," Barry whispered. "It's the only one in this area. I've got a hunch that it might be a headquarters building of some kind, although I didn't see any activity about it."

They crept in that direction, Barry leading the way. They walked noiselessly across fields and over a road. They had just crossed another road when Barry stopped to listen. There was no sound except the rumble of the guns atop Gardemont. He pointed ahead.

"I think that's the house. Move on it carefully. Can't see any lights but you never can tell."

They came to the back wall of the house. The roof at one end was caved in with age and the walls were crumbling.

"Doesn't look like anyone has been in here for years," Barry hissed. "Let's go inside and look around—or rather feel around."

THEY entered through a window that was smashed and gaping. They heard rats scurrying across the floor. Barry moved on ahead. With Sika behind him, he made a complete tour of the little stone place. Everywhere were signs of decay. In the end of the larger room a pile of debris lay heaped halfway to the ceiling.

"Well," he ventured, "there's nothing here. We might as well move up closer to the mountain and see what we can learn."

Suddenly Sika gripped his arm and hissed:

"Master, hear something? Somebody come. A car, master!"

Barry tensed. There was a car coming down the road that ran in front of the rotted house. Sika stood like a statue.

"We fight, master?" he almost pleaded.

"Wait. No, look. The car has stopped. I think they're coming in here. We'll hide under that pile of debris and listen."

Hastily and with as little noise as possible they dug their way under the pile of rubbish at the end of the larger room. From there they could hear voices. Then the thudding of feet.

"*Ach, nein.* This will not do," said a guttural voice.

"But Excellency, this is the only house about here."

"*Jawohl,* but what is wrong with establishing our headquarters on the rear of the mountain top. We will be safer there than here. Shells coming over the mountain might strike us here."

A flashlight beam spread over the interior.

"Besides, it would take much work to put this back into shape for our headquarters. *Nein*, you are a *Dummkopf* for even considering it. *Ach Himmel*, rats, too. Let us get out of here."

Then the thudding of feet and the purr of a car. Sika jumped suddenly and made a rustling sound in the rubbish pile as the car drove away.

"Ouch!" he gasped. Then he made a quick grab for something behind him. "Rats bit me, master."

Barry leaped from the rubbish pile. He couldn't help but chuckle.

"Master, rats not bite me. Wires stick into me," Sika said next.

"Huh?" Barry blurted. "Wires? Let's see."

Sika tossed rubbish off the top of the heap. Barry was burrowing down into it. Then he stopped short, took out a small flashlight and examined the rubbish pile.

"Hey, look here," he gasped. "Here are two wires sticking through the side of the house. Looks as though they lead somewhere outside."

He pulled a slip of paper that was fastened to the two wires, held the light on it, and stared fixedly for a moment.

"Unless I'm nuts," he ejaculated, "we've found something. Look at this note. It must have been left some years ago—the paper is yellow.

> *If you want to learn the secret of these wires, get in touch with me. I am a press correspondent at present attached to the German army. I have some information about them given me by General von Dorf before he died. The shelling is preying on my brain. It is terrible. Perhaps by the time you find this note I will be—*

The paper was torn, and smudged at the bottom. He held it closer to the light.

"Say, this signature looks like 'Hartson', or something like that. What was the name of that lunatic back there at your regiment, Sika. That was like that, wasn't it?"

"Sika think so," the big black nodded.

"Come on." Barry was on his way out of the tumbled-down stone house with the piece of paper stuck deep in his pocket. He ran across the fields with Sika trailing him, leaped into the front cockpit of the Red Falcon plane, and a moment later they were thundering into the air, bound for the south and the field they had just left.

At the sound of their drone the Yanks of the truck depot lighted another gasoline flare and Barry and Sika landed.

Yanks came on the run. Barry ran through them with Sika on his heels.

"Take care of my plane while we're gone and don't let any Frogs touch it," Barry called.

Blacks appeared about them and bowed again before Sika. But now the Red Falcon and his aid had no time to receive the tokens of esteem.

"I want to see this lunatic named Hartson or Hatten," Barry shouted.

"But master." It was M'Gunda's voice. "The colonel, he after you!"

"To hell with the colonel," Barry snapped. "Show me to the jug where they've got Harten."

Then suddenly other dark forms crowded in and he felt the prick of a bayonet in his back. A flashlight beam smacked him in the face. A laugh came in a high-pitched, excited voice.

"*Mon dieu*, Red Falcon, you are not so clever after all." It was the colonel. "I have you now. One false move and you will be run through with our bayonets. Did I hear you say you wanted to see the insane one in the jail, *monsieur*. You will see him. Ha-ha! You will get your wish. I will place you and your black man in the same cell with him. You will see plenty of him."

A short march, and then they were thrust into the cell and the door closed.

A dim light showed them a slim, wild-eyed figure leaping at them from the far corner of the cell.

"Killed—they will be killed. Everybody will be killed. They can not live—killed, murdered." Then at the end came a piercing scream.

AS THE man tore at Barry Rand with his long fingers, Barry stepped back and to the side. He let go a right that had his whole strength behind the blow. It caught the madman right between the eyes. The fellow slumped to the floor.

Barry shook his head. "Sorry I had to do it," he said. "You're no good to us this way. Maybe that will take the terror out of you for a while."

He and Sika bent over the form. They worked on him slowly, then the man's eyes opened and stared less wildly than before. Barry stroked his head gently.

"Take it easy, Harten," he said. "You're all right now. Maybe you can remember something that happened in the past—a note you left on some wires north of Gardemont."

The eyes grew mild and the lips moved.

"Gardemont," whispered Harten. "Gardemont. Yes." He tried to sit up, but Barry pushed him down quickly.

"We're working with you now. We know that you know something. You can save the Allies—if you'll tell us what you know."

Harten brought his hand before his forehead.

"Yes," he said. "Let me think. Shell shock—" he shuddered "—but before that something else. A note. I was an American war correspondent with the Germans before America entered war. General—general—"

"Von Dorf?" Barry supplied.

"That was it, General von Dorf. Told me just before he died—I was the only one with him. Eccentric old fellow, but a clever general. He had a great deal of high explosive entrusted to him to get rid of. Let me see—long time ago. Old mine there inside Gardemont. He carried all that H. E. there."

Harten was sitting up now, acting much like a sane human.

"Yes, old mine under Gardemont. Von Dorf put all that H. E. under there. Wires running from there to a lone stone house about two miles north. Attach a battery to the two wires and up she goes. Yes, that is what I was trying to tell them.

"I slipped out of the hospital when I heard what was going on and tried to make them believe me. Scared I couldn't put it across. Shell shock came back. Got too excited over it. But that's it, I'm sure. Von Dorf mined it so if the Allies ever drove the Germans back and took the mountain he could blow them up from the stone house."

"Listen," Barry hissed. "We'll get a battery and go over. Want to go with us? You might be able to help if you think you can keep hold of yourself."

Harten leaped to his feet.

"Ye-yes," he choked. "Be good for me. Either kill or cure me. It's hell this way. But—how do we get out of here?"

"Leave that to Sika," Barry grinned.

The big black went to work on the old rusty bars. Several hours passed, then the bars were pried apart.

Cautiously they made their way to the Red Falcon plane. Barry found the sergeant, got a battery from him and climbed into the plane. The Liberty blasted out and they thundered into the night.

Surely the Germans wouldn't expect them to land back at the same field that they had used before that night, Barry figured. So they turned in that direction and glided silently, as before.

Then the landing and the roll. Barry lugged the battery while Sika came on with Harten under his observation. They reached the ruined stone house, dug out the wires from the debris pile, attached one of them to the battery. Breathlessly he applied the other. Nothing happened. They remained motionless for a moment.

"No go," Barry mumbled with a baffled expression. Then slowly he turned and faced the others.

"I've got an idea," he said. "Remember the drum, Sika? Get the drum. Harten, can you show us how to get into the old mine?"

"Ye-yes," said Harten. "I'm sure—if the guns don't—"

"They won't," Barry cut in. "Come on. Get the drum from the back of the plane, Sika. We'll take it up with us."

Slipping up on the north side of the mountain they had to move cautiously. They crossed roads that trucks came rumbling down. Once it seemed that they were completely surrounded by the enemy, but they lay still and the Germans moved on.

Harten had lain there on the ground trembling like a leaf. Barry's heart went out to him.

"Harten," he whispered. "Maybe you could tell us how to get into the entrance of the mine, then you wouldn't have to go any farther."

"N-no," Harten stammered. "I'll make it. You couldn't find it."

They were crawling on on their stomachs, the mountain almost towering over them. Harten stopped for a moment.

"This way," he said, crawling to the left. "It—it's over here."

They moved on beside him. For some unknown reason, they ceased to hear German soldiers. The terrain was too rocky for a concentration of troops, perhaps.

"H-here," gasped Harten. "Right ahead, I'm sure. There's a hole between those two rocks there."

For the last three hours the guns on top of the mountain had been booming. The sound was deafening and the three had to talk to each other at close range. The strain was cutting down Harten's nerves rapidly. He could hardly walk.

With Barry and Sika half holding him up, they worked their way toward the two great rocks.

When they reached the two boulders, Barry went first. There was an opening there, a good-sized one, but not until one had pushed around the larger of the two rocks could it be found.

Harten plunged into the opening behind Barry. It was pitch black now. They were going down a sloping passage. Harten breathed a sigh and choked a little.

A flashlight beam blinked ahead as Barry got out his electric torch. To the right, a longer passage was discernible. Barry stopped and stared.

There, as far as he could see, were cases lining each side of the passage. He bent down and tore at one of them. There was a fine whitish powder inside. One wrong move and the whole thing would blow them into billions of pieces.

Barry stared about. Rocks, large and small, were everywhere. Barry began piling rocks at one side. Under his orders Sika lifted the cases of H. E. and piled those up almost to the top of the passage on the same side.

Harten sat down jerkily, like an exhausted man, on one of the cases. He was breathing heavily.

On top of the cases, and above those heavy rocks, Barry placed the drum. He pushed Sika back.

"Get Harten toward the entrance," he said.

THEN he went to work with other rocks. He balanced round cobbles weighing three and four pounds on the edge of the drum so that when they were shaken off they would tip over and fall with a crash on the piled-up rocks below.

Now, lastly, for the most perilous task. He scooped handfuls of the powder from the case he had torn open and sprinkled it thinly over all of the rocks below the drum. Then he started for the door.

Sika and Harten moved on ahead of him. They were just dim shapes in the darkness. Suddenly, Barry saw Harten leap forward, away from Sika. And then, above the thunder of the guns overhead, Barry heard a wild, unearthly scream of terror.

Harten was running like the madman he had suddenly become. Sika was after him in a flash. Harten ducked and was almost lost in the darkness. Then a loud command from somewhere ahead,

"Halt. Was ist!"

A flashlight gleamed for an instant, Harten stood out against it in bold relief, still screaming. He tried to duck away.

Blam!

A gun barked just beside the flashlight. Flame spat right into Harten's face and his head snapped back. Sika ducked and dived to the right. Barry was running to the right too. Half crouched, he stumbled over the figure of Sika and sprawled. Lay still there for a long time while he watched the flashlight play on the blood-smeared face and figure of Harten.

"Poor fellow," Barry breathed. "Got him right in the face. Perhaps he's better off at that."

They were crawling on. It seemed an eternity they spent in returning to the ship, but at last they made it.

"Almost dawn now," Barry said when they had taken off. "Got to get back and get that other drum from M'Gunda."

"Yes, master, Sika get drum as soon as we land. They not notice Sika with other Wampana black men. You wait at field. I get drum."

They landed at that field near the Yank truck depot. Barry climbed into the rear cockpit and crouched behind the twin Lewis guns.

"Now if they come," he snapped, "if those Frogs come to take us, they'll get a taste of something."

They did come, too—a dozen of them with rifles and fixed bayonets. The Liberty was idling all of the time. Barry turned the machine guns toward them and fired over their heads.

"Stay where you are," he barked. "A step closer and you'll get it."

Then Sika came running from the rest camp. He had a drum under his arm and a pale expression on his face.

"Master," he panted. "Wampana gone. They go up to attack mountain anyway when sun come over the ridge."

Barry leaped into his own cockpit. Sika clambered in with his drum and two big drum mallets. As they roared into the air the big black chief hung the drum on one side of his cockpit and began beating it with the drum mallets.

They could see the Wampana advancing across the lowlands. Going to their death unless—

Boom-boom! Boom-boom!

Sika was pounding that drum for dear life. Then shapes with wings came hurling over the mountain. The air was filled with screaming Fokkers that were determined on destroying the Red Falcon plane. Barry lunged and darted about the sky, trying to drive them off, while Sika, his guns still, pounded the big drum.

Then suddenly Barry swerved and came slamming over the top of the mountain low down with all the Fokker pack riding him.

Boom-boom! Boom-boom!

Brrrram!

For a split second everything went black. Some giant seemed to be heaving the Red Falcon plane up, up, with a blinding black mist about it. Fokkers were blotted out and the earth seemed about their ears.

Then things began to clear as the blasted mountain settled to the earth once more, leaving a flat place where, before, millions of tons of rock had loomed.

Barry and Sika could look down and see the black warriors of the Wampana storming over the blasted area that had for hundreds of years been Gardemont.

They were running at top speed, their black skins glistening in the morning sun, taking new land from the enemy. And far to the north German reserves, unprepared for this surprise, were fleeing before them.

Then, when Barry Rand grew tired of watching the scene, he turned to the east, into the rising sun. And no Fokkers remained there to watch them. They had been over the mountain when it went up.

"Master," Sika ventured, "Sika hope the colonel not angry with my people."

Barry laughed.

"Don't worry about that, big boy," he chuckled. "That little colonel will take all of the credit for this. We don't care about that, but he'll be so puffed up about it that he'll forget all about what passed."

Then the Red Falcon yawned and began whistling his favorite tune, The Dark Town Strutters' Ball.

HENRY "HARRY" STEEGER PHOTOGRAPHED IN HIS OFFICE AT POPULAR PUBLICATIONS FOR *WRITER'S YEARBOOK 1940* (ALL RIGHTS RESERVED). The accompanying caption reads in part: "Tall, slender, and handsome, Harry Steeger, who owns not a Ford but a yacht and a bicycle built for two (he went pedaling through New England last summer on a vacation with Mrs. Steeger) runs his shop the way he'd like a shop to be run if he were working there as an editorial galley slave. Everything is congenial and informal."

Henry Steeger 1903-1990

by Don Hutchison

For those who grew up reading the pulp magazines back in the 1930s and 40s, the Popular Publications colophon—two letter Ps back to back—always promised something special in fictional thrills. We had no knowledge of publishers back then but we did realize that symbol identified some of the most exciting magazines ever printed: **Dare-Devil Aces, Operator #5, Adventure, The Spider, Dime Detective, G-8 and his Battle Aces**. The list could go on and on. Dozens of titles, thousands of vivid covers, most of them dreamed up by a resourceful young publisher named Henry (known as "Harry") Steeger, a graduate of Princeton University and the University of Berlin.

In late 1929, when Steeger was in his mid-twenties, he borrowed some money from his stepfather, and with a partner named Harold Goldsmith, created the Popular Publications pulp chain. Goldsmith handled the business side and Steeger the editorial. The first title chosen was **Battle Aces,** which was Steeger's choice since he had previously edited **Sky Birds** and **War Birds** for Dell Publications and knew most of the authors. Originally, he managed only four magazines, a western, two detectives and the air war, but by the mid 1940s he was running the biggest pulp publishing company in the world--and by his own admission, enjoying every minute.

The youthful partners at the upstart company ran a happy ship, their offices described as a madhouse of larks and bantering. The entire staff was under thirty and they played as hard as they worked. Steeger once described a typical high-level meeting with authors as "squatting down on the floor and shooting craps, or getting boiled on martinis or whatever else, and having a great old time. The whole thing was more fun that I can possibly have imagined."

Fun. I think that is the key word in describing Harry Steeger's line of pulps. They must have been fun to put out because they are still fun to read. Initially, Steeger handled the dual role of publisher and editor. He wrote reader's departments, dealt with authors, and invented the general story lines for all series. He instituted a sassy, extravagant style for his popular fiction and developed an instinct for cover art that bordered on genius.

As the Popular Publications titles grew Harry hired others to edit, but the chain's uniform excellence indicated a master's touch at the top.

To survive in the pulp jungle publishers had to be adaptable. As new fads replaced old, new magazines sprang up or disappeared like weeds. By 1933 Harry's once-popular **Battle Aces** magazine was nose-diving in circulation. The resourceful businessman realized that it needed some fast thinking to bail it out. Over at rival publisher Street & Smith, **The Shadow** and **Doc Savage** had proved to be instant successes. Steeger would counter with his own larger-than-life mystery hero **The Spider.** Why not, he reasoned, add a super hero of the air? What other publisher would have conceived of transforming an ailing air war pulp into a bizarre series about a World War I master spy who spent much of his flying time combating airborne zombies and vampires, along with hordes of Teutonic master fiends as bent as boomerangs?

To create such a hero Harry called upon the resources of a young New Jersey writer named Robert J. Hogan, who had already proved himself as the author of the high-flying Smoke Wade series in **Battle Aces** as well as that of Barry Rand, the freelance Hun fighter known as The Red Falcon in Popular's **Dare-Devil Aces.**

Steeger had a talent for transforming underperforming titles into something new. He literally invented the so-called "weird-menace" pulps in September 1933 when he revamped the bland and ailing **Dime Mystery** into a Gothic fright fest. Infused with new blood (literally) the magazine emerged as one of the best-selling titles in the pulp field with rival publishers rushing to push out similar works in a sanguinary vein.

While designing his flying super hero title, Steeger realized that a full-length aerial adventure series might bog down without stronger, more bizarre plots. In pulp magazine terms he conceived the new magazine as a hybrid of **Dare-Devil Aces, Amazing Stories** and **Weird Tales.** To this outre stew, author Hogan added a hero who, with the aid of disguise, could mask himself in any role. Jaded pulp readers found the blend irresistible.

Debuting in October of 1933, the new magazine titled **G-8 and his Battle Aces,** proved to be an instant success. Thanks to Steeger's inspiration and Hogan's fecund imagination, the title ran for an incredible 110 issues. For over a decade, while one air pulp after another went spiraling down, G-8 winged on, carrying his fight with the Kaiser's minions into the heart of World War II.

The author of a thousand-and-one horrific, action-packed encounters, Robert J. Hogan was one of the few men to write pulp hero novels under his own name rather than that of a "house name" supplied by the publisher. As publisher Steeger explained it: "In other cases we wanted a company name in case the author should become ill or otherwise incapacitated, so we could go ahead with the series under the same published name. In Bob's case he looked so healthy and he was such a good friend that we let him use his own."

Friendship aside, the canny publisher may have decided that identifying the G-8 yarns with the author of the popular Red Falcon series would encourage a cross-over readership between the ongoing **Dare-Devil Aces** magazine and that of the newly invigorated **Battle Aces.** In addition, ace air-war cover artist Fred Blakeslee was drafted to create for G-8 some of the most breathtaking aerial encounters ever imagined. Another important contributor was interior illustrator John Fleming Gould. His planes were less convincing than Blakeslee's but his black-toned sketches excelled in the vivid imagery of awesome aerial combat, shadowy Black Forest castles and ghastly moonlit monsters.

It must be said that Harry Steeger was as much responsible for the creative contributions to his magazines as that of any of his authors or artists. His relationship with them was entirely collaborative. I suspect that a number of Hogan's villains and their devices were the inventions of artist Blakeslee working in close collaboration with publisher Steeger. One of Popular Publications' greatest strengths was that Steeger made a near scientific study of readers' tastes and personally supervised the execution of each cover with a master chef's understanding of ingredients. There are occasions in which a cover scene is described graphically in the final pages of a G-8 story but sometimes with little conviction. Details are brought painfully into the scene, and then disposed of summarily, as if Hogan had achieved his goal of justifying some preposterous cover concept. This theory would explain such macabre villains as Baron von Todschmecker—a walking skeleton with the hilt of a dagger protruding from his gun-blue skull—as well as scores of insane aerial confrontations with the likes of flying dragons, tiger-men, defrosted Vikings, and giant, man-carrying bats from the Matto Grosso.

G-8's author was under orders never to rewrite or edit copy, but simply get the material in on time. To do that, Hogan realized he would need assistance because he also had commitments for 100,000 words a month in other material. He employed two local business school graduates to take dictation so that he could simply "talk out" his stories. In a 1962 article in the **New Jersey Sunday Herald**, he explained: "One secretary would come over in the morning. I'd dictate two chapters to her, and the other would arrive after lunch, and I'd dictate two chapters to her. It was up to them to get together and come up with a complete book. They told me later that often the one who had finished transcribing at home would wait for the other to return from dictation to learn what happened in her two chapters."

Edythe Seims was the first of the magazine's hard-working editors, succeeded by Bill Fay, with Alden Norton taking over in the late 30's. In the series final years diverse hands took turns smoothing out Hogan's increasingly frenzied prose. Science fiction author/editor Frederik Pohl once admitted that even he had once served in that capacity.

With a story set in mysterious Burma, "Wings of the Death Tiger" (June, 1944), the saga of **G-8 and his Battle Aces** finally came to an end. Harry Steeger's other air titles, **Battle Birds, Dare-Devil Aces,** and **Fighting Aces** were terminated that same summer, although the long-running **Dare-Devil Aces** was later revived to make a brief but unsuccessful post-war run from mid-to-late 1946. Within a decade, the pulp magazines themselves would perish from neglect and changing tastes. It was the end of a way of writing and a way of dreaming.

In his later years, Harry Steeger became a warm and generous friend to researchers striving to piece together some authentic record of the pulp fiction era and its participants. Although kept busy with vital social causes, he always made time to respond to nattering questions concerning pulp history. In June of 1988 I received a long, four-page letter from Harry supplying me with requested information about his friend Robert J. Hogan. It read in part:

"Bob was never complicated or burdened with any of the restrictions of the academic world. He invented everything from his own fertile imagination. To look at him you would say this is the last person on earth who could be an author. He had a long, thin face and he was a very thin gangling type of person put together with steel wire rather than glue. He had sort of pale washed-out eyes and thinning hair but was most active physically and, of course, his fertile mind never stopped for a moment dreaming up dramatic situations. He was most uncomplicated; he was really one of the simplest people you could ever hope to meet, with an enormous sense of the dramatic and the magic of a born story teller. Erudition was not part of Bob's life, either. He was in every way a very simple person, lived in a simple little home and had a rather simple life because there was not much time for anything else. I believe he had a daughter and, of course, I know he had a wife who helped him with his work and he had very little time for anything else but putting together his yarns, 200,00 words a month was, I believe, his basic production, but I'm sure that other work crept into that schedule as well.

"Bob was also, as you might suspect, a born talker. He could rattle along just as fast and dramatically as he did on the typewriter, but it was all down to business and all planning for future issues of how to make the best of what he had done. He loved talking over his characters and his plots and we spent a great time doing just that.

"Incidentally, I worked with the authors and the artists on every single cover we ever published. That was my essential duty in getting each issue started. Nobody else ever did any of the covers, so, no matter how horrific they might now seem, I at least was responsible for them. And I believe, as I told you, we worked on those covers as though they were fine Swiss watches, sending them back over and over again to the artists to improve. There were grumbles but never any real refusals. Fred Blakeslee, the cover artist, was a man of similar ilk, with a simple home life with a driving desire to paint the air covers which he did, I think, to perfection for our audiences.

"As you say, Bob was accustomed to spending a great deal of time at his home in New Jersey and also a good deal of time down in Florida and I'm sure, as you say, most of it was spent working on his stories. He was not a scholarly type of person and he was not much interested in going to the theater or to the galleries or any similar cultural activities because he didn't have time for them, so his conversations never ranged along these lines but he loved nothing better than telling me about new evil doings of his villains and also of the great heroics of his heroes. G-8 and his pals lived for us but for Bob Hogan I think they were more real than anyone else he knew.

"Two other flyers of the same era, O. B. Myers and Sidney Bowen, were also frequent visitors to the office and worked just as hard as Bob although, of course, with lesser production--and each of them had stories in almost every issue of our flying magazines. Ralph Oppenheim was also a regular and produced a series called "The Three Mosquitoes" which was extremely well known but he really blasted my concepts one day when he admitted he had never been near an airplane in his life and that his stories were put together in a fiction factory supervised by him. By contrast, Bob Hogan did all his own work and when he came to town we did as we did with the others--we closed up the doors and celebrated with lunch or whatever else was fun and we kidded around and just had a great time, none of it connected with putting magazines together except for the particular author involved."

Harry Steeger was co-owner and president of Popular Publications from 1930 to 1972. His pulp-paper magazines ran from 1930 to 1955. They were only a part of his publishing career and only one aspect of his long and colorful life. As a writer, he produced books on flying and civil rights and wrote short stories under various names. He was a world traveler and adventurer, a member of The Explorer's Club, president of The National Urban League, a lieutenant colonel in the Coast Guard during World War II, a pro-level tennis player, president of "The Society of the Facially Disfigured," and a member of several hospital boards. He hobnobbed with the rich and famous but never lost touch with his roots in the beloved pulp jungle. He and his wife, Shirley, were honored guests at the annual Pulpcon in Dayton, Ohio in 1988 and again in Wayne, New Jersey in July of 1990, where they renewed acquaintances with old friends and made many new ones.

Harry's extravagant praise for researchers and writers of pulp history was, I think, entirely sincere. Harry was an enthusiast. The zest that characterized Popular Publications was Harry's own. He loved life, he loved people, and he loved to reminisce about those action-packed years when The Red Falcon and G-8 the Master Spy commanded our loyal attention.

Made in the USA
Lexington, KY
16 September 2011